# PRAISE FOR *ONLY WAY OUT*

"Small-town crime, big-time stakes, and the twists and turns aren't only in the plot. If there's an inheritor of Elmore Leonard, it's Tod Goldberg."

—Stephen Graham Jones, *New York Times* bestselling author

"In *Only Way Out*, Tod Goldberg takes us to the washed-out edges of the Oregon coast, where lost souls, small-time hustlers, and true believers collide in a derelict resort town. This is a story about escape—what we'll do to get free, who we'll become to stay gone—shot through with black comedy. Sharp, strange, and unexpectedly moving."

—Ivy Pochoda, author of *Ecstasy*

"Tod Goldberg has redefined the noir genre with *Only Way Out*. An unapologetic gripping view into criminal schemes gone bad, bad lives gone even worse, and sad lives redeemed. No beat is skipped as the exquisitely drawn, tragic characters repeatedly cross paths along an epic crime noir journey."

—Steven Konkoly, *USA Today* bestselling author

# PRAISE FOR TOD GOLDBERG'S GANGSTERLAND SERIES

## An Amazon Best Book of the Year (*Gangsters Don't Die*)

## Southwest Book of the Year (*The Low Desert*

and *Gangsters Don't Die*)

Finalist, the Hammett Prize (*Gangsterland*)

Finalist, Strand Critics Award (*The Low Desert*)

"Goldberg is one of the best (and funniest) crime writers working today."

—*Orange County Register*

"The most improbable and remarkable series of Mob fiction ever written."

—*Los Angeles Times*

"A stirring portrait of the region."

—*Time*

"A gloriously original Mafia novel: 100 percent unhinged about the professionally unhinged."

—*New York Times*

"With verbal riffs that echo Pynchon and DeLillo—but funnier—this is hard-boiled violence on an ambitious scale."

—*Times of London*

"Tod Goldberg is the literary offspring of Elmore Leonard and Charles Portis, which means he's smart, deep, and profoundly funny."

—*CrimeReads*

"Twelve spare, stylish contemporary crime stories that exemplify the craft."

—*USA Today*

"The work of a master storyteller."

—*Publishers Weekly*, Starred Review

"Clever plotting, a colorful cast of characters, and priceless situations make this comedic crime novel an instant classic."

—*Kirkus*, Starred Review

"One of the year's best hard-boiled crime novels."

—*Booklist*, Starred Review

"As sharp as a straight razor. But a lot more fun. Count me a huge fan."

—Lee Child

"Infinitely readable, infinitely funny, and infinitely better than anything else you'll read this year!"

—Craig Johnson

"*Gangster Nation* is a razor. It will slice you open and reveal your insides. And like the best of Tod Goldberg's work, it'll show you everything you are at your core."

—Brad Meltzer

"Tod Goldberg is a terrific writer, and *The Low Desert* is a smart, surprising page-turner."

—Don Winslow

"Tod Goldberg is one of this nation's sagest storytellers."

—Attica Locke

"Tod Goldberg has written a book that's impossible to put down and impossible to forget."

—Lou Berney

"Tod Goldberg's talent and compassion extends dignity even to the most fucked-up and misbegotten lives."
—Daniel Woodrell

"*The Low Desert* is a master class in how to write great noir."
—Dan Chaon

"Tod Goldberg seamlessly marries violence and grace to understand both the root and the aftermath of crime. And in doing so he tells a damn fine tale over and again."
—Ivy Pochoda

"Tod Goldberg's stories are full of humor, pathos, and sharp knife-twists of plot and insight. Featuring best-laid plans that have gone horribly awry, and heartbreakingly authentic characters broken by violence, longing, and hope, *The Low Desert* packs a heady, emotional wallop. More of this, please."
—Paul Tremblay

"Tod Goldberg's brilliant *Gangster Nation* is hilarious, complex, and a total page-turner. It's also a little insane, in the best possible way."
—Lisa Lutz

# ONLY WAY OUT

A NOVEL

## ALSO BY TOD GOLDBERG

### Gangsterland Series

*Gangsterland*
*Gangster Nation*
*Gangsters Don't Die*
*The Low Desert*

### Burn Notice Series

*The Fix*
*The End Game*
*The Giveaway*
*The Reformed*
*The Bad Bead*

### Stand-Alone Novels

*The House of Secrets* (with Brad Meltzer)
*Other Resort Cities*
*Living Dead Girl*
*Fake Liar Cheat*

# ONLY WAY OUT

A NOVEL

# TOD GOLDBERG

THOMAS & MERCER

This is a work of fiction. Names, characters, organizations, places, events, and incidents are either products of the author's imagination or are used fictitiously.

Text copyright © 2025 by Tod Goldberg
All rights reserved.

No part of this book may be reproduced, or stored in a retrieval system, or transmitted in any form or by any means, electronic, mechanical, photocopying, recording, or otherwise, without express written permission of the publisher.

Published by Thomas & Mercer, Seattle
www.apub.com

Amazon, the Amazon logo, and Thomas & Mercer are trademarks of Amazon.com, Inc., or its affiliates.

EU product safety contact:
Amazon Media EU S. à r.l.
38, avenue John F. Kennedy, L-1855 Luxembourg
amazonpublishing-gpsr@amazon.com

ISBN-13: 9781662534089 (hardcover)
ISBN-13: 9781662525629 (paperback)
ISBN-13: 9781662525636 (digital)

Cover design by Damon Freeman
Cover image: © lizhorwitt, © KadirKARA, © MVelishchuk, © Spectral-Design / Shutterstock; © Matthias Kulka / Getty

Printed in the United States of America

First edition

*For Wendy. You pick the century, and I'll pick the spot.*

# PART 1

# CHAPTER ONE

*Fifteen Years Ago*
*Granite Shores, Oregon*
*The Day After Thanksgiving—Black Friday*

The problem with being a crooked cop? When shit inevitably goes sideways, you're on your own.

This truth came to Officer Jack Biddle way too late. But what to do? Wasn't like he could go state's evidence. If he tried to cut a deal, he'd end up doing *less* time, but he'd still be doing time, and cops don't do well up in gen pop. Not even in some medium-security spot like Shutter River down in Bend. He'd be somebody's chew toy in about fifteen minutes.

He couldn't go to his friends. Only a few knew he possessed such a . . . fungible . . . moral center, and none knew the extent of his mendacity. Most of his true friends couldn't even define *mendacity*. His wife was way out. She just got elected to the city council. Rest of her family were dentists, save for her cousin Tommy, who was a DA up in Corvallis.

Was there something he could put into the water supply? Didn't Putin have some kind of chemical that could erase people's memories? Some old Soviet-era shit? Had he read that somewhere? He'd look into that.

Jack fired up a joint, took a big drag, tried to find a better solution. He'd parked his cruiser-rigged Tahoe near the top of Patterson Summit on the east side of Yeach Mountain, then backed up into a dense overgrowth of towering evergreens that obscured him from sight. Jack had to be careful, though, because if he backed up too far, he'd be ass over teakettle into Patterson Gulch, and that would be that. He'd be lucky if anyone *ever* found him. The gulch was named for the Patterson family, who disappeared into it in 1848 during a snowstorm; miners ended up finding one living family member seven months later—Yeach Patterson, an eleven-year-old boy, who later gave his name to the mountain—starving, stark raving, and with tales of eating the family dogs and then, eventually, the family to survive.

Seven months was a long-ass time. Could Jack survive that long? Maybe. He'd need more weed. More beer. More shotgun shells. Absolutely would need to figure out a Wi-Fi situation. A better coat, for sure. Tonight was the start of the bad weather. Freezing rain. Forty-mile-per-hour wind gusts that swirled across the grade.

Jack's granddaddy claimed the Pattersons were distant cousins, but Jack had never seen any proof, not that he gave a shit, since he'd never tell anyone that he came from some creepy-ass stock, though if Jack had his way, there'd be a Yeach Patterson Festival every summer.

Amp up the crazy. Get the tourists to flood into town. More tourists meant more traffic tickets. More traffic tickets meant more drug seizures. More seizures meant more people spending the night in County. More people in County meant a larger county jail, which meant a construction boom, which meant more housing, which meant more cars, which meant even more traffic tickets. Turn Granite Shores into something more than a dying resort town—turn it into a real destination! Get a little film festival. Close the streets around the boardwalk and let people walk around with beer. Maybe eventually they'd legalize weed, and that would mean more bakeries and deep-fried food places.

People had to get to know Granite Shores for more than its shitty nickname. The city was shaped like a capital *L* with the boardwalk and its rickety old amusement park rides, the farmers market, the marina, Granite Shores Bay, and the main businesses running north and south along Beach Boulevard. Most of the original neighborhoods, littered with Craftsman houses and clapboard bungalows, were situated to the east, in the foothills of Yeach Mountain, near the old quarry. The new developments, the nice part of town, where the Canadians and retirees bought houses and condos, where there was talk of maybe a new mall and a miniature golf joint, maybe a surf park if the locals didn't mind the Japanese funding—that was all located along the short leg, beside the village of Granite Park, which was what the world would look like if Pottery Barn was a recognized religion.

None of that mattered when you looked at the place on a map—the topography made it strongly resemble a giant *L* carved into an old man's forehead. So of course, kids started calling it Losertown as soon as they were able to get a look at it. Then the internet came along, and that was that. You lived in Granite Shores, you lived in Losertown. There were mugs and T-shirts sold on the boardwalk.

It was, in Jack's opinion, a fucking disgrace. He was a goddamn winner.

Jack's personal cell phone rang.

Bobby C.

Danny Vining's collections guy.

Shit.

*Ignore.*

Any idea of starting a festival was out the door if Bobby C. found him, that much was for sure.

Not that Bobby C. would have any notion where to even begin looking for him, since the only person who knew about this spot was Jack's father, Owen, who showed it to him in the first place, and he wasn't telling anyone anything anymore. Not without a Ouija board. Back in the day, Owen told Jack that if he ever went missing to come up here and bring a cadaver dog.

The cell rang again.

Bobby C. again.

*Ignore.*

Usually you couldn't get two bars up here, so the storm had to be messing with the signal. Normally, if he needed to make a call, he used the department cell phone, which was wired to the SUV. The department cell would mark his location and everything else about the call itself. Which was fine if he was up here during business hours. This was technically still his jurisdiction for another thirty yards or so, when it became county business, which was the provenance of the Sheriff's office, who only showed up if there was an accident with a body.

Off time? Jack unhooked the phone and the GPS unit and left it back at his house, or in the basement of the Sno-Cone Depot, a drive-thru snow cone shop the Biddle family operated for going on fifty years, over in the "cool" part of downtown, by the used record store and comic shop. It was a little side business that Jack inherited from his father—the only thing worth a damn the man ever gave him, other than training on how to use a gun—and that was a bit of a summer institution in these parts; when the giant neon sign that read **Treat Yourself and Treat Your Kiddies**! was lit, that meant it was vacation time. Anyone looked at his GPS right now, his car was parked right where it was supposed to be parked.

If he was a different kind of guy, Jack wouldn't drive around in his Tahoe when he was off duty, and this wouldn't be an issue. But the way Jack saw it, he was always on duty. Some shit went down, you wanted Jack Biddle to show up. He didn't mind using force. Didn't mind putting one in someone. Rob the bank? Be prepared to get rammed off the road by Jack Biddle. That was the nice thing about living in a shitty little beach town like Granite Shores: Jack Biddle got to be an action hero.

Plus, Jack *liked* rolling in his Tahoe. His father was the chief of police. His grandfather was chief before that. They never got a Tahoe; they just had shitty cruisers. One day, Jack Biddle would be chief, too, if he could unfuck this situation in time to not end up in a shallow fucking grave somewhere.

Jack took another deep drag.

Held the smoke.

At the bottom of the grade, which you could only see from this vantage point—another little trick his pops taught him years ago—he spotted a pair of headlights beginning their long and winding journey. It would be another fifteen minutes before the vehicle reached him—way the headlights looked, he guessed it was a van—provided the driver was familiar with the mountain and didn't freak out on every switchback. A newbie might take thirty minutes in this rain. A Canadian tourist might decide *fuck it* and turn around, keep going south until they hit Grants Pass. The beach would be there some other time. No sense trying to die for a thing you couldn't see at night, anyway.

The cell. Again.

This time it was Danny Vining himself.

Shit fuck motherfucker.

*Ignore.*

First thing tomorrow, Jack was getting a new cell phone. He didn't like the fact that every dirtbag in Losertown apparently had him on speed dial. He'd tighten that shit up. Second, he couldn't hide up on top of Yeach Mountain forever. Eventually Bobby C. was going to do some Bobby C. shit and kill his dog or abduct his wife, Caroline, or maybe both.

One more hit.

What to do?

The obvious answer was he should probably kill Danny Vining.

Jack did two tours in Iraq, first during Desert Storm—he'd enlisted in the army after high school, like a dumb fuck—and then he'd re-upped right after 9/11, found himself fighting house to house in Fallujah, and got to sort of liking it, so killing wasn't hard for him. It was part of the game.

Hell, he ended up getting popped by a nine-year-old with a .22, which got him sent home with a Purple Heart, a parade along the boardwalk, and then a few years of unceasing darkness . . . but he didn't hold a grudge against the kid. He was doing what he was told. Sure, Jack's brain was runny scrambled eggs for a time, which led to him doing some things for people maybe he shouldn't have. But it wasn't like he didn't enjoy doing those things.

These were out-of-town jobs that left Jack feeling like he was back kicking in doors. That rush. Had he taken it too far a few times? Yes. Did he like it, maybe too much? Yes. Did he have some bodies on his sheet?

Well, sure, but war was war. What was the difference between doing it for the government and doing it for Danny Vining's father? Iraq or Beaverton? Let God sort them out—that was the saying he was taught in the army, and that seemed like a good enough mantra all around. It's probably what the nine-year-old was thinking these days, too.

Anyway, that was years ago now. And anyone who knew anything about it was gone, even Danny Vining's father. Once Jack re-devoted his life to law and order (ish), he cleaned up those old messes, and that meant Mr. Vining went off Suicide Ridge one night. He was close to eighty. Didn't put up much of a fight. Body washed up a few days later; everyone figured it was dementia, the old man got lost and ended up in the drink.

But still.

Jack had been friends with Danny his entire damn life, so it wasn't like he could break into his crib and put one between his eyes and feel good about it. He had a real fondness for Danny. Everyone did. The fucking asshole. When he tossed his father off Suicide Ridge, he thought Danny would eventually see it as a kind of gift, an end to the suffering, or whatever.

Anyway, Danny being dead wouldn't solve the real problem—that Jack bet with money he didn't have and lost, again—since Danny surely kicked up to someone out of town. Maybe in Portland or Seattle or Las Vegas. Someone with real juice. Danny ran his book out of the shitty bungalow right behind his family's boardwalk confectionery shoppe—Sunshine Fudge—which was ballsy and told Jack everything he really needed to know: Everyone knew Danny's spot, which meant people more powerful than Jack were interested in his long-term existence. If Danny were to suddenly drown or get electrocuted or something, it wouldn't change the fact that Jack Biddle owed . . . someone . . . an additional $50,000 and had already lost about $200,000 this year alone.

$200,000 he simply did not have.

Never had.

But which the evidence locker did, from a case in the '90s when a local pharmacist and his family disappeared and left half a million in cash in their house. Bodies got found a few years later, disemboweled, buried, and frozen on Yeach, but the killers never turned up. This was back when his pops was still on the job. So he'd borrowed a little cash now and again, since he was in charge of the evidence locker, what with being the senior officer and because he was Jack-fucking-Biddle.

But that was a different problem.

Jack exhaled smoke out the window, into the rain. The blue plume hung there for a moment, like a thought, then was gone. Poof. Wouldn't that be nice. To just go POOF! But Jack had duties now. A life. They hadn't told anyone yet, but Caroline was pregnant. A miracle. They'd been told by doctors that they couldn't conceive, that Jack's swimmers were drowning, and so they'd basically given up hope until forty-eight hours ago, when Caroline got the positive test, right after her last city council meeting of the year.

Which is when Jack fucked it all up. Everything seemed ripe with possibility! Everything seemed miraculous! So when he saw that the Cowboys were favored to beat the Seahawks by twelve in the late Thanksgiving Day game, he knew it was a sign. The Seahawks were dogshit, but it was Thanksgiving, and Jack was feeling lucky, so Jack called Danny at home after he didn't pick up his cell, since even crooks celebrate Thanksgiving, and told him he wanted fifty K on Seattle to cover the spread.

"I want to see a bank statement first."

"I came into some cash," Jack said. "Sold some stocks. Just need twenty-four hours of credit."

"I'm not taking any bills stained from dye packs."

"It's not like that," Jack said.

"No old cocaine, either."

It wasn't like that, either. Not this time. No, this time, it was the universe communicating with him. He was going to win. He didn't need to put real cash on it. Danny would extend him credit for the night. He'd win. He'd be ahead.

Jack heard laughter in the background. Kids. A dog barking. During the tourist season, Danny's family had a monopoly on the fudge game up and down the Oregon coast. There was a town with diagonal parking, there was a Sunshine Fudge moving big product.

"I'm about to mash the potatoes," Danny said. "If this is what you want, understand that if you lose, I will expect full payment tomorrow morning. Nine a.m."

"Bobby C. isn't up that early," Jack said.

"But you are," Danny said. "And if you win, you'll expect payment promptly, and I'll do just that. You see how this works?"

The Cowboys beat the holy shit out of the Seahawks. 34–9. Sure enough, 9:01 a.m., Bobby C. was pounding on Jack's front door. Thank God he shuffled Caroline out the door at dawn to hit the outlet stores, gave her a hundred bucks to get a Coach bag. Jack waited on the side yard, peeking through the fence to make sure Bobby didn't break in to steal the DVD player, but at the same time kind of hoped he might, so he could put one in his chest.

"If you're hiding," Bobby C. called out after a while, "know I'll find you eventually, and it will be worse." When that didn't draw Jack out, he pulled out his dick and pissed right there on the door. Classy.

Now here he was, hiding on Yeach Mountain. If it wasn't for the good news about the baby, Jack might keep going right down the other side, disappear into the woods like the Patterson clan had, minus all that cannibalism bullshit, and try to live a more simple life. At least one that wasn't predicated on the Seahawks ever winning another football game.

Another blink of light pierced through the trees, fog, and rain. That van was moving. Which meant it was a local. If he pulled over a local up here, then everyone would know Jack was patrolling up here, and then he'd be out of hiding places. He'd wait to see if maybe he'd misidentified the lights. Could be it was a tour bus filled with Japanese tourists coming to stay the night before hitting the new outlet mall. Now, that would be a good shakedown!

So Jack Biddle did what he always did: He made a bad situation worse and went ahead and fired up another joint.

# CHAPTER TWO

$489,120.

That's what Robert Green owed the federal government, private lenders, and his sister, Penny, for the right to fail the bar exam.

Ten years since graduating bottom of his class at Harvard Law, Robert had failed the bar exam in New York, California, and Washington a combined fifteen times. It's not that he was dumb. Far from it. In fact, he was probably the second-smartest person to ever come from Granite Shores. Wasn't that he was a bad test taker. The core truth, he'd come to realize, was maddeningly simple: He didn't want to be a lawyer. Never wanted to be a lawyer. It was a notion put into his head from birth, practically, by his late mother and later—in all meanings of the word—his father. He would be a lawyer. His mother, herself a prominent lawyer, clearly wanted that for her only son. His father, a criminal, clearly needed that, if only to keep him out of prison.

He'd been trained like one of those kids whose parents dream of having an NFL quarterback, except instead of throwing spirals into garbage cans, he was reading *Crime and Punishment* on winter break during seventh grade, which didn't make him exactly the most popular kid in school, but at least he knew how to argue . . . which he mostly did these days with collection agencies and himself.

He knew precisely when his debt would hit half a million dollars. March 17 of next year. His bottom line compounding every day, every hour, every minute. Because that was the thing about being in debt: You were always accruing. There were no holidays, not even actual holidays.

It was the sort of additional truth that perhaps made Robert both take and fail the bar exam for a sixteenth time. He didn't even bother to study. What was the use? For him, the American Dream morphed into the American Reality: You would work for the rest of your functional life, until your brain was instant oatmeal—add a statin and a macchiato's worth of blood thinner to taste—and then retire with a depleted Social Security, gutted Medicare, and a plundered 401K. If you were lucky, the water shortages would kill you before the universe suffered its heat death. Even if he'd managed to become a lawyer, his own hot air would likely have added to the heat death.

Even his father, who'd managed to spend his entire life beholden to absolutely no one—the advantage of being an aspiring major league criminal in an avowed minor league town—ended up broke, alone, and owing money to the most vicious mob known to man—his mortgage lender—before dying alone in a hotel across the street from a Chico's outlet.

There was simply no escaping.

And that's why Robert Green was getting out.

Getting way out.

He was midway up Yeach Mountain in a white van he'd bought for eight hundred bucks from a wrecking yard in Pendleton. In thirty, maybe forty minutes—if he didn't slide off into Patterson Gulch in this fucking storm, Robert thinking now maybe he should have checked to see if the tires were bald, thinking, knowing, of course they were bald—he'd be back in Losertown for the first time since Dad slipped this mortal coil and even then, it was only for the funeral.

His sister, Penny, was waiting for him at the marina, where she'd spent the last few weeks, getting their late father's thirty-six-foot Catalina—the *Pere-a-Dice*—seaworthy. They'd separate out all the cash and jewelry right there, get it on the boat. Everything else of value, Penny had their cousin

Addie involved, underage, undermotivated, under her mother's thumb, which made her more than willing to commit some minor crimes. She'd be in charge of the physical part of the blackmail he and Penny planned. As in, she'd put things in the mail for them when the time came. Robert even set up a secret messaging system for them: a dummy Gmail account where Penny or Robert could simply leave messages in the drafts folder, which Addie would be able to access as long as she had the account's password. It was a move Robert learned from some criminal lawyers at the firm, which they'd learned from their clients. Hard to intercept mail that was never sent, after all.

They were all set.

Penny made a concise spreadsheet that showed who was to be blackmailed and when, based on the contents of the boxes, which Robert meticulously cataloged ahead of time. She then got a storage unit in town, paid for five years of rent ahead of time, gave Addie the keys.

And even if Addie fucked it all up?

Robert Green was fucking rich now. Cash alone? He guessed it was probably something like three million. Jewelry bumped that up another two, maybe three million, at least retail, but Robert understood you weren't getting top retail prices when you sold diamonds to the kind of people who bought diamonds. And then . . . all the other shit. Everything from baseball cards to guns to legal documents to ashes to art to illicit photos to pills to rings of keys that opened god knows what. He'd taken everything. Whatever he couldn't use, he could still *use*. It was valuable to the owner, which meant it was worth something to them, and they'd pay to get it back.

As far as epic heists go, it was pretty easy. Robert Green was the only person at the law firm of Barer & Harris who knew precisely what was in every single safe-deposit box housed on the sixteenth floor inside the firm's Grade V vault. It was part of their exclusive services aimed at the rich and rarely inconvenienced. They offered it in their offices in Seattle, Beijing, London, and the Island of Gibraltar alike, which Robert thought was like hanging a neon sign that blinked **HIDE YOUR LAUNDERED CASH HERE**, but which apparently wasn't illegal. Or didn't have the patina of illegality, anyway, since it was at a law firm instead of a bank or a private safe-deposit box facility. Whatever you kept at Barer & Harris had to be declared to your attorneys, which meant it was covered by privilege, unless it fell under the crime-fraud exception, which overrode that privilege since even your lawyer is required to let someone know if you intend to kill somebody. Which also meant that your secrets weren't yours alone and, theoretically, stopped you from storing your illegal gains.

The firm started offering their own safe-deposit boxes in the 1980s to a limited number of high-dollar white-collar clients who didn't want to be seen walking into and out of bank vaults all the time, this being back when banks were getting robbed on the regular. Now, thirty years later, with clients of every color collar, but with one thing in common—assets, dubious and otherwise—Barer & Harris advertised the service on their website and everything. The office in Gibraltar boasted that their boxes were located within the office's own World War II–era underground bunker, enhanced with the latest biometric security but with the comfort and class of a top resort, replete with photos of models sipping drinks and going over documents. The Beijing office touted boxes that were secure even from Chinese government intervention as they were the property of US clients and covered by international law, which was true only if you believed the Chinese gave a shit about such things as international law, which they rarely did. But the notion of security was always that you were secure from outside forces.

Nothing was protecting you from the one other person who had a key and a spreadsheet that kept track of all deposits to make sure no one was dumping off cocaine or child pornography.

It was still a law firm, after all.

In Seattle, that man was Robert Green. Who could be better? Since landing a summer associate position at Barer & Harris over a decade ago, Robert Green slid, notch by notch, down the ladder at the firm, until he finally landed, five years ago, on the sixteenth floor, managing the three hundred and twenty-four safe-deposit boxes belonging to the clients of the 108-year-old firm. It was a job that normally required a background check and a security clearance, but Robert Green, if he could have passed the bar, would have already been a lawyer at Barer & Harris, so no need to check those things out.

Robert was a beloved figure, pitied yet admired for his circumstances: a small-town boy and brother of a troubled prodigy, who failed the bar exam despite his natural grasp of the law. His decade-long loyalty earned him a unique role at the firm: He was the go-to person for sensitive tasks, handling discreet requests and questionable items—a roll of undeveloped film from the 1970s, a locked cell phone, an encrypted thumb drive—with unwavering professionalism, always willing to look the other way for clients who needed secrecy.

Well, that's what the firm thought, anyway.

Which was a mistake.

Robert checked his side mirrors and saw nothing but blackness behind him. Good. This time of year, driving up (or down) Yeach Mountain was a terrible, stupid, no-good idea. It rained every day, from November through February, only taking breaks for snow and sleet. And after that, it rained every other day until April. Even in the bright sun in the middle of a summer day, driving Yeach was a dicey proposition. One side: the uneven granite face of a mountain that was prone to sudden slide. Other side: a plunge to your likely death in the lonesome valley below. In between? There was a saying the old-timers had: a white line and a prayer.

Which was precisely why Robert chose this route, shortly after making his final decision last month.

Sitting in his windowless office, which was a cubicle with high walls, an envelope from the Washington State Bar Association unopened atop his desk-top calendar, Robert Green did the one thing he knew he probably shouldn't: He called Penny.

"It's here," he said when Penny answered.

"Shred it," Penny said.

Penny passed the bar at twenty-two. Never went to law school. Never practiced an hour of law. Couldn't if she wanted to, what with the Moral Character Provision the Bar imposes, and the felonies. Took it to prove a point to their dead mother and their living father: Neither of them was any better than her. If she wanted to, she could best either one of them.

In the background, Robert heard an old country song—Johnny Cash was about to kill a man in Reno—and some light chatter. "Where are you?" Robert asked.

"Work," she said. A faucet turned on and off. A bucket of ice got dumped into something.

"Since when do you work days?"

"Since I punched a fucking poet."

Penny worked at a restaurant called the Copper Skillet in Walla Walla. It was one of those shitty dives that somehow became a hot spot when Walla Walla upscaled from the home of wheat farms, Whitman College, and the state penitentiary to vineyards, Whitman College, and the state penitentiary.

"What would make you punch a poet?"

"Time and proximity."

It was hard to argue with Penny. She had an answer that sounded almost logical to everything. This was the benefit and the curse of her existence.

Penny had an IQ of 216.

Graduated high school at twelve.

Finished the University of Washington at fifteen. Fluent in Russian, Mandarin, Spanish, French, and Theoretical Computer Science.

Was in *People* magazine for being the youngest grad student at MIT. The headline? "Goth Einstein," Penny dressed in all black, wearing her band's T-shirt—the Christian Undead Necro Teens—and holding a laptop. Wore the same outfit on *Springer* a few years later, for the irony.

Sixteen and a juvenile criminal record and federal file. Hacking, drunk in public, fighting, a little minor B&E—robbed a fraternity

## Only Way Out

house, beat up a frat boy on the way out, Penny was also pretty good with her hands and feet and possessed a vicious head-butt—and *People* covered that, too. MIT kicked her out, which was fine; she wasn't attending anyway.

Twenty-one and already had a felony charge. Stolen car. Got off on a joyriding misdemeanor. *People* even sent someone to the court hearing.

Twenty-two and passed the bar. The *People* headline? "Disorder in the Court."

Twenty-six and punching poets. Somehow, *People* wasn't notified. Must have new editors.

In between all that, she'd spent a year working for some Russians as an interpreter. At least that's what she said she was doing. She'd gotten the job through some douchebag friends of hers, the kind of guys who owned a casino in Granite Shores and went by American names, but their passports were all in Cyrillic. It was typical Penny shit. Always on the edge of criminality, like her entire life was a middle finger to their mother, even after she was six feet deep. He'd get a postcard from Cuba, a phone call from Alaska, a Christmas letter that asked if she sent a ticket, could he get his ass to Moldova for a party? It was going to be off the chain!

Penny Green was the smartest person Robert knew.

And a total, unmitigated disaster of a person.

Robert said, "I'm going in." He ripped the envelope open.

> Dear Mr. Robert Green,
> It is with our regrets that we inform you that your Uniform Bar Examination score fails to meet the requirement for admission in the state of Washington. In order to be eligible for the state of Washington, you must achieve a combined score of 270 . . .

When Robert didn't say anything for a time, Penny said, "Fuck them."

"Fuck them," Robert agreed.

"You're smarter than all of them."

"So are you," he said.

"Oh I know," she said. "Also, I hacked the Bar Association's website yesterday and got your results. Impressive failure on every level. Left no doubt. You'd make a terrible officer of the court."

"Penny."

"Don't worry," she said. "I did it from the library at Whitman. Left no trace."

"I'm ready," Robert said.

"No you're not."

"I am," he said.

"You just found out," she said.

"I knew," Robert said. "I think I've always known. And you know what, Pen? It's a relief." He stood up then, looked over the top of his cubicle, made sure no one was around. "There's one way into this life and one way out. I don't want to spend the rest of my life waiting for that one way to show up. I want to live a real life."

"Well," Penny said, "that's good, because I gave my two weeks this morning. So don't do anything stupid until you see me."

After Penny hung up, Robert sat in silence.

It wasn't just that he was going to rob Barer & Harris—that had been settled in Robert's mind months earlier. It was that he didn't give a shit if they found out it was him.

He'd let the cameras see exactly how he did it all . . . eventually. Because the reality was that no one was watching anything in real time. The firm's security office was down the hall, and at the moment, it was stone empty, save for a lingering smell: Gabino Jones, the firm's head of security for fifteen years—and a former local boxer and firm client—died of a heart attack at his desk sometime over the first weekend of October. Fifty-seven years old, which is about eighty-five in steroid and meth years. Went into his office on Friday. Robert started to smell him around Wednesday. Benefit and hazard of having steel-reinforced doors.

His replacement was to start December 15, supposed to be ex–military intelligence and not just some local who looked threatening in a suit. Gabino hired him before he left this world, was planning on making him his #2. And now, he would be #1. It was Robert who called Mitch Diamond with the bad news, since Robert and Gabino were pals, in the way anyone you work with and never see outside the office is ever really anything to you.

"Are you a partner in the firm?" Mitch asked him that day, after learning the particulars.

"No, no," Robert said. "I'm the guy you'll eat lunch with." Which was true. Gabino and Robert ate with each other whenever both were in the office, not that Gabino was a desk guy.

"That's the guy I want to know," Mitch said.

Not that Mitch would watch the security video, either, the head of firm security more like a fixer than a cop. A criminal client threatened a lawyer in the firm, it was the head of security who went over to have a talk with him, often with a hammer. A partner gets drunk, runs over the neighbor's fucking cat, Gabino—and soon, Mitch—would show up in an hour with a check and an NDA.

Gabino, though, did a little time on the other side, too, which is why the firm liked him. He could handle business for them. All kinds of business.

"Why bother yourself with the law?" Gabino asked Robert once. They were sitting in the kitchen on the eleventh floor, sharing some leftover cake from a receptionist's birthday that afternoon. Work in a big office, it's always someone's birthday. "Those safe-deposit boxes you watch. What's the oldest one?"

"I'd have to look," he said.

"Bullshit," Gabino said. "You know it's Ford Baker."

Ford Baker, a Boeing executive, had a box going on forty years now. The contents: a Rolex, fifty thousand in cash, keys to a storage unit in Chicago that the firm made payments on every month for him—since he was in Walla Walla doing life for murdering his wife—and a stack of family photos. Each item meticulously entered into an Excel spreadsheet once a year, when they did an audit. *They* being Robert.

"What's stopping you from opening up his box and taking his shit?" Gabino asked.

"Morality, to start with."

"He didn't have no morality when he chopped his wife up and fed her to his pit bull."

"My morality is not predicated on how good or bad someone else is," Robert said.

"See," Gabino said, "you're a different kind of cat than me." He leaned close. "Perfect crime, when you think on it. If you're keeping your shit at your lawyer's office, don't matter if you're a drug dealer or a venture capitalist, you are not going to the cops if someone steals it."

"You've given this some thought."

"These days? With this hip? I'd rather have the fantasy than the experience. I couldn't carry all that shit down the stairs, even."

"Hire it out."

Gabino gave him a look that made Robert realize he and Gabino were not friends, just two people who occupied the same space from nine until five. "You're the kind of guy," he said, "you want to know about how people like me did bad shit, but you wouldn't ever do nothing, now would you?"

He wouldn't.

"See, I know where you grew up, who your daddy was, all that. You not that."

"You know who my daddy was?"

Gabino leaned even closer now, invading Robert's space, like how cops do. "Head of security," he said. "You don't get a job here unless I say so. So yeah. I know all that mess." That "mess"? That's when Robert's father paid a college kid from Granite Shores to burn down some failing restaurants in town for his friends, everyone getting rich on insurance money, except the kid, who eventually went to the cops when he didn't get his fair cut, and then someone broke into his dorm room and broke both his hands. Next thing the law was kicking in the front door of the Green house in Granite Shores. But that was just what he got caught doing, Robert's father always good to help facilitate a scam. Good thing Mom was able to keep Robert's dad out of jail, even though they'd long divorced by that point, being the personal attorney for the former governor having its perks. "Your sister, too."

"You're 100 percent pure class, Gabino," Robert said.

"Suppose I know more about all of you motherfuckers," he said. "Just like you and all those safe-deposit boxes. You know who's guilty of shit they haven't even been charged with. Now that's power." He leaned back, finally, back into his seat, took a bite of cake. "But see, difference between us is," Gabino continued, "me, I wanted to see the blood. Respectfully? You're a pussy. You'll always be the guy who didn't do shit. And that's a good, safe way to live. Wish I'd listened to that a few times in my life." Gabino got up, gave his finger another lick. "Good cake." Smiled. "Anyway. Don't try anything. I'll be watching." He pointed at the ceiling, where the security camera supposedly was. "Always." Licked his finger again. "Good damn cake."

That was all a year ago. He hadn't done shit. Not once in his life. Thinking about that conversation still pissed Robert off. Made him feel like a coward in his own life.

Planted a goddamn seed.

Robert stood up on his desk, reached up into the ceiling, and ripped down the acoustic tile—it was painted to mimic an azure sky after some consultant told HR it would keep the staff calm to see the sky periodically—and there it was: a camera. Like Gabino said.

That was the beauty of it all.

He didn't need to break into anything.

He had a key.

He had security clearance.

He needed a U-Haul truck.

He needed a van.

He needed a boat.

He flipped through his desk calendar. There was a perfect day. November 28. It was thirty-two days away.

That was more than enough time to prepare.

Black Friday. The offices were officially closed. But the safe-deposit boxes were open 365 days a year. Robert Green was on call every one of those days. The cameras were on, but not even the building's security team was on the clock, not that they had access to the private servers. Their main job was to make sure no one got up an elevator who didn't belong.

Robert Green belonged.

That moment, before he gave it any more thought whatsoever, he wrote an email to Stella in HR letting her know he'd be taking a three-week vacation beginning on Monday, December 1, his first real vacation in five years, so he had accrued time. He'd arrange to leave his box key for Mitch in case of an emergency, but he'd inform their clients ahead of time that he'd be away from the office and if they could wait until his return for any deposits or withdrawals, it would be much appreciated.

*Send.*

Five minutes later, Robert booking a flight to Paris, another to London, another to Mumbai, maxing out his credit cards, Stella in HR got back to him with two words: "Have fun!"

Oh he would.

It could be a month before anyone noticed anything was missing. Or it could be days, if, say, Danny Vining drove up to make a deposit or withdrawal, but that was unlikely. He never came in right after Thanksgiving. His business was too fluid around the holidays, too many big games. And anyway, he always called first, made sure Robert was there so they could bullshit a bit, talk about the old days in Granite Shores, when they were kids, riding bikes, every day a summer day, back when the boardwalk was the place. Pronto

Pups and saltwater taffy and Danny's family's fudge shoppe, diagonal parking, and shitty paintings on balsa wood. All that tourist shit that seemed cool when they were kids but now made Robert feel sad. Grow up in a resort town, all you see when you go back is the grift.

So he texted Danny. Give him that personal service he liked. Hey buddy. Hitting the beaches of Rio. See you in the New Year. Etc.

*Send.*

Fifteen minutes later: You deserve it, homey! Give my best to Goth Einstein lol.

The memory of this made Robert laugh out loud behind the wheel of the van. He could see it all unfolding like the movie he was sure it would one day be: Robert leaning back in his chair, eyes wide open, everything open, shit happening, doing it, giving the camera a big smile . . . followed by two flipped birds, secure in the knowledge someone would eventually see him, and he'd be long, long gone.

# CHAPTER THREE

Jack pinched the fire out of his last joint, looked down the mountain again. Definitely a van. Those headlights were too low for a bus. He had to guess, he'd go classic Econoline. Probably some normie trying to get home before the storm hit in full force. Could even be a neighbor. Lex Jacoby had an Econoline. That's who it probably was. He'd seen him up here before. Lex picked up *The Oregonian* from their plant in Portland a couple times a week for his newsstand on the boardwalk. Nice enough guy, let Jack pinch *Soldier of Fortune* every now and then, so whatever.

He dropped the joint into a ziplock bag, shoved it under his seat, leaned back. Let the high take him for five minutes. Usually, shit he came up on was pretty good. Sometimes it was laced with a little something extra, though that was less often these days. Everything was *less* these days, truth be told. It wasn't as if Jack was busting cartel motherfuckers. He was usually rolling twentysomething Canadians working south, moving their weight to college campuses, Granite Shores a good halfway spot between the border and California or Nevada.

Jack would patrol the shitty motels in town, looking for Canadian plates or rental cars, and then would start doing pullovers or he'd fake a noise complaint and pound open a door at the Super 8. If they were just kids, he'd take their drugs and money and let them go, maybe put a gun on someone until they pissed themselves a little, which pleased Jack. Some nights he really had to work a kid over to get them to piss; other nights, he'd pull his gun and it was like a Piss Now button. If they were real movers, he'd make an arrest, which was how he'd earned such a solid reputation on the force as a no-bullshit enforcer of the drug trafficking laws and a surefire Chief-in-Waiting.

Problem lately was that word seeped out. You stopped in Granite Shores, you were paying a toll. And so the small timers were driving straight through as often as possible, leaving Jack to shake down recreational users, mostly Canadians. Benefit of robbing foreigners of their illegal drugs was that they tended to stay quiet about it.

Still, his secondary income had taken a real dive. One thing led to a fucking other, and now here he was. Jack turned up the radio, hoping to find some old Pink Floyd to take him to the next level, but only found the fucking Eagles, some radio station always playing "Hotel California." He closed his eyes. Tried to really listen for the first time. See what it was all about, and maybe it was the weed, but Jack finally understood that bit about checking out but never leaving, but then he thought: *California. Yeah, maybe escape to California, change my name, become a big wave surfer, meet a girl named Buffy or Skipper or something, beer for lunch every day, grilled shrimp for dinner, mixing sex on the beach cocktails every night, yeah, that could be my life tomorrow . . .* which is right when the glare of headlights shot through the darkness and brought Jack back to the present. He opened his eyes, sat upright. Found his orientation.

*Shit. This guy is really moving. He's hitting that switchback going pretty fast.*

Jack checked the outside temperature. It was 32 degrees. The rain was starting to freeze. The road would be black ice in mere moments.

*This dumb fuck better be careful.*

Officer Jack Biddle, who'd spent his entire life thinking he deserved more, thinking that he *was* more, leaned forward in his seat, watched the lights zigzagging up toward the summit, not braking, just moving, moving, moving. Thinking, high: *Those lights look cool bouncing off the trees and wet pavement, it's like the old laser light show they used to do over the bay on the Fourth of July!* Then thinking, like a lawman for one brief second: *Maybe I should pull this asshole over for reckless driving?*

Thinking, like a fucking human being for once: *You need to be careful, there, hoss* . . . right when the lights spun around in a circle . . .

Knowing: black ice.

Foot off gas.

Control the steering wheel.

Don't lock your brakes.

Aim for the granite mountainside. Destroy your car, save your life, probably.

The lights twirled, twirled, and then . . . darkness.

"Oh that's not good," Jack Biddle said, like he was watching it all happen on TV and not, in fact, from the front seat of a Tahoe emblazoned with **TO PROTECT AND SERVE IS OUR DUTY** across the entire driver's side panel. A real albatross, that.

# CHAPTER FOUR

*Black Friday*

Content that darkness was the only thing closing in behind him, Robert Green began to relax. He checked his watch. Everything was right on time.

He'd driven ninety minutes from Seattle to a parking lot behind an abandoned Carrows in Centralia, unloaded the box-truck he'd rented using the firm's account into his new-old-van, left the keys in the ignition, truck running, stereo on conservative talk radio, Rush Limbaugh talking his dumb shit into the ether. Sat there for a minute, staring at the Carrows. He'd come here a dozen times a year as a kid. Maybe more. The designated Friday night drop-off spot for weekends with Mom. She not only taught in the law school at UW, she was their top fundraiser. Even after her death, when Robert himself was still in law school, it was probably her name that got him the interview with Barer & Harris. Probably got him the offer, too. That's the kind of reputation she had, professionally. No one seemed to care she willingly left Robert and Penny with their father in Losertown after the divorce. Didn't even try for custody.

Not that Robert and Penny argued the point. Life with their father, it was a ride. When he was a kid, everything seemed electric and cool and filled with possibility. It was only in retrospect that Robert recognized how bananas it was, how what was electric and cool and filled with possibility looked a whole lot like criminal neglect.

Mom would pull up in front of Carrows in her Range Rover, Robert and Penny sitting inside sharing a Belgian waffle, watching their father eat liver and onions. Dad saying, every time, always a little sad, never angry or bitter, "There she is, queen of the world." He'd put a twenty on the table, walk them outside, they'd climb into her Rover, no words would be spoken, and Sunday night they'd be right back here, this parking lot like Robert's own safe-deposit box. Maybe that's why Robert took every single box, he considered, even the ones where he knew there was nothing of real value. A photo of a clown. A deed to some land outside of Spokane. A Tupperware canister of dog ashes. A pair of women's shoes. Just because something wasn't valuable to Robert didn't mean the item was worthless. Like when he found out this Carrows closed. It felt like a close cousin was run over by a bus, even though he hadn't been inside the place in years, maybe decades. But if he had a safe-deposit box, he would have dropped the memory of his father's liver and onions in there, preserving it.

If his father had a box, what would have been inside of it? Probably a wedding photo. A frozen memory that nothing could touch. Something he'd pay anything to get back.

Robert turned out of the parking lot, drove around the city of Centralia for a few minutes, to see if a SWAT team rolled up on him. When none came, he headed south, then swung east, all the way through Portland, to make sure nobody was pacing him or waiting to snatch him up, and then slid across the state, headed for the coast.

Robert checked his rearview.

The last thing he wanted was to bring the cops to Penny, and this ride up Yeach was the best way to know, absolutely, if anyone was onto him. If they were onto *him*, fine. He had enough shit on the players at Barer & Harris that they'd never prosecute him. They might have him fucking killed, but they wouldn't let him in a courtroom.

Nothing.

He flashed his brights on. Was there a roadblock ahead? Twenty cops with AR-15s pointed at him?

Nothing but trees and road and darkness.

For the first time all night, he turned on the radio, began to scroll through the stations.

Static.

Static.

Static.

And then, coming in faintly from somewhere, the lingering strains of "Hotel California." Terrible song. Supposedly the band's tour manager once had a box at Barer & Harris filled with pills. This was back in the '90s. The old key master—an OG named Spenser who'd been disbarred for a cocaine problem leading to some financial malfeasance, which lead to his job on the sixteenth floor—told Robert the band's manager would come in with bottles of vitamins, not like anyone was testing the contents in a lab, and then whenever they came through the Pacific Northwest on tour, they'd get a courier to bring the vitamins to KeyArena or wherever they were playing. Whenever this shitty song came on, Robert imagined how smart these dipshits must have thought they were. How everyone always thought they were so damn smart.

His cell phone buzzed.

Penny.

"Problem," she said.

"What?"

"This storm," Penny said. "I don't know if we can get out of the bay. The wind is forty miles per hour pushing into land. It's a full squall, Robby."

*Shit.*

"What do we do?" Robert asked.

"You in the clear?"

"I haven't seen another car in forever," Robert said.

"Where are you?"

"About halfway up the mountain."

"See any ghosts of the cannibals?"

"Not yet," Robert said.

"Then we wait," she said. "Unload tonight. Spend the night on the boat. Wait it out. Hit the water at first light."

"Okay," Robert said. "Okay. If that's what you think."

"It's not what I think," Penny said. "You're the sailor."

The shoreline up and down the coast was filled with jagged outcrops of rocks. What they couldn't have is a situation where they washed up onshore in a boat filled with actual pirate's booty. "What do we do about Addie?"

"I'll handle that."

"Do we really need her?"

"Yes," Penny said. "And she needs us, trust me." Robert didn't love the Addie part. She was their cousin Donna's kid. The idea of getting her wrapped up in this shit felt dicey. "What's the worst that could happen? She fingers us? So what. Everyone is going to know it was us. Roll on us for a crime we want everyone to know we committed. Make her mom happy. Keep her from taking an obstruction charge."

"You're right, you're right."

"You're a rich man now. And Addie hates her parents so much, this is the best day of her life. She's a minor. Nothing she's doing even counts. Tomorrow at this time, we'll be on the high seas, grilling steaks and watching old kung fu movies on the DVD player."

"You put in a DVD player?" Up ahead, his lights flashed on a sign—VERY STEEP CLIMB AHEAD 14% GRADE—Robert suddenly thrilled that he hadn't attempted this deal in hot weather. This shitty Econoline would overheat, for sure.

"Robby," Penny said, "wait until you see this bad boy. Dad would be proud."

This made Robert smile. "See you soon," he said, "I'm almost at the Grade," and in that moment he believed that to be true, believed he and his sister, whose lives were tethered together by both great expectations and profound dumb-fuckery, were about to become legends. The important part, the bit they didn't talk about all that much, because it was the bit that actually hurt, was that they both knew when they hit Ecuador, they'd need to split up. If everything worked out, they might not ever see each other again. But that's what family was for. To love you enough to never see you again.

"Hotel California" came to an end, and the car filled with fucking "Feliz Navidad," objectively the worst Christmas song ever recorded. Robert Green, worth a few million dollars, driving a few miles from freedom, and a few weeks from a beach in South America, leaned forward to change the station, his eyes leaving the road for a blink, half a second, if that, not that it mattered, because it was at that moment one of his rear tires humped over something in the road and blew out, cracked the axel, and sent the car into incoming traffic—of which there was none, thankfully—and toward the sheer granite wall of the mountain, Robert thinking, *This isn't good.*

He slammed on the brakes, the wrong move—he'd lived in a city for too long—sending the van into a spin, thinking, *This would be an ironic way to die.* The rear of the van smacked into something—*the guard rail?*—and then for a brief moment he felt nothing, the van in the air, coasting. *Maybe this will be okay.* Then: *As long as I can walk out of this.* And then the van slammed head-on into a five-hundred-year-old, forty-foot-tall evergreen, and Robert Green, in his final millisecond, the evergreen slicing the front end in half, about to slice his head clean off, saw he was right, after all: He was long, long gone.

# CHAPTER FIVE

***Black Friday***

Jack couldn't see shit looking down the mountain. No flames or anything, so that was good; the van hadn't blown up. Not that a forest fire would happen in this weather, but still. Did he even really know where the van had gone? Trying to navigate the Tahoe down the road right now, high as fuck, in the freezing rain? Might end up joining the van on the side of the mountain. He'd need to walk.

Shit.

Jack dug his rain poncho from the back seat of the Tahoe, pulled it on over his heavy coat. Found his Maglite, checked it: fine. Went around to the back of the Tahoe, popped the trunk, stuffed bungee cords into a backpack, along with some road flares and a blanket. Fished around for his snow boots, pulled them on while sitting on the gate. What he wasn't going to do was break his own fucking neck out here. Jack stepped out from the shield of the evergreens and stood there on the side of the road, the freezing rain punching him in the face. Jack, letting it happen, hoped it might sober him up, then started to hike down the blacktop, toward where he thought the accident might have happened.

If the driver was dead, so be it.

If the driver was alive, well, he'd have to figure that out.

It took Jack about fifteen minutes to find the spot. There was a three-foot-long tree branch in the middle of the road, bits of shredded tire everywhere, the stink of burning rubber. He shined his flashlight up and down the blacktop, hoped maybe the driver was out and walking around, cursing the mountain and the ghost of Yeach Patterson, but there was nothing. He dragged the branch off the road, tossed it into the darkness of the gulch, kicked a tire tread away. He shined his Maglite along the road, looking for skid marks, no easy task on the black ice, then tried to triangulate where a car might have ended up if a tire blew and started spinning in this general area.

Jack stood there in the middle of the road, placed himself in the spinning car, jogged back up the grade, arms spread wide, trying to get a feel for what the driver felt, the weed not exactly hurting at this point, then zigzagged up another thirty yards or so, Jack knowing the math of a car accident like he knew his own birthday—a car travels fifteen feet for every ten miles per hour, figured the car he saw was going thirty miles per hour, maybe forty, but the spin would drop it—and came to a stop. Inhaled. Walked over to the gulch side of the road, shined his light. Kept walking, slowly, up the grade. Breathed deeply, hoping to catch a whiff of something that didn't belong, an old trick his father taught him. Nothing should smell like electricity, gas, or rubber. Catch even a hint of those on the wind, you've found a car.

Jack walked another thirty feet—the equivalent of half a second of travel time in the car—the rain coming down now like plastic wrap, Jack still doing his breathing tricks . . . and there, right *there*, he smelled something acrid, like a wet battery. He banked his Mag back and forth into the darkness of Patterson Gulch. A van coming down here would have a clean flight off the side of the road, would probably be in the air for two or three seconds before it started hitting evergreens.

He took out three bungee cords, hooked them together, sidestepped down another fifteen feet, found a solid trunk, wrapped one end of the cord around the base, hooked the other to his tactical belt. Shined the light back up to the road. It was complete darkness behind him. He broke his leg or something? You could fucking die out here. What the fuck was he doing?

"Protect and serve," Jack said, to hear something other than his own labored breathing. Turns out, getting lit before hiking Patterson Gulch was not the move. He kept inching down, shining his light in a corona, trying to smell that battery smell again, when the wind kicked up through the ravine, and suddenly the air was filled with pieces of paper. Jack grabbed one as it blew by. It was a spreadsheet from the law offices of Barer & Harris in Seattle, listing items. A gold pocket watch. A birth certificate for Terry Thomas. A passport for Terry Thomas. It went on. Terry Thomas's personal history.

Smaller papers fluttered by. Jack reached up, grabbed whatever was above his head.

Shined his light on his closed fist.

A fifty.

"The fuck?"

Reached up again.

A twenty.

The part of Jack's brain that was still high said: *Maybe it does grow on trees?*

And then he heard . . . was that "Wish You Were Here"? Jack took his hood off, stood rock still for a moment, then turned his good ear—fucking Iraq—to the wind, and there it was, the unmistakable chorus radiating out of the forest below. Finally, some Floyd. Timing wasn't great.

Jack took another several sideways steps down, the bungee cords growing tight, shined his light down the canyon, and there, wrapped around the base of a towering evergreen, paper beating out of it, was a white storage van. The kind with no windows. Jack took another step, but the bungee was at its limit. He unhooked it, latched it to a tree branch. He took one tentative step and started to slide, so he sat his ass down, an old trick to not break your fucking legs, and managed to come to a stop against the van's bumper.

He pulled himself up, made his way around to the front of the van, which was cleaved by the tree, the evergreen halfway through the cabin, pushing the guts of the engine into the front seat, Jack thinking that no one could survive that, knowing that for certain, bracing himself for whatever he was going to find. The driver's side door was open, which for a moment gave Jack a smidgen of hope, which ended almost immediately when he shined his Mag inside the cab and found a man—khaki pants, white dress shirt, one arm crushed against his body, the other dangling at one side, a nice watch on his wrist, a Tag diving watch, pretty fancy considering the van was such a piece of shit—who looked surprisingly at peace, considering he was missing his head.

Jack shined the light into the back of the van. It was filled with bankers boxes, Redwells, sealed plastic crates, maybe half a dozen green garbage bags, some of which had come apart in the accident. When a gust of wind blew through the crushed front window, the bags rippled, and out came cash, paper, newspaper clippings, photos, Jack unable to make sense of it yet, since his big question was: Where's this guy's head?

Despite the damage, "Wish You Were Here" segued into a commercial for Lippman's department store in downtown Granite Shores, a Thanksgiving "DOORBUSTER on turtleneck sweaters from fashionable designers! Prices lower than the outlet mall!" and then into a promo for KOGS 104.7, "the OGs of Granite Shores ROCK!" Which meant the electrical system was still operating.

A great way to blow the fuck up. Jack couldn't wedge his arm between the body and the van's console to get to the ignition, the whole thing crushed together and sticky with blood, so Jack unbuckled the seat belt on the body—which had kept the body safe, right up until it was tasked with keeping his head attached to his neck, but what are you gonna do?—then pushed the body over a few inches, blood and god knows what dumping from that gaping neckhole and onto the passenger seat, giving Jack enough room to grab the keys, turn the van off, plunge the forest into its natural silence.

He saw that the driver had a wallet in his back pocket, so he pulled it out, flipped through it. There was sixty bucks in it, which Jack pocketed, a dozen credit cards, every kind of Visa and Mastercard on the market, a Costco card, Seattle library card, even a fucking Discover card—Jack thinking this fucking guy was way overextended—and a Washington driver's license all in the name of Robert Green.

He'd gone to school with a Robert Green. They'd grown up together in Granite Shores, Jack a few years older, but back then it didn't matter, everyone played with everyone until puberty and high school hit, Jack a senior when Robert was a freshman. Everyone made a big deal of the fact that Robert got a perfect score on the SATs three years early. Some kind of prodigy or some shit. And then his sister, too, ended up being in fucking *People* magazine for being like ten times smarter than Doogie Howser. While Jack was off fighting actual fucking wars, Robert and Penny were getting the keys to the city for being fucking nerds.

Unreal.

He shined his Mag on the license.

An address on Forty-Eighth Avenue NE in Seattle. Nice. Not too nice. But nice enough. Jack's in-laws were up in that area.

But what was all this shit in the van?

He looked at the photo again. He wouldn't recognize Robert on the street. But that didn't mean he didn't know him. Didn't mean this wouldn't all seem shady as hell if he got involved with it. He needed to find Robert's head, be sure of this.

Jack stepped around the back of the van, tried the door—locked—slipped the key in, yanked the double doors wide open, and out popped Robert's fucking head, right into the muck, face up. Poor son of a bitch. He had a strange little smirk on his face, like he'd heard an old joke he liked, except one of his eyes was a crushed mess, like maybe his ocular well splintered, so maybe it wasn't 100 percent entertaining. Jack opened up one of the bankers boxes, thinking he'd get the head in there before it rolled away like on top of Old Smokey, but instead came face-to-face with a stack of Tiffany jewelry boxes. He opened one. It was a tennis bracelet, circled with forty or fifty diamonds. Next one: diamond earrings. A spreadsheet was stapled to the front of the box, like what he'd caught in the air.

> Law office of Barer & Harris
> Itemization of Safe-Deposit Box Items for Bethany C. Patchett
> *Tiffany Metro Tennis Bracelet*
> *Tiffany Elsa Peretti Diamond Earrings*
> *Tiffany Victoria Graduated Line Necklace* . . .

The list covered a full page. In this one box, all of Jack's financial problems could be solved, plus he'd have some walking-around money, plus a little something to put on Caroline's wrist, and then maybe put some bets in on Christmas games, to see where things stood . . .

Jack shined his light on each of the boxes. Same thing. All of them were from the law offices of Barer & Harris. He was familiar with the firm. They had a big criminal defense division. How many times had he found himself getting grilled by some fucking asshole in a $10,000 suit from Barer & Harris on a DUI trial? It was always the kid of some Seattle robber baron afraid a DUI would ruin their kid's chances of getting into Stanford when the truth was that it was probably the pound of coke he *hadn't* charged the kid on that was the real fucking problem, neither the kid nor Jack willing to bring that salient detail up in court.

Fuck it. He grabbed the jewelry boxes up—about twenty in all—shoved them into his backpack. This wasn't Robert Green's property, after all. He'd find out who this Bethany lady was, but if she was keeping this shit in a safe-deposit box at a law firm—which Jack didn't know was a thing—she wasn't going to be missing it. And what was Robert doing with it in the back of this beat-ass van? He'd figure that out, too.

Meanwhile, he'd climb back up, take this box home with him, get Bobby C. on the phone, give him some diamonds, they'd be square. He'd come back up this way on Sunday or Monday, part of his normal shift, call it in, do some hero shit on the news. Maybe start taking meetings again at the Native American casino up in Brawton, work on his gambling problem, now that he had a baby on the way, think about being better, in general, so he wouldn't find himself in situations like this in the future.

And then a fifty flew by his head.

Jack pushed some boxes aside, climbed all the way inside the van, found one of the open green garbage bags. Three bankers boxes were stacked inside. The first box was missing its top. It was filled with cash. Fifties and twenties rubber-banded together. Jack counted five, ten, fifteen . . . thirty-seven rolls. There must have been $50,000 right there. Maybe more. All his fucking problems: POOF. There it was. The elusive POOF.

He pulled that box out, set it lightly on the floor, covered it with another box. Yanked open the second box. More cash. The third box. More.

How much?

He couldn't be sure. There were fives and tens and singles.

Enough to retire on? No.

Enough to start a new life? With the Tiffany jewels he already had in his backpack? With whatever was in the rest of these boxes?

Hell fucking yes.

Jack stood there for a moment. Was this what fate felt like?

Robert Green was dead. Whatever he was doing, Jack had the sense that it was highly illegal. Wherever he was going in Granite Shores with all this loot, it couldn't have been to sponsor the local pet rescue. He'd need to figure that out. But there was no sense leaving all of this stuff out here, subject to the elements. No, Jack would bring his Tahoe down the grade, grab as many boxes as he could carry back up, get them into his trunk. Hope that the rain died down, come back tomorrow, get the rest of it.

He'd get a body bag, get Robert into it. Get him on some ice. Figure out what he should do next.

Well, no.

That wasn't true.

He knew what to do next.

Jack checked the time. He had about an hour before Caroline started to worry about him.

He should bite the bullet, the one Bobby C. would probably be putting in his head eventually, get the coroner, a tow truck, about a dozen cops, probably the Sheriff's office, probably someone from Barer & Harris. Hell, probably the FBI eventually. Maybe he'd go to rehab. That would probably save his life, twice.

That's what he should do.

Jack Biddle shoved as much cash as he could into his backpack, grabbed up the empty green garbage bag, crawled out of the van, picked up Robert Green's head, the poor son of a bitch, shoved it inside, spun the bag around, tied it in a knot, took a deep breath, and began to hike back up the side of Yeach Mountain.

# CHAPTER SIX

*Saturday*
*Klamath Falls, Oregon*

California was a done deal for Mitch Diamond. Not that anyone in California knew him by that name. Didn't even bother to tell his mother he was leaving, figuring that when the time came, she'd understand he'd done a good thing for her.

He ended up in Klamath Falls working for his ex-cousin-in-law, Dale, who ran the night shift at the Purple Flamingo casino, a bar with six video-poker machines, nightly keno and Tuesday night karaoke, and then a fairly active meth and sex trade in the parking lot. The place was owned by the Golubev brothers, Fred and Rodney, who were twins. Dale claimed they were connected to some organized shit over in Russia.

Mitch didn't buy it. They drove Subarus.

Dale had him working the grill, which he was good at, and for the first few months, Mitch thought maybe he could spend some time in Klamath Falls. Maybe get some cash together and buy a trailer over at the Casablanca Trailer Estates, which had its own bowling alley, according to the flyer pinned up in the break room.

But then Mitch's homey Gabino—who he knew from his Golden Gloves days and then when Gabino needed some help getting out of a situation with some Samoans in Spokane—tracked him down, told him about a sweet deal going up in Seattle, salary, benefits, all that, and if Mitch could get up there before Christmas, he could get in on it, too, because Gabino needed a guy he could trust. A straight job with a crooked side, mostly legal. Gabino would fix up some hiring paperwork. All Gabino needed from Mitch was some cooked documents, and then he'd get it all set, Gabino would make it right, keep it safe for him. Get up to Seattle by the middle of December, man, they'd be running a game like the old days, but with health benefits.

But then Gabino went tits up a few weeks after Mitch got him what he needed to set up his identity. Mitch still had the job, that wasn't a problem, it was just that now he had to pull it off on his own. He'd have to fake it, not get tossed up on anything before December 15, then figure it out as it went. What's the worst that could happen?

"Anyone looking for you in Granite Shores?" Dale asked. He'd brought Mitch into his office at the Purple, which was surprisingly spacious. There was a big desk that Dale shared with the other assistant managers, a minifridge, a sunken caramel-colored leather sofa that had the imprint of every ass that ever sat on it. There was a window that looked out to the parking lot and the street beyond. It was raining outside, like every other night in Klamath Falls, so the pavement glowed a dreamy purple from the neon lights out front.

"No one I'd recognize."

Dale said, "Turn around, I need to open the safe."

"I don't do that shit anymore."

"Humor me," Dale said.

"Fine," Mitch said. He turned around, took a paperback from inside his apron pocket. He'd started reading in San Quentin and told people it gave him a profound sense of empathy, but the truth was that the biggest thing he got from books was that even though his life was prone to dumb-fuckery, there were opportunities out there to fuck up that far exceeded his own limited imagination.

This wasn't one of those books, though. An ex got Mitch hooked on Richard Bach books when he was getting clean and somehow, they'd become comfort food. This was maybe the tenth time Mitch read the one about the talking seagull, so when the words started to jumble on the page—a sign of how fucking exhausted he was, his dyslexia showing back up like that—Mitch closed his eyes. He heard Dale's chair creak, heard the spinning of the combination, counted the seconds . . . figured the combo was something like 6, 9, 19. You break into enough cheap safes, you never forget precisely how long it should take to get to every number. It wasn't about the eyes, not really, it was about the ears and your fingertips and dumb luck. In this case, it was also knowing how predictable Dale was. Anyway. If he was going to rip a safe, it certainly wasn't going to be the Purple Flamingo's.

"You can turn around." He'd put an envelope on the desk between them. "You have a driver's license?"

"Of course."

"Valid?"

"It'll pass," Mitch said.

"Cop runs it, what happens?"

"If we get to that point," Mitch said, "it means someone found a body."

Dale considered that answer for a moment, shrugged. "I got an errand for you," he said. He handed Mitch the car keys. "There's a Caddie in the parking lot. You drive it up to Granite Shores, drop off the keys, get a hotel for the night, catch the grey dog back to Klamath Falls. We'll give you $500 plus whatever the hotel runs. Stay somewhere nice, even. Easy-peasy."

"Whose Caddie is it?"

"No one you know," he said.

Mitch set his book on the desk and went to the window, see if he could spot the Caddie in question.

"It's the red one," Dale said.

Mitch recognized it. It belonged to a regular named Paul Copeland, who the girls in the lot called Poochie, because he owned Paws & Reflect, the dog grooming place up over on Wantland Avenue. He tended to show up around dinner time covered in fine dog hair and smelling vaguely like pet shampoo. He'd get a burger, play some video poker, get a hand job, and head home. Mitch saw him maybe six times in the last month, but not recently.

"Nice ride," Mitch said.

"Don't be thinking of running off with it," Dale said. He got up, looked out the window for a moment, then dropped the blinds, went back to the desk, put his feet up. "So you're good?"

"Who is 'we' in this situation?"

"What are you talking about?"

"You said, 'We'll give you $500.' Who is 'we'?"

"You're just driving a car," he said, not answering the question. "You get to Granite Shores, you hand the keys to a little old lady, she hands you a cashier's check, you come home, we're all straight."

"A cashier's check?"

"She's a little old lady." He shrugged. "It was either that or like a dozen money orders."

"This doesn't sound straight."

Dale cleared his throat. "Between us?"

"No one else in the room."

"I've run into some trouble. Some money trouble. But I figured out a way through it. This is the conclusion," Dale said. "You do this? Everything comes clean, we'll get you off the grill, get you into something more lucrative. Isn't that what you want? A shot? Isn't that why you called me when you needed a place to stay?"

Mitch hadn't told Dale about Seattle.

"When would I leave?" It was a six-hour trip.

"You want some crank? You could leave right now."

"That shit makes me paranoid," Mitch said.

"Oh *that's* what makes you paranoid, okay." He picked up Mitch's book, flipped through it. "Why are you always reading?"

"Keeps me from thinking about my own death," Mitch said. None of this seemed right. "I want a thousand. Up front. I'll find my own lodging."

Dale nodded, then ran his tongue over his front teeth. It was a weird habit he had, from back when he had a habit. "So this bird. He talks?"

"That's right."

"Crazy," he said. He slid Mitch's paperback into his back pocket, like it was his own fucking book, then said, "Fuck it," pulled out a wad of cash from the envelope, counted out ten bills, put them on the table. "Two things. Go the speed limit. Don't let anyone in the trunk."

Mitch left Klamath Falls after 2:00 a.m. and even still the six-hour drive took him eight hours, Yeach Mountain on the other side of Granite Shores covered in ice and snow. Highway patrol and Granite Shores cops were escorting five cars at a time over the pass, make sure no one crashed out. When the highway patrol officer came to Mitch's window, he played the rube, kept it calm, thinking this wasn't a scenario that was likely to end poorly. Highway patrol and cops, they didn't fuck with white dudes in Cadillacs. Not out here, anyway. Their racism was consistent over the years.

"Pretty treacherous up there," the highway patrolman said. He was maybe twenty-five. "Do you absolutely need to get into town today?"

"My auntie's all alone," Mitch said.

"What's her name?"

Mitch, as a rule, didn't answer questions from people in uniforms. So he said, "Auntie Dora. On my wife's side." Dorothy Copeland was the name Dale gave him. "You know her?"

The highway patrolman peered into the car for a moment, Mitch thinking maybe he'd fucked that up, but then he said to Mitch, "Oh I know her. We all got that one, right? Lives alone, you gotta go over to fix her VCR from blinking, that whole deal. Married your wife, married her whole family, right?"

"Right."

"Wifey says you take care of her auntie," the patrolman said, "you take care of her auntie."

The patrolman patted the roof of the Caddie. "Say no more. Be safe." He pointed up the mountain. "Patrol car will be back in fifteen. Wait on the side of the road. Under the grade sign."

Mitch drove another twenty yards, pulled over beside a sign that said **Very Steep Climb Ahead 14% Grade**.

Sat.

Waited.

Fifteen minutes became twenty. An SUV parked behind him, another pulled in front of him.

He was about two-thirds of the way up the east side of Yeach. Off to his right was Patterson Gulch, where supposedly some kid ate his whole fucking family and maybe a cat or dog or maybe it was a donkey? It happened in the 1880s or 1840s or 1760s. One of those. Mitch heard the story a bunch of different ways over the years in about ten different bars in the region. He'd never believed it.

Mitch took down the passenger window to get a better look at the environs. Peered out into the woods. The gulch was too far down to see through the wall of trees and the thick mountain fog even this early in the day.

Ice pelted the car.

The wind whipped.

Mitch decided, you know, maybe the kid roasted his family for warmth and didn't eat them or the pets . . .

. . . and then a gust rolled up from the gulch and swept damp and muddy debris in through the window: Leaves, twigs, soggy trash, and dirt spattered onto Paul's rich leather interior—he really kept his ride nice—and got rammed between the windshield and dash and into the air vent. The defroster blowing the dirt up against the window.

Mitch reached in, yanked whatever all the crap was, expecting to see mulch and big maple leaves in his hand, which he did, but also, inexplicably, a twenty-dollar bill and two fifties. Wet and one of the fifties was missing a corner, sure, but all the cash would still be good in any decent establishment and all the disreputable ones, too.

If Mitch was a betting man, he would have gone somewhere and put that twenty down on black.

But he wasn't.

Not anymore.

This was his practical era, after all.

So instead, he got out of the Caddie, walked around to the passenger side, checked the soft shoulder for more cash. He didn't find any. But he did find someone's wedding photo from what looked like the 1950s—it was embossed with *1953* on the white border—and a torn envelope stamped PERSONAL AND CONFIDENTIAL. There was a boot print across both. Mitch took another step along the shoulder and felt the dirt give, so he hopped back against the Caddie as the edge gave way. Jesus-fucking-Christ. What he didn't want was to die an ironic death, even if the irony was only in his own mind.

"You all right there, partner?"

Mitch turned and saw that a Granite Shores Police Tahoe was idling beside his car, window down, cop looking at him with crazy eyes.

"Yeah," Mitch said, "thought I'd take a quick leak."

"Good way to break your neck, like a real yahoo," the cop said. "What do you have there in your hand?"

Mitch looked down. He'd practically forgotten the photo and envelope. "Nothing," he said, "just some garbage. Litter makes me crazy. Keep America beautiful. All that Lady Bird Johnson shit."

"I'll take that," the cop said. He put his hand through the open window. Mitch came around the Caddie, handed him the trash. The cop looked at the photo. "Look at that. Probably been sitting by the road for fifty years."

"Boot print is fresh," Mitch said.

The cop tore the photo in half and in half again, dumped it onto the floor of his Tahoe. Weird. Did the same with the envelope. Smiled at Mitch. "You'll be over the hill soon enough. There's a nice toilet in Shake's bar. Turn right on Beach Boulevard. Can't miss it. I'm here to get you over, if you want to get moving."

Mitch sure did. He got back into the Caddie. The cop pulled ahead of the SUV. Mitch examined the cash for a moment. Fairly new bills. The twenty was a series 2006. The fifties were series 2004 and 2001. He took one last look out the passenger window before putting it up, in case another gust of cash came his way.

Nope.

Just ice and wind and leaves.

Mitch put the cash behind his fake driver's license. A little lucky money.

Maybe today was going to work out okay.

Maybe today was going to turn fortune's way for once.

Maybe may be.

When Mitch finally got into downtown Granite Shores, the streets were mostly empty. The blue and yellow beachside resort motels flashed vacancy signs, a few already getting fancy with Christmas lights and decorations. The only places with any signs of life were the comic book shop, the fudge store, where there was a guy in the window boxing up candy, Shake's bar—where he did, in fact, stop to piss—and Lolly's Diner, which advertised a breakfast special of three eggs and three sausage for six bucks—**FOR A LIMITED TIME!**—on a banner that looked like it had hung in the same spot for a decade.

The boardwalk attractions looked cartoonish in the distance, the ancient roller coaster—the Demon—and the Ferris wheel, both bright red against the gray of the Pacific. The storm was stuck on the other side of the mountain, however, so by the time Mitch turned down E. Madison, he found himself in a sun-dappled village called Granite Park filled with diagonal parking, artisan ice cream shops, too much green space, and women in Juicy tracksuits pushing strollers and sipping from Starbucks cups. It felt like a Meg Ryan movie from the '90s, but not the one Mitch saw. Everything was a shade of J. Crew. Mitch fished out the Post-it note Dale had given him with the directions to the address he was looking for, and a few minutes and about a dozen strollers later,

Mitch found the Shore View at Granite Park. A six-story complex on a bluff that hung right over the Pacific. If there was ever a tsunami, everyone was fucked.

Dorothy Copeland. Apartment 403.

Apartment 403 was down a long hallway that smelled like cooking meat and cleaning solvent. There was a stack of three newspapers at the door, a Christmas wreath hung around the peephole, and even from outside Mitch could hear the TV blaring. Mitch rang the doorbell. Waited. Knocked. Rang the doorbell again. When no one came to the door, Mitch checked out the handle. Standard colonial reproduction from the 1970s. Maybe late '60s. Cheap. He'd never let his own mother live with one of these.

Took him forty-five seconds to pick the lock.

He cracked the door.

"Hello, Mrs. Copeland?" he said. "I'm here with your car."

Nothing. He slid in, locked the door behind him.

To the right was a short hallway leading to a bedroom, which is where the TV was playing. The door was open, and Mitch could see the corner of a bed and a dresser, but nothing else. In front of him was a great room, which was surrounded by floor-to-ceiling windows with a view of the Pacific and the floating bridge to Loon Island, where the rich people lived. Mitch stepped a few feet in, sniffed. There was a bad smell somewhere in the house. One he'd smelled a time or two before. Mitch went down the hall, but all he found in the bedroom was an immaculately made California king, covered with about fifty pillows, and an old-style TV, the kind that was also a piece of furniture, shoved into a corner. A woman in a floral dress was telling Pat Sajak about how she'd never been to Hawaii but that was all about to change!

Mitch found the remote on the bedside table next to a glass of something brown, clicked the TV off, smelled the glass. Coke or Pepsi. There was a dead fly in it and no carbonation. Mitch took a look in the bathroom. The tub was empty. No one was dead on the toilet. So that was a relief. Opened the medicine cabinet. Found all the usual suspects. Emptied the bottles of the good stuff into his pockets. A little something for the bus home. Found a hand towel, dampened it, wiped down everything he touched.

Mitch made his way back down the hall, through a pocket door into a galley kitchen, found a Coke in the refrigerator, drank it down. Checked the milk. Good for another week. The yogurt. Same. There were green bananas on the counter. Back into the great room. The smell was stronger here. No blood on the floor. Maybe it was a dead rat in the wall? There was a sliding glass door to the patio, which wrapped around the apartment in an *L*. Mitch opened it up, stepped outside, and found what he was looking for: There was a woman on a chaise longue, a towel pulled up to her hips, hat and sunglasses on, a crow standing on her chest pecking at what was left of her fucking face.

After wiping everything down again, Mitch found a cordless telephone in the kitchen, called Dale at home. When he didn't pick up there, Mitch tried his office. "The fuck you calling for?" Dale said.

"Mrs. Copeland," he said. "You know her?"

"Not . . . directly." Whatever the fuck that meant.

"Okay, well, she's dead."

"What do you mean she's dead?"

"I mean there's a bird eating her fucking face. Dead."

"How long?"

Mitch walked over to the sliding glass door, looked at Mrs. Copeland. She hadn't started to liquefy, but bugs were starting to work at the open bits, plus of course the birds. The weather was fairly cool and the patio was protected from the elements by a wide overhang, so that was a help. "A day or two."

Dale lit a cigarette. "That's a real problem."

"For who?"

"You see a cashier's check anywhere?"

"Not in plain sight."

"Open some drawers. See if maybe you can find a checkbook."

"Let me ask you a question," Mitch said. "You of the opinion you want my fingerprints all over this apartment? Because I'm not."

"You on her phone?"

"I am."

"Probably gonna be pretty clear she wasn't making calls today, so you've already fucked up, hoss. For both of us."

Shit.

"What do you want me to do?"

"Best thing would be to find that cashier's check. Second best thing, figure out if she has a safe or some diamonds or something. Anything easy to move."

"You think I can move a safe?"

"I think you can do whatever you want," Dale said, "but maybe you've gone light on me."

"Light? I did five at San Quentin and don't want to go back. So don't talk to me about light."

"Look around," Dale said. "I'm gonna need to call you back in fifteen minutes. Don't leave."

Mitch found some cold cuts in the fridge, a loaf of Jewish rye, made himself a sandwich, flipped through a *People* magazine in the living room. Poked around for a safe or some stash of expensive jewels. Found some shoeboxes filled with receipts, a couple of old rings that someone would miss if they were gone, that kind of family heirloom shit that Mitch was averse to stealing. Mrs. Copeland's purse had some credit cards and thirty-six bucks in it and a sleeve of photos, all of a German shepherd. Mitch took the credit cards, left the cash and the photos. Went through some drawers in the kitchen, found photos of Mrs. Copeland with the same giant German shepherd. Went into her bedroom. Opened drawers. Looked under the bed, half expecting to find the German shepherd rotting away, but there was nothing but dust bunnies and socks.

After twenty minutes, Mitch called Dale back. Nobody picked up. Twenty-five minutes, he called the general line at the Purple Flamingo. Same. Mitch seeing the obvious: Dale was in the wind, the fuck. Mitch stood there for a moment, tried to figure out his next move. He had to get the fuck out of there. Fucking Dale. Put this shit on him? All that, Mitch realized, and he stole his fucking seagull book.

When Mitch got to the parking lot, there was a teenage girl leaning against the Caddie, licking an ice cream cone. She was dressed in all black, thick white pancake makeup on her face, black lipstick, hair teased like she'd recently been electrocuted. Mitch hit the key fob to unlock the ride, which got the girl to look at him with vague interest but didn't make her move.

Instead, she said, "You're not Paul." She wore a T-shirt with the logo of a band called the Christian Undead Necro Teens. She was maybe sixteen. Maybe seventeen. Certain point, it's hard to know how old anyone is anymore, except to know that they're too young.

"Isn't it too cold to be eating ice cream?" Mitch said. The sun disappeared and the rain he'd driven in all day was beginning to sprinkle down.

"Oh god, no." The Christian Undead Necro Teen shrugged and rolled her eyes at the same time. It seemed to be the most physically taxing thing she'd ever done.

Mitch looked up at the apartment building, see if he could make out Mrs. Copeland's balcony, but the angle, thankfully, was wrong. Which was probably why no one noticed her up there. "You live here?"

"Loon Island," the Christian Undead Necro Teen said. "We came over for Thanksgiving. My nana lives on the third floor, so I saw the car pull up. Thought it was Paul. But guess not."

"What's your shirt about?" Mitch said.

"The Christian Undead Necro Teens? That's my cousin Penny's band."

"Never heard of them."

"Penny Green? You don't know her?"

"Should I?"

The girl shrugged. "She could have been bigger than Nirvana ever was but like, lived to spend the money."

"'Could have' is doing a lot of work for you."

"Google her. You'll be impressed. Like the most famous person to ever come out of Losertown."

"Where's that?"

"Right here. It's what we call it."

"Why?"

"Dude," she said, "look around."

He did. It seemed nice enough. Mitch said, "How do you know Paul?"

"We hang out sometimes during the summer," she said. "He's real cool." This made her laugh. "Well, okay, not *cool*, but like, nice. Not a creeper." Then she laughed again. "When he's here for the holidays and we're here, he'll always drive me to Frontier Square and like, pick me up and take me for Sunshine Fudge and all that."

"What's 'all that' entail?"

Christian Undead Necro Teen eyed Mitch for a moment, then said, "You a cop?"

"I look like a cop?"

"Undercover, maybe. Do you have any tats?"

Mitch rolled up his sleeve. Showed her the ace of diamonds card he got in prison. He wanted an ace of spades, but the fucking guy who did the ink, Kiko, convinced him a diamond would be more distinctive, every asshole has the ace of spades. So ace of diamonds it was, and this was before he'd stolen the dude's name. Luck worked out that way for Mitch.

The girl examined the ink, went back to licking her cone, presumably satisfied. "Paul helps me sell my Adderall and Xanax and shit. My loser mom is trying to turn me into an addict. So I'm turning a profit on it."

"That's no way to talk about your mom."

"She's not much of a mother." She shrugged again, this time as if there was a thousand-pound yoke over her shoulders. "My mom went to high school with Paul, so it's like, whatever. He's like an uncle. Everyone in Granite Shores knows everyone."

"I get that sense."

"My cousin Penny?" she said. "I'm helping her with something big."

Mitch had the sense that if he asked her one question about whatever that big thing was, she'd eventually get him digging for Hoffa's body. Girl had a weird energy. Not bad, just weird. Reminded Mitch of himself, back before he started getting caught for shit, when it all seemed cool and dangerous, but not consequential.

"Where's your mom now?"

"She and my nana are screaming at each other upstairs. So I decided to get a cone and wait it out, hoping Paul would see me and come save the day. But guess not." She took another lick of her cone and then tossed it into a bush. In the distance, Mitch thought he heard a siren. Probably a coincidence.

The siren got louder. Mitch took a step out onto the street, looked down the block, then back toward E. Madison Street. On the corner, a woman stood talking on her cell phone, pushing a stroller back and forth with her foot. Except there was a corgi in the stroller, not a kid. The corgi heard the siren, too, his head up, ears perked, Mitch thinking: *I need to get the fuck out of Granite Shores.*

"Why are you driving Paul's car?" Christian Undead Necro Teen asked.

"I was dropping it off," Mitch said.

"That doesn't make sense," she said, but with no real conviction behind it, even though she was correct. It didn't make any sense. "How old are you?" she asked.

"Old enough not to be comfortable with this conversation," Mitch said. "How old are you?"

"I'll be nineteen," she said. She didn't give a timeline. "I don't suppose you want to drive me to Frontier Square, do you?"

"Sorry, kid," Mitch said. "I'm not the kind of guy you're supposed to ask for rides."

A police Tahoe turned down the street. The sirens blared for a moment and then abruptly turned off. The cruiser came to a stop in front of the Shore View.

Mitch said, "What's your name?"

"Addie."

"That's an old lady name," Mitch said.

"Maybe I'm really an old lady." She flashed Mitch a peace sign. "See you never," she said and then took off down the street.

"Friend of yours, partner?"

Mitch turned and the cop was out of his cruiser now. It was the same guy from on top of Yeach, except he wore reflective sunglasses now.

"Just met," Mitch said. They both watched Addie stomp another twenty yards or so up the block, then plop down on a bench with a view of the Pacific.

"Guess she doesn't like cops," the cop said. He walked over to Mitch, stood beside him. "Never got that goth shit. Like why pretend to be dead? So weird. What was her shirt about?"

"She's related to a Christian Undead Necro Teen," Mitch said, figuring answering questions about the kid would make him seem less suspicious. Just two dudes amused by the youth of America.

"Penny Green?"

"Yeah." How the fuck did he know that?

"No shit," the cop said. He looked around. "She here, too?"

"I wouldn't know her, but I'm told she's famous."

"People got a skewed sense of what fame entails."

A window opened on the third floor of the building. A woman stuck her head out, shouted, "Finally! They're making me crazy!" and then closed the window.

"You live here?" the cop asked. Mitch caught a whiff of something on his breath. Was that . . . weed?

"Nope," Mitch said.

"Nice ride," he said. He took off his sunglasses. His eyes were slits. Was this cop . . . high? "Haven't seen it in town. You visiting from somewhere?"

"Klamath Falls."

"That's a shithole," he said.

"You get used to it."

Mitch saw that the cop had a name tag. Officer Biddle. He'd been in a slicker when they were on the mountain.

"Eat shit for long enough," Officer Biddle said, "it's just a meal." He looked up the length of the building. "Hope they've got an elevator; my knees are cooked today. And do me a favor, partner, when you head home, stay in your car this time. Don't want to have to pull your body out of the gulch later." And then he was off, disappearing inside.

Mitch waited a minute, made sure Officer Biddle, blazed to the roots of his hair, didn't show back up. Popped open the Caddie's trunk. Inside was a white Igloo cooler. Mitch took the top off. There were several ice packs stacked on top of something. Mitch peeled away the top layer, and that's when he saw the pointed ears, the long snout, the dead eyes.

The German shepherd.

So that's where he was. There was a Post-it note stuck to his head. It read, in all caps: NEXT TIME IT WILL BE YOU'RE SUN IF YOU DON'T PAY UP.

Fucking Dale couldn't spell for shit.

Mitch repacked everything, closed the trunk, locked the Caddie, walked up the block, found Addie, sat down next to her. She was smoking a clove cigarette, offered him a drag.

"I was told they make your lungs bleed," Mitch said.

"I heard that, too," she said. "That like, they have fiberglass in them or something."

"Give me one," Mitch said. Lit it up. Inhaled. It was like smoking a yoga mat dipped in formaldehyde. Mitch dug the keys out of his pocket. "You want to get out of here?" he asked.

"Like nothing else in the world," she said.

"You do me a favor?" he asked.

Addie took a long drag on her clove. "I'm actually seventeen."

"You know how to drive?"

She took another drag. "And a half. Seventeen and a half."

"Yes or no."

"I crashed in driver's ed," she said.

Mitch handed her the keys and a couple of Mrs. Copeland's credit cards, all of which she took without question. "How much you think you could get for those cards?"

"They're not reported stolen?"

"No."

"Kids at the Square will go nuts on these. But not if you're around." She flipped over a gold American Express card. "You could buy a plane with this, probably."

"I need about three grand," Mitch said. Three grand, he could have some walking-around money for a few days before he got to Seattle. Maybe get a gun if he needed one.

"When?"

"How soon you think you could get it for me?"

"Two, three hours," she said. "Oooh, this is nice." She waved a Nordstrom card in the air. "They just opened one over by the outlet mall."

"It's all yours. Finder's fee."

"How long these good for?"

"Couple days, I'd guess." Another cop car came down the street, lights rolling, but no sirens, parked in front of the Shore View.

"My mom for sure called the cops," Addie said.

"That one I was talking to," Mitch said, "he was high as fuck."

"He robs drug dealers," Addie said. "He's a real piece of work. Everybody knows him."

"Why doesn't someone do something about it?"

"Like what? Call the cops?"

Right.

"I need to worry about him?"

"Are you a drug dealer?"

"Not this week."

"You're not his type," she said. "He likes people he can scare easy."

"I don't scare easy."

"Like I said."

"How about we drive downtown," Mitch said, "you drop me off over by that comic book store, come back with the money, and we're square."

"How do you know I'll show back up?"

"Well," Mitch said, "I know where your nana lives. I presume you don't want her to wash up somewhere."

Addie smiled. Her teeth were perfect. Living on Loon Island must have included orthodontia. "You're so much more interesting than Paul," she said.

# CHAPTER SEVEN

*Saturday*

Penny Green didn't put much faith in instinct, gut, or intuition. It was all too preternatural for her. Not that she hadn't taken some mystical journeys over the years—a little ketamine under a desert sky did wonders to broaden one's spiritual horizons—but none of that crap ever solved any real problems for her.

And yet, this late morning, she found herself in Mel's Cosmic Comics looking for answers.

Over twelve hours since she'd heard from her brother, and Mel's was the only place she could think to go, sitting on the *Pere-a-Dice* making her stir crazy. If Robert was being followed, or if he chickened out, or if he simply needed to reconfigure his reality, this is where he would go, no ketamine for him. Half of his life was spent on the ratty sofas in the back of the shop, eating shitty slices from Driftwood Pizza, the now-shuttered joint across the street, guzzling small-batch Losertown cream soda, bottled in the old RC Cola facility off of Sandy Avenue in the industrial district, playing D&D until well beyond the shop's posted closing time. Mel's was a de facto clubhouse for all the local misfits—the goths, the skaters, the gamers, the straight-edge punks, and anyone whose parents thought they were talking to the devil. Goons of all stripes were welcome, plus, of course ardent comic collectors.

Not even the most fervent klepto dared fuck with Mel's. It would have been like robbing Santa on Christmas.

All those years, Mel herself worked the front counter, one of those women who seemed permanently twenty-five, sandy blond hair parted straight down the middle, a Rolling Stones tour shirt that never became too small, jeans frayed at the ankle, flip-flops on her feet all summer, a rainbow of Chucks the rest of the year.

The store, and Mel herself, was a kind of sanctuary.

If he wasn't here, he wasn't anywhere. Mel would give him a soft landing.

So when Penny walked into the shop and found a shaggy-haired man behind the counter, she did a double take. He was maybe thirty, wore a black T-shirt and blue jeans slung low on his hips, flipped through a copy of *The Granite Shores Mercury*—the free alt-weekly that used to be owned by Danny Vining's father before he (supposedly) took an Alzheimer's-induced dive off Suicide Ridge—drank from a mug of hot tea.

"Where's Mel?" she asked.

"I'm guessing heaven."

"She's dead?"

"Two years now," he said.

"From what?"

"You know," he said, "the things that kill you. Smoking, eating, drinking, never using SPF."

"Are you her . . . son?"

"Not unless you know something I don't," he said, not unpleasantly, like he'd had this conversation before. "Her nephew. Also Mel."

"Really?"

"No." He laughed then. "I'm Corey. But Corey's Cosmic Comics sounds ludicrous, so, that's one change I'm not making."

"Okay," Penny said, "okay." Penny hadn't set foot in the shop in years. She'd moved from Granite Shores more than a decade ago and only returned periodically. Yet she half expected to walk in and find herself sitting in the corner with her headphones on, watching her big brother play Magic: The Gathering, old-school Cure songs pinging in her head to help quell her inner narrative, the one that constantly did mathematical equations so that she wouldn't need to think about anything else.

The building was once a textile warehouse, back when Granite Shores had an actual working harbor. All that business moved up the coast, leaving behind these old husks, most of which sat empty for years. Mel, however, liked the cement floors and brick walls, which made the joint impenetrable to the whims of teenagers and burnouts. At least those were still in place. The ratty old sofas were replaced by beat-up recliners perched in front of televisions, each hooked up with a gaming system. There were still racks filled with new and collectible comics; however, all the D&D books and figures were gone, replaced by bins of video games. The rear of the store—which used to have a pretty decent head shop hidden behind a purple velvet curtain—now was stacked with used books. They'd also built out an ersatz Starbucks, including a sign proclaiming it STARSUCKS!—where you could get espresso drinks and oversized muffins served by a teenage girl in her dad's Ramones T-shirt.

A fortysomething man browsing the New Age paperbacks met Penny's worried gaze for half a second, gave her a quick what-are-you-gonna-do shrug, and went back to the stacks, Penny thinking he didn't look like the kind of guy who read a lot of New Age books. Sort of looked like the kind of guy who might rob a comic book store, in fact, just to have the story to tell down the line.

Corey leaned across the counter. "I know it's weird to see the changes. Did you hang out here a lot?"

"For a time."

"Mel loved you kids," he said. "She kept these scrapbooks filled with photos stretching back to the 1970s. It's really something. When were you here?"

"Not that long ago. Ten, fifteen years ago?"

Corey patted the counter. "Wait right here," he said, then disappeared into the back of the store, the man in the New Age section watching him the whole time, Penny thinking, *Okay, he's going to make his move now.* And in fact, he did. He walked up to the counter where Penny was waiting, set down a twenty. "You mind letting him know I got two Mack Bolan novels?" He fished them both out of his back pocket, like he thought Penny needed to see the proof.

"You could just wait," Penny said.

"Don't want anyone remembering my face," he said. "You understand, don't you?" She did, strangely. And then he was gone. Corey came back a few minutes later, a scrapbook in hand.

"Here it is!" he said. He cracked open the book. Started flipping pages. "Ah! This you?" There was Penny, in a Bauhaus T-shirt, her hair a sweet shade of purple, sitting on one of the old sofas, Robert in profile beside her, a twenty-sided die in his hand. "How old were you?"

"Too young," she said. She flipped through the book until she found a photo of Robert that showed his full face. "You haven't seen him, have you?"

Corey put on a pair of glasses. Maybe he was older than he looked. Must have run in the family. "Don't think so," he said.

Penny pulled up a photo on her phone. "That's him now."

"Doesn't look familiar. Is he local still?"

"Sort of."

"You want to leave a note for him, or something?"

What would that note say? *Did you forget we were skipping the country?*

"No, no, that's fine." Penny closed the book. "I'm sorry about Mel. She was a nice lady."

"She had a good life. Left me this place, and now I have a good life." He leaned forward again, now stage-whispering. "Mel bought Microsoft stock at twenty-one bucks in 1986."

"You're lucky," Penny said. She slid the scrapbook back across the counter.

"You're someone I should know, aren't you? I recognize you, but I don't know why."

"No good reason."

"I've offended you," Corey said. "I didn't mean to."

"No, no, *I've* offended me." She showed him the twenty on the counter. "Guy that was in here bought a couple Mack Bolan paperbacks while you were in the back."

"They're only fifty cents." He rubbed the bill, like he thought the ink might come off. "Didn't seem like a Mack Bolan guy. He spent ten minutes educating me on the history of Richard Bach."

"You never really know someone until you see their bookshelves," Penny said.

"Isn't that true," Corey said.

Penny stepped back outside. A Granite Shores Police cruiser rolled by, the cop with his arm out the window, cigarette between his fingers, tunes blaring.

This fucking loser town.

# CHAPTER EIGHT

*Saturday*

Mitch had Addie drop him off at the comic book shop near the boardwalk farmers market, told her to find him at the clam chowder spot in ninety minutes.

"How do you know about the clam chowder place?" she asked.

"Is there one?"

"Yeah," she said. She pointed down the block. "Sanford's Soups & Chowders."

"See?" he said. "There's always one."

The boardwalk farmers market was a sprawling bazaar and tourist trap across from the closed amusement park. It was filled with Japanese fishmongers, local produce dealers, people selling cashew butter, water-stained paperbacks, candles, hemp clothes, shitty paintings, and way too much turquoise jewelry. Still, Mitch liked the mood of tourist traps. Reminded him of those few years growing up when his mom and dad were still married and had a beach house in Capitola, right until the ocean swallowed it up during a winter storm.

Mitch spent the first twenty minutes in the bookstore looking for a new old Richard Bach book, the guy behind the counter no help, said he'd never heard of him before, Mitch explaining to him that he was a fucking national treasure for a few years, before he grabbed a couple of shitty, ancient Mack Bolan paperbacks, found the clam chowder spot, sat down with a bread bowl, the chowder feeling good on his teeth, read twenty pages to calm his mood, watched the rain fall into the ocean, then his cell rang. Caller ID said it was Dale. His home phone.

Problem was, it wasn't Dale.

"Motherfucker," Rodney Golubev said when Mitch picked up.

"Easy with that motherfucker business," Mitch said, still feeling bad about running out on his mom. "I'm presuming Dale isn't with you?"

"Motherfucker," he said. "It's a figure of speak. Where are you?"

"Taking a vacation day in Granite Shores."

"Dump," he said. "We own a casino there. The White Pelican. You know it?"

"No," Mitch said. "They looking for a cook?"

"Summertime it's big business with trashy Canadians. Maybe I can send one of our bouncers by and chat with you."

"That wouldn't be good for your bouncer's health."

"So you're a tough guy now, motherfucker? Please."

"I don't think you know me," Mitch said.

"You dumb motherfucker," Rodney said. "You think I let just anyone work for me at a casino? I know exactly who you are. Mister bank robber. Mister forger. Mister crook. Mister thief. Mister killer of old men. I know you."

So he did. "He wasn't old," Mitch said.

"Your motherfucker friend departed Klamath Falls," he said, "with my money. Cleaned out the safe and all the registers."

"He has my book."

"Your checkbook?"

"No," Mitch said. "A novel I was reading."

"We hang him by the balls," he said. "Motherfucker, I know you were literally helping him with some dumb shit. This dumb kidnapping scam. This house. There any secret hiding places?"

"There's an entrance to the crawl space in the hall closet," he said. "Only thing down there are raccoons and kit fox pups."

"Kit fox pups?"

"I heard them crying the other day," Mitch said.

"You *are* a dumb motherfucker." Rodney laughed for a few seconds. "Did you see these foxes?"

Mitch hadn't. He'd woken up one night the previous week and heard them mewing and slamming around all night and went back to sleep. The next morning, which was actually the afternoon, Dale told him what was what, Mitch thinking now that he *was* a dumb motherfucker, that he believed anything Dale said, that he heard crying and yelping and wanted it to be an animal, because he didn't even get out of bed and check, so fucking tired from an overnight at the Purple Flamingo that he didn't give a fuck about anything.

"I'll call Animal Control if you like," Rodney said. "I have a feeling this will be an experience you'll want to be here for." Mitch heard a car door open and close. An engine started up. "Your cousin stole the drop from the Purple Flamingo."

"Cousin-in-law," Mitch said. "Ex."

"Family is family. I presume you have some money that now belongs to me," he said.

"That didn't work out."

"No?"

"Lady was dead when I got there."

"How?"

"I'd guess eighty years of fatty foods," Mitch said.

"My advice, motherfucker?" Rodney said. "Make good choices. Come back to Klamath Falls. I'll let you work off the debt. I'm not reasonable—run, you'll always be running. You don't want that."

An hour later, and a full thirty minutes late, Addie walked into the clam chowder spot holding two huge Nordstrom bags, sat down across from Mitch, picked up his spoon, dug some damp bread out of his bowl, swallowed it down.

"You're late."

"Did you report me missing?" She dug another hunk of bread out. "That's good."

"Always get the bread bowl," Mitch said. "That's my motto."

"So," she said and leaned forward conspiratorially, "that car got stolen." She reached into her jacket pocket, came out with a handful of cash, set it on the table between them. Mitch counted it. There was five grand there.

"A terrible shame," Mitch said.

"I told the thieves they had forty-eight hours."

"You're going to be a real problem for your parents," Mitch said.

"My mom finally called me," she said. She reached into her bag, pulled out a man's shirt, a heavy coat, sport coat, slacks, some socks, a beanie, even a new watch. A Movado. Nice. "Paul's mother apparently is dead. Mrs. Copeland? So there's like, a whole thing going on."

"What a time for the neighborhood."

"She was outside. On her patio. I guess it was pretty bad. For like a few days she was out there. You wouldn't know about that?"

"Sounds pleasant. Nice view. What a way to go. That's what I know."

"Someone called the building manager, my mom said."

"That sounds like a person who made a good choice."

"Well," Addie said, "anywho, I thought you might want a new outfit. In case you needed to not match any descriptions of you."

"I didn't kill her," Mitch said. "That's not the kind of person I am anymore."

"Anymore?"

"She was dead when I got there," he said. "I couldn't stay. For a variety of reasons." Mitch extended his hand. She shook it, firmly, while staring directly into his eyes, which Mitch appreciated. Good manners went a long way with him, especially with kids. "It was nice meeting you, Addie."

She stood up. "Weird day, yeah?" She looked around the restaurant. "My cousin was supposed to meet me down at the shore last night, but she's not there, either. I thought for some reason you might be with her. Like this was a test."

"I'm sure she'll turn up."

Addie said, "Did you Google her?"

"It's been a dog's year," he said.

Addie started out the restaurant, then stopped, like she realized she'd forgotten something, came back to the table. "You reminded me," she said. "Whoever killed that dog, that's fucked-up. It's irredeemable to kill a dog. You can't even do that in a book or in a movie. You know? You shouldn't abide that. Whatever you are."

"I don't," Mitch said. "Someone else did that. Not me."

"Did 'someone else' do Paul, too?"

"I'm thinking so."

"Why are you so casual?"

"I didn't know Paul like you did. He's just a guy who made friends with the wrong people. That should be a lesson for you."

Addie took that in, then shrugged. "Anywho. What are you going to do about it?"

"I've been sitting here trying to figure that out."

"I vote revenge." She gave Mitch the peace sign again. "See you never."

That night, Mitch took the last Greyhound out of Granite Shores, which was a red-eye to Walla Walla, where he still had some family, if you count dead people as family. His grandparents were buried there along with a handful of cousins, back when rural Jews were a thing. Mitch hadn't been back in decades, but when he saw it on the destination board, it was the one place that made any sense to him. He wasn't due in Seattle for another two weeks and needed the five grand he had in his pocket to stretch. He was asleep by the time the wheels started turning.

When Mitch woke up, the bus was outside Wallula Junction, the Snake River black in the darkness. He dug out his cell phone and went into the bus's shitter, snapped the phone into pieces, dumped everything into the toilet. It was 5:12 a.m. He had enough money to get from one bad situation to the next. He also had a few of Mrs. Copeland's credit cards, which might be good for another couple days. But that was it. Did he believe this gig Gabino sold him on? It all sounded legit. No reason to think Gabino was setting him up for a fall.

Mitch stepped out of the bathroom. He counted fifty-three people asleep in their seats. They were forty minutes from Walla Walla. If he moved quickly and quietly, he could probably get a dozen wallets. With enough time and enough driver's licenses, he could make some passable magic. Proper materials? He could forge the *Mona Lisa*.

People riding the grey dog, though, weren't the kind Mitch was comfortable screwing over. You were on a midnight ride to Walla Walla, you were in the middle of some shit, that was certain. So he'd make do. Get a room at the Super 8 near Whitman College, lift a laptop, figure out all the lies he'd need to pull off working at a law firm. He could fake anything. Might as well start with his past.

# CHAPTER NINE

*Monday, December 8*

It only took Penny Green ten days to realize she was deeply fucked.

First nine days, after her jaunt to Mel's, she hid out on the *Pere-a-Dice*, ducking even her cousin Addie, worried about getting her tossed up in something beyond her control, subsisting primarily on Pronto Pups and funnel cakes she stole from the boardwalk stand next to the Tilt-A-Whirl. The boat was stocked with provisions, but Penny reasoned that if she started digging into their supplies and then Robert showed up, they wouldn't have enough food to get them to South America.

Not that she expected Robert to show up.

Not anymore.

When Robert failed to show after three days, Penny convinced herself that the firm figured out what happened, and her brother was apprehended on Yeach. Yet, there was nothing in the newspapers, no chatter on the radio or TV, no locals gossiping in the marina. Had he gotten into an accident? She called the local hospitals. Did he lie to her? Had he never left Seattle? She called his apartment, his cell, even called his office, and got nothing but voice mail. She sent pizzas to his apartment, got only angry calls from Domino's in response. She even made a call to the Granite Shores coroner to inquire if there were any John Does in the fridge.

And still she waited.

Yeah, she had a boat, but she'd never sailed a day in her life. That was Robert's thing. She could watch some YouTube videos, see if she could Neo that shit, but that didn't seem entirely realistic. She was smart, but she wasn't that smart.

The other pressing problem was that Penny was broke. She'd dumped all her cash and everything in Robert's savings into the *Pere-a-Dice*, fat lot of fucking good that was. Penny wasn't a wanted criminal yet, so technically she could go about her business in the light of day, but she knew trouble was about to come down. Maybe four days left to get some cash in her pocket and get ghost. Once it became clear what went down, it wouldn't just be the cops that were after her; it would be every scumbag Robert ripped off, too. Cops she could probably avoid for a bit. The scumbags wouldn't wait for evidence or probable cause.

So on the tenth day, Penny called the only scumbag she was sure didn't have a safe-deposit box at Barer & Harris, because Robert checked it out ahead of time: Freddie Golubev. Told him she needed his help.

"Help," Freddie said. "That means money?"

"That would be a good start," she said.

"Sister," Freddie said, "how have you fucked up this time?"

"Not on the phone," Penny said.

"You think you are so important FBI is listening in before you've even been fingered for a crime. Now that's an inflation of ego. I will send a car. Where are you?"

Twenty minutes later, Penny sat in Freddie's office in the White Pelican, his shitty video-poker casino. When she met Freddie in college, he and his brother, Rodney, owned a hookah lounge near UW, but even then he was trying to get diversified into gaming and protection rackets. Once she was of age, Freddie got her hooked up for some translation gigs . . . which is to say, she sat in meetings with Freddie's father in Odessa as he brokered deals with Triad gangsters, Penny the only person

## Only Way Out

they knew who spoke Mandarin, Russian, and English and was morally dexterous. It wasn't a bad gig. She managed to earn enough money to loan some to her brother and pay off most of her father's debts. She was all set to go back to Russia so she could get the family home out of foreclosure, but then Dad up and died, and Countrywide took it. The fuckers.

Penny explained her situation to Freddie. Spared no details, figuring, fuck it. What was Freddie going to do? Turn her in?

"Can I give you advice?" Freddie asked. He was behind his six-foot-long faux oak desk, which Penny suspected was a remnant from when the White Pelican was a United Furniture store.

"That's why I'm here."

"Go to police, turn in your brother. He is gone. Has left you out here like a dog. You turn him in, they won't think you were involved. You end up the hero. He shows back up, you'll explain that the heat was on you, he'll understand. When they make the TV movie, maybe they cast Alyssa Milano. She would be good in this. I liked her growing up."

"That runs counter to everything I've ever done in my life. You don't think that would be suspect?"

Freddie came around his desk, sat down across from Penny, stared into her eyes. She'd seen this move before. He wasn't inconsiderate to people he liked. It's how they'd become friends in the first place. She'd wandered into his hookah lounge when she was fifteen, and he was a perfect gentleman to her. Thought she was a runaway. Didn't know she was a genius until he read about her in *People* at his dentist's office. And then he gave her a job figuring out the math on slot machines in the Native American casinos in Vancouver. That was a nice payday.

"Police look into you, they're going to eventually show up in my life, asking questions, and what will I do? To save my ass, I will give you up. Snitching to me, that means nothing. It's some kind of dumb code you learned from movies. My country, different rules."

"You've lived here since you were seven, Freddie. This *is* your country." Penny didn't even think Freddie's accent was legit anymore, that he and his brother kept it because it was cool, like they were gangsters in some shitty cable movie.

"And everyone here snitches. It's how you know it's a thing. And it's why you should do it on your brother."

"Would you flip on your brother?"

"To save myself? Yes. A hundred times. A million times. He's a fucking idiot. Will eventually get us both killed if I do not eventually turn him in, so, you see, it's part of my long-range plan. You should adopt it. It's a solid plan."

Penny considered this. Robert was a good person. This was the first time he'd ever fucked her over. How many times had she let him down? Countless times. And yet, he'd always remained steadfast. Was he getting her back? She couldn't imagine that. He'd taken care of her for her entire life, in return only ever asked for love and some money to pay off his law school tuition. Some years, she'd been shitty with that love part, the problem with being a young person being that you always assumed the people you cared about would accept your petty bullshit. She'd taken him for granted.

"I can't, Freddie."

"You will regret this. It is good advice." Freddie sighed. "So what do you want?"

"Fifty thousand dollars. That will be enough to get me into Canada, lay low for a little bit, get my shit straight."

"You will be spotted at the border. You'll be on camera. There is extradition from Canada. They'll find you in forty-eight hours if they want to."

"You have a better idea?"

"You were going to go to sea? Do that."

"I told you I'm not a sailor."

"No," Freddie said. "Take a cruise. No one ever expects anyone has hopped on a cruise ship. Best way to escape. My advice? Cruise to Hawaii. No passport needed. Get off on the Big Island. Buy one of those stupid excursions into the wild, get off the bus, never come back. Make your way to Honolulu, it's a real city; you need help, I can help you from there. Lots of friends on the islands. Easy to hide there, easy to get a tourist's information, make it your own. Could probably live happily in Hawaii for the rest of your life, changing identities every few months."

Penny had to admit, it wasn't a terrible idea.

"And what do you get?" Penny asked.

"You find your brother," Freddie said, "I get 25 percent of your take."

"And if I don't find my brother?"

"You pay me back, with interest, of course."

"When?"

"You don't find your brother in a month," Rodney said, "you'll never find him. So you make it right."

"Police come to you, what will you say?"

"The truth. I loaned you money, and you skipped town. Makes it all sound pretty believable, doesn't it? And then you realize, you don't pay me, our friendship? It is moot."

"That's my problem, not yours."

"You do not want me as your enemy."

"I'm not worried."

"You do not want Rodney as your enemy, either." Well. Shit. "He's the kind who forgets but does not forgive. Even after you make it right, if you've fucked us over? He might still kill you. This is truth I am speaking." He leaned close. "What do you have for collateral?"

"My boat," Penny said.

"Okay, and for the other $49,999?"

"Everything in my head about you and your father's businesses."

"That's not collateral."

"Not in a traditional sense," Penny said, "but isn't it worth a lot more than $50,000?"

"This sounds like extortion to me."

"It's not. I'm giving you a reason not to cut my fingers off or something."

"You think I would torture you? You wouldn't be able to earn my money back without hands. That's silly. I'd sell you for parts to the

Chinese. Your liver alone would cover my debts." He closed his eyes. Breathed in deeply, let it go, Penny thinking if she was smart, she'd push him through the floor-to-ceiling window and hope he broke his neck when he landed. "Because now you have given me something to worry about, the deal is changed. Thirty-three percent of your take if your brother returns. If he does not, you eventually come back here, maybe you do a favor for me, now and then, and you work your debt off. Fair? Threaten me again, it goes to 50 percent."

"Fair."

"You do not show back up," Freddie said, "I go to police with this whole story you've given me, probably there will be a reward, which I will claim, and then I will have you killed in prison when you are caught, because you will be. Fair?"

"Fair."

Freddie went back to his desk, clicked on his computer, scrolled around. "Okay," he said. "Celebrity has a cruise leaving tomorrow, but they are crap, midnight buffet will give you illnesses that came over on the *Mayflower*."

"Why do you know this?"

"I am a cruise person," Freddie said. "Very cathartic. Lose yourself in the rhythms of the sea." He clicked around some more. "Okay. Here we go. Next Wednesday. Royal Caribbean, departs Seattle. *Quantum of the Sea*. Beautiful boat." Click. Click. Click. "I have points. I'm getting you an upgrade." Hit a button. Printed out a full itinerary. Shuffled through it, brought out a yellow marker, highlighted a few things. "Balcony room. You'll love it. Get to see whales." Stuffed it all into an envelope, slid it across the desk for Penny. "You have cut a terrible deal. Do you understand? This is a terrible deal for you. Because if you end up finding your brother, I could rob you both. You understand that? You should not trust me, Penny. You should leave here right now."

He was right, of course. So she said, "Can I get that money in twenties?"

# CHAPTER TEN

*December 8*

Jack Biddle came to two conclusions: Number one, he was now a rich person. After paying off Danny? Cash alone, he had a couple million dollars.

Number two: Jack Biddle needed to kill Penny Green. Provided he could find her.

He'd made that decision a few days after realizing how fucking rich he was, once he'd gone through all the shit Robert Green had in that van, including his laptop and his BlackBerry, and realized Penny would be looking for her brother and her cut. How long would it take for her to backtrack Robert's steps and eventually find herself up on Yeach, poking around? The van was still up there, kind of. He'd been going up there every night at 2:00 a.m., told his wife he was on a stakeout. He'd power-washed the interior with every chemical he could find, then set the interior on fire, which wasn't much of a fire since the interior was all metal with a scoop of carpeting. He knew that in some controlled cases, luminol found blood traces even after fires burned as hot as 1,000 degrees, but this was no fucking controlled case.

He was going to dismantle the van, piece by piece. He'd already ripped out the front seats. All he needed was a decent 60V reciprocating saw, some nine-inch-thick metal blades, that old Econoline would be scrap in a couple hours. Maybe a blowtorch, if he wanted to make less noise, but the reality was, middle of the night, out there? All he needed was time, which was something Jack had plenty of, provided Penny Green wasn't lingering around.

So she had to go.

Jack didn't have a good idea how he'd do it.

The law firm hadn't even reported the crime yet, Jack checking the blotter, watching the news, nothing. Part of Jack wanted to do some hero shit, get *his* photo in the newspaper, maybe get another parade—he liked parades—maybe parlay that into a gig with the FBI? Wouldn't that be sweet. He had all this money now, all these jewels, a fair number of guns and coke, heroin, pills, all the weed on the planet, a shitload of baseball cards and family photos, an inordinate amount of ashes, some deeply weird Nazi shit, some super troubling pedo-level materials that he could probably go to prison for possessing—that was a concern—a lot of computer disks he couldn't make heads or tails of, and then a gazillion stock certificates, passports, marriage licenses, divorce agreements, prenuptials, diplomas, password-locked laptops, and countless other items he hadn't even started to look at, all of it locked up in the basement freezer of the Sno-Cone Depot, along with both parts of Robert.

What he didn't have was Penny. Jack figured she was somewhere in Granite Shores. There was no reason for Robert to escape this direction if she was still in Walla Walla. He'd found several spreadsheets on Robert's computer that the metadata indicated Penny had created. Meticulous lists calculating street and retail values for items in various boxes, which was helpful to Jack, one less thing to do, plus lists of items to be examined for potential long-term extortions, which Jack *really* appreciated. One thing was certain: they were working together. He didn't have any legal way of showing that. No probable cause to run up on her and in the process, somehow, reveal the heist and then . . . boom . . . cue the floats and high school bands!

Hence, she'd probably need to end up floating in the Pacific. He'd like to go kicking in doors to find her, but that was sort of frowned upon, so he had to hope for a lucky break.

And then he got one this morning. MaryAnn Scofield, who owned the Pronto Pup Hut on the boardwalk, called 911 to report a break-in.

Jack showed up and found MaryAnn smoking a cigarette, sitting with her laptop open on one of the dozen cement picnic tables behind the Hut. The rain stopped for the first time in days, but Jack could see storm clouds over the bay. It would be wet by lunch.

"Where's the damage?" Jack asked.

"Look at this." MaryAnn walked Jack to the back door. "Someone removed the existing doorknob and replaced it with a new one." She put her key into the hole, tried to unlock the door. No luck. "You believe that?"

He tried the doorknob. It was a classic ball-style, keyed-entry doorknob. Brass finish. Kind you could buy for about ten bucks. "What did your previous doorknob look like?"

"Exactly the same."

"Smart," Jack said. Nice attention to detail.

"Smart? You think that's smart?"

"Would you have thought to do that?"

MaryAnn said, "I'm not a criminal, so no."

"What about the front door?"

"Left that alone."

"How often you come in through the back door?"

"Never. We use it to go out, like to take the trash to the bin. But we do that from inside the store."

"And then you lock it from the inside, too?"

"That's right."

If someone wanted to watch the Pronto Pup Hut surreptitiously, all they had to do was plop down at one of the picnic tables with a paperback, like the one old man in a windbreaker was doing right now, about a hundred pages into a Clive Cussler novel. Jack liked that one about the *Titanic*. "So could be you'd never notice that doorknob was replaced," Jack said, "until you checked the lock from the outside. Right?"

MaryAnn stared at Jack for a long moment. "I guess that was smart," she said. "I see your point."

"So what's missing?"

"I'll show you," she said. He followed MaryAnn back to the picnic table. "We don't keep any cash on the premises," she said. "Don't even have a computer we keep here. I take this laptop home every night. All we got in here is frozen Pronto Pups, frozen funnel cakes, mustard, sugar, and oil. Some canned pop. I've got a camera over the doors, the register inside, and one in the dry storage, make sure we don't get rats in the night." She clicked open a file. A grainy video popped up. Time-stamped at 11:25 p.m. "Couple days, I've been noticing our inventory has been off. Thought my son was giving away food again, something he does on occasion because he doesn't value hard work or my money. So I checked my cameras. I see this."

There was Penny Green, not even bothering to cover her face, wearing the same T-shirt her cousin wore last Saturday, walking up to the back of the Hut, screwdriver and Allen wrench in hand, backpack on. Looked the same as she had on TV all those times, except here she was doing some crime. In two minutes, the doorknob was off and she was inside. Once inside, she goes to the freezer, takes out a few Pronto Pups, a couple funnel cakes, three Cokes, puts them all in her backpack. Walks over to the counter, leaves something in the loose change tray. Exits. Unpacks a new doorknob, installs it, locks it. Disappears into the darkness.

"You believe the audacity?" MaryAnn asked. She clicked forward. "Four days in a row, same thing. Walked in like she owned the place."

"You mind?" Jack clicked the rewind button. Watched it all over again. "What did she put in the change plate?"

"I thought she took some coins out." They both watched it one more time. Penny absolutely dropped something in. "Well shit." MaryAnn disappeared around front. Jack watched the next few videos. Same thing. Walked right up, unlocked the door, grabbed up some hot dogs and cakes, a couple sodas, yesterday she preferred two Orange Crush cans. Out the back door, locked it up, walked off into the night.

Not a care in the world. Jack could probably hide in the parking lot with a long gun and pop her from a distance. But then he'd need to go collect her body. That might be cumbersome. And a hassle. He didn't need to have two bodies to take care of. Better to see if he could drown her, dump her in the ocean, let the sharks figure out the rest.

A minute later, MaryAnn returned holding the change tray. She dumped the contents on the table. And there, among a hundred pennies, nickels, dimes, and quarters was a single key.

Jack picked it up, walked over to the back door, inserted it into the keyhole and the door popped open.

"The audacity," MaryAnn said again, this time with a bit of wonder. She shook her head. "Do you recognize her?"

"Probably a homeless person."

"She seemed familiar to me."

"You've probably seen her around," Jack said. "You know how it is with the homeless these days. All up in your face. We need to get them all out of town, you want my opinion. When my wife is mayor, that's job one."

MaryAnn pondered this. "They do bother my regulars. What are you going to do about it?"

"We'll position a SWAT team on the boardwalk tonight. She shows back up, we'll take her down."

"Jesus, I don't want her *hurt*," MaryAnn said. "I just . . . don't want her stealing my stuff."

"How about," Jack said, "I patrol for a few nights, see if I can scare her off."

"Would you do that?"

"Of course," Jack said. He gave MaryAnn that famous Biddle smile, the one that got Caroline to fall in love with him, the one that drug dealers thought meant he'd let them slide, the one that he gave that nine-year-old in Fallujah, right before the kid fucking clipped him. "It's my honor to keep this town safe, MaryAnn."

There was no fucking way Jack was going to waste his night watching the Pronto Pup Hut, so what he did instead was that afternoon he pulled up the city's CCTV feed from along the boardwalk and tracked Penny Green all the way back down to the marina, where she vanished through the front gates and into the labyrinth of slips. There were two hundred boats parked out there. Houseboats, fishing trawlers, a couple actual yachts, sailboats, catamarans, the whole nine. She could be hiding out on any of them. He supposed he could go to the office and see if there were any new rentals, but what Jack didn't want, or need, was any record of him looking for Penny before her bloated corpse washed up somewhere.

So instead, Jack clocked out, dumped his GPS at the Sno-Cone Depot, put a sweatshirt on over his uniform—look a little less like a cop—then parked across from the marina in the crowded Fleenor's supermarket lot and waited for Penny to walk in or out. He'd pop her for the break-in, get her in cuffs, drive up to Suicide Ridge, let God sort 'em out.

That was the plan, anyway, but then a black Subaru wagon pulled up, Freddie Golubev in the passenger seat, some meat driving it, Freddie's absurd personalized plate—FRED4FN—surrounded by a bedazzled frame on the rear end, and five minutes later, Penny Green came walking through the marina's front gate. Freddie and his brother, Rodney, owned the White Pelican and kicked Jack a grand a week and signed off on a monthly blow job from the prostitute of his choice to keep his eyes away from their girl business. It was a fair-enough trade, Jack thinking there were probably a good number of other cops who had something similar working, since no one ever hassled the White Pelican. But still, those guys were bad news. If Penny Green was in business with them, this whole thing had the potential to go sideways five different ways.

So.

He'd need to kill Freddie, too, he supposed. He'd figured that all along, what with his desire to eventually be chief of police and Freddie being privy to a whole host of Jack's dealings. This, however, made it more pressing. Once Penny was taken care of, that would be simple enough.

Freddie got out of the Subaru, popped the trunk, took out a Priority Mail box, handed it to Penny. She opened it up, checked the contents, seemed content. The two talked for another minute, she hugged him, Freddie kissed her on both cheeks—fucking Russians and their weird kissing—and then Freddie got back into the Subaru and drove off. Penny stood there for another few seconds, watching the Subaru drive away. Looked up and down the block, disappeared into the marina. Jack watching her through binoculars, saw her climb aboard a good-sized Catalina.

Well.

That confused things.

There was only one thing that could be in that box.

Jack could confiscate it. That would be a nice little additional haul.

So maybe . . . he wouldn't kill Penny. He'd arrest her for the break-in, seize that cash, let her sit in jail for at least seventy-two hours, get a warrant to search the boat for other stolen property, that cash being a good bet to get the judge interested, hope the heist got discovered by the law firm by then, but if not, surely that boat would have some intel about Robert Green on it, and then Jack could *really* be the hero.

He wondered what it took to get a street named for you? Maybe you had to be dead? He'd add that to the list.

# CHAPTER ELEVEN

*December 8/9*

Jack waited until right before midnight to make his move. He dressed quietly in the dark, being careful not to wake up Caroline, who was feeling queasy all evening, Jack wondering if this was how it was going to be for the next nine months. They'd spent dinner going over potential names for their miracle baby. Caroline liked Grace, Holly, or April if the baby was a girl. Jack liked the idea of a boy named Travis, Brad, or Cooper. Travis Biddle, Brad Biddle, or Cooper Biddle all sounded like quarterbacks. Jack liked that. Caroline went to bed early, and Jack stayed up, getting ready, took a couple tokes, formulated his plan.

He checked his look in the bathroom mirror. All black. Kevlar on. Sig Sauer service weapon on the hip. AR-15 with a laser/light attachment over the shoulder. Sunglasses, even though it was dark.

"Where are you going in your tactical gear?" Caroline asked.

Jack looked behind him. Caroline was sitting up in bed.

"Go back to bed, honey," he said.

"You look like you're going to war."

"Got a tip on a wanted felon," he said. "Need to do a stakeout."

"Another?"

"Busy time."

"You're dressed like the Russians are going to attack the aquarium."

He came over to the bed and kissed Caroline lightly on the forehead. "Get some rest. We've got eighteen big years coming."

"Are you going with backup?"

"No," Jack said. "Solo."

Caroline said, "Are you sure?"

If Jack called this in, he'd be laughed off the job. Sending a blackout team for a theft of snacks? What was the actual value of the Pronto Pups, funnel cakes, and sodas? Street value was, what, about thirty bucks? Actual cost to the Pronto Pup Hut was probably about nine bucks? And Penny replaced the doorknob, which she could likely argue increased the value of the Hut, and since she was only breaking and entering the first time, she could probably plead this down to a misdemeanor shoplifting citation. He needed to get whatever was in that box from Freddie into evidence. Plus whatever was on that boat. Plus maybe Penny would try to act tough, and she could then maybe get one in the chest and everything would be solved.

"Acting on a hunch," Jack said. He kissed her again.

"Have you been smoking? You smell funny."

*Shit.*

"That's the oil from cleaning the AR," he said. He gave her arms a squeeze. "If you can't sleep, maybe look up how the city awards street names."

"Oh that's sweet. Are you thinking for your dad?"

Rain soaked downtown Granite Shores. Every few minutes, Jack saw a burst of lightning, the blackened sky briefly marbled in the current, and heard a rumble of thunder. Jack found it oddly calming. The streets he drove down were empty, his blue light bouncing off the storefronts. Yeach was lost behind clouds. It was like he was the last man on earth. No. No. No, Jack corrected himself, he was the last gunslinger! The Tahoe was the horse he rode through the lonesome town . . .

Lonesome Town. Now *that* was a good nickname.

He reached into his glove box, took out one of his one-hitters, took a quick hit.

Yeah. The Last Gunslinger of Lonesome Town. That's who he was tonight. Hell yes.

Jack drove under a canopy of golden lights the Soroptimists and 4-H hung each year across Beach Boulevard. Down by the entrance to the boardwalk, there was a giant Christmas tree and fifteen-foot-tall Santa. Couple days was the annual lighting ceremony, provided the rain ever let up. Caroline would be down there in her official capacity; maybe she'd even start to tell everyone about their baby. Jack thinking if he played this right, turning down the frontage road to the marina, maybe he'd be in the news by then, too, and he'd join his wife at the tree lighting, get the handshakes, the back pats. Maybe he'd drop some cash on a new suit. Now that he had the cash. The Last Gunslinger of Lonesome Town would look nice in something tailored from the Macy's in Portland.

He parked the Tahoe in the marina's lot, left the blue light on—let everyone know who might be looking that this was official cop business, including the security guard in the shack near the dock entrance. If Jack was lucky, it was someone he knew, which was possible since Jack knew just about everyone. The Last Gunslinger of Lonesome Town was a popular man, despite his name.

After a minute, the guard came out of the shack, popped open his umbrella, ambled over. If Jack were a more courteous sort, he'd have parked closer . . . but Jack didn't have much time for these corporate cops. Better to have a couple Rottweilers.

"Help you, Jack?" The security guard was Del Francis. Retired Granite Shores PD. Old-timer. The kind who let you pay off moving violations on the side of the road. When it came to that kind of *Dukes of Hazzard* shit, Jack was of the opinion that you should do it on a grand scale or not at all.

"Looking for a suspect," Jack said. "Woman. Late twenties. Been living on a boat out here about two weeks or so. Long black hair. Five six. Hundred and thirty pounds."

"Penny Green?"

"Is that who it is?"

"You know it is," Del said. "If you have her description, you know who it is. What did she do?"

"Not at liberty to say."

Del said, "You're rolling out at 12:17 a.m. for Penny Green? Come on, man. I'll have to go to the station and make a statement tomorrow. I got my grandkids coming by. Unless she killed someone, why not come back in the morning when the staff is here. I'm contract labor."

"You don't work for the marina?"

"Naw," Del said. "I work for Raleigh." Raleigh was a private security outfit out of Portland. All ex-cops was their selling point. "I'm getting twelve bucks an hour here. I don't got time for some bullshit, Jack." He paused. "You waiting on a detective?"

"Doing some recon."

"Not how it was done in my day."

"Your day is done," Jack said. He checked his watch. "What time is your break?"

"I typically get a sandwich and thirty minutes of sleep around one a.m."

"Maybe grab an hour of sleep." Jack took a twenty from his wallet, tried to hand it to Del. He didn't take it. Put it on the dashboard instead.

"Tonight they got steaks at Shake's. Serving until two a.m.," Del said. "Runs 29.99."

This fucking guy. Jack put another twenty on the dash. Del picked up both.

"She's in slip 52," Del said. "Ninety minutes enough?"

"Should be."

"Don't think you need that AR," he said. Jack had it across his lap.

"No?"

"Tends to make a lot of noise. You want to make a lot of noise, that's going to be something I need to worry about. Because that seems to me to be more of an assault-type situation. That's a lot of property damage."

"I see your point." Jack racked it behind him. One gun would be enough. Two was probably overkill.

Del headed back off into the rain. A few minutes later, he switched off the light in the guard shack, climbed into his F-150, and pulled away. Jack grabbed another one-hitter, took a big toke. It was some strong shit. He felt like he could climb Mt. Everest, backward.

He opted not to wear the sunglasses. Fuck it. He looked cool enough. He'd put them on when the press came.

The Catalina in slip fifty-two was named the *Pere-a-Dice* and was parked between a houseboat called the *Cruise Control* and fishing trawler named, weirdly, *Just Kevin*. Jack never did understand boat names, but Jack recognized the *Pere-a-Dice*. The boat belonged to Mort Green, Penny and Robert's dipshit father, an insurance fraud expert—as in, he was expert in burning shit down for insurance money—who pretended to be a community activist, who nevertheless was pals with Jack's father, Owen, because they all grew up on the same block, back when Granite Shores only had like five blocks. Last time Jack saw the boat, it was under a tarp in the backyard of Mort's house when Jack was there evicting him. A fucking mess. Poor fucker was dying of cancer and had to spend his last days in the Hampton Inn across the frontage road from the outlet mall. No one wants to die in view of a discount Chico's.

Now, though, the *Pere-a-Dice* looked . . . good. New sails. Two satellite domes. A full suite of Garmin navigational computers in the cockpit, all under a brand-new Bimini top fastened with metal rails. No shitty nylon. This was all top-notch material. This boat was getting ready to go somewhere. Provided the squall ever gave up.

Jack stepped on board at the stern . . . right when Penny Green opened the hatch, an Orange Crush in one hand, an orange flare gun in the other, and not surprised at all to see him.

"That you, Jack Biddle?" Penny asked.

"Hey, Penny," Jack said. "You remember me?"

"Saw you walking up."

"Thought maybe you were too famous to remember us little people." Keeping it cordial. They might both be in the paper tomorrow. Wouldn't that be ironic.

"You evicted my dad, didn't you?"

"That was Countrywide," Jack said. "I was there making sure things didn't go south."

"How much further south can something go when you're losing your house?"

"That was between your pops and the mortgage people." He pointed at the flare gun. "You want to drop that flare gun?"

"I don't, no," Penny said. "What if things go south? Need a way to alert the proper authorities."

"I am the proper authorities."

"That so?"

"It's making me nervous. You understand. I know you've dealt with the law before."

"What kind of law shows up on someone's property like this? Without even saying why you're here? I could have shot you already and been in my rights."

Jack was beginning to think tonight was a mistake. Lightning crackled in the distance. Man, that sure was bright. He should have grabbed his sunglasses, after all. He said, "I saw you on the Pronto Pup Hut's security cameras breaking in. Because our pops were friends, I'm coming by as a courtesy to talk to you. But that flare gun, I'm telling you straight up, it needs to be tossed overboard or I'm in *my rights* to shoot you right now."

"I'm not pointing it at you, Jack," Penny said. "Also, according to federal law, since this can only shoot a pyrotechnic charge, it's not even considered a weapon. I could be holding a popsicle. Same difference. So no, you're not in your rights."

Was that true? It sounded kind of true. Looked to Jack like it was an Orion 12-gauge flare. Probably $39.95 at Target and about as accurate as shooting a water gun. About as damaging, too. It would be bad to get hit in the face with it from an inch away, might burn his eyebrows off or break his nose, could maybe put out an eye, but wasn't going to brain him. But from the fifteen feet between them, and in the darkness and in the pounding rain, Jack seriously doubted Penny could even hit him center mass. And the amount of time it would take her to cock and fire, he could put two between her eyes. If she tried to reload another flare, he'd be able to dig her a proper grave, give her last rites, and prepare a deli plate for the wake.

"You want to tell me what you were doing at the Pronto Pup Hut?"

"Community service," Penny said. "I saw the door was open, so I went to the hardware store and bought a new doorknob for them, installed it and everything. Didn't want to ask for payment, you know, so I took a few Pups and a couple sodas. Kept meaning to come by during the day to let them know where the key was, but with the weather, I kept missing them." She took a sip of the Orange Crush. "What's with the Kevlar?"

"Standard uniform."

"To ask questions of someone after midnight?"

A roll of thunder echoed over the water, Jack thinking it would only be a few seconds before another round of lightning hit. That would be a good time to put one in her, if he was so inclined. But he liked the idea of being a hero. Of solving this whole deal . . . even before it was a deal to be solved. But it was getting to the point where he was aware Penny was wanting to make this a whole incident. She wouldn't have grabbed the flare gun if she was sitting on the boat reading romance novels. Which told him all he needed to know. She knew what she'd done. What her brother did. She probably thought Jack was onto her. Probably was feeling pretty paranoid, Jack vaguely aware that maybe he was projecting a bit, because man, there was something fuzzy in his head right now. That one-hitter was coming on strong. It was weed he'd found in one of the van's boxes, Jack thinking that would be some primo shit, and it was, it was, but maybe it had PCP in it? Or some crystal?

Jack said, "I'm going to place you under arrest for breaking and entering, Penny. I need you to drop that flare gun, get down on your stomach, and put your hands behind your back."

"Or what?" Penny asked. "You're going to shoot me over some corn dogs, Jack? Really?"

"I've done it for less," Jack said.

Penny tilted her head, like she couldn't believe what she was hearing, Jack not sure he knew why he said that, either. It sounded hardcore. He knew that much. It was also *true*, but that wasn't typically Jack's barometer for conversation. He had no damn idea what was happening between his brain and his mouth. Shit. But whatever. Jack Biddle was in it now.

Lightning cracked over Granite Shores Bay then, the world illuminated in a shock of blue-white electricity, Jack pretty sure he saw Penny raise up the flare gun, pretty sure, almost positive, and in the end, the courts wouldn't care much. Jack dropped into a firing stance, pulled his Sig, not sure how long it would take a flare to reach him, everything super slow now, pretty sure he could see the flare heading his way. Just as he was about to fucking smoke Penny Green, about to show her that her IQ wasn't shit compared to his Sig, everything in his brain went cattywampus—that was something his mom used to say, what a time to be thinking about his mom—and his feet slipped out from under him on the slick deck, and then another roll of thunder—that's what he thought, *that thunder sure is close*—and that's when he realized, no, that wasn't thunder, that was a gunshot, and that Jack Biddle blew a hole in his own damn leg.

# CHAPTER TWELVE

*December 9*

Jack Biddle was going to bleed to death. This much was certain to Penny. He'd somehow shot himself on the inside of his left thigh, above his knee. If he hit the femoral artery, he was probably about three minutes from seeing all his ancestors. The amount of blood pouring out of him was not good, no matter what he hit.

The thing to do was grab his keys, drive as far north as possible, ditch the ride in the woods somewhere, and get to the border. She had Freddie's cash. She'd need to figure out a different out, because a dead cop on her boat was going to be a manhunt, and so a leisure cruise to Hawaii was not in the cards.

She could let him die and then roll his body into the water. Clean the boat. Go about her life as planned. He'd wash up eventually. The water was pretty shallow right here. Twenty feet deep. Maybe twenty-five. He'd wash up in a day or two, if that.

That was the thing to do.

"I shot myself," Jack said. He was flat on his back, blood pooling around him.

"You did," Penny said.

"Am I going to die?"

"I'm deciding that right now."

"I'm going to have a baby. My wife is going to have a baby. I'm going to die. And my wife is going to have a baby. Travis. I'm going to name him Travis. I can't believe this." He tried to sit up but couldn't, his body sliding in the rain and blood. "I am the last gunslinger, and my son will never know."

Jack was clearly starting to lose reality. Now was the time to go.

But she couldn't.

"Remember this," Penny said and then unfastened two bungee cables from the dock tie, rushed over to Jack, yanked the nightstick off his belt, wrapped the bungees around his ruined thigh, once, twice, three times, knotted them in a square, slipped the nightstick through the knot, like a windlass, and twisted, and twisted, and twisted, until the rush of blood stopped. Turned out she did retain something from Girl Scouts.

"Did I do that right?" Penny asked.

Jack lifted his head up. "I can't see. What did you do?"

"I put a tourniquet on you."

"Why?"

"So you wouldn't die." She took out her cell phone. Tried to decide what the rest of her life might look like on the other side of the call she was about to make, saw that some blood was still leaking out of Jack Biddle, just a drip. Who knew how long this tourniquet would hold?

So Penny Green did something she'd never done in her entire life, would never do again, and would regret acutely, particularly during her time at the penitentiary in Gig Harbor, when she realized those moments with Jack Biddle were her last, that she wouldn't see the sky like this again for a very long time, that what she did changed the trajectory of her entire life. If she waited five minutes, Jack would be dead by his own hand, and yeah, there'd be some explaining to do, but she'd have already tossed her computers, wiped her phone, burned the maps, canceled the storage unit contract, told Addie to keep her fucking mouth shut, melted her flare gun and come up with believable answers to questions she should have known were coming.

All that would have changed the trajectory of many things. Many bad things.

But Penny Green did not wait.

Penny Green called 911, told them that Officer Jack Biddle was down. That she would wait with him, of course, because all she'd done was steal some corn dogs and so she believed she would be out of custody in twenty-four hours, if that . . .

"If that" was over thirteen years.

# PART 2

*Fifteen Years Later*

GREEN DAYS FESTIVAL EXAMINES THE COMPLICATED HISTORY OF OUR LOCAL ROBIN HOOD
By Seema Nitch
*Granite Shores Daily News*, Friday July 14

Get ready for the wildest party of the summer, Granite Shores! Green Days are back and bigger than ever, this year celebrating notorious local Robert Green's birthday and the fifteen-year anniversary of his daring heist.

30,000 visitors will invade our sleepy resort village starting Wednesday for five days of events featuring Food Network stars, HGTV tours, Granite Shores' own podcast queen Addie Green (Robert's cousin!) appearing live at the historic Green family home, and a blockbuster boardwalk fireworks and drone show.

Green's claim to fame? Cracking over 300 safe-deposit boxes at the Barer & Harris law firm, swiping millions from powerful (and notorious!) bigwigs from across the region, then disappearing and (virtually!) reappearing to demand good deeds in exchange for secrets kept. Call it extortion or genius—either way, it's the stuff of legend now. Seattle chef Tom Tucker owes Green for the safe return of his nana's secret recipes: "Guardian angel with a criminal bent . . . I paid a $10K ransom to Seattle Food Bank, got the recipes back—now I donate $100K annually!" Tucker's upscale diners in Seattle, Portland, and his newly opened Granite Shores location still serve up his nana's famous coconut and banana cream pies.

Granite Shores transformed from "Losertown" to a vibrant community thanks to Green's audacious crime and local lawman Jack Biddle's role in cracking the case. Mayor Caroline Biddle—Jack's wife—walks a diplomatic line: "We condemn Green's methods but celebrate community spirit." The town's quirky charm, generosity, and rebellious streak have made it a thriving destination in the aftermath.

Festival backers like Danny Vining of Sunshine Fudge agree: "Green Days boosts business—Robert Green may be a thief, but he's our thief. This festival is equally a celebration of our law enforcement partners and our indelible grit." Events kick off Wednesday with the annual carnival and street fair, including:

Food demos featuring local and celebrity chefs!

Exclusive architectural tours of Granite Shores' unique homes!

Panel discussions and documentary screenings!

Live music from the Neil Diamond hard-rock cover band Street Caroline . . .

# CHAPTER THIRTEEN

*Wonder Valley, California*
*Saturday, July 15*

The Creosote Saloon looked condemned, but then everything out this way looked condemned, even the kid sitting out front on the bumper of a truck, playing a game on his iPhone. He was maybe thirteen, wore checkered Vans with white socks pulled up his calves, cut-off jeans, no shirt. It was 110 degrees outside, but the kid wasn't sweating. When Mitch got out of his Caddie, the kid didn't even look up from his game.

"This place open?" Mitch asked.

"You're not from here," the kid said.

"Not even close."

The kid's phone made a buzzing sound. "Shit. You made me fuck up."

The Creosote used to be a house, but where the front door should be, there was a wall of cinder blocks. There was a banner, however, that said they had cold beer, which sounded good. "There a way in?"

"Until six," he said, "you gotta go around back." He motioned with his thumb over his shoulder. Mitch made out a rusted water tower, the Texaco logo still visible on it if you sort of squinted, the wreck of an old service station beside it. Then nothing but open desert. The kid saw where Mitch was looking. Sighed. Hopped off the truck. "Sorry. Other side. Unless you're one of those assholes who moved here during the pandemic. Then it's closed."

"That wasn't me."

He pointed at the car. "You have a spare tire? There's nails and broken glass all over here."

"Run-flats," Mitch said.

"No offense, but that's kind of pussy, don't you think?"

"I don't think, no," Mitch said. Ever since he drove Paul Copeland's Caddie to Granite Shores, Mitch had a thing for them, so when the firm told him he could have any car he wanted—within reason—on his ten-year anniversary, he immediately went for an XTS, though what he really wanted was a 1979 Seville. Maybe he'd buy one of those with his own money one day, but Mitch was still not in a place where he felt great with his government paperwork, his fake names only as good as the person looking into him. He wasn't about to try the DMV, much less TSA.

Mitch took a twenty out of his wallet, offered it to the kid. "Why don't you make sure no nails jump into my tires." The kid pocketed the cash like he was expecting it. "Something else," Mitch said. "Is Bonnie working today?" Intel Mitch had was that Penny Green was going by Bonnie Clyde. Clever.

"You'd have to ask inside," the kid said.

"You don't work here?"

The kid tapped something on his phone, turned it around. There was a photo on it of three women sitting inside a giant kiddie pool filled with water and ice, bottles of beer floating between them. One of them wore a Christian Undead Necro Teens T-shirt. "If she's one of these women, then yeah, I guess."

"You walk around snapping photos of women?" Mitch asked.

"They don't mind."

"Do you ask?"

The kid said, "It's the desert," like that explained everything.

Mitch started off toward the back. Stopped. "What happens at six?"

"Huh?"

"You said at six there's a different way in."

"Oh yeah," the kid said. "They knock the cinder blocks down."

Penny was still in the kiddie pool when Mitch came around the rear of the building, but the two ladies with her were now inside the bar, one lighting candles inside mason jars and setting them up along the L-shaped bar, the other straightening up the bottles and glasses, wiping down the spider-webbed mirror on the wall. There were four other kiddie pools in a semicircle around the property, all filled with water, ice, and bottles of beer. There was a man in one of them, eyes closed, head tilted over the rim of the pool, face flush to the sun. His chest was covered in two tattoos—on one side, a wolf's head, on the other, the words *HANK FOREVER*. He snored out of his open mouth.

"Good way to go blind," Mitch said.

Penny said, "You want a beer?" Mitch told her he did. She took one from her own pool, twisted off the cap, handed it to him. "Odds are he'll drown first."

"Optimistic," Mitch said.

Penny watched the man for a few seconds, then said, "Want to put some action on it?"

"Sure."

Penny got out of the pool, went inside the bar, came back with a chair for Mitch. "Five?" she said.

"How much is the beer?"

"$4.95."

"Well, let's make it interesting," Mitch said. He took out everything in his wallet, set it on the ground under a bottle. "Thirty-three bucks."

Penny cocked her head. "Do I know you?"

"Not yet," Mitch said.

"Then you'll have to trust me," she said. "I don't have any pockets." All she had on was the T-shirt and a bathing suit bottom. There was a pair of shorts on a chaise longue a few feet away. "But I'm good for thirty-three bucks."

"Oh," Mitch said, "I bet you're good for a few million." He sat down, sipped his beer, let that hang there, Penny watching him with no more interest than before. In the distance, a single coyote strolled through the desert, planes crisscrossed the deep blue sky, heading into and out of Palm Springs, which was just over the mountain. Somewhere, the smell of cooking meat wafted through. All that and the passed-out man didn't move an inch.

"What's his name?" Mitch asked after a while.

"We call him Yard-Shitting Sam," Penny said.

"To his face?"

"You'd be surprised."

"And no one drops the *G*?" Mitch asked.

"Only way I've heard it said. What do people call you?"

"Mitch Diamond." He put out his hand. She let it sit there. Okay. "You really going by Bonnie Clyde?"

No reaction.

"Trying it on," she said. "Kids don't seem to know it."

"You got paper with it?"

"Don't you know?" He did. She didn't. No court in the land would grant Penny Green that change. "How long did it take to find me?"

"A bit," Mitch said. She'd been out of prison for almost two years and moved around a fair amount.

"I guess Keith Morrison wants to interview me," she said.

"The guy from *Dateline*?"

"That's him," she said. "Thought I'd wait to see if he showed up one night." Penny pointed at Yard-Shitting Sam. "Oh no." He was trying to turn over. "Here we go." Yard-Shitting Sam shifted in the pool, his head slipped off the rim, and then he was thrashing underwater, sending bottles of beer and waves of ice water over the side and onto the desert floor, before he burst out of the pool, gasping for air.

Penny went inside for a minute, came out with a towel, gave it to Yard-Shitting Sam. He dried his face, his hair, his arms.

"You good?"

"Guess I fell asleep again," he said. He picked up one of the beers that had sloshed away, cracked it, walked into the bar.

"Again?" Mitch said to Penny when she returned.

"I may have had some previous experience with this situation."

She picked up the bottle, gathered up the cash, waited for . . . something. "That it?" she said.

"All thirty-three dollars."

"Don't you have some papers to serve me with or something?"

"Why would you think that?"

"Well, according to my security detail in the parking lot, the Cadillac out front is registered to the law firm my brother and I robbed," she said. "And then there's the scars on your knuckles."

"I'm not here to bother you," Mitch said. "Can I buy you dinner or something?"

"Are you asking me out on a date?"

"No," Mitch said, but the truth was, once he subtracted out her notoriously bad qualities—she'd spent half her time in Gig Harbor in solitary owing to her propensity for violence—Penny Green did seem like the kind of person he could make some bad decisions with, if the moment were right. The moment was certainly not right. "I want to talk to you about a chance to get back on your feet."

"You work for Barer & Harris and you . . . want to help me?"

"I work for a law firm. To not act in the interest of our clients is not what we do. That would be like asking someone with a 200 IQ to act like a moron when they're clearly a genius." Mitch paused, let that sink in. "Which is why I'm here, today."

She looked at her watch. "I get off at ten," she said. "There's a Black Bear Diner in Yucca. It's open twenty-four hours. I'll listen to you for as long as it takes for me to eat a stack of blueberry pancakes that your thirty-three bucks is going to pay for." She picked her shorts off the chaise, slid them on. "And it's closer to 220."

"I rounded."

"You rounded down. No one rounds down. My IQ is 216," she said, "but you knew that, too."

He did indeed.

# CHAPTER FOURTEEN

*Saturday*

Penny Green was pretty sure her life was in danger.

Fortunately, she didn't think anyone knew where she lived.

Not exactly, anyway.

Someone named Bonnie Clyde paid cash, monthly, for an apartment in Twentynine Palms, a few miles from the marine base. It was a two-story dingbat that held four tiny units, each the same: a galley kitchen, a living room, a bedroom, a bathroom. All crammed into 450 square feet. There was a single cement staircase surrounded by iron railings that ran up the front of the building to the second story walkway, which was appealing to the person calling herself Bonnie, since that way she could see someone coming. Each apartment also had a tiny rear balcony, which was also nice, since this Bonnie could leap off and probably survive and then run off into the desert. Which was another bonus. The building was on an undeveloped block surrounded on all sides by desert, Penny Green making sure Bonnie was no dummy.

One of her neighbors was a cook at the Creosote, Victor, who did twenty years in Corcoran on some biker gang killing and now was damn near the best short-order cook in the region. Another was a sex worker named Jolly. Her territory was the Pilot truck stop near Needles, a good two hours and half hours away. She didn't like working near where she lived, she told Bonnie. It was a job, it didn't need to be her life. And then the building manager stayed in the last place, but he was rarely there. His name was Brent. He was about thirty and one of those guys who said, *No worries*, when he really meant to say either *Thank you* or *You're welcome*. It was one of those terms that Bonnie wouldn't think much about, but boy, Penny Green sure did.

The apartment also had a front door painted a nice shade of forest green, which was enough for Penny Green to believe it was a sign. It was the little things that she'd come to appreciate now that she was free again.

A shame she'd need to leave. And change her fake name. She kind of liked Bonnie Clyde.

Now, close to 10:00 p.m., standing in her kitchen, Penny was throwing all her shit into garbage bags, sure that this Mitch Diamond fellow was going to show up at any minute and put one between her eyes. He worked for Barer & Harris, so he had a legit job, but that didn't mean he wasn't there to collect for one of the firm's more *angry* clients.

She'd walked from her shift that night at the Creosote with a hundred bucks. She'd gas up, buy as many groceries as she could get, and hit the road. Where to?

Yuma, maybe?

No one wanted to be in Yuma. Not even to kill a person.

Salton Sea?

That seemed too obvious. If she was going to look for someone hiding from society, she'd start there.

Maybe she'd say *fuck it* and go to Los Angeles. A city where everyone was so inured to famous people, her name might go unrecognized.

Her cell phone rang.

She looked at the caller ID.

*Mitch Diamond. Barer & Harris.* Calling from his company phone. She was sure Mitch was the kind of guy who had three or four phones for different purposes.

Thing was, she hadn't given the guy her number. She took the phone and went outside to her balcony and looked out into the black desert. Half expected a red laser light to fix on her chest. But all she saw were stars.

She let the call go to voice mail.

And Mitch Diamond, it looked like, was leaving a message?

Which was oddly . . . calming. What was *that* about? Was her tuning fork out of whack? Was it ever *in* whack?

Penny Green was nineteen the first time she felt this kind of fear for her life. She was in a supper club called Krym in Odessa, Ukraine, sitting in a meeting with Freddie Golubev's father (who everyone called Puka, which Penny knew meant *honest* or *reliable*, but which was the exact opposite of Puka himself) and a Basque separatist named Ameztoy, which Penny understood to be his last name. Ameztoy was in town to see about getting a tank or two. Penny's job was to translate for both men, literally sitting between them at a long table in a private room that overlooked the Black Sea.

The two men were cordial, talking about each other's families, Penny getting the sense they'd done business before, had a decent-enough knowledge of each other to feel comfortable discussing their children, share a bottle of red wine, eat plate after plate of grilled lamb dishes, and even politely share baklava. Puka excused himself to the bathroom, leaving Penny with Ameztoy.

"Do you want wine?" he asked Penny, his English flawless. Which was odd since Puka spoke passable—if uncomfortable—English, too. So why was she even there?

"No," Penny said. "I'm working."

"We are all working." He poured her a glass of wine. She ignored it. "How old are you now?"

*Now?* Immediately, Penny felt something change in the room. He hadn't said *now* accidentally. "I'm nineteen," she said.

Ameztoy said, "Smartest teenager in the world, right? Wasn't that you?"

Around the world . . . and here she was. "That's me," she said.

"I remember you on *Dr. Phil*." So did she. It was all bleeped out. "You shouldn't have come here. You're smart, you'll get up and leave now."

He poured himself another glass of wine, too. Drank it down. "I have a sister. She's a moron. Wants to be a pop star in America. So she's in school in Boston." This made him laugh in a way that Penny found intensely uncomfortable. "But you know what she would never do?" He waved his hands around the room. "This. Do you know why?"

"I'm going to guess," Penny said, "that she has decent parents who love her."

"No," Ameztoy said. "Our parents are imprisoned. Each in solitary confinement. Which ruins you. Ruins you. Barbaric. I raised my sister from the time she was nine. Not to say our parents didn't love her. They surely did. I am sure they are so brain addled now that they wouldn't know what love even is." He drank the glass he had poured for Penny. "She would not be here because my sister, who we have established is a moron, would have been smart enough to figure out who I am, and she would not be in the same room with me."

"I'm working," Penny said again. "My job is not to do deep research. It's to translate."

"Is your job worth your life? Because if this does not end up how I want it to end up, you are not safe anywhere on this planet. I will kill you. If I cannot find you, I will kill your brother, Robert. Your father, the grifter? He is also a dead man. I will dig up your kind and recently deceased mother from the Jewish cemetery in Seattle and will kill her again." He took a piece of baklava and chewed it slowly. "I do *my* research, Penelope. Choose your words carefully."

Before Penny could respond—that this was 100 percent not worth her life—Puka came back into the private room. Sat down. They got back to negotiating. Puka in Russian. Ameztoy in Spanish. Penny between them, speaking both, carefully. The men shook hands at the end. Puka would not sell the tanks Ameztoy wanted because, in the end, Puka did not think Basque separatists rolling tanks into Seville would go unnoticed by the world community, and that would be bad for Puka's business. Penny watched from the window as Puka walked Ameztoy out of the restaurant, down a long sidewalk next to the beach, into a yacht that waited nearby.

Puka returned ten minutes later and sat back down at the table.

"Sit," he told her in Russian.

She did.

"Understand," he said, "that man you met? He is already dead. His body is dumped in the Black Sea." He poured her a glass of wine. "You're shaking. Take a small sip."

She did.

"I did not like the way he spoke to you," he said. "You are my son's friend, and that means you are my friend, while you are here. Tell me you understand, Penny."

She did.

"My business is binary," he said. "Yes or death, I think of it that way. The way he spoke to you, I saw that he was not to be trusted. Too stupid to know I was listening, even, so he is sloppy and had to go. You are not sloppy, Penny?"

She was not.

Puka said, "I'll have one of my guys get you back to your villa. Do you wish to stay? Or do you want me to send you home?"

*Yes or death*, Penny figured, so she said, "The villa."

"Good," Puka said. "You are smart, aren't you."

"About some things."

"Here," he said, "we have a proverb. If you are as smart as they say, you'll remember it. The past is a lighthouse, not a port."

For years, she wondered if what Puka told her was true. She never searched for news on Ameztoy. If he was alive or dead was irrelevant. She'd spent the rest of her life checking her back regardless.

Until today. When she got caught slipping.

Well, no.

Soaking.

Mitch Diamond could have walked up and put one right behind her ear and she'd never even know it.

And now here he was, giving her a courtesy call?

She played the message.

*I know you're scared,* he said. Which was true. *So if need be, we can split the check. I'll be there about eleven.*

The sound of her own laughter echoed out into the desert.

She went back inside.

Put her cutlery away.

Went out front, knocked on Victor's door. His boyfriend, Dom, opened the door.

"What's up, girl?" Dom said. He and Victor were two of the scariest-looking dudes she'd ever known. Neither had an inch of open skin on their face, every pore taken up with ink.

"I was wondering if you and Victor could do a little security work for me tonight."

# CHAPTER FIFTEEN

*Saturday*

Penny was sitting in a booth, her back to the wall, drinking an iced tea and listening to something through her earbuds when Mitch arrived at the diner. He'd watched her walk in from across the street, made sure she was alone, Mitch not wanting any witnesses, but also he didn't want this to be some situation where he ended up in a fistfight with a woman who could probably beat his ass, Mitch in his fifties now, still willing to do what had to be done, but not so willing to do it with his bare hands. He had an arthritic thumb and something going on in his neck that shot pain up through his right eye and down to the arch of his left foot. That couldn't be good.

So he waited a few minutes and then followed her in, but first he popped his trunk, took out a duffel bag he had for her, pondered whether or not to grab the little drop gun he kept back there, a shitty .38 that he kept one bullet in on the off chance he had to literally get away with murder. Decided, fuck it, if she was going to go crazy, she wasn't gonna do it in the Black Bear Diner and risk going back to prison. He'd trust his ability to get what he needed without getting fucking shot in the process.

The diner was packed, a mixture of LA hipsters in town to hike Joshua Tree, locals coming off their bar and dispensary shifts, tweakers coming down from their meth, teens working through their edible highs, and then some RVers coming in off Highway 62 and just happy to see people again. When Mitch slid in across from her, Penny took out her earbuds, set them on the table, started talking like they were already in the middle of a conversation.

"You believe in aliens?" she asked.

"Do they believe in me?"

"They surely do," she said. "They're not so up in their own passivity and denial to believe they're alone."

"I guess I've never spent too much time thinking about it."

"Oh that's total bullshit." She pointed out the window. "You walk out of here tonight, look up there. Purest sky you're ever going to see out here. I mean, you can see the fucking satellites if you have decent eyesight. Look. Really look. And try to tell me you've never wondered if there's someone else out there."

"I have too many earthly concerns to worry about what's cracking on Jupiter," Mitch said.

"No, no," she said. "Don't be so egocentric. Our solar system is a fucking dump. We live on the one planet that hasn't been doomed yet. We're the last mansion in New Orleans after the ocean rises. The universe is infinite. You can't begin to comprehend its size. And you're looking out your window and deciding what's what." She turned her phone around, showed Mitch the screen, which said *ALIENATION* with *DR. BOB AND DR. TRAVIS*. "It's this podcast by these two astrophysicists at Stanford, these thirty-year-old too-smart-for-their-own-good-douchebags, and what they keep coming back to is if we're being visited, we're being visited by, basically, aliens who have failed driver's ed and stole their drunk stepfather's truck to go joyriding and boom, they found Midland, Texas, or whatever. And now they want to party. Because we're depleting our natural resources so quickly, any benefit we have to the aliens was mined a million years ago, which is basically a dog year to them."

"I like that term," Mitch said. "My mom used to say it."

"Well, your mom was probably a very smart woman who is now wildly disappointed." Penny pointed at Mitch. "Shit. Is she dead?"

"No." She was eighty. He hadn't seen her in a long time, but every month he got cash to her, made sure that the assisted living facility she was in was first-class, that she didn't have too much salt in her meals.

"Whew. Anyway. Point is. None of this shit you see on YouTube is because Martian Einstein is behind the wheel."

"So not the best of the best," Mitch said.

"Not even the best of the worst. But that's the thing, right? Here we are, trying to figure out all the mysteries of the universe, and we've got Beavis and Butthead, essentially, blasting through wormholes in time and space to put on a light show to some farmers in Azerbaijan and we can't even figure out a way to get basic medical care for people in need. When I was in Gig? I was getting regular teeth cleanings, saw my gynecologist every nine months, and even got a troublesome mole removed off my back." She slid a menu across the table. Mitch couldn't quite tell what she was working toward. But it was like she'd practiced this whole thing in case she ever had to deliver it in a convincing tone. "Anyway. Whenever I feel more significant than I should, I look up and remind myself I am but a speck of dust in a vast history of specks of dust."

"How centering," Mitch said.

"Cheaper than seeing a therapist."

A waitress came over to the table. She was in her sixties and wore a T-shirt with a black bear on it, jeans, and garish suspenders. She set a coffee down in front of Mitch, kept moving.

"I ordered for you," Penny said. "I figured you for a black coffee guy."

"Why is that?" Mitch said.

"Well, there's this whole laconic asshole thing you've got rolling," she said. "Hard to imagine you inside a Starbucks getting lattes."

He dumped three creamers into the cup, stirred it with a knife since there wasn't a spoon on the table. Plus, he liked the image. Poured two sugars in, tasted it, poured two more in. Took a satisfied sip. "And yet. I'm a normal, twenty-first century man."

"Your crooked nose tells a different story. And you should get those scars under your eyes Botoxed. What did you fight? Middleweight?"

"Light heavyweight."

"Miss it?"

"Sometimes I dream about it and I'll wake up and I'm sweating like I've been in a fight and my bed's all messed up. So maybe subconsciously, sure. But no part of me misses having strangers scream at me for falling after getting hit in the face."

Penny nodded like she understood. And maybe she did. Her file from her bid at Gig Harbor included more than a dozen fights, none with her on the losing end. She didn't seem to start fights, but she finished them. "My father used to say, 'Every man's got to figure to get beat sometime.'" Mitch couldn't stifle his laugh. "What?" Penny asked.

"Your father didn't come up with that," Mitch said.

"No?"

"Joe Louis said it."

"Well," Penny said, "my father was a liar. So that tracks."

"We all have something." Mitch took his encrypted iPad out of his duffel. His tech guy swore it was impenetrable. If he entered the wrong password twice, he was pretty sure it would blow up and send a robot from the future to kill the president, too. Tapped it twice. "For instance. Did you really gouge out a woman's eyes while you were in prison?"

"Tried," Penny said. "If I'd been successful, she wouldn't have been able to ID me. Does your iPad have the detail that she'd been paid by some Seattle Crip shotcaller that your firm represented to attack me? Or was that left out?"

Mitch said, "Let me check," then scrolled for a few seconds. "Oh there it is. Guess they didn't lead with that." He showed her the story. It was in *US* magazine. Headline: "When Prodigies Attack." She took the iPad from him, typed a few words. Turned the screen back around. It was a Google search for "Mitch Diamond Seattle."

"Funny thing," she said, "you don't show up in any news stories. No social media. You don't even show up in court records, which is odd since you'd think that Barer & Harris would use you as an expert witness, what with your background in covert intelligence, according to your bio on their website, which is the only speck of you I could find when I did this little charade from home."

"Did you try my middle name?" He rolled up his sleeve. Showed her his tat. "Ace of?"

"What kind of Jew gets a tattoo?"

"Who says I am one?"

"Diamond? Come on. Plus we look like we fell out of the same tree in Ukraine. You could be my cousin."

"It's my job to not be easy to find. I show up in your life, you've done something shitty. So I keep it low. Use PO boxes. That sort of thing."

"Except that from nine to five, most days you're in an office with terrible security. Enterprising person could hide in the parking structure and shoot you when you pull in."

Mitch didn't respond. Penny wasn't fucking dumb, sparring with her like sparring with Mike Tyson, getting hit in the face, realizing your whole plan needs some readjusting.

"You seem like the type of guy," Penny continued, "who got some money and scrubbed himself up, but then got bored, maybe forgot to leave some crumbs around the internet for anyone who might be interested enough to look into you. Your boxing record would be a good one. Or, you know, a high school yearbook photo maybe? An old Facebook profile? Any of those would make you seem more human."

"Oh yeah?"

"Yeah." She pointed out the window at Mitch's car. "Fiftysomething years old driving a seventy-five-year-old's car. That's a level of comfort. Normally, that would tell me you got money late in your life and were scared that you'd lose it, so you deposited it all into a car big enough to sleep in if you needed to. Except it's not registered in your name, which is weird, because if you lost your job, you'd lose the car, so you must feel confident you're not about to lose your job."

"I feel pretty good."

"It's not a very inconspicuous ride," she said. She finished off her iced tea, reached across the table, grabbed Mitch's coffee, poured it over the ice in her glass. Waved the coffee mug in the air. The waitress swooped by, filled it back up. It was like being in some kind of Russian diner ballet. "I saw you parked across the street. You think I was bringing the cops?"

"I was more concerned about Yard-Shitting Sam."

"You've got an answer for everything, don't you? What about those $500 loafers you're wearing in the middle of the desert? I'm guessing your arches failed about twenty-five years ago, but now you can afford the good insole, no more Dr. Scholl's for you. And that watch. What is it, a Rolex?"

Mitch slid it off his wrist. Flipped it around. "So it is." He examined the face. "What time do you have?" he asked Penny.

She looked at her phone. "11:13 p.m."

"Yep," Mitch said and put his watch back on. "That's what I've got, too. Except I'm not being tracked by the Chinese every time I check." Penny's cheeks flushed. Mitch didn't know what exactly was going on between them right at that moment, but he sort of enjoyed it. "Anyway, it was a gift."

"From a woman?"

"No. I bought it for myself." Which was sort of true. He pulled it off an ex-con's wrist on Mercer Island about five years ago when he went to go collect on a seriously past due notice for the firm. Firm was so impressed, they let him keep it.

"It's too showy. Tells me you put it on when you want people to take you more seriously than maybe you've earned. Put you on an even line with assholes that might otherwise think you were trash."

"I do come from a long line of trash," Mitch said.

"I thought I recognized you from the Old Country." Penny stared at Mitch again, like she was trying to place him in a lineup. "When you came around the back, you didn't even look at me twice in the pool. Practically averted your eyes when I got out. You were even nice to Jeff, the kid out front. Seems like you might be what we used to call a gentleman, but you're not that gentle, something tells me. So maybe that just means you were raised with women. Gave you some innate respect. Probably got a family who's disillusioned by you somewhere, now that you've turned out to be a good guy."

"That's where you're wrong," Mitch said, thinking: *Finally.*

"You're not a gentleman?"

"No," Mitch said. "I'm not a good guy. It's important for you to understand that, Penny. I'm not here because I want to be friends. I'm here because you're the only person on the planet that I think can help me solve a problem."

The waitress came back before Mitch could continue, Penny's head angled like a confused puppy's. "You want to order, or do you want a referee?" the waitress asked.

Penny kept her eyes fixed on Mitch but said, "I'll have the full stack of blueberry pancakes, two scrambled eggs, country potatoes, and wheat toast, burnt. My friend Mr. Bad Guy will have the chicken-fried steak, extra gravy."

The waitress glanced at Mitch. "That true?" she asked.

"Which part?"

The waitress said, "The only thing I care about is the food, hon."

"I'll have some cottage cheese," Mitch said, "and some egg whites. Box the steak to go." When she was gone, Mitch said to Penny, "Are we done now? Have you established whatever dominance you wanted to establish? You're smart and perceptive. You don't need to prove that to me."

"Was I wrong about anything?"

Mitch thought for a moment. "I think aliens have always been here," he said. "Makes more sense, doesn't it? If they're traveling through wormholes in time and space, those didn't get built overnight. So maybe Earth has been a rest stop for, say, a hundred thousand years? Or as little as a thousand years, right? In our time? That feels pretty old, but these guys live light years away. If they can get here over light years, gotta assume time doesn't mean to them what it means to us. So what I'm saying is, I don't have to *believe* in them. I might fucking *be* one of them."

Penny Green pinched her bottom lip, Mitch thinking she was trying to stifle a smile, then pointed at two big motherfuckers sitting at a booth across the restaurant. They looked like bikers, but not of the weekend warrior variety. Mitch noticed them when he walked in, the way they'd mad-dogged him from the moment he opened the door but didn't bother to get up and say anything, which told Mitch they were probably with Penny, because Penny Green wasn't stupid. She said, "I'm going to send my friend Victor and his boyfriend home, cool?"

"Cool," Mitch said.

She walked over to them, handed each a twenty, gave them both a hug, followed them outside, then came back inside once they got into a white Honda Accord and roared off, Mitch thinking Harleys must not be practical in the desert during the summer. Penny sat down, her breakfast waiting for her.

"They were out of wheat toast, so I got you a burnt English muffin instead."

"Who *are* you?" Penny said.

Mitch said, "Do you want to make some real money, Penny?"

For the next hour, Mitch explained to Penny his problem. In the years since Robert Green robbed the safe-deposit boxes of Barer & Harris and then disappeared into the ether, there'd been every manner of television special, movie of the week, cold-case documentary, podcast, true crime book, and feature story possible. By all rights, a never-ending series of media hits where his face was plastered across everything would have resulted in him turning up . . . somewhere. Or at least being spotted. Even Whitey Bulger only got sixteen years on the run and he had the fucking FBI working with him.

Least that was Mitch's opinion.

Plus, every so often Robert *did* show back up, either to blackmail someone or to Robin Hood for some good cause. The last time, it was a tech oligarch with an external hard drive with five thousand pictures of himself fucking Thai hookers. At least they were of age. He got shaken down for $500,000, Mitch making that cash delivery himself. Mitch handed a ten-year-old boy who stepped off a Carnival cruise ship at the Port of Seattle a duffel bag filled with cash in exchange for the drive. Which of course was duplicated, the residual data from the cloning software sitting there like a waving flag. A subtle warning that if the dude fucked around some more, he'd be finding out, directly.

Time before that, though, a floundering Planned Parenthood project in Portland received a check for $2 million from a former Republican congresswoman, made with the proviso that her donation be made public, which after a career of demonizing Planned Parenthood was quite the coup. Her crime? Turned out her safe-deposit box contained both her sainted mother's ashes—returned in full—and a gun used in a drive-by shooting allegedly involving her son, Deuce. Thing was, Deuce was already doing ten in San Quentin for robbing a Wells Fargo in Oakland. If that news got out, he'd be looking at the rest of his life behind bars. It didn't. At least not yet, anyway. These were two of thirty different like events that Barer & Harris handled over the years. Plus however many didn't go through the firm. It was the agreement the firm had made. Keep this shit away from the cops if Robert came to them directly, Mitch thinking Robert must have a reason for how he decided such things, but there was nothing obvious. Periodically, Robert contacted the Granite Shores PD, who then contacted the firm. Periodically, he contacted the firm, who handled house business in-house. Regardless, very few clients wanted the law to look too closely at what they were keeping hidden, which Robert seemed to understand.

For the most part, news of this sort was kept out of the media, but every now and then, Mitch would place a call, shoot out an email, contact a friendly at *The Seattle P-I*, particularly if somehow the transaction made Barer & Harris look good and it might get this fucker found, finally. Because as soon as that happened, the whole story would get retold, how a small-town cop making a routine arrest stumbled on evidence of something much larger and . . . and . . . and . . . Though all the details were so well known now that Mitch wondered why anyone really cared . . . except, of course, it was obvious.

Robert Green got away with it. Only person who got physically hurt was Jack Biddle, and he'd managed to turn that into a cottage industry.

"So how is this my problem?" Penny asked.

"Your commissary account was refilled every month," Mitch said. "Every month, someone using a different prepaid Visa made the payment online from a different IP address. Never the same person. Never even in the same city. The receipts are all on the iPad, if you want to see them."

"I don't," she said.

"Meanwhile, you were in prison, your brother made no effort to disappear from the public consciousness, yet also didn't do anything to help your case. Never sent a letter saying, *Hey, go easy on my sister, it was all my idea, she was an unwitting accessory.* He let you carry that whole weight."

Penny said nothing, Mitch thinking maybe he should move her fork and knife, in case he managed to piss her off too much. "So that gets me curious. If he wanted to reach out to you covertly, how would he do it? That got me thinking about your commissary payments."

"Robby and I," Penny said, "we always spoke in secret codes buried deep in the recipe for Funyuns, so you cracked that, Nostradamus. How much did that cost you?"

"Nothing," Mitch said. "Benefit of being the aggrieved party. State of Washington gave us everything. Last payment, it was a guy named Dexter Turner. That name mean anything to you?"

"No."

"And your name meant nothing to him. He answered a help wanted ad on Craigslist. Ended up getting paid in one-carat diamond earrings that we traced immediately back to the theft. You wanna guess who they belonged to?"

"No," Penny said.

"The first lady of Washington. The governor's wife."

"Those would have looked nice on me, I bet."

"Not your style," Mitch said.

"Diamonds are everyone's style."

"Thing is, anyone who did even a rudimentary amount of digging would eventually find Dexter and those earrings and then you'd be on the front page again, right when you were about to get released, when the governor was forced to answer questions about why he was keeping precious jewels in a safe-deposit box at a law office."

"And why didn't that happen?" Penny asked.

"Because I was tracking your commissary payments for a year," Mitch said. "Thirty-six hours after your last credit hit, I was on Dexter's front porch in Centralia with a check and an NDA."

"Centralia?"

"Yeah. You ever been?"

Penny said, "We used to go there twice a month when I was a kid. That's where our mother used to pick us up for weekends."

"I know," Mitch said. "Keith Morrison told me. The *first time* he did an episode about you."

Penny closed her eyes, did some kind of deep-breathing exercise, silently counting to twenty-five, muttered, "Fucking *Dateline*," then leaned against the back of the booth, spread her arms across the top of the vinyl banquette. The Black Bear Diner was mostly empty. It was after 12:30 a.m., and the only other patrons were buried silently in their phones and pancakes. Single men and single women eating alone, Mitch thinking that this was a fate that he needed to avoid, but that he was speeding toward. Even their waitress was sitting by herself at a table on the other side of the restaurant, going to work on a short stack of pancakes.

"Let me ask you something, Mitch Diamond," she said, eyes still closed, voice calm, using Mitch's full name like he was a character in a *Snoopy* comic strip, but also, Mitch knew, because she didn't believe that was his name. Then, eyes wide fucking open, voice still calm, but something about her reminded Mitch of a tea kettle, the steam starting to come out now: "When you motherfuckers turned my brother into D. B. Cooper, what did you think was going to happen?"

"That wasn't my decision."

"Bullshit," she said. "Respectfully? Your entire physical reality is owned by that law firm, so their decisions hang on to you like a second skin. You're their emissary. You don't like how they do business, seems to me you'd be the kind of guy who'd go get another job."

"Like Robert did?"

"Yeah," Penny said, "exactly. He even put his signature on his resignation. Clearly."

That was true, Mitch knew.

Which was part of all this. Mitch's own time was running short. His past was running up behind him. He could feel it. Last couple years, he'd been doing what he could to pave over that road. Nevertheless, one of these days, there was going to be a knock on his door, and a cold-case detective with questions about Paul Copeland was going to be standing there with way more questions than Mitch was prepared to answer.

So.

He'd taken pains to fix that. Penny was right: There were no photos of him online. His tech guy washed away everything. It was happenstance and time and age that worried Mitch these days. None of those things could be controlled. If he was going to get away with it, he needed to force the issue.

Because it wasn't just Paul Copeland.

There was his dead stepfather, whose name he took. There were all the old-timers he ran with down in Pajaro, who maybe he'd screwed over a time or two when he was a younger man and prone to such things, and maybe they get pinched and start throwing his name around.

As it was, he couldn't confidently set foot on a fucking plane with his fake IDs. If he got pulled over and someone ran his license? Maybe he'd be fine until they realized they should be looking at an eighty-year-old man. Since Gabino hired him as an independent contractor fifteen years ago using the name and social he gave him—that's where his dead stepfather factored in, the asshole scattered in little pieces, a favor he'd done for his mother before skipping California, the abusive fuck getting what was coming—he'd continued to pay his taxes like a good citizen. Even stayed out of trouble.

Or, well, hadn't been caught for his trouble.

But how much longer could he do that?

"I'm just trying to live my life," Penny was saying. The Black Bear had emptied out. "I'm tired. I've had a long day. It's 300 degrees outside and the aliens refuse to come and get me. And for some reason, the one thing none of you ever bother to ask me is how it felt to be left behind to rot in fucking prison while my brother became a mythological character. Are you under the impression that I *wanted* to martyr myself for my brother's cause? Because I've got news for you: He didn't have a cause. He wanted the fucking money. We both just wanted the fucking money. Where he went? I have no idea. When he didn't show up? I was heartbroken. I *am* heartbroken." She slapped the table. A spoon clattered to the floor.

"Let's take it easy," Mitch said evenly.

Their waitress came over, dropped off their check. "My shift is over," she said, so Mitch handed her a C-note, told her to keep the change. She took a marker from her pocket, drew a line through the bill, held it up to the light.

"That doesn't work on new bills," Mitch said.

"How do you know that?" the waitress said.

"I'm a criminal," Mitch said. He was in a truth-telling mood.

"I don't even know what I'm looking for, anyway," the waitress said.

Mitch stood up when the waitress left, grabbed up his duffel bag. "Let's get out of here," he said to Penny, but she didn't get up right away.

"Robby is the only person I have ever loved," Penny said, quietly. She looked up at Mitch, and for a moment he thought he saw the kid he remembered from the old news stories and documentaries. "There was nothing to gain by leaving me behind. If you've got something to offer to me, put it on the table, or let me go, please, and don't come back. I've got maybe thirty years to live. I want to live them in obscurity."

Mitch reached into the duffel bag, took out a mailer inside a clear, sealed plastic evidence bag, set it on the table. The address label was made out to Dexter Turner. "This is what the diamond earrings came in. We've tested every single piece of mail your brother has sent for DNA and trace materials. Sometimes, we'll find a hair of your brother's, a fingerprint. Some dandruff. He's not hiding, even though he's hiding. But this time? He fucked up. Beyond his control, but he fucked up." He pointed at the postmark. "Says here it was mailed out of Elko, Nevada. That means that's where he—or someone working for him—dumped it in a mailbox. But when we swabbed it for evidence, on the seal, in addition to one of your brother's eyelashes, we found traces of *Ammophila arenaria* pollen. You know what that is?"

Penny said, "I look like an arborist?"

"It's found in a kind of beach grass."

"Okay," she said. She picked up the evidence bag. Flipped it over. Examined everything. Set it back down.

"Thing is, this kind of grass, it's indigenous to North Africa, coast of the Black Sea, the Baltic, the Mediterranean. You know, other side of the world." He let that sit there for a moment. "More the seas rise, more natural dunes are disappearing. Last few years, the city of Granite Shores has been importing these heartier dunes and planting them surrounding new beachside construction, so the coastline doesn't slide into the ocean and take two hundred condos along for the ride."

Penny looked up. "Go on." Interested. Working through it. Mitch thinking he was close now, so he sat back down, lowered his voice, leaned close.

"It means this envelope was sealed outside, most likely, on a windy day, somewhere fairly near to some sand dunes either in North Africa or Granite Shores. Maybe use your Chinese surveillance machine and check what the weather was for Granite Shores the day before the postmark on that envelope."

Penny did just that, Mitch waiting for her to see what he already knew: On March 13, two years ago, weather in Granite Shores, Oregon, was a blustery 56 degrees, with wind gusts out of the west of up to twenty-six miles per hour. "Jesus-fucking-Christ," Penny said.

"Thing of it is," Mitch said, "two weeks ago, one of our clients got a letter from your brother demanding a significant cash payment for the safe return of a child's ashes. We tested that for the pollen, too, even before scraping for DNA. It was right there."

"Robby would not extort someone for their child's ashes."

"Our client doesn't have a child," Mitch said.

"I don't get it."

"She declared it was her child's ashes. There was an urn and everything. We have no idea what was actually in there. But it was enough to get our client excessively concerned and willing to pay."

"Did they pay?"

"Not yet. Money is supposed to be deposited in an account in Gibraltar in two weeks."

"Or what?"

"The contents of the urn will be released online."

"But then," Penny said, "Robby would get nothing. I don't get it."

"Yeah," Mitch said. "Tells me Robert knows she'll pay. Me, I'm not so sure. This client? Government job, mailing address is the Pentagon. Home address, it's an apartment in Seattle. Not a millionaire by any stretch of the imagination. Client tells the firm the firm has to front the money. It's their fault, after all."

"Reasonable."

"Yeah," Mitch said. "Thing is, firm is prepared to pay, but they want to take a moon shot first. So on your brother's birthday, Barer & Harris are going to announce a significant reward for the safe return of the items still missing from the heist."

"His birthday is Wednesday."

"That's why I'm here."

"You couldn't have called?"

"Would you have picked up?"

"No," Penny said.

"So here we are."

"How much?" Penny said.

"That's not been released yet."

"How much?"

"I'm not approved to say."

"How about this," Penny said, "you tell me how much, and I won't spend the rest of tonight figuring out who the fuck you used to be. I'll pretend you've always been named Mitch Diamond and ignore the fact that your tattoo looks like it was done in prison, probably by Kiko Pocotillo in Quentin."

*Shit.* She really was on a whole other level. Mitch said, "How do you know Kiko?"

"His homegirl was in Gig with me," she said. "Her entire back was his canvas. He's got a website now. Went legit. Rappers pay him top dollar to give them upscale tats that have that prison patina. His girl put them up on her IG. They're nice."

Mitch underestimated Penny. In a strange way, that made him admire her.

Penny said, "So it's a couple calls, Mitch Diamond, and your whole story is blown up. Maybe get some laser work, now that you can afford Italian loafers."

"Two million," Mitch said.

Penny whistled. "I can't imagine I'm eligible to collect that."

"No," Mitch said, "but I am, provided I quit my job first."

"And?"

"Gainfully unemployed as soon as you agree to help. Got the email saved in my drafts, ready to go."

"You have the list of items?"

Mitch patted the duffel. "Right here. Got it from your laptop, in fact."

Penny ignored that. "Two million dollars, everyone on the planet will come looking for it."

"We'd have a head start. And each other. Who is more qualified?"

Penny looked out the window. "I find my brother," she said. "What then?"

"I'm not the police. All I care about is the loot."

"What's the catch?" Penny asked.

"When we find it," Mitch said, "you can't claim the reward."

"You're saying I have to trust that you'll give me what's mine."

"That's right."

"You don't see the irony in that?"

"This time, it's not a criminal situation. I fuck you over, you go tell Oprah."

"When I was seventeen, Oprah told Dr. Phil I was destined for prison," Penny said. "She can get fucked."

"Turns out," Mitch said, "she knew what she was talking about."

Penny dug into her purse, pulled out a pack of cloves, got up, walked out of the restaurant. Mitch grabbed his silverware, his coffee cup, and his napkin, put them in his duffel bag. Poured a glass of water on his dinner plate, followed that with the rest of Penny's coffee, wiped down the table, then followed Penny outside, where he found her sitting on the curb. She lit up, blew smoke into the desert night, Mitch thinking he hadn't even smelled a clove since . . . well, since that fucking day. If only he'd known then what he knew now, maybe he'd already have all that stash.

# CHAPTER SIXTEEN

*Saturday*

The Black Bear Diner was right on Highway 62, which was also the main four lanes through town, but at this time of night, there were only a few cars going either direction, so Mitch sat down beside Penny, stretched his legs out, put the duffel on his lap. When was the last time Penny sat on a curb? When she was seventeen? Eighteen? Certain things you didn't do after a while.

"You know," Penny said, "when I was a kid in Granite Shores? We had the boardwalk and all that, of course, but people cared about the coastline, really took care of it, protested when those oil company assholes wanted to start drilling in eyeline of the shore, really made it clear that they were not wanted in our area, and when developers wanted to build condos, it was like the Troubles. I think my father may have blown up someone's car. That's what basically ended our parents' marriage." She took a deep drag on the clove, held it in, blew it out slow, like it would choke the memory. "The world is near collapse. Fascists running half of the government, morons running the other half, masses of garbage in the world's oceans the size of Rhode Island, the seas are rising, the sun is getting hotter, we're all deeply fucked, and yet your law firm is willing to spend two million dollars to get back the personal items of a bunch of millionaires and crooks?" She finally turned back to Mitch. "It's blood money. You understand that."

"If someone else finds your brother, he's likely to end up in a body bag. You and me, we'll do it right."

"He's already dead to me."

"No he's not," Mitch said.

"He has to be," Penny said. "Do you understand? He has to be. The only way I could survive prison was to give up hope."

"And get good with your hands."

"Neither are the best of me."

"I'm giving you a chance to be whoever you want to be."

"You're the fixer for Barer & Harris," she said. "You put me away."

"I prefer 'corporate security,'" Mitch said, "and let's be clear, you put yourself away." That was true. She pled guilty to robbery, conspiracy, and assault on a peace officer. With her prior convictions, she got ten to fifteen years, ended up getting out in a little over thirteen. Beat the shit out of a cop, you're going to do a full bid, or close to it, even if you have good behavior . . . and Penny didn't have good behavior.

"I said I'd never go back to Losertown," Penny said.

"What if I told you I had some information you might want?"

"Like what?"

"Who put out the hits on you inside."

"It wasn't you?"

"We're a law firm, Penny," Mitch said. "We don't sanction prison beatdowns." Well, not often, anyway, but never on a woman, at least.

"I'm listening."

"You know someone who goes by Bobby C.?"

"I figured he was dead or in prison."

"Nope," Mitch said. "Operates a limo company in Granite Shores. You got seventy-five bucks, he'll drive you to prom. Also has a lucrative service driving people out to Gig and Walla Walla, and down to Bend for visiting hours."

"You have to be kidding me."

"Drives Shirley Turner's family out once a month."

"She tried to stab me with a bar of soap. I'd never even seen her before, and then she was in my cell with a Dial soap shank." Penny lifted up her shirt, showed Mitch a scar near her belly button. "Got me pretty good."

"How'd you get out of that?"

"Drowned her in my sink. Didn't want a manslaughter on my sheet, though, so I pulled her out. She now gets spoon fed." There was part of Mitch that Penny saw was impressed by this story. Another part of him was deeply frightened. This man was not a poker player. "Bobby C. doesn't have anything against me. He's a bagman. Who paid him?"

"Figured that would be something you might enjoy finding out." He took the iPad out of his duffel. "Everything you need, it's on here."

"I need a day or two," she said.

"Twelve hours," Mitch said, "I'm out of here."

"That should be enough."

"You won't find anything on me in that time," Mitch said.

"Twelve hours, I'll know how your grandparents met. Eighteen hours, I'll know where they're buried. Twenty-four hours, I'll be using Bubby's social to get credit."

"That isn't the life choice you want to make, Penny, respectfully."

"Respectfully? How bracing."

Mitch walked over to his Caddie, popped the trunk, stowed away his shit. "I'm staying in Palm Springs at the Margaritaville Hotel. If I hear that 'cheeseburger' song one more time, I'm likely to do something I'll regret, so don't wait too long with your answer." Mitch looked up at the desert sky. "I think I saw the space station."

Penny followed his gaze. All she saw were dreamy-looking stars, streaks of light against the blackness. She needed to get some glasses.

Mitch got inside the Caddie, started it up, pulled out, but stopped beside Penny, rolled down the window.

"Kiko's dead," he said.

"Really?"

"He is if you contact him. Just being real with you."

"You really think Robby's been in Granite Shores all this time?" she said.

"No," Mitch said. Penny knew they'd found Robert's DNA at minor crime scenes in France. In Albania. Croatia. On a cruise ship in the Azores. In eleven different states. That was on *Dateline*, too. "But here's the thing. I went back and had all the old envelopes we had from Robert rescanned for pollen. It's not something that's normally tested, degrades quickly, needs to be caught in the glue. Last five years, that pollen has turned up about 50 percent of the time. So is he there? I don't know. But he's *been there*. And he's not trying to hide. I think he's waiting for you to find him. That's my guess. He was planting evidence so someone like me would find it, find you, and make this deal."

Penny considered this. "Sixty–forty," she said.

"I was going to offer you an even split," Mitch said. Penny thought she heard a siren in the distance, but that might be PTSD. "But forty is what you want, forty is what you get."

# CHAPTER SEVENTEEN

*Saturday*

Mitch knew hope was a dangerous thing.
> But he kind of hoped this worked out.
> This Penny Green?
> He liked her.
> Sassy.
> Possibly crazy. If he was going to get what he needed, he needed her.
> Plus, that sixty–forty thing? That felt like flirting.
> Well.
> Shit.

# CHAPTER EIGHTEEN

*Sunday Morning*

If Penny Green had one regret, it was that she didn't shoot Jack Biddle. She'd watched the video a thousand times in the months since being released from Gig Harbor—YouTube had the grainy CCTV from the marina, plus there were the fan videos, recut to the *Curb Your Enthusiasm* theme music, and then the Lifetime movie recreation, Penny played by an ex–Disney Channel heroin addict who talked like some kind of cereal-box gangster, which was embarrassing. They even had the videos of her robbing the Pronto Pup Hut, which was what caused this whole dumb thing, though at least that was sort of amusing. And Oregon now also had a law on the books where it was still considered B&E even if you improved the property, so that was nice. Good for the community and all that.

But even now, in the dim light of dawn, sitting on the wrought-iron balcony of her studio apartment, Mitch Diamond's iPad on her lap, the desert sun rising orange in the eastern sky, rewatching it all, the one thing she still couldn't figure out was *why* Biddle came to look for her.

It never made sense. It never came up in court because there was never a trial. She pleaded guilty to her role in the Barer & Harris heist, the B&E charge at Pronto Pup, and resisting arrest, even though she hadn't, not in a good way: They pinned a weapons charge on her for the flare gun. Apparently, it was illegal to point that at an officer of the law, even in whatever fucked-up capacity Jack was in at the time. Jack said he believed she fired it at him. Which was bullshit. It was lightning, but in the end, it was all irrelevant. There was no sense prolonging what *was* true. With her priors, she was going to do real time. Best to start it.

Besides, being in custody kept her somewhat safe from the Golubevs. Granite Shores Police seized the fifty G's, still in the box it was delivered in. Not that Penny rolled—she wasn't like that—but the marina's CCTV told the same story Jack ended up delivering on the topic. And then, a few weeks later, Freddie seemingly up and skipped town, which meant there was no one to ask for the money back. Rodney wasn't about to go show his face inside a police station asking for cash.

That didn't mean Penny didn't still owe that money. Rodney made that clear enough when he came to visit her. This was four years ago, Penny living in the K Unit, the minimum-security wing, had a prime job grooming dogs for the Prison Pet Partnership, so when she sat down across the table from Rodney, she was in a smock covered in spaniel hair. All the other women were in the same gray sweatshirts and sweatpants, save for those nursing babies.

"You smell like dog," Rodney said.

"It's nice to see you, too, Rodney," Penny said.

The visitors' room at Gig was bright and airy, practically felt like a Build-A-Bear or Color Me Mine with all the kids doing crafts and the amount of junk food being consumed. That said, it was the nicest room in the place, other than the law library, which had comfortable chairs and, if the librarian liked you, access to the good coffee she brought from home. There were skylights in the visitors' room and a patio under a pergola for the smokers. Penny didn't get to spend much time here, her only semiregular visitor was her nana, and now she was dead. Anyone else who came along wanted something from her.

She was done giving interviews. She was done meeting with actors. She was done talking to anyone that didn't have something to give her. Something to help her. A job. A chance.

She figured it was good to meet with Rodney, however, in light of the fact that she wanted to keep living.

"I got you a roast beef," Rodney said. He pushed a sandwich and a Coke from the vending machine toward her. "The other choice was egg salad, and I do not think anyone should eat egg from a vending machine, not even you." He also had two Butterfingers in front of him, which he pointedly didn't offer Penny.

"What's with the candy?"

"You give me what I'm looking for," Rodney said, "maybe I give you prizes."

"I'm not a performing seal." She started to get up, but Rodney put up both of his hands.

"Easy, easy," he said. He unwrapped one of the Butterfingers, split it in half, gave one half to Penny. "Peace offering. I come as friends."

"We're friends?"

"How long we've known each other?"

"Since I was fifteen," Penny said.

"That's two decades. You know other people for two decades that you do not consider your friend?" He broke a piece off his half of the Butterfinger, ate it. "Friends are the kind of people who understand that debts are hard to pay off when you are making, what, fifty cents an hour washing dogs? Is that right?"

"Forty-two cents an hour."

"This is why I cannot go to prison," Rodney said. "I would demand a raise."

"Something tells me you'll get your chance," Penny said. "Look, I don't know where your brother is, if that's what you've come about. And I don't know where mine is, either."

Rodney leaned back in his seat, took a long look around the room. Penny wondered if he noticed he was the only person wearing a full Adidas tracksuit. "Spirit realm, is my opinion."

"Really."

"Freddie is my twin," Rodney said. "I no longer feel him in this reality. So I live for both of us now. You maybe do the same." He snapped off another piece of Butterfinger, popped it in his mouth, chewed it thoughtfully. "Does your brother write you letters?"

"No."

"He is a very active writer of letters to others," Rodney said. "Why do you think he doesn't reach out to you?"

"Even if he did," Penny said, "they'd confiscate the letters before they ever reached me."

"How many more years do you have?"

"Two to four. Depends on my behavior."

"What are your plans?"

"To behave."

"After that."

"I was going to start writing pop-up books," Penny said. "What are you doing here, Rodney? I mean, it's nice to get a visitor, but we aren't friends. Shouldn't you be at the White Pelican selling crank to little kids?"

"I sold the White Pelican to the city," Rodney said. "Made a handsome profit. They're going to build a new police station on the land. I love that. Granite Shores, nothing but shitty memories there. It is Losertown. But my wife, she loves beach, so we take a little bit of money, buy a nice place with a view." A little boy ran by, Rodney watching him for a moment. "Freddie, that was his place, so we'll keep a place, in case."

"You're worried he's sitting in a hospital somewhere with amnesia?"

"This life is not a soap opera," Rodney said. "Missing is dead. This is truth, too. But truth and hope, they do not match so good. This little boy that keeps running by? He will remember this as fun times. Not the reality. See what I mean?" He pointed at Penny then, like he realized something suddenly. "Long time, I did not understand why Freddie was so fond of you. More than me, this is a true story. Made deals with you I would not have. Our father, he appreciated the work you did for us when you went to Odessa. Even the Chinese liked you. And all this time in here, I appreciate your silence. Very much. You could have said many things, and you haven't. Could have made deals."

"I wouldn't."

"Truth again? This is why you are sitting here and not doing this conversation during a séance." Rodney gave a big smile, in case one of the COs was paying attention, but there was such a baby cacophony that they could have been planning to dig up Hoffa and no one would have noticed. "But see. Freddie and Papa are gone, and so I'm what's left. And so I want you to understand, two years, four years, fifty years, your debts stand. Your deal with Freddie, I have inherited that, too. You remember the terms?"

"Yes, Rodney."

"Now those were made before your brother was famous," Rodney said. "Before his face was on shirts. Before they make Hallmark movies."

"Lifetime," Penny said.

"What is the difference?"

"Violence and sex," Penny said.

"Well," Rodney said, "your earning potential is increased when you are out. Maybe HBO or something. So what I want you to understand, long term, is that we are business partners. One-third of your heist now includes all media and licensing rights. Action figures, lunch boxes, life rights, podcasts, all that. That is the new deal."

"So I understand," Penny said. "You came to see me in the penitentiary to shake me down? Are you for real? You want . . . podcast money?"

"It's the twenty-first century," Rodney said. "We must all adapt. Your brother will not return, but he is making money, so you owe on that."

"And if I don't give you your cut?"

Rodney leaned across the table, so close now that Penny could smell the Drakkar Noir cologne he'd likely been bathing in since the 1980s, said, "Then you get cut." He sat back. "And now, so you know, I am on your books here, too, keeping you alive. You'll face no more problems from the general population. You keep busy shaving poodles and know that when you get out, you come to me, I get you a nice place, maybe you even move in with me, and we begin investigating how to properly monetize."

"I'm not moving in with you, Rodney," Penny said.

"Freddie, he always had a little crush. Caused him to be stupid. Probably could not take you being in here, probably blamed himself for being so dumb as to give you all that cash in plain view of the world, knew I would be mad at him, and so he ended it." Rodney sniffed. Was he . . . sad? Maybe. "I don't know for sure anything, but I know he is no longer. I know that. But you are right here, and we will maybe get a chance to make his story into something cool, embellish it? We'll figure it out." He got up to leave then. "Don't run, Penny. This is advice I give people too often, and they don't listen. Be the one who listens."

That was all Penny needed to hear to know that her biggest job upon getting out was to come up missing. Not like how her brother went about it, with his ransom notes and Robin Hood act. No, Penny Green needed to go somewhere people simply didn't ask questions. She couldn't get face-altering plastic surgery, like in the movies. She didn't want to cut her hair, or wear glasses—though she needed them more and more these days. That Clark Kent shit seemed whack in the comics Robert read, seemed silly in real life.

She needed to vanish her name as much as she needed to vanish her face.

And for nearly two years, she'd been able to do that, particularly in this part of the desert where you could still pay cash for a room. A desert life suited her. She liked a place that challenged you to live, life always one blown AC unit away from a literal heat death. Working at the Creosote maybe wasn't using 100 percent of her brain, but Penny didn't need a job to do that work. She needed her books, her earphones, and the time to just *think*. People were a nice bonus, provided they didn't piss her off. No one simply ended up somewhere that gets to be 120 in the summer; you have to pull over one day and stop. Penny made that choice, and it was the right one, she found. The desert gave her space and a minimum of intersection and that was . . . good.

But then along came Mitch Diamond.

If he found her, that meant Rodney likely wasn't far behind.

Could be he'd show up tomorrow.

Could be he was already in town.

Could be he was walking up the stairs right now.

What she should do is pack all her shit, right now, and get as far away as possible . . . but that was the problem, wasn't it? There was nowhere far enough anymore. She was literally in the middle of the desert, and Mitch Diamond came rolling up in his pimped Cadillac with a deal to offer her.

There was no good reason to trust Mitch.

He had no good reason to trust her.

Though, she must admit, there was something appealing about the guy, like if Kris Kristofferson had never started songwriting, ended up doing a little time and then got a dubious job with a law firm known for representing the notably corrupt, and now was a strange combination of amiable and threatening.

Because Penny did what he told her not to do.

She'd looked into Mitch Diamond. It took her about two hours using Ancestry.com, a newspaper archive, and a website filled with old yearbooks, cross-referencing a list of open warrants in California and inmate records from San Quentin . . . and there he was. If he was really the Mitch Diamond she found, he looked fucking great for eighty. And it was a little weird that he was his own stepfather, too . . .

What was his angle on this? Other than wanting the money. He must have come to the conclusion that whatever retirement he might have earned at Barer & Harris would eventually look odd to someone at the IRS when he was 106 years old. Never mind Barer & Harris. The alarm on his clock was about to go off.

Penny set the iPad down on the tiny, white plastic table beside her.

Everything in her body was telling her the same story: *Run.*

But: The sun was rising, casting shadows across the Pinto Mountains, the light an ethereal pink and orange. She'd never seen colors like this, certainly not in Oregon growing up, but also nowhere else in the world, back when she was able to travel from continent to continent, acting the fool in each one. What was she trying to prove back then? It was a question that dogged her all the years she spent locked up. What did she think was going to happen? For a smart person, Penny knew well how dumb she'd been, how her anger and cynicism led her to self-destruction. Who was she even trying to hurt? Mom was long dead. Dad was dead years before he died. It all seemed so silly, so pitiless now. There was something in this light that soothed her, that made the old shit drift away. She missed her brother desperately. And if she was being honest, like Rodney, she didn't feel him anymore. It wasn't merely the emotional distance.

*Run,* her body said again. *Never look back.*

Thirty yards away, two coyotes loped across the open desert, slipping between the shadows, nipping back and forth at each other in that high-pitched whine of theirs. What were they after? Where were they going?

If she ran? There would always be someone behind her.

Penny read all the true crime books about her brother. She watched all the documentaries. She read all the theories on the internet. She watched the shitty Lifetime movie. Since getting out, she listened to about a dozen different podcasts, including one that cousin Addie did, the little fucking turncoat. She'd even watched the presentations Jack-fucking-Biddle did at various crime conferences around the country and the world, captured on YouTube, where he expressed his own expert opinions, the fucker exaggerating his limp every time, sometimes seemingly forgetting which leg he'd been shot in. Never once did he mention that Penny saved his shitty life.

What all the content had in common was the same: The chase would never end. It was the not knowing that made it romantic. Everyone in their shitty jobs, trying to figure out how they could heist their employer. They needed to know that it was possible, if unadvisable.

The coyotes came to an abrupt stop. Looked up at the brightening sky. Four black helicopters from the marine base at Twentynine Palms soared across the sky.

*See if you can outrun them,* her mind said. *Do it. Run.*

Maybe she was being paranoid.

Maybe no one was really looking for her.

Maybe Rodney gave up his hopes and dreams.

Maybe . . .

Maybe . . .

Maybe she was looking at this all wrong.

Maybe the place to be wasn't out in the world alone.

Maybe the safest place for Penny Green was the one place she never wanted to be: right back in the public eye.

Maybe if she didn't want to get hurt, it would be a good idea to be surrounded by witnesses, not palm trees and apex predators.

But something was bothering her.

Penny found the phone number for the Margaritaville, asked for Mitch Diamond's room. He answered on the second ring.

"You didn't ask me why we did it," Penny said.

"The heist?"

"Yeah."

"I don't care," Mitch said. "Motive is stupid. You did it. Motive is for the newspapers. Makes for a better story."

"All the movies and books? They have it wrong."

"I told you," Mitch said, "I don't care."

"That student loan stuff? That's bullshit."

"Great," Mitch said. "What time is it?"

"About six," Penny said.

"You sound alert."

"I've been up," Penny said, "reading."

"Any questions?"

"A few hundred," she said, "but first: Ask me why I did it."

"Why'd you do it?"

"Because I wanted to," Penny said. "No higher purpose. No mythology. I wanted the money. And I wanted to disappear. But mostly? I wanted to do it." It was something Penny spent a long time thinking about. The why of it all. There was a therapist at Gig who wanted to attach it to her mother and then maybe to her father, but Penny knew the reality of the situation was that she wanted to do *something*. Be known for anything other than being smart. To be defined by her brain wasn't so bad. Solving a Rubik's Cube in twenty seconds was impressive the first couple times someone saw it, but then it made her a freak. Being able to recite pi literally forever was useless since no one even knew if she was lying. Being the smartest fuckup, however, seemed like the sort of thing criminologists would study, and that appealed to her at twenty-six. Made for better bar stories than her ability to speak all those languages.

Now, at forty-one, her prevailing thought was she should have gotten a rescue dog and taught it to help the blind.

"Why'd you save Jack Biddle?"

"I didn't have anything against him," Penny said. "I'm a crook and I'm a thief. Or I was. But that's the part of the game that intrigues me. Hurting someone, that's for preservation only. Jack Biddle was doing his job. Kind of. Dude was always sketchy. But I'd done the crime he came to talk to me about, he'd figured that out. Hat's off. Didn't anticipate he'd pull a gun on me and then shoot himself."

"You didn't think that would make the cops search the boat?"

"I couldn't let him die right there. It wasn't right."

"Well," Mitch said, "it's good to have a code, I guess."

"I do this with you," Penny said, "there's a high probability I fuck you over."

"I'll risk it."

"I need a first-class ticket," Penny said. "Somewhere nice to stay. Not under my name."

"Fine. Anything else you need to tell me?"

"There's some bad people looking for me," Penny said. "They find out I'm in Granite Shores, it could be a real problem for you to be with me."

"You want a gun?"

"I'm not legally allowed to possess a firearm in the state of Oregon."

"That's not what I asked."

Penny thought about it for a minute. If she had a gun, she might well use it. "No."

"Okay," Mitch said. "You don't mind if I carry a couple?"

"No."

"Then we should be fine."

"Okay," Penny said. "You already have a plan in place?"

"For a few years, yeah," Mitch said. "How far are you willing to go with me?"

"You really think you know where my brother is?"

"Maybe not your brother," he said. "But I got a feeling about the loot."

Penny thought about that. "How far are you willing to take it?"

"Those bad people looking for you? They Russian?"

"Some of them." He must have looked at her visitor logs from Gig. Or saw the video of Freddie meeting her with a box of money. Probably both. "I take it you've done business with Rodney in the past?"

"You could say that." He paused. "I put a tracker on the iPad. I saw every page you visited. So what I can tell you, he doesn't have business in Granite Shores anymore."

"Every page?"

"Every page. So whatever you're going to ask, ask."

Penny closed her eyes. Of course he tracked her. Why hadn't she considered that?

Because, of course, he wanted her to look.

Because, of course, he hadn't shown up here by accident.

Because, of course, he already knew she'd go with him.

He wanted her to know what he was. He couldn't tell her. He needed her to figure it out on her own.

"The original Mitch Diamond." She paused. "Alive?"

"No."

"Bad guy?"

"Hit my mother," he said. "A lot. And worse."

"But you took his name?"

"His name didn't hit my mother. His hands did."

"You worried someone will find him one day?"

Mitch said, "You ever been to Capitola? Out near Santa Cruz?"

"We didn't vacation much. When we did, it was somewhere with a racetrack."

"I lived out there as a kid. Mom would get married, we'd move inland. Mom would get divorced, we'd rent a place at the beach with whatever her settlement was. Then she met Mitch, and he lived at the beach. So that worked out for a while. And then when it didn't, turns out there's more white sharks off the coast there than anywhere in America. If you know where to go, near Soquel Cove, you can even see them congregate. They don't really school. Not in the traditional sense. And they get real competitive if there's food in the water. It's something else to see them get set into a frenzy. So. To answer your question: No, I'm not worried."

"I guess that answers my other question, too." She stood up then, leaned over her balcony railing, stared across the open desert. She could still hear the coyotes, somewhere, but the sun was blazing now, and everything was coming alive. Lizards. Rabbits. Snakes. That was the remarkable thing about the desert. From a distance it looks dead, but up close it's a giant, pulsing ecosystem that can and will kill you. There were no good guys and bad guys. Just animals fighting to survive.

"What's the plan?" Penny asked.

"We're going to shake a couple trees," Mitch said, "and watch the rats scurry out. Starting with Jack Biddle."

"Why?"

"Because Robert has sent ransom letters directly to the Granite Shores Police Department for about half of his shakedowns. Most of the time to Jack. And that seems out of character. Am I right?"

"Robert called him Jack Shit, so yeah, it's odd."

"Did they know each other well?"

"Everyone knows everyone," Penny said. "Our dad and Jack's dad used to go fishing together. Or whatever it was they were doing out there on the water." Penny thought about this. "The letters he sends. Does he address Jack directly?"

"No. It's not like a letter from camp. They typically say the same thing: X person has Y amount of time to deliver Z amount of money for the return of their box. No FBI. No media. And then Jack contacts us."

"And you don't contact the FBI?"

"FBI could give a shit," Mitch said. "Our clients getting shaken down want no law enforcement involved at all. You know what was in those boxes."

She did. It was the golden part of the plan. Extort people who would never go to the cops.

"So then I have to wonder: Why does your brother go through the cops? Particularly now that Jack and his wife have commodified your brother's very existence? If anything, wouldn't he have tried to use you? Get some leverage to keep you out of prison? If he was paying for your commissary, why not use some of the power to get you into Camp Fed somewhere? Or was this in your plan all along?"

"No, no," Penny said. "We didn't have friends on the police force in Seattle or here, I promise you." It was something Penny hadn't pondered too much while in prison—this process Mitch clarified—because she didn't know the extent of Robert's activities, since most of these extortions were kept quiet. The things that made the news were the good causes. Not the millionaires with their hooker problems. After reading through the files Mitch gave her, it was at the front of her mind now, that was for sure. "What are you getting at, exactly?"

"I don't know," Mitch said. "I'm working through a concept. It might not see fruition without breaking someone's fingers."

"Metaphorically?"

"No," Mitch said.

She waited for him to laugh.

He never did.

"I'm not going back to prison," Penny said.

"Me either," Mitch said.

And then he told Penny a story about an errand for an ex-friend that went bad, about a dead woman, a dead dog, a dead man, a seventeen-year-old girl named Addie, who it happened was Penny's cousin, and a friend in Seattle with a job for him . . . and then enough ellipses to fill every crater on the moon.

# CHAPTER NINETEEN

*Granite Shores, Oregon*
*Sunday*

Police Chief Jack Biddle constantly had to piss. He assumed it was something to do with his prostate, but he was too scared to go to the doctor. What if something was seriously wrong and they put him under to stick a camera up his wazoo and he babbled the entire time he was under? Woke up surrounded by FBI agents? Nope. He'd have to wait until his next "business trip" or vacation, like he always did with anything he thought might require more than a prescription or a local anesthetic. Somewhere with decent socialized medicine and a language barrier. He heard Lithuania was nice. If he went on vacation, he'd need to convince Caroline that she and Travis would like the place, not that Travis liked anything. Fourteen years old and with the general countenance and effervescence of a budding serial killer. Caroline placed him in an Outward Bound program for the summer, which was sure to bring him back either cured or filled with fresh ideas.

Something to worry about later.

As it was, today was his day off, and he was up early, waiting on Danny Vining in the parking lot of the old muni golf course, which by next year would be two hundred condos, a Chipotle, a Dutch Bros coffee drive-thru, a Chevron, and a Salad and Go. Used to be he'd come out here on his day off and play eighteen with his neighbors, show everyone he was a regular guy, but now that he and Caroline were living in their new gated community, the Dunes at Granite Shores, he mostly avoided the golf course altogether. He'd go hit a bucket of balls every now and then, but the idea of talking to his neighbors for two hours did not sound like fun. They were all transplants from California, and all they wanted to talk about was how Granite Shores wasn't anything like what they were used to in Sacramento or Burbank or Riverside and when would someone open up a decent Chinese place? It was exhausting, and Jack was afraid one day, he'd pull out his revolver and plug someone.

And then of course, someone would want to talk to him about Robert Green, his theories on the case, and naturally, if they felt bold enough, they'd ask what it was like when he arrested Penny Green and didn't he try to shoot her but ended up . . . shooting himself? Wasn't it something like that? What was that like? *Not advisable*, he'd say every time, which made it sound like he didn't think about it every day, like he hadn't tried to get Penny killed in prison half a dozen times, like he understood when you're a cop sometimes shit gets dicey and you have to move on and keep protecting and serving or some bullshit, like it was something that he could joke about easily these days—which he did every year during the Green Days Festival, which he'd championed in the first place, helped fund on the down-low, and profited handsomely from—when in fact it was the exact fucking opposite.

It was all his own fault, on a lot of fucking levels.

Chief Biddle reached into the Igloo he kept on the passenger seat of his civilian Tahoe, felt around for his favorite ice pack, found it surrounded by a couple tall boys, slid it between his ass and the seat, and before too long everything from his taint to the tip of his dick was one solid frozen block. *Sweet frozen relief.* The pack managed to numb the Urge (which is how he always thought of it—like it was some kind of Godzilla monster) for a little bit, which was good because it was pouring fucking rain. He wasn't about to go searching for a public toilet to dribble piss in. End up soaked to the bone.

He popped his glove box, found the Altoids tin he kept filled with Oxy and mints, put two Oxy on his tongue, chased them with ten mints, chewed them all up together. Not that he was in any pain. Not really, anyway. He liked the way the Oxy took the edge off his meetings with Danny. If he *was* in any pain, he had enough Oxy stored away that he could survive being the last man alive for a cool decade, or if another pandemic hit and he had to hide in his doomsday shelter.

Danny Vining pulled up beside him, driver side to driver side, cop-style, in his black Range Rover, put down his window. "You look like shit," he said to Jack.

"My prostate is acting up," Jack said.

"I'm on that saw palmetto," Danny said. "You should try it."

Jack didn't particularly enjoy talking about his plumbing problems with Danny, but they were both in their fifties now, and that's just how it was. "I'm not much for that holistic shit," Jack said.

Danny shrugged. "Well, the dispensary has some good edibles that are supposed to help, too. It's all legal now, Chief. No worse than going to the liquor store. Who knows. You might like it."

"It's a bad look for me," Jack said. He simply could not get used to the idea that smoking weed was legal, that he didn't need to sneak up Yeach to get high, he could eat a gummy while walking down the street.

"Can't be seen consorting with my kind?"

"You know what I mean," Jack said.

"Ironic," Danny said. "What have you got for me?"

Jack reached beneath the passenger seat, where he kept two portable compact gun safes. One was for his gun. The other was for Danny. "Fair amount of heroin. Eight, ten bags. A bit of coke. Some pills. Not much."

Danny opened the box. Looked in. "Canadians?"

"No," Jack said. "Some country band playing a show in Reno later in the week. Raided their bus."

"Anyone good?"

"I'd never heard of them."

"Nice work. Probably good shit." He tossed the box onto his back seat.

"What's that get me?"

"Call it ten."

"Ten? That heroin was primo shit, I'm gonna guess. The guitarist wept when I took it."

"Did he autograph it? Maybe I could get ten on eBay."

*Fucking Danny.* For the last few years, Danny and Jack worked out a nice deal where Jack gave Danny a cut of the drugs he confiscated in lieu of cash he owed for his gambling losses, since Jack came to understand that he had an addiction but was hesitant to move actual cash to Danny. He didn't know what was marked and what wasn't these days, and washing it through Danny seemed like a dubious proposition. On the off chance that he actually won, Danny gave him credit that he could gamble with or theoretically cash out at some point in a distant, unlikely future.

Jack lost way more than he won. Way more.

He'd initially thought this whole . . . thing . . . would be over by now. But Travis was in private school, Caroline ran for mayor—won, ran again, lost, ran again, won—they'd bought the new house, turned the old house into an Airbnb, then refurbished Caroline's mother's place after she died, turned *that* into an Airbnb, too. Renovated the Sno-Cone Depot. And that was the aboveboard shit that he admitted to.

He had shell companies buying up land around town that he was then selling to the new developments popping up that his wife was approving, he was paying off half a dozen assholes who knew too much—like Bobby C., who had a kid with muscular dystrophy now, so he needed good insurance, plus some decent life insurance and 401K set up so his kid would be taken care of when Bobby C. was invariably murdered by someone, which meant Jack had to put him on an actual payroll, not just give him drugs and cash, so he bought a limo and an Expedition from the city seizure pool, cleaned them up, started a limo company, put Bobby C. behind the wheel, and now the dumb fuck was a part-time limo driver and a part-time getaway driver for his other dumb fuck friends, a never-ending headache. Jack had half the thugs and lowlifes on the coast hooked up to one LLC or another so they could have dental and vision just to keep his name out of their mouths.

So while he had money, he also had expenses, both real and created, plus he kept a reserve in case one of the aforementioned lowlifes tried to get funny on him. That happened a few times. Problem with being in business with criminals, they do criminal shit, and so either Jack would have to pay them off or kill them to keep them quiet, though the health benefits mitigated that some. No one wanted to lose a decent Rx plan these days.

He was waiting on a pretty decent blackmail situation. Something he'd learned from the detailed plans Robert and Penny hashed out, even identifying good potential boxes. In this case, he gave the lady three weeks. Clock was ticking. Might get a couple hundred thousand. That would disentangle some worries. There was no way out but through, he kept telling himself, but now he didn't even know if that was true. Maybe there was no way out.

"I was thinking fifteen. That bottle of Dilaudid is full."

Danny rolled his eyes. "Can I give you some friendly advice? You can do Gamblers Anonymous via Zoom now. You don't gotta go to the community center or anything. Because the day is gonna come when I retire, and then what are you gonna do?"

"I'll think about it."

"You go," Danny said, "I'll give you twelve."

"So now we're on the barter system. I'll just take ten." Jack started up his SUV.

"Wait," Danny said. "I need you to look at something." Danny handed him a letter still in its certified envelope. "This came the other day. What do you make of it?" Jack opened it up. It was on Barer & Harris letterhead. "What are my rights on this?"

Jack tried to make sense of what he was reading. To coincide with Robert Green's birthday and the upcoming Green Days Festival, Barer & Harris was putting up a "significant" reward for the return of the remaining stolen property and/or the capture and prosecution of Robert Green. Due to "new evidence which suggests Mr. Green and a notable amount of the stolen property have been in the Granite Shores region within the last month."

*Shit.* How had he fucked this up? What did he do in the last month that would reveal . . . anything?

Nothing.

He'd done nothing.

Well, other than that blackmail letter to Melissa Ruby, a Barer & Harris box owner. But he'd done that literally dozens of times. He was following Robert and Penny's action plan, which was helpfully stored in Robert's computer: He extorted some folks just for cash that went to him, extorted others that went to a CAUSE, Jack always thinking of it in all caps, since it was always some do-gooder shit. It was kinda elegant, curry favor with the world, make them seem like Good People, and, in fact, that shit worked. But what a time suck to make it work.

This time, he didn't bother to have it go through his own precinct, which he often did so as to burnish his own reputation as a crime fighter in touch with the greatest heist of all time etc., etc., etc. ad nauseam, and instead sent it directly to Barer & Harris, which he'd done periodically, particularly when he didn't have the time to playact through the whole shenanigan. Jack liked to imagine people thinking of him like one of those big-city profilers on TV or in movies who develop a symbiotic relationship with the killer they're hunting, until such time the darkness subsumes them both, though by that time Jack was usually asleep so he wasn't 100 percent on how that all ended up, but anyway, it was all a lot of work. And he didn't have that kind of time these days. So instead, he'd put some dandruff on the stamp, some fingernail skin on the letter, all that good stuff, and shoot it over to Mitch Diamond to handle.

This letter? A bluff. A ploy to get people talking again. Not that anyone ever stopped talking.

Green's birthday and the Green Days Festival were kicking off on Wednesday. The festival, that was his brilliant goddamn idea. What got him to be police chief and got Caroline elected, twice, as mayor. Turned the whole city into a tourist destination, brought in the developers, the fucking Chipotle. There were tours, symposiums, guest speakers, panels. They even got the approval to get the boat they were going to escape on—the *Pere-a-Dice*—out of dry dock, where it had sat as evidence all this time. They'd preserved it exactly, right down to the Orange Crush sodas in the fridge. For fifteen bucks, people could come on board to take selfies and such. City was estimating they might make $150,000 from that alone, which would pay for new computers for every cruiser on the force.

There was some podcast producer coming to town who wanted to do a show focusing on Jack's role in everything, Jack thinking that might be cool, might get him speaking gigs out of the region, maybe get a movie deal, figure out a way to get Keanu to play him, that would be fucking badass, get him enough cash to maybe go legit, let him burn the rest of the shit, be done with it, finally, Jack thinking *Biddle to the Bone* would be an awesome title.

And now this bullshit?

Jack said, "You need to talk to a lawyer."

"They *are* my lawyers, dumb fuck," Danny said.

Jack Biddle could shoot this motherfucker right here. Dump his body in the ocean. Go home and watch a baseball game. You didn't disrespect a person like that.

Chief Jack Biddle, however, was a man who could take an insult. Kind of.

"Tone down the disrespect," Chief Biddle said.

"You gonna cry? Jesus fucking a dog on the beach, Jack. This is a real problem. Someone comes up on my box and turns it over? I'm cooked. You're cooked. We're all cooked. Can you help me, or do I need to find another chief of police?"

Jack needed to read this all again when he wasn't high as fuck. "Can I keep this? I need to confirm what's happening here. This could be a public safety issue." *My own.*

"Be my guest."

Jack folded the letter back into the envelope, stuffed it into his pocket. "I'm sure this is a publicity stunt. Nothing will come of it."

"Could be, could be," Danny said, "but if someone happens to recover what I had in my box? We all got fucking problems, okay? Me. You. Half this town. My guy in Las Vegas. His guy in New York. Your favorite Trailblazer growing up. And then probably someone in Sicily gets a phone call, and who knows what happens next." Jack knew Danny was overstating this somewhat . . . but not too much. The shit about his favorite Trailblazer was true, though, and now whenever he saw the motherfucker on ESPN talking about how close they were to greatness back in the '90s, he had to take a fucking Ativan. "Someone comes up on my shit? I need you to handle that, understand? The old way. Understand?"

He did. He and Danny, it was more like a partnership now. A hostile partnership where one guy had the other guy in a fucking vise grip, but a partnership no less.

"Sure, Danny," he said.

"I need my name not to appear in anything, understand?"

"Of course."

Danny said, "It never ends, does it? Just when I think we're done with this guy, something like this happens. I considered him a friend, right? He texted me before he disappeared with my shit. I mean, I saw Robert all the time. Every two weeks. You know how that hurts? To have someone you think you know rip you off? He fucking texted me like the day before! Reminded me! He wanted me to know he was taking my shit. Rubbing it in my face, turns out. Fucking slick, gotta give him that. But I'll tell you what, this taunting business, I don't support that. We're all out here doing our thing and he's sending crazy letters to the victims and cops and shit? That's not right. That's out of pocket. His pops would be sick about this, all I'm saying." Danny pointed out the window, toward the bridge connecting Loon Island to the mainland. "You know me and Greeny, one summer we painted that fucking bridge. True story. Fifteen years old. Every morning, start at five a.m. Both ended up getting a grand, which may as well have been a million dollars."

"I didn't know that," Jack said, though he'd heard the fucking story five hundred times, always with some new nostalgic detail thrown in. This time it was the "Greeny" bit.

"That's what I'm saying. Basically cousins, and he does me like this." Danny pounded his steering wheel. "Whatever evidence they've turned up, you need to act like a fucking cop and get your hands on it, too, and you find my shit before some kid with AirPods and one of those dumb gold chains and fucking bangs in their eyes does, understand? And then you bring Robert to me first, okay? You owe that to me." Danny Vining sighed. "Knew him his whole life. His sister was like my sister. Anyway." He reached into his back seat, came back with a Sunshine Fudge candy box. "Made Caroline some of the toffee she likes. Tell the mayor I appreciate the zoning ruling for the new dispensary. She's a doll."

"I will." Something Danny said was still ringing in his head. That bit about getting another chief of police. "I ask you something, you need to promise me it won't piss you off."

"This should be good. Fire away, Chief."

"You got someone I don't know about?"

"Like a mole or some shit?"

"No," Jack said. But now he worried about *that*. "Like somebody who owes you money and does shit for you on the slide. I can't be the only one."

"Are you fucking crazy asking me this? You wired?"

"You don't need to be wired anymore," Jack said. "All you need is a cell phone. So yeah. I'm wired. So are you. The Chinese, the DOJ, and any fifteen-year-old with skills could be listening."

Danny said, "This is stupid. You're stupid. I'm more stupid. What do you want, Jack?"

"I need a someone who is willing to do some . . . errands. Possibly related to your recent correspondence. I'm chief of police. I can't be running down leads on this. You understand. People know me. I go out shoe-leathering this, people are going to talk." What he didn't need was Caroline asking what the hell he was doing, either.

"Shit." Danny drummed his fingers on his chin. "I don't normally miss the good old days when Bobby C. could get business done, but here I am, wistful for his unique personality traits." He looked in his rearview mirror. "I ever tell you my five-year plan?"

"No."

"Five years from now," he said, "I only want to be in the actual fudge business. Been saying that for going on twenty years. But now my daughter has two years left at Stanford, and she's not exactly expressing an interest in running a crime family, but sure does love fudge. I can't have my books floating out there. I need that shit back. Because those books threaten her existence, so here we are."

"That your way of telling me yes, you've got someone else on the payroll?"

"It's my way of telling you to solve this shit, or we're both looking at a real different five-year plan, you understand?" He told him he did. "And go see a doctor, you look like you're in toxic shock," Danny said. "And I'm sorry I called you a dumb fuck."

"I'm still the law here," Jack said. "One day, we're going to be in public, and you're going to say something, and it's not going to be cool, Danny."

"I said I was sorry," Danny said. "Don't make me a liar."

Jack waited for Danny to drive off before he popped another couple Oxy, then took out the letter and read it again, slowly, took a few notes, made sure he understood everything, made a couple calls, including one to the cell phone of Mitch Diamond, Barer & Harris's head of security, who'd signed the letter, but Jack didn't figure he'd written it. It was too literate and filled with legalese. *Herewith* and *forthwith* and *in lieu of*.

They'd had a cordial-enough relationship over the years, he and Mitch, which is to say Jack did a little background on him, nothing too deep, found that his online biography was either all made up or,

## Only Way Out

alternately, was 100 percent true: Either he was ex–military intelligence, or he wasn't. If he was in deep, no one would confirm that. If he wasn't, there was no real way to find that out definitively—you couldn't ask HR if someone was running black ops. Jack tried to surreptitiously grab his DNA one time when Mitch came to town to do a cash drop on one of Jack's better extortion jobs, but the motherfucker wiped down every piece of silverware he used at every restaurant he went to, plus in his hotel, he either burned his garbage in the sink or somehow hid it.

But whatever. Maybe that's just what you did when you were some kind of super spy. Couldn't have Chechen assassins rolling up on you while at a seaside resort.

Mitch wasn't running for president, and he never seemed to cast any suspicion on Jack for anything, even shared the DNA tests the firm did on the mail they'd received when Jack asked out of professional curiosity, Mitch happy to fill him in, particularly since Seattle cops weren't even investigating anymore. They knew who did it. He was gone. No one was murdered. Cops didn't even know the value of what was taken. And of course, Jack Biddle was the goddamn hero of this story. The one who cracked it, the one who Robert Green now periodically trusted to do his bidding. Jack was beginning to think he might be the greatest crime fighter and criminal mastermind to ever live. Superman and Lex Luthor, all in one.

Anyway, it all helped Jack figure out what was and was not working. Hair, dandruff, skin from under the fingernails: great. Reconstituted saliva: more difficult, which made sense, that fucker's tongue seemed to be disintegrating, no matter how cold the freezer. But now this? What the vigilante fuck was he thinking with this letter? Every bounty hunter, true crime dipshit, and podcaster in the galaxy would be in Granite Shores by the time this hit the internet.

Jack very carefully crafted this con. Well, after he stumbled on it, anyway. He had a year left until he could retire, both from the force and from this Robert Green business. Mitch-fucking-Diamond was not getting in his way.

Jack cracked a tall boy, downed it, pissed into the can—because now the Urge was threatening to become the Accident—tossed it out the window. He looked up at Yeach Mountain, looming off to the east. It was capped in clouds today, trapping the weather along the coast. It was probably clear blue skies on the other side of the peak. That's how it was this time of year. He hardly got up there anymore. Couldn't chance it. Too much to lose. But he could still see his spot there tucked in the trees in his mind, could remember how it felt to be up there with himself. How he thought everything would be different after that night. How he thought everything would be better. And sure, he had money now. He had property. He and Caroline had a life. Were goddamn admired citizens of Granite Shores! Everybody in town knew and respected them . . . or, well, at least knew them.

Now this.

If he'd been nice, Jack would have set fire to all of Danny's meticulous records, particularly since they implicated him, too. But there was too much there. Too many get-out-of-jail-free cards. Danny may have seemed like a small-town gangster in Granite Shores, but there was a reason he had a Seattle lawyer: Sure, half of the Pacific Northwest bet illegally with him, but who really cared about that anymore? You could do more damage on your phone playing fantasy football for money, and sure, you might not get your legs broken by Bobby C., but your credit would be for shit, and in the long run, fucking with Experian was worse than a slight limp in wet weather.

The bigger problem was that Danny fixed games for years.

If not him personally, whomever he worked for and with.

Football, basketball, baseball. Even the fucking PGA. Professional, collegiate, he probably took high school action and had a fourteen-year-old dropping passes for free Starbucks.

Danny put all their names down in his little books, protecting his ass, not even bothering with nicknames or aliases. The statute of limitations was long over on the crimes themselves—it was only five years on RICO shit, another five if the Feds could tack on some additional conspiracy charges, so ten total in the best-worst case—but Jack knew Danny was still in that business. And revealing that this beloved point guard, that big-game quarterback, who was now in every insurance ad, and that gritty pitcher who now hosted his own talk show on ESPN weren't just cheats but in the pockets of organized crime? That would likely be the sort of thing that the IRS would be interested in, too. And more saliently: the general public. Criminal law might have limitations, but public shame was a whole different sentence.

Jack knew those records being out there kept Danny up at night . . .

. . . and Jack liked that. The fucking asshole.

All his life, he wanted to be Danny's buddy. From grade school on. AYSO. Little League. Scouts. Playing football with him at Granite Shores High. Danny always everyone's favorite, brought fudge to all his teachers at the end of the school year, his family hosting fundraisers and car washes, donated money to get the preschool rebuilt after the floods, all that. And now here they were, grown-ass men, and all Jack desired was maybe an invitation to watch the Super Bowl together. Maybe fly down to Arizona and catch spring training. Hell, he wouldn't mind doing a BBQ on the beach one night, everyone's families, making s'mores, crushing some tall boys. Just a touch of kindness from the man. A little of that shine he gave everyone else.

But no.

Still, today, he's calling Jack names! Disrespecting him!

Jack took down another tall boy. Feeling good now. The Oxy and the beer hitting together.

Clarity. Lucidity. The throbbing in his taint a low hum.

Danny went down, Jack went down, with or without his books. Difference was, if Danny snitched him out, those books were Jack's way out. Could probably get Jack immunity. Yeah, he'd lose his pension, and Caroline would leave him, and his son would probably hate him, and Danny would probably have him killed, eventually, but Jack had money stashed around the country and the world, Jack smart enough to use safe-deposit boxes himself now, and he'd get some distance and time. California. Washington. Idaho. Nevada. Florida. New York.

Mexico City. London. Virgin Islands. Even in Green Bay, for fuck's sake. Everywhere he and Caroline vacationed over the years, every place he'd gone to a conference, everywhere he'd managed to get a speaking gig, he'd opened up a box. Partly out of irony, partly because the heist Robert pulled off improved security of those boxes exponentially! He probably had fifty keys and codes stored away. A million dollars spread around. Maybe more.

If he ran, he had options.

# CHAPTER TWENTY

*Klamath Falls, Oregon*
*Sunday*

Back in the day, Mitch wouldn't have counted on the Purple Flamingo still being in business, but there it was, right where Mitch left it. There were still a few working ladies in the parking lot, but not like it used to be when it was like an open-air market, Mitch thinking if these last couple ladies were smart, they'd get an OnlyFans and be done with it.

He found a parking spot, left his engine running, hit Play on Chief Jack Biddle's voice mail. It came in when he was already on the road heading north, making the fifteen-hour drive to Granite Shores, rolling up the interior of California on old CA-99, bumping through the Central Valley on cruise control, a POW/MIA cap in the back window to keep highway patrol from pulling him over, a little trick Dale taught him back in the day.

Mitch hadn't been up that way in years and part of him thought about veering west, sliding into Santa Cruz, playing a little Skee-Ball, hit the used bookstore he liked in Capitola, check in on his mom, but knew that would only lead to bigger issues. If he got out of this situation the way he imagined, he'd get his mother out of the assisted living place, maybe get his own place at the beach, get her some live-in help, like she deserved.

It was a nice thought, interrupted when Jack Biddle started barking, "Diamond. Chief Biddle. What in the vigilante fuck are you thinking . . ." so Mitch hit *Delete*. He'd be in Granite Shores tomorrow in person. He'd make an appointment to hear the rest of the message. One thing Mitch knew? Danny Vining was the only Granite Shores resident with a box at Barer & Harris. Which answered a few questions for Mitch and brought a couple more to the fore. Penny landed in Portland an hour earlier. He hoped she didn't get into any trouble before he got into town, because he was still six hours away and now that Penny was in the fold, he could handle a little business of his own. Start working his plan. She was actually step two.

Step one? Put a tight cap on this Paul Copeland and Dale business. Last thing Mitch wanted was to come up on the property from the heist only to spend the rest of his life in prison for Paul's death, a crime he didn't do—for once—nor actively obstructed—for once—or to constantly be searching crowds for Rodney Golubev. The guy with Mitch's old name was wanted for questioning on Paul's murder. So the last thing Mitch needed was to be sitting in an interrogation room across from Klamath Falls homicide cops who'd want to know how he ended up sporting the name Mitch Diamond and where he'd been for fifteen years.

It took a good long while, but he'd done the hard part already.

Which was finding Dale and avoiding Rodney.

Word for years was that Rodney caught up to Dale and dropped his body out of a plane into Crater Lake, which sounded apocryphal because it was. The kind of story Rodney would make up to scare the dumb fucks in his employ.

Mitch was on Dale's trail for years, finally tracked one of the aliases Mitch cooked up for him to an American Legion Hall in River Falls, Wisconsin, where he'd been working as a cook, up until he got fired for stealing thirty pounds of ground beef, precisely the kind of dumb shit Dale would do, and which landed him in their online newsletter. This was five months ago, in February.

Dale lived in a trailer with the bartender from the Hall, a woman named Glory.

Glory answered the trailer door in a tank top, low-rise jeans, flip-flops. It was about 13 degrees outside, snow thick on the ground, but Mitch could feel heat bleeding out of the trailer.

"Your man around?"

"You a cop or something?" Glory asked.

"Something," Mitch said. "You have a fire in there?"

She pointed over her shoulder. "Central heat shit out. So I'm using the oven."

"Gas or electric?" Mitch asked.

"I'm not an idiot," she said. She took a step out onto the enclosed patio, looked down the block, Mitch thinking maybe she was expecting a SWAT team. "You here about the meat?"

"I don't give a shit about the meat," Mitch said. "Just looking for my cousin. Legion told me he was staying with you. Can I come in?"

Glory watched him for a few seconds, said, "Your cousin. What did you call him?"

"Dale."

That got Glory laughing. "I wondered about that tattoo on his hand. He said it was his mother's name." She stepped aside, let Mitch inside. "If he owes you money, get in line." She pointed to three green garbage bags in the corner. "You're lucky. I was bagging his shit up. You looking for anything in particular?"

He snapped on a pair of medical gloves. This place felt like a fully inhabited antigen. He also wasn't interested in leaving any of his own shit behind.

"His kids," Mitch said, "they want something to remember him by."

"Kids?"

"Oh yeah," Mitch said. "Six of them. That's how it is with Mormons, you know."

"Mormon? Jesus fuck."

Mitch opened one of the bags. It was filled with clothes and paperbacks, which reminded him of something. He started unpacking the books, and there it was, his talking seagull book. Flipped it open, saw that the asshole took a yellow highlighter to it. No respect.

"You mind if I take all this?" Mitch asked.

"I could give a shit. Got a feeling he's not coming back." Glory stood a few feet away, in the galley kitchen, where the oven door was open. She lit a cigarette. "Mormon. You sure?"

"Hundred percent." He didn't think Dale believed in any god, much less a Mormon one.

"What's your name?"

"Mitch," he said.

"He never mentioned you."

"He might have called me something different."

"What is it with you guys and your names?"

Mitch walked into the bathroom without answering her. There were two toothbrushes, one electric, one manual. The electric was clean and with new bristles. The manual looked like it was used to scrub tires. A razor, a nice hairbrush, and a shitty comb.

"You want some coffee?" Glory called from the kitchen. "Or I've been working on a bottle of Goldschlager this afternoon."

"I'll take some coffee."

"I thought Mormons didn't drink coffee?"

"That's old-school," he said. He grabbed up the razor, the manual toothbrush, the comb. If he'd learned one thing about searching for Robert Green, it was that DNA was the golden ticket. Cops needed to find some of Dale's. Mitch wasn't having that. Not before he found him. Opened the drawers. Found a roll of small plastic garbage bags. Dumped everything in. "Church owns every Starbucks in Utah."

"Is that so?"

"Yep," Mitch said. Looked in the tiny shower. Found the soap. Took that, too. When he came back into the living area, Glory was standing there with a mug of coffee.

"I put in a splash of Goldschlager, for flavor, since it's instant." She looked at the bag. "What do you have there?"

"Evidence," Mitch said. Figured, why not?

Glory thought for a moment. Said, "Well. I guess that's fine." Handed Mitch the mug. He took a couple sips, stifled his gag reflex, thanked Glory for her hospitality, and then hauled all of Dale's belongings to the Caddie. Came back, gave Glory a business card. Wrote his burner number on the back.

"If Dale comes back, tell him I can help him."

She read the card. "Corporate security. Fancy. I picked the wrong cousin."

Mitch said, "Remember that. Make better choices if you can."

It was a little show. Because Mitch waited for Glory to go to work, broke back into her place, turned the oven back on, tossed a gasoline-soaked rag into the kitchen. Even called 911 when he saw the smoke in the distance.

He spent another week in the region, hitting the places he knew Dale would visit. Truck stops, Native American casinos, strip clubs, Dale a walking cliché, but the man had his tastes.

It wasn't until Mitch was three hours away, outside Okojobi, where he heard there was a cockfight with big action, that his cell rang. Caller ID said it was coming from the Bayfield Carnegie Library.

"Hey, cousin," Dale said.

"There you are," Mitch said. He pulled off the side of the road. Sign up ahead said Spirit Lake was only five miles away.

"You burn down my lady's trailer?"

"I did," Mitch said.

"That wasn't nice," Dale said.

"You skipped town on me, left me with a dead body. Two, if we're being technical. So I'd say we're still working toward even."

"That was like fifteen years ago. You're still pissed. Incredible."

"No statute of limitations on murder."

"Hey, hey," Dale said, "we're on the phone."

"If your line was tapped," Mitch said, "you'd already be in prison. Same with mine."

"Look at you, with business cards. And a real job. Isn't that something." He paused for a second. "Mitch. That was your stepdad."

"Still is."

"Oh he's alive, is he?"

"Death doesn't make someone not your stepfather."

"Listen," Dale said, "I'm out of options here."

"You kill someone else?"

"Got into a situation at a gas station up the highway. Could be a body. I don't know. Shit."

"You know."

"I could use a familiar face."

"You could use a lawyer."

"Ain't that convenient," Dale said. "You work for a law firm."

Mitch didn't respond. Smart thing to do here was to call the cops. Ten minutes from now, Dale's problems would be over, one way or the other.

"Any way you could come get me, we could let it all go?" Dale asked.

"Where is the Bayfield Carnegie Library?"

"Last stop before I walk into Lake Superior." That was north of River Falls. Way north. Mitch figured he was about six, seven hours away. "Glory said you took all my clothes and books. Is that true?"

"You stole a book from me."

"Which one?"

"Talking seagull book."

"That was yours? I sure liked it. Listen," Dale said. "I need a little bit of cash, maybe a car if we can get one, and I'm out of your hair for life." He paused. "If you had a gun, that wouldn't hurt my cause, either. One I had, found its way into a river."

That was the problem. Long as Dale was anywhere out there, Mitch couldn't be sure his life was safe. Particularly not if Dale had a gun.

"How do I reach you?" Mitch said.

"Well," Dale said, "library is closed until ten a.m. Monday. So I'll be right here."

"You broke into a library?"

"Yeah," Dale said. "You got me into reading. Turns out libraries don't have much security and nothing worth stealing, so they're pretty easy to get into. Clean bathrooms, usually got snacks in the breakroom, comfortable sofas." That's why Mitch couldn't find him. He'd failed to case out the better libraries in the state. "You get here, I'll be inside. Honk three times, I'll unlock the back door."

"Can I trust you not to kill anyone in the next six hours?"

"I'm losing it, cousin."

"Don't do something stupid."

"Entire life has been something stupid."

Mitch didn't like the sound of that. "How about we drive down to Florida, get you some sun."

"Man, that's a twenty-hour drive. You'd dump my body in St. Louis. Don't forget. I know the real you."

"I'll be there. Wait."

"We had some good times together back in the day. I helped you when you had to get out of California." All that was true. "I mean, we were family for a while. I could use some family."

By the time Mitch got to Bayfield, it was already dark. The Bayfield Carnegie Library was, in fact, the last stop before Lake Superior: It was three blocks from the shore, on what was probably a leafy street in the spring, but that night it was 19 degrees outside, and the trees up and down the block looked like witches' arms, all sharp bones and long, crooked fingers, Bayfield Pier glowing in the distance. Sign out in front of the building said it was built in 1857.

Mitch parked and walked around the rear of the lowercase t–shaped building, trying rickety doors as he walked, until he found the one Dale busted through off a small loading dock. Busted through, in this case, meaning that he'd taken a fireman's axe off the back wall and put it through a single pane of glass in an eight-pane panel and then unlocked the door. He'd replaced the pane with Scotch tape, which was thoughtful, and hung the axe back up.

Mitch pushed through the tape, popped it out the glass, turned the deadbolt, let himself in. Dale was sitting in an overstuffed chair, a floor lamp articulated above him, a brick fireplace with a five-foot-high surround behind him, the mantel covered in classics. *Moby-Dick. Red Badge of Courage. Grapes of Wrath.* Dale looked peaceful, which was weird because he was one of the least peaceful guys Mitch had ever known, the man always a ball of anxiety and bad choices, but being dead certainly helped the matter. There was a paperback with library binding in his lap. *Jonathan Livingston Seagull.* A catalog card covered in Dale's fifth-grade handwriting (and spelling and grammar) was bookmarked twenty pages in. Mitch yanked it out:

> *Couldn't weight 4 you to get here to do this 4 me. Didn't want some stranger to find me. Sorry about you're book, I wrote in it, butt this one is pretty clean. Tell Glory I'm sorry I was such a shit. Tired of the hussle.*

There was a can of Coke and a bottle of Ambien in Glory's name on the little side table. She didn't need this bullshit. But also, Mitch didn't need this bullshit. No one needed this bullshit. This was a real Dale move. Leave your dead body in a place where someone else had to deal with it.

He put his thumb on Dale's neck. He was still a little warm.

Mitch knew that Dale's body in this library would lead to even bigger problems. There would be news stories. It was weird enough that it would eventually be on one of those cold-case documentary shows, and that would lead to Paul Copeland, and that would lead to Mitch's old name put on blast. They'd run his old booking photo, and someone would recognize him and then . . . and then . . . and then . . .

Mitch found a rolling flat shelf utility cart behind the checkout counter, hoisted Dale over the top, pushed his body down into a V, covered him with green garbage bags, dragged it out to the loading dock, pulled his Caddie around, dumped Dale into the trunk.

Mitch then went back inside, yanked the pillows off the overstuffed chair Dale died in, put those in the trunk, too. Carried the rest of the chair outside, hurled it into the dumpster, covered it in a bunch of trash, went back inside one last time. Dropped two hundred bucks into their donation box. Grabbed up some local maps. Seems he was about three hours south of Superior National Forest. Looked like there were plenty of lakes out there.

He grabbed the axe off the wall, took that with him, too. Figured he was going to need it, a good plan taking root.

And now he was back in Klamath Falls, happy he was a man who thought ahead.

After about five minutes, a security guard came out of the casino, knocked on Mitch's window. He was one of those body builder types, all arms and chest and neck on top of chicken legs. He wore a polo shirt with a badge printed on it and then a windbreaker that said SECURITY on the back, a flashlight and some zip ties hooked to his belt, a baseball cap with the same fake badge as his polo shirt tugged low on his forehead, probably had a tattoo of an upside-down flag on his back.

"You can't park here," the guard said when Mitch lowered his window. "Unless you got any questions."

"Is Rodney on the premises?"

"No, he don't work nights."

Mitch looked around the parking lot, saw something familiar: a black Subaru Outback with the personalized plate FRED4FN. Fred disappeared about when Mitch did. Everyone thought Fred was in witness protection. If that was the case, however, Rodney would be in prison or dead.

"Isn't that Fred's car?"

"Rodney likes seeing it, like a memorial or some shit," he said.

"In the parking lot?"

The security guard shrugged. "Grief is weird, man." *True enough,* Mitch thought. The security guard gave Mitch a strange look. "Do I know you?"

"You have so many friends you can't remember who you know?"

"You look familiar."

"I've been by in the past," Mitch said, which is when he flipped open his wallet, showed the security guard a badge from the United States Department of Agriculture. The kind carried by consumer safety inspectors in the Food Safety and Inspection Service department. Used to belong to one of Barer & Harris's clients, Jimmy Kochel, currently doing time for taking bribes to sign off on trucks of subpar meats. Was ordered to give up his badge. Mitch charged with getting it from his house. Turns out it wasn't there. Never did turn up. Real shame. "I need these girls out of the lot, and I need everyone out of the building in fifteen minutes. There are federal violations at work here, and if you don't want to be arrested for the steroids and HGH in your medicine cabinet at home, I'd get ghost."

"You've been to my house?"

"We've been collecting your garbage for six months. We have your DNA on every single needle you've used."

"Dude," the security guard said, "I'm part-time here. I'm not even on the payroll."

"That's why I'm going to let you walk out of here." He looked at his watch. "Fourteen minutes and thirty seconds from now, I'd be somewhere else and not in that uniform."

The security guard whistled. One of the girls came sashaying over, probably thinking she had a job, Mitch now getting why this fucking guy asked if he had "any questions," as in: How much for the night? He was security and pimp. What a fucking world. Even when she was in his headlights, Mitch couldn't tell if the woman was eighteen or fifty. She probably couldn't tell you, either. "Marcy," the security guard said, "get all the girls out of here. He's a Fed. I'm out of here. I'm trying to get into the marines." He stripped his jacket off, dropped it on the pavement, and took off in a dead sprint.

Marcy looked at Mitch. "You're really a Fed?"

"That's right." He showed her his badge. "You want to hold it?"

"Yeah, sure," she said. He handed it to her. She pulled it from the sleeve. Turned it over. "Department of Agriculture? They have their own cops?"

"Even the post office has cops."

She handed him back his badge, then walked around the rear of his Caddie, returned. "Why don't you have government plates?"

"Undercover."

Marcy nodded. "I'm gonna go ahead and let you do what you do, because it's cold and raining and tonight's a loser and fuck Rodney Golubev. I *wish* someone would call the Feds on him, but your photo is in the break room with a note to call Rodney immediately if you ever show your motherfucking face, okay? So whatever it is you're doing, stay in your car, and I'll get everyone out. And then do what you do."

"It really says 'motherfucking' on it?"

"Spelled wrong, but yeah. Been there forever. It's laminated."

Mitch took all the cash from his wallet, handed it to Marcy, said, "That's about three hundred bucks. Appreciate it if you told the cops I was five seven, three hundred pounds if they come asking."

"I don't get down with cops," she said, "unless they're here off shift."

"Then Rodney," Mitch said.

"He don't talk to me," she said. "I'm over nineteen." Marcy counted the cash, handed him back ten bucks. "You'll want coffee for the rest of the ride," she said and walked off.

Once everyone was gone, Mitch figured he had about twenty minutes, tops, to get what he was looking for—anything with his name or likeness on it, any old employment records, that sort of thing—and to leave some of Dale behind for the investigators. He had one of his thumbs and a foot on ice in the trunk, wrapped up like pieces of salmon from Whole Foods, even had a price sticker for salmon on the brown paper packaging. Sell by next Wednesday. Worth the five minutes he spent in the Whole Foods across town, even Klamath Falls getting uppity with their markets. Anyway, a little authenticity was good. He'd pop the thumb into the safe. Probably had the same combination. And even if it was a new safe, with a digital pad instead of a combo, he could bust into a common business safe in under five minutes. Digital pad was easier these days than a combo lock. Maybe he'd even get some traveling money for his efforts.

He'd leave the foot somewhere else, less obvious. Like in one of the bathrooms. Hard to burn tile. Both the thumb and the foot were in pretty bad shape. A couple months in his freezer at home after traveling across the country in an Igloo, followed by a road trip to the California desert in the summer hadn't exactly preserved them like King Tut. But that was fine. A situation like this, a surprising bit of decayed corpse was the vibe he was after. It would take the investigators some time to figure out. Couple weeks at least if they rushed the DNA. But it wasn't like TV. Could take months.

Then a thought occurred to him.

Surely one of the working girls would be on social media in minutes talking about the bust. Maybe one of the patrons. There was likely a video ready to drop on TikTok. Shit. Used to be criminals couldn't shut up and that's what did them in. Now, they posted video.

So maybe not twenty minutes.

Maybe more like fifteen.

Fortunately, he knew what he was doing.

Twenty-seven minutes later, he was passing the Super 8 and the Pilot Travel Center off route 97, where Dale used to sell his trucker speed. The Purple Flamingo was fully involved, according to the police scanner app on his iPad, officers going on about a short, fat Asian woman seen in the area with a gas can.

# CHAPTER TWENTY-ONE

*Sunday/Monday Morning*

Everything in Shake's was wood paneled. The walls. The floor. The bowls of nuts. Even the ancient juke box in the corner by the bathrooms had a wood veneer. Sounded like the needle on the record player was wood, too, Dolly crooning in the distance about someone trying to take her man. It was just as Penny Green remembered it. Her father used to sit her in the booth under the neon Rainier Beer light with a plate of french fries and a coloring book while he did his business, whatever that was, Shake's a kind of Switzerland back then of off-duty cops, off-duty crooks, off-the-clock boardwalk workers, and worse: real estate agents.

Now, it had more of a retro vibe for the tourists, which they achieved by changing absolutely nothing except for the people inside. There was a Japanese tourist couple sitting in Penny's old booth, along with a baby in a highchair, finishing some fish and chips; two women in matching horn-rimmed glasses and sleeve tattoos sat at one end of the bar reading books and sipping Rainier from the can; and then at the far end of the bar, as she hoped when she saw the white limo parked in the handicapped space, was Bobby C.

Penny half expected that Bobby C. would be wood paneled by now, too, but in fact he'd gone to flesh. He used to be coke-thin and vampiric, sort of cute if you liked the living dead. Now, he looked burger-fat and beer-fed dressed in a cheap black suit, a white shirt that strained against his gut, the collar open to reveal way too much neck and chest, black shoes that were oddly shined to high gloss. He also wore a nice watch—a Movado; not going to break the bank but showed a modicum of taste—and a wedding ring. Alternating gold and platinum bands. Penny tried to imagine who would crawl into bed with Bobby C. every night without a gun to her head.

The answer tonight seemed to be "no one," since here he was with the sports page spread out in front of him, a plate with some parsley sprigs and a ring of grease where some mystery meat used to be off to one side, a bottle of Jameson he was pouring from, and a glass filled two inches high with Pepto-Bismol. He had on a pair of readers and was highlighting box scores with an orange marker. There was a gun on him somewhere. Oregon was open carry, but Bobby C. wasn't one of those guys who walked around with a legal piece all polite. He'd rather surprise you, make you beg, treat you like a punk.

Penny sat down beside him. She'd spent the last two hours walking through downtown, gawking at what it had become, which was . . . a quaint village. Even the Airbnb Mitch reserved for them was knocking her for a loop. The rental was Scotch Thompson's old house over on West Quarry, which was notable in those days for the Confederate flag he flew 24/7 and the Dobermans he kept chained up in his front yard, but which was now done up like an ode to the 1970s, with themed bedrooms and everything, including the one she was sleeping in, which was covered in child actor and teen idol posters—David Cassidy, Bobby Sherman, Rodney Allen Rippy—and stacked full of old board games. Risk. Sorry. Stratego. She was curious which themed bedroom Mitch would take—Evel Knievel or *Saturday Night Fever*?

Used to be Granite Shores had a rough edge to it after dark. The carneys who worked the amusement park rides and con-job games would walk up Foyle Hill from the boardwalk, still in their sweat-stained uniforms, smelling of cotton candy, salt water, and secondhand weed smoke, then spread out to the bars downtown for the couple hours before last call. Two a.m. would come around, they'd fall out into the street to finish the party. Summer nights always good for a stabbing or a curb stomping, a head-on collision, a liquor store robbery, an anonymous tryst behind the drive-thru snow cone place, until the cops showed up to chase everyone off. They'd be back on the boardwalk by 9:00 a.m., hungover and in charge of the Tilt-A-Whirl, while the shop owners swept up the glass and teeth and puke and started all over again.

It was kind of appealing, in a *Lost Boys* sort of way, though even Penny recognized it wasn't a sustainable tourism model. Eventually, you needed people to come and spend money, buy second homes, invest in the region. Granite Shores couldn't exist on Sunshine Fudge alone.

Thing about gentrification, it's doesn't half-step. Most of the mom-and-pop shops and dive hotels that used to line Beach Boulevard, the main drag through what they were now calling Old Town Granite Shores, were mostly gone—save for Sunshine Fudge—replaced by West Elm, Banana Republic, Panera, two Starbucks, the Ace Hotel, a sign for a new Hobby Lobby being built, a Super Target that took up a full city block and even had underground parking, a Tesla showroom, a Patagonia store, a cigar joint that was also a sports bar, and about a half dozen places where you could get an eighteen-dollar cheeseburger or a thirty-dollar local cheese plate. Penny wasn't even aware there were cows nearby. There were also three dispensaries that catered to different tourist subsets: HighLife, which looked like an Apple store; Buddy, which looked like a record store from the '70s; and Lotus, which looked like a Bath & Body Works.

But the most disturbing thing, by a long-fucking-shot, were all the sundry shops and minimarkets filled with T-shirts and mugs and posters emblazoned with her brother's image—most of them from the now-iconic video still of him flipping off the security cameras at Barer & Harris offices—and then the full mural on the side of Mel's Cosmic Comics . . . which gave Penny an even worse thought: What had they done to her childhood home? A quick Google search on her phone revealed that she could take a tour first thing tomorrow morning, which is when Penny decided she needed a fucking drink.

She was pleasantly surprised to find Shake's was still in business.

She was less surprised to see that Bobby C. hadn't given up his seat. Nothing pleasant about it, particularly now that she knew he'd middled for whoever wanted her fucking dead. She guessed there were about 324 of those people floating about.

The bartender came around, Penny ordered an old-fashioned, the drink her father used to order from Shake himself, back when both were still alive, sipped it for a few minutes, watching Bobby C. in the Jack Daniels mirror behind the bar, trying to decide if she wanted to smash a glass into his face, drill his face into the bar rail, or maybe break into his limo out back, wait for him in the back seat with some piano wire—granted, she'd need to go find a piano, but whatever, it was a fantasy all the same.

Bobby C. met her gaze in the mirror. "Like what you see?" Bobby C. asked. He slid the bottle of Jameson over to her, reached over the bar, grabbed a clean glass, slid that over, too. "Have a drink on me."

Penny finished her old-fashioned, gave herself a generous pour of the Jameson, sat for a bit listening to Dolly, who was now wearing a coat of many colors, saw that Bobby was still watching her, like he was trying to place her. Penny decided to help him out.

"When I was thirteen," Penny said, "you used to ask me to flash you for weed."

"Gotta be more specific than that, sister," Bobby C. said. Which made him laugh. Hard. Penny felt her skin get up and sprint away.

"The other thing you did," she said, "is you paid a woman named Shirley Turner to show up in my cell and try to gut me with a sharpened piece of soap. Do you remember that?"

The bartender turned on the houselights then, flooding Shake's in way too much brightness. "Fifteen minutes," the bartender said.

Bobby C. put the cap on his highlighter. Closed his newspaper. Folded it up nicely. Took off his readers. Stuffed everything into a satchel on the floor. Turned his stool and faced Penny. Gave her an exaggerated look up and down. "You got old."

"You got fat."

"I can lose weight," he said.

Penny took his measure. "You sure about that?"

"You were a cute kid. What happened?"

"Maybe I'm not your type anymore, short eyes."

"You also got a smart mouth while you were away."

"I always had that."

Bobby C. took a deep breath. Gathered his surroundings. "You thinking of hitting me with that Jameson bottle?"

"I am now."

Silence.

"You been thinking about this meeting a while, imagined how it was gonna go, what you were gonna say, how mean old Bobby C. was gonna get his comeuppance? That sustain you in Gig?"

"Your existence is meaningless to me."

"Yet here you are."

"I'm taking the free tour of Green family hot spots," Penny said. "Internet suggests Shake's provides a truly authentic opportunity to meet a real-life scumbag."

"You should visit your house," Bobby C. said. "Went to a wedding there a few weeks ago. Took a shit in your daddy's closet, for old time's sake." This made Bobby C. laugh. "Don't suppose you've got the money he owed me when he kicked?"

"He took it with him."

"Tell you what. A few years ago, when I was pretty low I thought about digging your daddy up and taking that Rolex he wore," Bobby C. said. "Then I figured, well, probably was a fugazi. If it was worth something, he would have hawked it. Plus, my lung capacity is shit, probably would have keeled over before I even hit the coffin." Bobby dug a pack of Nicorette out of his pocket, offered a piece to Penny. She declined. He chewed his piece for a few seconds, thinking. "You been to the cemetery?"

"No."

"You should go," he said. "True story. Whenever I go there, I stop by and chop it up with your dad for a few. He's buried down from my pops. That's the funny thing. Our parents, they had the gall to go and die on us, leaving us here in all this shit, and they're down there laughing like maniacs, that's what I imagine." Bobby C. put two twenties on the bar. The bartender swooped by, pocketed them. "Because, sister, look at me. You're basically angry with the UPS driver. I drive places and drop things off. That's my job now. I'm out of the leg-breaking business. I'm sure I dropped some money off for a lady you were locked up with, okay. I'm sure I did that. Way back home, I might have swung by three different county lockups and done the same. You hear me? It wasn't about you, okay? You and me? We don't got a problem. You and your dumb fuck brother pissed off every crook in the Pacific Northwest and then half the millionaires, too. I'd rather have the crooks on my ass. Those assholes, they give up. The millionaires, they'll chase you until you're both dead, and then they'll send their fucking heirs after you." He blew a bubble with the Nicorette. "Can I tell you who paid that lady? Probably. Probably. But then I'm dead. Here we are now, free people, out having a drink. Why court problems?"

Bobby C. poured himself the rest of the Jameson, took it down in a couple swallows, wiped his mouth with his coat sleeve.

"My A1C could power the space station, I've got neuropathy in my right foot. I take so much Lipitor, I should probably have an advertising wrap on my limo for it. I got a kid at home, if you can believe it. Ten years old. Got muscular dystrophy. A fuckin' Jerry's kid. So I'm paying for whatever it is you think I've done, okay? You're alive. You made it through. Count your blessings you still got your health. When it goes, it just keeps going."

Penny began to clap, slowly. "Incredible performance, Bobby. Incredible. You should have done the Summer Playhouse. You could have been Hamlet."

Bobby C. got up from his stool, took one step toward Penny, close enough that she could smell the onions and cigarettes on his breath, could head-butt him and break his nose if it didn't look like his nose was missing all the cartilage already. "I don't hit women anymore. But I'm willing to change my ways." He smiled then in a way that made Penny want to rip her own eyes out, the vampire still there, all right, hidden under layers of sediment. "If you see your brother, let me know. Would love to catch up." He tried to button his suit jacket. No luck.

"You better hope your coffin fits better than that suit."

Bobby C. lumbered out of the bar. Penny thought about catching up to him, knocking all his fucking teeth out, but judging from the gape-mouthed stares of the Japanese family and the two bookworms, the houselights and her conversation with Bobby C. revealed to them a local celebrity in their midst. Penny didn't have her own T-shirts or mugs, at least not with her face on them. All the money she made from her line of Christian Undead Necro Teens merch? Her band that never recorded a single song? That all went straight to her lawyers, the only people she kept in semiregular contact with, and who she still owed, since she was constantly being sued by Barer & Harris clients. The judgments against her were in the millions. She'd never get out from under it. She kept a PO box in Seattle. Every few months she'd drive up and check it for letters, handle what she could, sending five bucks here, ten there, to stay active. She was guilty. She was trying to do what was right.

"You okay?" the bartender asked. His back to her, but he was watching her in the mirror while he mixed a drink.

"I'm fine," Penny said.

"We're on camera," he said. "But don't think I wasn't on top of the situation." Penny looked around. Sure enough, there were Ring cameras in every corner of the establishment now. That was a *real* change from the old days, Shake's the kind of place where you didn't have to worry about leaving behind any evidence.

"Who owns this place now?"

"Danny Vining. He owns most of the block."

Danny Vining was exactly who she thought paid Bobby C. In terms of minor league crime bosses, he could have his own stadium and mascot by now. Robert stole a good sum of his insurance money—which is to say, insurance against any big losses—but Penny knew it was worse than that: Once every two weeks, Danny drove all the way up to Seattle to make a drop, then his sister, who lived up in Laurelhurst in a mansion across the lake from Bill Gates, would swing by and make a pickup and a drop-off, too, the box essentially their walk-up teller. Robert estimated the amount in the hundreds of thousands, Penny entering it all into a spreadsheet of their projected earnings. And then there were customer rolls he kept there, too, and stacks of notebooks detailing years of illegal activity. "I think he's maybe trying to write a book," Robby told her one night before the robbery, after he did a quick dry run of boxes he was most interested in. Good to know where the really good shit was in case for some reason their timeline broke down. "He's keeping detailed notes on everything."

Penny figured he was taking contemporaneous notes, dated and time-stamped, because when shit went down—and it would, it always did—he wanted to have all the state's evidence in a tidy place. She imagined that those client rolls were worth as much as the cash to the right people.

Which made her wonder why Robby hadn't extorted Danny. The iPad Mitch gave her detailed two dozen different extortion, blackmail, and "Robin Hood" events over the course of the last decade alone. Robert hadn't returned anything to anyone without a dollar figure involved for himself or someone else . . . which simply did not sound like how Robby would act.

Mitch's detail of missing items showed four boxes containing animal remains. What the fuck was Robby doing with Trixie the cat's earthly remains? He wanted to curry good favor? He'd send those back. The plan was always to extort awful people. There was no reason to hurt people that didn't have it coming. If Robert wanted to be an asshole, sure, he'd hold those ashes hostage for a payday. Truck them around for fifteen years? No way. They took all the boxes because that was the easy thing. Addie's job was going to be to return what they didn't need. Hurting innocent people wasn't job one. It wasn't even job 324.

It didn't make any sense.

Asshole like Danny Vining? Robby would relish that shakedown.

Likewise, if Danny wanted her dead, Penny imagined he wouldn't have failed. He had enough money, enough petty desire, enough of everything that he'd keep coming for her. He wouldn't have been dissuaded by time or distance. Like Bobby C. said. So if it wasn't Danny Vining . . . who was it?

The bartender turned around, set down another old-fashioned in front of her. "I've never seen anyone talk to Bobby like that," he said. "So that one is on the house. And then any drink you have for the rest of your life. I hate that fucking guy."

"Then why do you let him in?"

"Not my bar, not my drunks. I'm indebted to fifteen bucks an hour and tips. Plus we get medical, dental, and vision. And not even Kaiser. That good PPO shit."

Penny downed her drink.

Crooks giving health benefits.

What a fucking life.

Three a.m., drunk, standing on the front lawn of her childhood home—open from 9:00 a.m. to 5:00 p.m., seven days a week, for public tours and private events; general admission tickets were seventeen dollars, seniors eleven dollars, and children under twelve were free—Bobby C.'s words pinging around in her head, Penny Green decided to do a misdemeanor. She wasn't paying seventeen bucks to go inside her own house, so she hopped the fence, ignored the **ARMED RESPONSE!** private security sign, knowing full well that you could buy those online for less than a cup of coffee, and walked around the property to the backyard. From there, she knew she could climb up on top of the old shed, hop onto the porch roof beneath her bedroom window, and then jimmy the frame, which she'd done ten thousand times beginning at age five, pop open the window, and slide under her covers undetected. That the house was now operated by the Granite Shores Historical Society didn't seem like a huge hindrance. It was still the two-story modified farmhouse built in the 1940s that her father "improved" over the years using wood that washed up on the beach and then buckets of glue and old nails. The only thing to code was of the penal variety.

Still, Penny wasn't expecting to see the backyard turned into an event space. Under a louvered pergola was a dance floor, a stage big enough to accommodate a wedding party or a decent punk band, and a roped-off bar and outdoor refrigeration unit. They'd ripped out the shitty aboveground pool and replaced it with a rose garden that featured a fountain and a meandering walking path that circled the rest of the property, which was frankly an improvement over the series of discarded washing machines and dishwashers that used to litter the space, dad convinced he could fix them and make a killing on the resale market.

Five minutes later, Penny busted her bedroom window open and stood in a meticulously recreated version of her '90s childhood and early teens.

No Doubt, Garbage, and Alanis Morissette posters above her bed. A closet door dedicated to pinups of Rider Strong.

Bookshelves weighed down with Russian literature—she never was one of the *Sweet Valley High* types, particularly since she could read by the time she was three—and theoretical physics textbooks.

There were even clothes littered on the floor and tumbling out of a laundry basket. How many babydoll dresses did one person really need? Everything familiar, none of it original. A diorama of her life.

Penny stepped into the hallway. Her brother's bedroom, directly across the hall, had also been recreated, right down to the yellow shag carpeting, the stacks of D&D books on his bed, *Star Wars* action figures guarding his bookshelves, Beastie Boys and Metallica posters, and an ancient PC on his desk. The third bedroom—which was ostensibly for guests, if they ever had any—was now a gift shop replete with prints of Robert flipping the bird, postcards of Penny's booking photo, renderings of the *Pere-a-Dice* on decorative plates and trivets, stuffed bears colored green, holding stacks of cash in their paws. There was also a stack of books for sale, including cousin Addie's companion photo-memoir to her hit podcast, *Stolen*

*Childhood*, which a sign said she'd be signing on Thursday at 1:00 p.m. If Penny wanted to avoid a murder charge, she figured getting out of town by then would be the move.

The Historical Society knocked down a wall in the guest room, so it wasn't all historically accurate, but now the hall bathroom was a fully operational concession area serving burgers, hot dogs, soft drinks, and the Penny Special: a Pronto Pup and an orange Fanta for $9.99. Penny thought she should sue somebody but wasn't entirely sure who that somebody would be.

None of this made any sense. This wasn't what Robby wanted. He'd be mortified to see all of this, wouldn't he?

When was the last time they'd both been in the house, even?

Right before their father died. Which was about eighteen months before all that shit went down. Penny was in King Salmon, Alaska, when Robert called her.

"I need your help," he said. Penny was working at a bar called the Reindeer Saloon after getting fired from a freelance tech gig for a Slavic guy who demanded to be called Neo, which was a bad sign, and who skipped without paying her, which she should have known would happen. She tried to land a civilian job at the Air Force base, but her criminal record made her a no-go, same with the National Weather Service, so she was waiting out the spring and dating a guy named Jamie who read palms and did tarot for a living, which was surprisingly lucrative up there. "Dad's lost the house." Somehow, Jamie didn't bother to predict this turn of events.

"How?" Penny asked. "It's paid off."

"He took a loan on it," he said. "Then several more." That was Dad in a nutshell. Do him a solid, he'd try to make it liquid.

"Do I want to know why?"

"No," Robert said. "Same shit as ever. Seventy years old, still trying to hit a lick."

"How much does he owe?"

"Countrywide is taking the house May first, so next Tuesday," he said. "That part is settled. The people who want cash aren't the kind of people who put a bill on paper."

"These people. Do they speak Russian?"

"Been known to."

"You want me to talk to them?"

"If you think it would help," Robert said. "There's some concern about people coming to break Dad's legs. Why is it always broken legs with these people?"

"Would you prefer they poked out one of his eyes?"

"Might make him finally change his ways."

"Nothing," Penny said, "is going to do that." She looked out the window of the bar. A man locals called Smoker stood outside, shirtless, with an acoustic guitar slung over his shoulder. It was maybe 37 degrees, but at least the sky was clear. Practically spring break in Cancún. Was he . . . singing? "Russians are more interested in knees, in my experience," Penny said.

"Well, Dad had his replaced already, so they're out of luck."

"Maybe let them try," Penny said.

"Look, I know you and Dad don't see the world the same way. We still have to do something."

"I'm in a fishing village in Alaska," Penny said. "I don't even like fish. He fucked us up, and I *still* paid off the house when I had the money, which I don't anymore. You can understand my frustration about having to do anything when I was sort of counting on that house being my equity down the line."

"This isn't permanent," Robert said.

"Countrywide taking the house sounds permanent."

"No," Robert said, "I mean . . . his time will come to an end. And then you can get up at his funeral and tell anyone who shows up that he was dogshit."

"Anyone who would have shown up," Penny said, "is dead or in prison." Penny opened the window. Smoker was, in fact, singing.

Sounded like James Taylor. "Fire and Rain." He had a nice voice. "I don't know how soon I can get out of here, anyway," Penny continued. "I'm working a new job. Dating a guy I might marry. Why don't I send someone to talk to Rodney. I assume it's Rodney making the threats?"

"It's not Rodney I'm worried about." Robert didn't say anything for a moment, Penny thinking the call dropped until he said, "I can't do this alone, Penny."

"What is 'this,' exactly?"

"Get Dad to eat. Get Dad to bed. Get Dad out of bed in the night. All of it. I can't do it, Pen."

"Hire a visiting nurse or something."

"You're not listening. I need you. Okay? I need you."

Jamie didn't predict that, either. Penny was going to need to break up with him. He'd probably figure that part out when she didn't ever come back to Alaska.

Penny was in Granite Shores the next day. One look at their father, Penny could tell he wasn't long for this life. Liver cancer turned him inside out. He couldn't hold food down, would only take painkillers and Ativan, which Robert said he got off the streets, which explained his debts to Rodney Golubev, and at night he'd treat the disease with Dewar's and a pack of Camel Straights. He'd die in a Hampton Inn a month later. The front desk clerk called Penny's cell to let her know that a cleaning lady found him in the tub, where he'd been for a few days.

That week in the house, however, Penny and Robert got as much shit as possible moved out, set up a place for Dad to live for a few weeks while they tried to get him into an assisted living place, paid what bills they could, and listened to their father while he flipped through snapshots in his mind, tall tales and truths and everything else in between, until the Dewar's put him to sleep. The two of them would then decamp to the living room floor for a slumber party. Their childhood rooms hadn't yet received the historic treatment and were instead filled with goods that looked either stolen—there were fifty slow cookers in Penny's closet—or indefinitely borrowed from since-closed big box retailers—the dozen or so Sears-brand toaster ovens on top of Robert's bed seemed dubious, to say the least, since the Sears went belly up three years prior—and then a decade of newspapers and unopened mail.

Yet, despite it being the most depressing week of Penny's life, it ended up being . . . well, oddly pleasant.

She and Robert would wake up early. Eat bowls of Peanut Butter Cap'n Crunch. Drink buckets of Folgers. Sift through the detritus of their father's criminality and mental decay, play their old CDs too loud—which was fine because Dad was mostly deaf, the entire house raging against the machine until the neighbors called the cops and Jack Biddle showed up with his lights on, that fucking guy—and remind each other of How It Used to Be, like the past was an old sitcom and not the grist of their future therapy appointments, if either bothered to try to get fixed.

Instead, they robbed a law firm.

Maybe not the greatest decision.

Penny wandered around the gift shop, gathering up snacks—three bucks for a mini carton of strawberry milk ("as found in the *Pere-a-Dice* fridge!"), two bucks for a Butterfinger ("Penny Green's favorite candy bar, according to prison records!"), five bucks for a bag of the Green Family Home Caramel Corn ("featuring Nana Green's famous recipe!"), so she left a twenty on the counter, since she didn't want to get pinched for robbery—and then returned to her bedroom, curled up on her doppelgänger bed, and had her favorite drunk meal. How had it all come to this? If she could do it all over again, Penny thought she'd do it all essentially the same . . . but maybe she wouldn't have let Robert hit those boxes alone.

Why had she waited here?

She trusted him.

It was that simple.

And now . . . this?

Penny leaned back against her headboard, closed her eyes, room spinning from booze and strawberry milk. Endless nights she'd spent right here, stuck in this drift. Endless nights she told herself she'd never let herself be trapped in this place, with these people, only to spend her entire adult life trapped because of this place, these people. Endless nights, her headphones on, she sat in the darkness with a flashlight in her hands, reading the same sentence, making the same vow.

Penny clicked the flashlight app on her phone, beamed it into the darkness above, her memory a broken dam now. After a minute, she clicked the light off, and there, illuminated in the popcorn ceiling, was a message she'd left for herself three decades ago, in glow-in-the-dark stickers:

*I Will Get Out.*

Turned out the Russians were right all along. The past *is* a lighthouse.

# CHAPTER TWENTY-TWO

*Granite Shores, Oregon*
*Monday*

Used to be Mitch Diamond only went to a police station if he was in cuffs. Mitch still went ahead and put Super Glue on his fingertips before going in to meet with Chief Biddle, even if he wasn't being interrogated and was, in fact, merely standing in a well-lit conference room on the second floor of the sparkling new Patterson Center Public Safety Building, surrounded by floor-to-ceiling windows and a wall plastered with photos of missing dogs and cats.

Old habits.

Plus, he figured Biddle had looked into him over the years. It's what Mitch would have done. He'd certainly looked into Jack. Was curious how he'd gone from a negative bank account to him and his wife owning half the town's available real estate, a controlling interest in the Green Days Festival, a house on the water, and about a dozen LLCs, all on civil servant salaries.

He had some ideas.

He'd emailed the chief the previous night, once he got into town, Mitch not wanting his IP pinging in Klamath Falls, let him know he'd be by around 9:00 a.m., then showed up at 8:30, because that's how you don't get caught slipping, particularly since he'd never been in this specific conference room before, needed time to understand the layout, the Patterson Building brand-new, the result of some tourism tax bond a few years back. He kinda missed the old precinct. It was across town, by the high school, and had the charm of a Soviet prison, right down to the rings on the floor for leg irons and the stink of piss and industrial cleaner. This new place was more like a really nice community college, albeit one with a jail.

In all his visits in the last decade or so, Mitch met with the chief of police several times—Jack Biddle on the job the last seven or eight years—but he'd never met the actual mayor, who he imagined didn't want to spend too much time in that old joint's urine stink. But now here she was, sitting beside her husband, reading through a stack of files embossed with the Barer & Harris logo, while Mitch stood beside the window watching the Pacific eat at the coast, sipping coffee from his own thermos. He wasn't leaving any genetic material behind.

"This is some bullshit," Chief Jack Biddle said. He took off his reading glasses, rubbed at his eyes with his palms. "Pollen? You think he's here because of some pollen? That's what you're going on?"

"And enough DNA to clone him."

"Pollen?" Jack said again. "Would that even hold up in court?"

"We're not going to court," Mitch said.

"No, you're gonna end up sending a bunch of fucking bounty hunters to my city. This isn't happening, Mr. Diamond. I'm being real frank with you, it's a no-go."

"You don't really have any say," Mitch said. "I'm here as a courtesy."

"You think it's a courtesy to me that you've brought Penny Green into town with you? That woman tried to kill me."

That Jack was aware Penny was in town didn't surprise him all that much. He figured Jack had his spies. That he knew Mitch had brought her was not entirely expected. How would he have known that?

"Didn't you shoot yourself?" Mitch said.

"It was legally adjudicated!" Jack said. The mayor put her hand on her husband's wrist, gave it a squeeze, Mitch thinking this wasn't the first time she'd had to do that little move. "She caused me to shoot myself," Jack said, slightly calmer. "She tried to kill me is the point, and now you're bunking with her?"

There it was.

Mitch hadn't done a deep dive on who owned the house he rented for the week. That was a mistake. Jack Biddle struck Mitch as the kind of guy who liked to watch his tenants on a secret camera. He'd need to get Penny out of there, quickly.

"I don't think she's come to finish the job," Mitch said.

"This is about to be our biggest tourist week of the year, and you're fixing to turn it into a circus," the mayor said. "Green Days is for families. Do you know how much we raise for the schools?"

"Don't worry," Mitch said. "I'm not telling you to close the beaches."

The mayor and the chief shared a look, Mitch wondering what their home life must be like. Jack Biddle looked like he carried his concerns around in the bags under his eyes. He'd also lost about thirty pounds in the last year or so, which was odd, Jack Biddle always a pretty big guy, but now he looked . . . baggy. Caroline Biddle, on the other hand, looked like the best Chico's manager in the country. Probably ran the flagship store.

"People must think you're clever," the mayor said.

"People usually think I'm an asshole," Mitch said.

"And here we're in agreement," Jack Biddle said. An alarm on his cell phone dinged. "I need to take a piss and get on some ice for a few minutes," he said. By Mitch's count, that would make it four times in ninety minutes that this guy had gotten up to take a piss, unless he was going into the bathroom to take bumps, which, to be fair, Mitch wasn't putting past him. Jack Biddle did seem . . . unloosed. "And then I have real police work to do. I'm telling you right now, you're making a mistake with all this." He squeezed his wife's hand. "Caroline, you're not required to sit here and listen to this bullshit."

"Oh his bullshit fascinates me, honestly," she said.

Chief Biddle pointed at Mitch. "Then you'll be respectful of the mayor, or I'll impound that fucking Caddie of yours. Be riveted to know what you keep in that giant trunk."

"How about I call the ACLU preemptively."

"If you think they can get here before the dogs rip out your back seat, be my guest."

"You'll soon be rich in Redwells and manilla envelopes," Mitch said, which was true. He'd taken everything . . . interesting from the Cadillac and moved it into a rental that he'd picked up earlier that morning and that he'd preemptively parked down in the public lot by the farmers market. Anyway, Mitch didn't figure they'd be getting a warrant anytime soon, Biddle more about the bluster than the actual illegal search and seizure, at least for those affiliated with law firms. "I think you're overreacting, Chief. You'll sell every room in this city. I'm sure the tourism tax alone will pay for another wing on this lovely law enforcement campus. And maybe some seventeen-year-olds will show up with some meth you can confiscate. Get yourself on the front page with the score."

"Careful," Chief Biddle said, because what else could he say? Mitch had done his research, too.

Once the Chief was gone, the mayor took a vape pen from her purse, hit it, and exhaled a plume of vapor that smelled like chocolate chip cookies, Mitch guessing the **NO SMOKING** signs everywhere didn't apply to elected officials.

"You're very disruptive," the mayor said.

"Do your constituents know you vape?"

"It makes me relatable," she said after taking a second hit. "It's not illegal. It's just . . . ugly, I guess." She leaned back in her seat. Closed her eyes for a moment, Mitch with the sense that she was gathering something up. "Why have we never met before?" she asked.

"I was wondering the same thing," Mitch said.

"How long have you been on this job?"

"I started right after . . . everything."

"So why this charade now?"

"We've never been this close to Robert," Mitch said. "If he's not here, fine, but he's been here recently. Someone saw him. Someone helped him. Robert might be a great criminal mind, but whoever is helping him isn't, and they're going to start making moves to not get caught. Or they're going to start feeling scared, or guilty, or maybe they'll want the reward themselves."

"How much is it? Your letter doesn't say."

"Between us, right?"

"Of course."

"Because those cameras up there?" He pointed up at the ceiling. There were cameras in each corner, focused on the conference table. Which is why he was standing at the window. A natural blind spot. He wasn't going to make it easy on Chief Biddle. "They're on mute, right? Because it would be illegal to record my voice without my consent, right?"

Mayor Biddle said, "I'm sure they are."

"I'd hate to sue the city if this got out." It didn't actually matter to Mitch. He'd come here for a reason, after all. "Two million dollars."

The mayor took another hit from her vape pen. Held it. Released it. "Well," she said. "Well." Took one last hit before dumping the pen back into her purse. "And you believe Robert was here? You believe that?"

"Follow the evidence," Mitch said. "Your husband could do the same."

"The crime wasn't committed here, Mr. Diamond. That's Seattle PD's business. If they're so interested, they can come down here and make an arrest. Have you given them your information?"

"They're not interested. They view it as a no-human-involved case at this point. Penny Green did time, and I think that's enough for them. He didn't hijack a plane. I've been happy to share information with your husband in the past because of his heroism, obviously, and connection to the case. Plus, that way when he goes on TV, he's already prepared." Mitch fucking with Caroline. Caroline fully aware. "Look, Robert has chosen both Jack and the firm as his middlemen. Good to make sure we don't step on each other's dicks."

The mayor placed her thumb between her eyes and rubbed. "Maybe I should call the FBI, then," she said, though without much conviction behind it.

"And tell them what?"

Mitch knew that the FBI was equally disinterested. The vast majority of Barer & Harris clients hadn't revealed what was stolen from their boxes. Those that did? Most of them had sued Penny, which kept her from profiting off all this. To keep them from suing the firm, Barer & Harris paid out internal settlements to a dozen clients, but the majority of clients who had real things of value stored at the firm—be it actual or blackmailable value—didn't want anyone knowing about it. That was the whole purpose of the boxes, after all.

The FBI wasn't interested in chasing down someone who stole granddad's pocket watch and a Rickey Henderson rookie card. The only person who was actively looking for Robert Green was Mitch Diamond. He'd crisscrossed the country in his Cadillac, whenever and wherever a new piece of mail showed up somewhere or in the instances where some minor crime took place and Robert's DNA showed up, Mitch as comfortable now in small-town precincts as he was in his cell in San Quentin. An unceasing irony.

That was an odd thing, though.

It was always a small town.

Never in Los Angeles or London or Manhattan. Might be a town near those places, but never in the jurisdiction of a major league department with deep pockets to do an investigation on their own.

The mayor came over to the window where Mitch stood. "Do you see that area over there?" She pointed at a spot north of them: A bluff perched out over the beach where earthmovers moved like ants. "We're thinking of calling the development Granite Highlands. Have you ever been up there?"

"I don't believe so."

"Best views in the whole city. Hundreds of years, people have lived here, and yet no one ever built homes up there, not even the tribes who settled here. Do you know why?"

"Because a view that beautiful shouldn't belong only to those who can afford it?"

"Agreed, agreed," she said, in a way that Mitch did not believe one iota, "but the other issue is that the city simply could not afford to bring infrastructure up the hill, so there wasn't even a drinking fountain or public restroom, never mind a paved road. So you know what ended up happening, I'm sure."

"Teenagers hiked up there to drink and have sex?"

The mayor smiled, and Mitch thought he saw a real human being flash under her skin. "Plenty of that, Mr. Diamond. Plenty. But the flipside is that those same kids started to jump off the edge to kill themselves. Got so bad in the '90s, people started showing up here to kill themselves. The city earned an actual reputation as a nice place to die. Cheaper and prettier than Las Vegas." She shook her head. "The kids started to call it Suicide Ridge and pretty soon everyone started calling it that. It's even in guidebooks to the city. There's Yelp reviews. It's quite insidious. City would put up a chain-link fence, and that didn't stop anyone, of course. During the mortgage crisis? Three real estate agents jumped off at the same time. Thank God the media didn't learn about that!"

"There's still time."

The mayor ignored him. "One of the things I ran on was that we were going to change the whole view of this place. Do you know what we called this place when I was growing up?"

"Losertown," Mitch said.

"That's right. Can you imagine the odds stacked against young people growing up here when they believed that they'd been raised in Losertown? This is why Robert and Penny were so special. They both got out. Robert to Harvard. Penny to MIT. They were the smartest kids in town, and I'll tell you something, they let you know. They let you know. I wanted all the kids growing up here to get the same chances those two squandered. And we've done that. Granite Shores is becoming a place to be proud of again. It's become a tourist attraction for the right reasons, finally." She went back to the table, picked up a copy of the letter he'd sent Danny Vining. "This? This is going to ruin it."

"You'll excuse me," Mitch said, "but the reason tourists come here is you've commodified a criminal. You have a week of events tied to a fugitive. And then you've taken the bed taxes from the hotels to build Chipotles and cookie-cutter mansions."

"A fugitive who stole from a lot of corrupt, awful people," the mayor said. "That's practically the American Dream! Sticking it to the bad guys!"

"Getting away with it," Mitch said.

"That's exactly it," she said. "He got away with it." She paused. "This is going to make me sound a little crazy, but let's be clear here: From the British perspective, George Washington could be viewed as a seditious traitor. It's all about point of view. In our view, he's the father of our country. Heroes and villains, Mr. Diamond, depend upon who tells the story."

"Robert Green robbed people to pay off his student loan," Mitch said. "Isn't that the story you guys sell every year? A real Robin Hood."

"That's right, that's right, a thing many of us can understand. You see?"

"I do see what you mean," Mitch said. "Catching him would put a real dent in your economy. How much property do you own in town, Mayor?"

The mayor started to respond. Stopped. Started. Stopped. "I apologize," she said, finally. She went back to her purse, took out the vape pen again, took a hit, put it away. Looked at her watch. "I'm going to be late," she said. "I have a pancake brunch to attend at the Rotary."

"Feel free to take any of those files with you. There's plenty we didn't get to," Mitch said. "I brought them for you."

"We all grew up together," the mayor said, flipping through the files, like she was looking for something specific. "Penny, she was younger than us, so not in our peer group. Robert always thought he was better than everyone else. We used to say he was conceited. Do people even use that word anymore?"

"Too many syllables."

"Well. You ask me," the mayor said, "he stole all that to prove a silly point, that he could do something the rest of us couldn't. All of us could *fail* the bar. I mean, never becoming a lawyer must have been very embarrassing." Opened a file. Closed it. "His mother, you know, was a very prominent lawyer in Seattle. And here Robert was, unable to even pass the bar." Opened. Closed. "So now what is he? Never underestimate the perils of pride in a person's undoing. Which is why I don't believe he's here. He doesn't need to come back. Part of him never left." Opened. Closed. "He's still the second-smartest person from Granite Shores." She flipped open one last file, found what she was looking for: an artist's rendering of what Robert would look like now. She held it up. "His father was bald. You might want to recede his hairline a bit."

"Noted."

She closed the file, dropped it back on the stack, Mitch feeling like she was stalling for some reason. "What are you going to do if you find him?"

"Personally? All I care about is what belongs to our clients. If it happens that he's standing between me and that, I'll encourage him to move."

"And if he doesn't?"

"I'm not a cop, Mayor Biddle. I'll call your husband if it comes to that."

"Mr. Diamond. This area? It depends on this story. It depends on the notion that he got away with it. People come here to visit the mythology. I don't know if whatever was in those boxes matters. In Granite Shores, however, the story is now a lot of people's livelihoods. This reward has the potential to turn a weird bit of Americana into a dark end. Would that be worth it to you?"

# CHAPTER TWENTY-THREE

*Monday*

Jack Biddle closed the video feed of the conference room on his iPhone, flushed, zipped up. *This fucking asshole.* Opened the video feed from inside his rental on West Quarry. There was Penny Green eating scrambled eggs, like she had no cares in the world. He wondered if he could get a cleaning service into the place this week that could sneak in some more cameras. He had the one in the kitchen because there was a door leading into the backyard, so it was theoretically security, like the one on the front door and the one on the roof. But he sure would like to get a look at what these assholes were up to. The house was technically in Caroline's portfolio—she was all about designing them to be whimsical trips down *blah blah fucking blah*—so he had to be gentle with this situation. It would be bad for their Airbnb rating if people found out the mayor of the damn city was peeping on them.

When Bobby C. texted him last night at 2:00 a.m. with the news Penny was in town, he immediately did a search of their properties and there she was. It wasn't exactly serendipity. They owned eleven rentals. That she and Mitch Diamond were staying together, however, immediately made him feel nauseous. These were not people who should be friends. What the fuck was happening?

He still didn't have a good idea. There was no good reason they should be helping each other.

He wondered what that Russian fucker Rodney Golubev would think if he knew Penny was in town. That Jack had managed to kill his brother *and* buy his property for the very police station he was standing in was some gangster shit that he didn't give himself enough credit for accomplishing. He did miss those blow jobs, but he couldn't very well be police chief and let an open-air flesh market operate unimpeded.

Jack checked his appearance in the mirror, didn't bother to wash his hands, locked his private bathroom's door so no one busted in while he was on the phone, not that anyone ever used it but him, called Danny Vining from his personal cell.

"This letter," Jack said. "It's a problem."

"That's your expert opinion?"

"The law firm," Jack said, "they've sent their guy into town. Mitch Diamond. You know him?"

"I met him ten, twelve years ago. When it became clear I wasn't getting my shit back. Had me sign an NDA in exchange for $100,000."

"And you took it?"

"That's the thing about NDAs," Danny said. "You'll never know."

"You ever spend any time looking into him?"

"I literally pay his salary," Danny said. "So no. What the fuck is your problem, Jack? I'm at Sunshine. You worried he's a criminal?"

"He brought Penny Green with him." Jack could hear Danny's breathing. In the background, someone was ordering rocky road fudge, which sounded good. "She ran into Bobby C. last night."

"Where?"

"Shake's."

"Best thing that could happen to Bobby C.," Danny said, "is maybe he takes a long drive one night. He worries me. I'm just saying. All this old shit coming up. He knows too much, and that kid of his has him acting like a more responsible citizen, which is not good. Put some thought on that. What else?"

Jack wasn't opposed to Bobby C. maybe being . . . unalive. He'd give that some mental attention. It was a few years since he'd needed to . . . engage . . . in such a way, at least on an intentional level. There'd been a few drug dealer types who ended up getting gone, but no one files missing persons reports on drug dealers. Bobby C.'s wife would probably miss him.

"He said Penny's not some little smart girl anymore," Jack said. "He's concerned about his family."

"What I'm saying." Another long pause. "So do something. You're the law."

"She tried to kill me," Jack said.

"Did she? The *Dateline* episode was pretty damning on that one, sport." Fucking *Dateline*. "Anyway, she *succeeded* in robbing me," Danny continued. "Do they, or you, have an actual reason to believe Greeny is within reach?"

*Greeny. Jesus-fucking-Christ.*

Jack told him about the pollen.

Told him about the most recent blackmail.

Told him about the diamond earrings.

Told him about the commissary payments. All that. Told him that it was, on balance, pretty believable.

Which made Jack fairly certain Mitch Diamond wasn't merely doing the firm's bidding. There was something about him—shaking hands with him was like shaking hands with a Ken doll, every surface was smooth, for instance—that raised Jack's cop radar. He had too much confidence and not enough trackable history. What *was* that on his hands? Glue? Emu oil? Some spy craft? There was no one he could call at the law firm to get more information about this—Mitch was his point of contact all these years—and what would he say? *Please don't help us solve this crime?* That would seem . . . dubious.

Still.

It would bring a lot of people to town.

So there was that side of it.

He would make money from this whole thing.

But . . .

What if someone found something?

This fucking pollen thing *was* some Jason Bourne shit, after all. *Pollen!*

Who even knew you could track that? This yahoo Diamond? *Please.* There was no reason he'd know! Fifteen years Jack had stayed abreast of all things DNA evidence, had gone to every conference and symposium he could find, even got to go to France and Spain to talk about small-town law enforcement using big-city science, his newfound specialty what with Robert Green sending him all those crazy letters. And of course, his own stellar record for stopping the local drug trade. He'd become such an expert, he was even called in to consult every now and then on cases in Portland! When they caught that Golden State Killer using familial DNA? He got to appear on Glenn Beck for a minute and four seconds. He still had the clip on his phone.

And now this asshole undoes him . . . with *pollen?*

This Penny Green business, though, that complicated matters. Jack thought he was pretty slick with the commissary stuff. Show that Robert was still interested in his sister's well-being, even if he wasn't in communication with her. Keep Penny feeling indebted to big bro. Over a decade, he kept Penny rich in Hostess, even pushed a few extra bucks in during the holidays. When she got the gig working on the dogs, he dropped a fifty spot in her account to get her the nice scrubs. She'd saved his life, after all.

What had Mitch Diamond ever done for her?

It didn't make sense these two were working together unless they both had something to gain.

Jack Biddle had to tighten his shit up.

"But look," Jack said, "if he were here, we'd know. You think he's living in the caves? Come on."

"So what? Someone's planting evidence? Why don't you pull in every fucking scumbag in the city and get them on a lie detector. See what we see."

"Because there's still something called the United States Constitution," Jack said.

"Why didn't you have this pollen information?"

"We don't have the kind of manpower or the money to be running that kind of testing," Jack said, which was true, but also he wasn't exactly going out of his way to indict himself. "We know it's him that's been sending letters. He's not hiding his DNA. It's all right there."

"Why do I bother paying you, then?" He didn't literally *pay* Jack. Maybe extended him credit. But . . . shit . . . this disrespect was starting to bother him. "I've got someone for you, okay? You're not gonna like it. But you asked for it." And then he hung up.

This hanging-up-on-him bullshit was starting to get tiresome.

Jack stepped out of his private bathroom just as Caroline was sitting down behind his desk.

"That went well," she said. "How many people received those letters?"

"There were three hundred boxes," Jack said. Three hundred twenty-four to be exact. "So I guess three hundred people."

"These people could have spouses? Children?"

"Of course."

"So we're talking those three hundred boxes, a wife and two kids for each, close to a thousand people have read this letter. Have you checked social media? Someone must have tweeted or TikTokked about this."

"The people who got robbed," Jack said, "aren't the TikTok kind."

"But their kids are."

"I'll look," Jack said.

"Don't bother," she said. "I just did." She flipped her phone around. What was he looking at? There was some fifteen-year-old girl dancing with her dog. "There's nothing out there. Not one word. You don't find that unusual?"

"I guess I do," Jack said.

"After all, Danny came to you with questions. Other B&H clients don't have questions? Their heirs don't have questions? What was in Danny's box, recipes?"

"Yeah," Jack said. "Recipes."

Caroline tapped on her phone. "Who else had things stolen? Hold on. We can get a good idea of who might say something."

Jack said, "We don't need to do that." He took his wife's wrist, gently. Took the phone from her. "Listen. Maybe it's not so bad. Maybe they catch Robert, and we can, I don't know, get an RV and drive around the country for the rest of our lives."

"You're fifty-three years old," Caroline said.

"And I'll have twenty-five years on the job next summer. Maybe this is what Travis needs. Change of scenery. Don't tell me you haven't thought about it."

"I haven't thought about it," Caroline said. "I have three more years on my term, and we have a new house and now you want, all of a sudden, to buy an RV and drive around the country? What are you going to do to occupy yourself, stop in and solve crimes for people along the way? And I remind you, you can't drive thirty minutes without needing to pee. Your prostate is the size of a raccoon, and you want to start driving all the time? Please. Be real, Jack." She picked up her phone. Tapped again. "The governor of Washington had his box stolen. That's right. And he's strangely silent about all of this. So. There you have it."

"What is 'it' in this context?"

"Your answer. If anyone solves this, it's *you*. Then we can control the narrative. You let someone parachute into town and figure it all out? You'll look like a moron. And you're not a moron, Jack. You're the chief of police! You are Granite Shores royalty! Do you hear me, sweetheart? Do you?"

He did. He wasn't entirely certain how he was going to pull this off.

"You handle this, people will forget the whole shooting thing." *Jesus fucking hell on a Ritz cracker.* "Anyway. Do you believe what Diamond said?"

"That Green is here? No."

"Well, that's a relief. Who is this Melissa Ruby person? That got the blackmail letter with the pollen?"

"One of the three hundred and twenty-four," Jack said, because he couldn't find shit on her. Soon as the letter was received by Barer & Harris, however, they immediately sent an email saying the deposit would be made by the desired date and the stolen materials should be sent to the firm directly.

"I can't find her online."

"Could be she's dead."

Caroline set her phone down again, seemingly satisfied. "How do you explain the pollen?"

"My guess? It's his cousin Addie."

"Oh Jesus, Jack," she said. "How many times are you going to defame that poor girl?"

"Number one, she's a woman now. Number two, I've never believed a word she's ever said."

"I don't want the city to have to go to court again," Caroline said. She took out her vape pen. "Do you mind?"

"Yes," Jack said. "I can't have you giving me cancer on top of everything else."

"Too bad, you're stressing me out by saying that poor girl's name."

The last time Jack said something about Addie Green, he did it on a crime show Geraldo Rivera was hosting. He made sure to implicate Addie in as many aspects of the heist as possible, including the notion she might have even been the mastermind, might be helping Robert Green stay hidden, and could very well be posing as Robert. In short, he framed her for the crimes Jack was committing on a regular basis, the claims so profound she'd have to sue . . . which is exactly what she did, much to Jack's glee.

She sued the city for defamation, and Caroline ended up cutting her a check for $375,000, cheaper than trying to defend the chief's (bogus) claims of qualified immunity. Jack wasn't about to allow discovery. Who knows what they'd turn up? That was why it was called "discovery," after all.

Not that it was ever going to get there. Jack had a good idea how much Addie owed on the loan she'd taken out to open Fitness4Moms, her soon to be foreclosed upon yoga studio and cardio gym she owned across the street from the Sno-Cone Depot, since Burt Flawson leased the building to Addie instead of him, because Burt wanted to give the girl a leg up or some shit, though the real reason was Jack had arrested his son on a DUI. Problem was, there weren't a lot of moms in Granite Shores, at least not ones for whom fitness was a priority, and Jack figured even Addie could see that she wasn't going to change that trend.

She needed a way out.

So Jack encouraged Caroline to offer her a number roughly double the amount of the loan, figuring that it would be enough to get Addie to pay off what she owed to get out of her business with a little walking around money for her troubles.

Which was important to Jack, because he needed to access the electrical system of the gym to help run his freezer without it seeming weird how much power he was using. So once Addie was gone, he planted some drugs on Burt himself, ran up his legal bills for a few months, then bought that building, too, eventually renovating it into a performance hall that he named the Evergreen Spot, a little private joke, hired Bobby C.'s long-haired nephew Dip Shitaroony—he could never remember his name—to book crappy concerts with big light shows—like the country band he rolled for their drugs—and then tapped into their electrical, paid the bills, no questions, no problems.

It all worked out better than his other plan, which was to have Bobby C. toss Addie off of Suicide Ridge after torturing her into writing a suicide note.

What Jack hadn't counted on, however, was that Addie would take that money to remodel her nana's old condo at the Shore View and build a true crime podcasting empire from there and would then diversify into books. Word was she was planning on launching her own bus tour. All of which was pissing Jack off.

"So what are you going to do?" Caroline asked.

Jack felt like he'd done a damn good job covering his tracks all these years. He wasn't going to be undone by some fucking pollen and an eventual press release. If someone was going to figure out what happened to Robert Green, they would have found him already, that was Jack's thinking. Jack had gotten away with it better than Robert Green ever could have, that's for damn sure. D. B. Cooper couldn't hold Jack's dick.

"I'll handle it," Jack said. He felt a sudden brightness. Like he'd woken up from a long sleep, finally fully alert, as if he didn't have untreated sleep apnea all these years. "Don't you worry." He opened a drawer in his desk, pulled out some pages he'd printed out from the internet that morning, waiting for that asshole Diamond to arrive. "Sweetheart, did you know they have cruises that stop in Lithuania?"

# CHAPTER TWENTY-FOUR

*Klamath Falls, Oregon*
*Monday*

Rodney Golubev stood in the parking lot of what used to be the Purple Flamingo.

A fireman came out of the rubble pushing a safe strapped to an appliance-sized hand truck. The safe was dripping with soot but otherwise undamaged.

"This it?" the fireman asked.

"There is another one in the basement," Rodney said.

"Fire didn't get through the floor."

"No?"

"Burned hot and fast," the fireman said. "But whoever torched this place didn't care too much about not showing how he did it or doing a complete job. He even left the gas can on top of that Subaru over there."

Rodney turned and looked at his brother's car. "Motherfucker," he muttered.

The fireman slid the safe off the hand truck. "Anything else you want me to look for?"

Rodney had some coke in his desk and a gun. He presumed the coke melted. The gun was registered. He could get another. Oregon didn't care much about background checks. "Cameras?"

"Cooked," he said. "You rebuild, get the system that records to the cloud."

"Cloud can be hacked. People who come here, they want to know it's private."

"Then don't have cameras in the first place," he said and then headed back into the rubble.

Rodney got down on one knee, spun the combination. Opened the safe.

The night deposit drop bag was still there. Felt about the right weight, but he didn't feel any coins. Unzipped the bag. All the money was gone, even down to the rolls of pennies. Replaced by . . . an Alaskan salmon fillet from Whole Foods? Still wrapped in brown butcher paper and everything?

"The fuck?" Rodney said. He smelled it. It didn't smell like salmon.

Rodney looked around. The firemen were doing firemen shit. The cops were taking a statement from the dumb fuck bouncer. That kid didn't know it yet, but he should have been planning his funeral. At least putting together a will.

He unrolled the butcher paper. Stared at what was inside. Tried to make sense of it. Realized it was a human thumb cleaved from a hand.

"Motherfucker," Rodney said. Rodney had seen some shit in his life, no doubt, but this was grisly even to him. Who the fuck's thumb was this?

There was something tattooed on the patch of skin that would be between the thumb and index finger.

A name.

*Dale.*

Well.

Rodney wasn't sure if he was happy or upset about this. Clearly, someone had taken care of the Dale problem, so that was nice. And clearly someone wanted it to look like Rodney was complicit in said eradication.

Framed for a murder people already figured he did.

He liked that shit, on a conceptual level.

On a practical level, not so much.

Only one person capable or willing to do that shit. To hold a grudge for that long . . . and then pay it off? He liked that shit. Respected it.

That clever motherfucker.

Whatever his name was.

He'd kill that motherfucker.

Whatever his name was.

Rodney shoved the thumb back into the bag. Tossed it into the safe. Spun the combination. Where was the rest of Dale? Now he had something to worry about. He headed over to the rubble, grabbed a dolly. He needed to get this safe somewhere . . . safe. He'd load it into his Outback, then maybe he'd BBQ the thumb when his wife wasn't home.

A detective walked over. His name was Haskell. Rodney had dealt with him in the past. Used to pay him off to keep the girls working. But didn't want money or sex. Came in on steak night, brought his whole damn family. He was a vice guy then. Now he must be major crimes. His suit was nicer than when he'd come to not bust the girls.

"Mr. Golubev," he said. "You have a few minutes to come down to the station to talk?"

"I don't talk to police."

"Someone burned down your business. I'm trying to help you."

"Someone did. Do you know who?"

"That's why we want to talk."

Rodney said, "Have you found my brother yet?"

"That's not my job."

"You find my brother, I'll answer questions."

"He's been missing, what, fifteen years?"

"Yeah, you see the problem."

Detective Haskell said, "Are we going to find anything illegal on these premises? Be honest here. Better for you long term."

"My business burns down and you're worried about what illegal things of mine have been burned?"

"I'm trying to help you."

"I don't talk to police," Rodney said again.

"We find something," Haskell said, "you'll want to reevaluate that. A steak dinner won't help."

A fireman said, "Hey, we need a cop over here. We've got partial remains."

*Partial remains?*

Haskell said, "That doesn't sound good."

The fireman said, "Is that . . . a foot?"

*Motherfuck me.*

# CHAPTER TWENTY-FIVE

*Monday*

Many of Jack Biddle's best ideas came to him on the shitter. Like the idea he just had: If Jack was going to skirt this whole situation, he'd need to frame someone for murdering Robert Green. Like, today. Tomorrow at the latest. He'd have to hope for some more inspiration on this topic since this first bit came to him a moment ago, after he convinced Caroline that a quickie in his office bathroom would make her feel better before the Rotary's pancake brunch.

He couldn't figure out a good way to get Penny pinched on this. That seemed sort of cruel, anyway. She had saved his life, after all. And did her time. And survived all the attempts on her life he'd arranged while she was in prison, which was pure vanity on Jack's part, the desire to not have her ruin his rep when she eventually got out of prison and started telling her story. But that hadn't even happened! She'd gone completely dark! She must have known that Jack Biddle was not to be played. Still. Things *would* be easier if she was dead.

There was also the reality that Jack wasn't, in fact, guilty of killing Robert Green. He was dead when he found him. What was he truly guilty of? Well, a lot, of course, but as it related to the death of Robert Green, he'd tried to save the man. He'd never be given credit for that. All anyone would ever see was that he'd profited in a deeply fucked-up way from the man's death.

So telling the truth was out.

The only way to keep the heat off him was to put someone else in the fire. Framing someone for Robert Green's natural death was kind of cool. Only an amazing combination of law enforcement know-how and criminal ingenuity could result in something so inspired. Jack Biddle really deserved proper study. Alas. He'd probably die an unknown legend. Maybe one day, though, they'd rename Yeach Mountain for him? Biddle Mountain? Hmm. Not hardcore enough. Chief Mountain? Probably not. Gunslinger Mountain? And then maybe they'd put up a bronze of him, a big plaque explaining everything he'd done? Yeah. Now *there* was an idea. He'd investigate how that might happen. Had to be a lengthy process. This could be the way Travis really paid homage to his father. He'd get that in his will: *See about getting the mountain renamed for my heroism.*

First, the job at hand.

Caroline was putting her makeup back on, talking to him about . . . something . . . and Jack was on the toilet, watching her, thinking about how good their life was these days, minus the whole Travis thing, and how if he had to do it all over again . . . well, hell, he'd do it all over again. For moments like this. The small perfect joy of three minutes of friction.

The next thirty years were going to be his coasting period. Just moving through, unencumbered by . . . all this shit. No more long cons. That was like a second job, and Jack barely had tolerance for his first job.

His way through was right in front of him.

Rodney Golubev always scared Jack. He knew Rodney probably had video of him getting blow jobs back in the day, Rodney the kind of guy who probably kept good records to blackmail people down the line, which Jack respected. Which is partly why the city overpaid to get Rodney to sell the land the new station was on. It was a penance Jack was ready to sign off on, particularly after Rodney suggested it would be good for his long-term health and marriage if the city paid a "local's premium" on the land, which Rodney punctuated by making the universal sign for blow jobs.

But also? Since Jack was instrumental in getting that $50K seized after the whole Penny incident, which Jack went ahead and got reinvested into his tricked-out department Tahoe, he figured, well, scales were even.

For a time, anyway.

Time came, scales don't fucking matter much, turns out.

Jack was surprised he hadn't thought of this plan earlier. But often good ideas came slowly to Jack. Hence the toilet. He thought maybe it had something to do with the Oxy and all that backing him up. Or maybe it was because he had so much on his mind these days. All the evidence was already there. Why else would Rodney's (dead) brother give Penny that cash? For the jewels. For the passports. For . . . whatever was in those boxes. Maybe Penny dropped the dime on her brother, sold him out for the $50k down payment? And then part of the profits from all the blackmail to follow? But then everything went south on the boat, and she was cut out of it all?

It was a case Jack could surely make. It would help if Rodney was dead while Jack was making the case. Less cross-examination. But if Rodney-fucking-Golubev managed to get out of this alive, it would be up to *Rodney* to figure out how he hadn't pretended to be Robert. Hell, Rodney had a house at the Dunes, too. Asshole was probably covered in pollen from his head to his Commie toes.

If Jack could solve all this without anything ever appearing in a court of law?

Oh he'd get a statue for sure.

Could he suggest text for the plaque? *For his dedication to the people of Granite Shores . . . to protect and serve . . . for solving the greatest unsolved crime of the century . . . taking down the Russian mob . . .*

Jack could see his speaking fee increasing tenfold.

But . . . then there was the Bobby C. issue.

Well.

That was easier to handle.

Or.

Or . . . no.

Could be, he'd plant some evidence on Rodney. Plant some on Bobby C. Hell, maybe he'd plant some on Mitch Diamond. Arrest them all. Let God sort them out.

The toilet was his spiritual lodestar. Maybe he'd write a self-help book? *The Toilet Meditations*. He'd investigate that.

"Are you listening? Baby?" Caroline said.

Baby? When was the last time his wife had called him *baby*? Years.

Why was she calling him *baby* now? What even was she saying? He'd need to go back and watch the tape later, in case she brought something back up at dinner or something. For now, though . . .

"Yes, baby," Jack said.

She dropped her lip liner into the sink. "Oh thank you, Jack! Thank you, I'll contact the agency tomorrow." Wait. What? Caroline came over to the toilet and kissed him hard on the mouth. "Maybe a girl?"

"Maybe?" Jack said.

She kissed him again. "It's what Travis needs." One more kiss. "We'll talk more at dinner. We're getting a baby! I can't believe it."

# CHAPTER TWENTY-SIX

*Monday*

Mitch sat in his rental van at the bottom of Dune Shores Parkway waiting for Jack Biddle to drive by. He'd followed him from the office, saw him turn up the parkway, which was the only way in or out of the Dunes at Granite Shores gated community, and decided to see where this fucking guy went next.

Because that meeting had clarified a few things.

First, that Jack Biddle was sick. As in literally ill. Anyone who needs to piss that often and then needs to sit on an icepack, at work, has a problem that needs correcting. And that he's not correcting it? Well. That was to be examined, too.

Second, that his wife had no idea who she was married to. And maybe that was for the best.

Third, that Jack Biddle was on . . . something. He was Parkinson's-level twitchy, but also a bit more acutely paranoid and unpredictable.

Which brought him to his last thing.

The Jack Biddle he met on those days fifteen years ago. Both on the mountain and at the condo. But also? How and why he ended up on that boat with Penny.

Mitch took out his wallet, slipped his fake-ass driver's license out, and there it was: his lucky money. Fifteen years he'd kept that money he found on the side of the road, his money of last resort, money to spend when he knew his luck was gone. What could a person get with $120 these days?

A night in a hotel.

Put it on a hard eight, get $1,080 if it came up. Maybe that would buy a desperate man a week more.

A shitty gun with one bullet.

Enough Ambien to kill yourself.

One last good meal.

Two dances at the Crazy Wolf strip club in Portland.

A hundred and twenty bucks wasn't much. But it would solve a problem permanently if it came to that.

It never was far from Mitch's mind these days how weird it all was. He found that cash, that was lucky, but there was also that wedding photo Jack Biddle tore up. Even more things that didn't make any sense . . . unless you knew that Robert Green, driving a van filled with cash and documents and pictures and guns and god knows what else, slipped from this reality somewhere near that very spot.

Mitch rubbed one of the fifties between his thumb and index finger. Could still feel bits of dirt. The money well preserved all these years, moving from one wallet to the next, but going nowhere else.

So strange.

Mitch put the cash back behind his license. Closed his eyes for five seconds. That's all he was giving himself. Could he order this all up yet?

He couldn't.

Good thing he was used to waiting.

As it was, it took Mitch Diamond most of a year to figure out where all his meticulously created documents ended up after Gabino died. He found digital copies of some of the materials stored on Gabino's old laptop—copies of the Social Security card he'd used, another of the driver's license, for instance—but Mitch had given him an entire life. Three entire lives, in fact, so that Gabino could choose which documents were most likely to pass muster. From there, they could slowly build an online past, Gabino telling him he had a guy, an ex-Microsoft drone who owed Gabino big favors, of the kept-him-out-of-prison variety.

That was the plan, anyway.

They'd build an actual footprint Mitch could walk in for the rest of his life.

Childhood photos uploaded to ancestry sites.

College records.

Military records.

Comments on blogs from the early part of the century.

They'd even get him an old Myspace if he wanted it.

He did.

He wanted it all. Had even given Gabino some cash to make sure it was all first class, even though Gabino said it wasn't needed, that his guy was happy to do it, but Mitch believed in compensating for jobs. He was old-school like that. Man, he missed Gabino. He'd been one of Mitch's only true friends. Mitch had helped him out of a bad situation, and Gabino said that he'd never forget him for that, that he'd save his life if he ever got the chance . . . and then, when he got the chance, he'd legitimately done so. In his own way.

By the time Mitch got to work that Monday in December fifteen years ago, no one much cared about his paperwork one way or the other. They'd held the job for him since Gabino's death, and now he needed to hit the ground. They'd found out on that previous Friday, after a woman was arrested for robbing a Pronto Pup shop in Granite Shores, Oregon, and then possibly shot a cop, that she'd been involved in a heist that emptied out all their safe-deposit boxes, and now they needed Mitch to help get things secured in the firm while they tried to figure out what the hell happened . . . and keep as much of it under wraps as possible. The crime was going to get known. What was taken needed to be on the way down-low.

Forever.

It took Mitch months to finally track down Gabino's "guy." Not because he was that hard to find, but because that's when things finally calmed down at the office long enough for Mitch to go take care of that problem, Mitch not the kind of guy who liked strangers knowing his business, but also not the kind of guy who'd ever really had an office job, as opposed to what his fake-ass résumé said. Twenty years in military intelligence? Oh boy. He had a lot of reading to do.

The guy's name was Sylvester Sullivan, he was one of the first two hundred employees at Microsoft and lived like it: a massive house on Mercer Island, near the Mercer Island Beach Club, right on the water. Zillow said the house was worth about eight million. It also gave a nice satellite view of the entire property, which let Mitch know the easiest way to break in. Mitch went and cased the joint, make sure what could be seen from space was accurate: The front of the house was a fortress of gates, locks, intercoms, and cameras. Rear of the house? Backed right up to a dock on Lake Washington. No fencing at all. Maybe some cameras, but avoiding cameras was not really Mitch's concern.

Mitch selected a day in April, when it was reasonable he might be on a boat on Lake Washington. Docked. Walked up the rolling lawn to a sliding door. Picking the lock on a sliding glass door required exactly one tool—a screwdriver—and involved no picking whatsoever. A flathead screwdriver, shoved between the door and slide, and a quick push, and you were in.

Mitch didn't want to toss the whole place, leaving his DNA everywhere, so he simply sat downstairs, in a giant "playroom" filled with old stand-up video games—Defender, Galaga, Pac-Man—a Buck Rogers pinball machine, 60-inch flat-screen TVs, and shelves filled with DVDs and books, Mitch selecting an Oprah-approved hardback off the shelf—it was about a man in the South who owns a magical pizza shop—and waited for Sylvester to come home, which he did a few hours later, his Bentley pulling into the garage around 6:00 p.m.

Mitch came up behind Sylvester while he prepared two drinks, Mitch hoping there wasn't a woman, or another man, showing up soon, put a gun to the back of his head, and said, "If you're going to scream, do that now, get it out."

Sylvester didn't. Instead, he said, "These are salty dogs. You like those, right?"

He did. How did he know that? "With gin."

Sylvester said, "Only have vodka."

Mitch checked the bottles Sylvester had. Top-top-shelf shit. "That Beluga Epicure will work." $10K a bottle. He'd drink slow. Mitch said, "You knew I was here?"

"I've been expecting you," Sylvester said. "I have about five hundred cameras in this house. So. Yeah. I knew."

Mitch spotted them, too. He wanted to see if Sylvester would be honest.

"And you didn't call the cops?"

"Not a thing I do," Sylvester said. He kept mixing the drink, back still turned. "If I wanted the cops to know about you, I wouldn't have waited for you to show up."

Mitch took the gun off him. "You can turn around."

"I'd rather not," Sylvester said. "I'm terrible with polygraphs. If I don't see your face, I feel like I'm better poised to pass. You want to know where your things are, yes?"

"Yes," Mitch said.

"Gabino put them in a box I paid for. I don't know the name. I imagine Gabino didn't run the invoice through the firm."

"No, probably not."

"There's an encrypted flash drive with all your materials. It's all there. What Robert Green can do with those materials? I have no idea. Nothing profitable. Even if he put it on the dark web, it's useless. It's not real. Whoever bought it would need to know your past, which I don't."

Of course he didn't. *Of course.* Like how he didn't know what kind of drink to make him. Sylvester set one of the drinks down on the counter. Mitch took a sip. It was a damn good drink. "How was the book?"

"It was too unbelievable for my taste," Mitch said. Took another sip. He'd need to go through the declared inventory of all 324 boxes and try to figure out which one contained his shit. Or at least make an educated guess. That could take weeks. Months. And even then? It would only matter if the firm found out, he supposed, or Rodney Golubev, or the Klamath cops. Or anyone looking for his dead stepfather.

"Let me ask you something," Mitch said. "For not killing you, and since you know nothing of my past, would you be open to periodically helping me with some long-term internet-related concerns?"

Sylvester said, "Gabino was a dear friend. We had an agreement. He kept me out of prison, I kept him and his close friends out of prison. I feel like that could be a lasting relationship with you."

"What would I have to do?"

"The sorts of things Gabino did," Sylvester said. "I don't imagine you're averse to a little blood every now and then?"

He wasn't, though he was less prone to it now, generally. Happier to get things done with his brain than his hands. But a job is a job. "I'll need that bottle of vodka to go," Mitch said.

It took Mitch six more months to get handed the file of a client no one could find on their rosters: Melissa Ruby. Contents of her box: an urn theoretically containing a child's ashes.

Mitch went to find her. And in about thirty minutes, realized he was looking for himself.

Took another decade-plus for Robert Green to send a ransom letter, a postmark from Sacramento. Which was unusual. Most of the time, the letters came from foreign countries or states far away from Oregon. In fact, the last time anything from Robert Green was postmarked within a thousand miles of Granite Shores, it contained those diamonds, a shitload of DNA, and all that pollen.

So he sent the envelope and letter off to be tested by the private firm they used. Normally, all Mitch wanted was the DNA, to make sure it wasn't a hoax, and then any environmental fibers or notable plant life, Mitch looking for carpet, native trees, anything to give him a clue where Robert was *now*. It had gotten to the point that he expected the DNA to be there—that Robert was likely leaving it intentionally, so that there was no question as to the veracity of anything.

The results that came back were as expected . . . until they weren't. Three eyebrow hairs positively identified as Robert Green's DNA. Skin sample positively identified as Robert Green's DNA. Pollen identified as *Ammophila arenaria*.

And then, another page that Mitch was not expecting:

> Evidence Item #17: Glass
> Description: A total of eleven fragments of curved, laminated glass were collected from the hair and skin samples.
> Location and Context: The glass fragments were found embedded in the skin samples (attached) and attached to hair found within the envelope.
> Quantity and Characteristics: The glass fragments ranged in size from .025 mm to .029 mm in diameter and exhibited a green tint.
> Comparison to Known Sources: The glass fragments were compared to known samples of commercially available glass and were shown to be comparable to commercially available windshields and consistent in terms of curvature, tint, and laminated structure to those currently available through Carlite and the like.
> Analysis Results: Refractive index (RI) measurements were performed on three fragments, yielding values of 1.518, 1.520, and 1.522. These values are consistent with the RI of standard commercial windshield glass.

The next morning, Mitch went to the offices of Centrax, the outside forensics company Barer & Harris employed. He'd never shown up to their offices in person, but in this situation, it felt smart to maybe have that personal touch, particularly since he wanted to limit the paper and digital trail. He imagined their offices would be like something from *CSI*—some darkened lab with flat-screen TVs everywhere running data, lots of hot young things running around in designer jeans, solving crimes and making bad personal decisions.

In fact, their offices were in an office park across from what looked like an especially nice senior living facility in Bellevue, Mitch thinking that maybe he could get his mom up here, closer to him, away from the bad memories—if she still possessed any—from those years down south in Pajaro. He found his way to the fourth floor of the office building and found that Centrax wasn't dark nor filled with high-fashion model scientists. It was exceedingly well lit, and the scientist in question, Jillian, who he'd traded emails, phone calls, and Zoom meetings with a hundred times over the years but had never met in person, had her own office at the end of a long corridor filled with even more exceedingly bright labs. She was in her forties, wore a white lab coat, and had long black hair that was pulled away into a precise ponytail. She was one of those scientists who spent her entire life looking into the worst instincts of people whittled down into microcosmic bits, and so liked to decorate her office as if it was perpetual Christmas. She even had a fake tree in the corner that she redecorated every few months, even during the pandemic when it was her Zoom background, Jillian one of those people who still went to her office every day during that period, since it's hard to do DNA testing from your bedroom.

If she was surprised to see Mitch at her office door, she didn't act like it. She looked up from her laptop and said, "You're taller than I thought." She pointed at a chair. There was a stuffed Santa sitting on it. "Feel free to move St. Nick and have a seat."

He did. Looked around the office. "Let me guess," he said. "At the holidays, you do your house up like a forensics lab?" She didn't laugh. He set down a copy of the report she'd sent the day previous, along with a box covered in fancy Christmas wrapping. "I brought you a little something for your tree."

"I like to buy my own ornaments," she said. "I have a particular taste."

"I respect that," Mitch said. "But I thought if I had to ask you to do some extra work, maybe a gift was in order."

"'Extra,' meaning?"

"Meaning between us. In the holiday spirit." He slid the report across the desk. "Tell me what I'm looking at here. We've never had any glass particles in anything I've sent you. I need to understand it better."

"Pretty standard stuff," Jillian said. And pushed the report back. "If I knew the situation where this skin and hair were recovered, maybe I could be more helpful."

"You know as much as I do," Mitch said. "It was in the envelope I sent you." Barer & Harris didn't tell the lab which cases they were working on, though Mitch was fairly certain the various techs they worked with had a good idea. The samples were coded. No names. "You know the rules." He pushed the report right back to her. But also, tore off a corner of the box wrapping, revealing the logo of Christopher Radko. The tree behind Jillian was filled with his glass ornaments.

"You're good," Jillian said.

"I do my research."

Jillian picked up the report, read back through it. "My husband handles the decorations at the holidays," she said, still reading. "You a *Star Wars* guy, Mr. Diamond?"

"I got my own dad problems. Don't need someone else's."

"My husband goes all in at the holidays with the *Star Wars* stuff. Plays the 'Imperial March' music every night at sundown. The kids in the neighborhood love it. Just saying, Radko has a *Star Wars* line. Some pretty rare finds, at that. There's a C-3PO-and-R2 ornament from 1999, for instance." Kept reading. "If I had a larger skin sample, we'd be capable of figuring out velocity and angle of impact, but what we found in the skin was very small, microscopic, obviously, so nearly impossible to generate significant data beyond what's on the page. What do you need?"

Mitch wasn't sure.

"How big is .025 mm?" he asked after a moment.

"Half a grain of salt," Jillian said. She turned her laptop around. "See those pixels?" Mitch leaned close. "Not really."

Jillian took a pair of readers from her desk. "Try these." He did. That worked. "Each pixel is slightly larger than .025."

"Okay," Mitch said, "which means what?"

"This person was hit with glass traveling at an exceedingly high velocity. Typical for someone in a car accident. I mean, it's basically always there in bodies that get recovered. Finding bits in the hair and skin, all standard, nothing unusual in that."

"But it hasn't shown up on any of the previous samples we've sent you from the same client. Is that odd?"

"Why would it?" She looked at the report. "We've been comparing skin and hair samples to this DNA record for years."

"I don't understand."

"These were eyebrows we tested. Very thick, easy to embed substances in there. The skin, that's scalp skin. Dandruff basically. Again, very thick area, easy for glass to get caught in that mess. But if the sample is coming from someone's arm or their beard, big open spaces, lots of room for the glass to fall out, gravity being the great equalizer to forensics."

"How long would the glass stay on the body, though? Like if I'm in a car accident and then take a shower?"

"Likely all gone. But if it stayed, we'd find things like bits of soap attached to it. Normal environmental changes. This is untouched. This person was recently in an accident. I'd wager the same day."

"So this glass . . . has been on this hair all this time?"

"What do you mean 'all this time'? I just told you. This person went through a window or had a window go through them the same day as these samples were dropped."

Mitch unwrapped the box completely. It was Radko's Rosse Lamp Drop Ball. Went for about a grand on eBay. He'd been holding it for a good bit. In case he fucked up royally, as he may have, or needed a good favor, as was his original intent. He'd had Sylvester get him her eBay and Amazon searches. Answered everything.

Jillian unpacked the ornament. Looked at it from every angle. Sighed. Then put it right onto her tree. Took a moment to really admire the work.

"What am I not asking?" Mitch said.

"Where's the blood?" Jillian said. "This much glass, this recently, it would have been bloody."

Mitch thought about this. "Is it possible to find out what kind of car had that glass?" he asked when Jillian turned back to him.

"The actual car? Probably not. The kind of car? Yes. Within reason. Old car, probably had the windshield replaced at least once, so if it's an aftermarket window, could be any car on the road. But let's say it's a Honda. Honda manufactures and sells four million cars every year. Maybe they use the same windshield type on all those cars. We can't tell the size of this windshield, only the composition, so you're now looking at four million cars a year."

"I don't need to know the exact car," Mitch said. "But what if I had an idea of the possible make and model of the car?"

"That would narrow things considerably."

"A 1984 Ford E150, half-ton cargo van," Mitch said. He knew that by heart. The van Robert purchased from a junkyard was a thing of great conspiracy theories online. Could it be he'd been living in it all this time? How do you disappear a half-ton cargo van between Yeach Mountain and Granite Shores? Do aliens want our cargo vans? Does Bigfoot? "You want the license number?"

"No," Jillian said. "This is going to cost you."

"How much?"

Jillian leaned back in her seat. "The droids I mentioned I was looking for, to start." She twirled around, amused. "Limited-edition, Darth Vader ornament, 1999. They made seventy-five hundred of them. You find me something in the first five hundred, you're golden with me for life."

"I think that can be arranged." He didn't know how, but he'd find one. "Might take me a bit."

"You're good for it, I can sense that." Jillian spun back around. "I'll be in touch." She pointed at the door. "If you could give Father Christmas back his chair, I'll see what I can do for you."

Mitch had an email waiting for him the next morning: Ford used the same window glass on their Econoline vans from 1975 to 1991, the samples found on the hair and skin matched the chemical tinting and the RI index in their accident database for those same Carlite windows . . . however, the same glass was also used on millions of other cars, of all makes and models.

Which didn't really matter.

What mattered was that for some reason Robert Green had broken glass in his hair and embedded in his flesh from a car produced between 1975 and 1991.

Which made no sense.

And still didn't, weeks later, Mitch thinking about all this while waiting on Jack Biddle's car to reappear.

Mitch didn't bother to fill in the Seattle authorities with this new information.

Or anyone in the firm.

Or Penny.

At least not yet. He had a couple theories, which is why he was in Granite Shores in the first place.

Why he'd started this all up.

Could it be that Robert Green wasn't missing at all? That he'd never left Granite Shores?

Not that he was walking around. He was too famous for that. Not that he'd had his face replaced, because that required doctors and nurses and bills and healing, and the one thing Robert didn't have was anonymity or health insurance.

But what if Robert Green was being held captive? Could that be? In some form or fashion? Mitch knew a lot of forms and a lot of fashions for terrible things. He wasn't sure anyone else was as fucked up as he was or as inclined to get away with something for as long as it humanly required.

Maybe that was the wrong way of thinking.

Maybe, Mitch considered, captivity wasn't about keeping someone alive.

Maybe it was about keeping an idea alive.

After thirty minutes, Jack Biddle finally came hurtling down the Dune Shores Parkway, now behind the wheel of his personal Tahoe, not looking around at all, the situational awareness of a man who didn't think anyone would ever suspect him of anything, ever.

# CHAPTER TWENTY-SEVEN

*Monday*

Jack clocked out for the day, told Gil Olney, his deputy chief, he had some doctors' appointments, would be gone until the next day, maybe the day after, he was feeling a little "not good," and then drove home, changed out of his uniform, left his cop Tahoe in the garage, climbed into his civilian Tahoe, swallowed about five Oxys and Altoids and then headed across town to the Sno-Cone Depot to start fixing this situation.

Not that the Sno-Cone Depot was open.

In fact, it hadn't reopened in fifteen years.

Not since Jack realized he was going to need to keep Robert Green on ice, literally. And needed a secure place to keep the contents of 324 safe-deposit boxes.

Back then, during the off-season, the Depot was surrounded by a flimsy chain-link fence and was boarded up with plywood, nothing too aggressive, since teenagers liked to sneak onto the property to get high and dry-hump, and the Biddles were about serving the community, after all. But once Jack realized this was all going to be a long-term proposition, he slowly fortified his position, first getting some better doors and locks . . . and then better fencing . . . and then better security cameras . . . and then, well, he realized he needed to make the freezer system a bit more secure and advanced.

These days, the Depot was encircled by a twelve-foot-high fence, topped with barbed wire, and fitted with the best security system he could find. A pigeon landed on the roof of the Depot, Jack got an immediate text. Caroline had been on his ass about selling the place since they started dating, particularly since it occupied a prime bit of corner real estate, but once they had Travis and he started to accumulate problems, their little plot of nothing had become less of a strain on her mind. Still, Jack kept her satisfied by telling her once they both retired, they'd move the property, fill out their nest egg. And to show he wasn't a shitty father, he kept the business shuttered even during the summer so he could spend weekends with his sociopathic fucking son.

He didn't want anyone to feel suspicious about his visits to the property, so he always went over in broad daylight. Caroline was under the impression that it was his man cave/personal office, which it was. He had a trailer behind the Depot fitted with a bathroom, a couple sofas, a flat screen, an old Sega system because he dominated at the hockey game back in the day, plus of course a PS5, a pretty serviceable bar. Sundays he even went over and watched football with Travis sometimes, back when Travis could stand to be in the same room with him and when Travis wasn't busy poisoning birds or whatever the fuck he did in his free time.

He also didn't want anyone to be suspicious about the fact that the property was now more secure than the actual Granite Shores jail, so he told everyone that they'd found unusually high amounts of lead and manganese in the soil surrounding the Depot, likely from having been built on a former scrap metal operation from the turn of the previous century, which was true, and hell, maybe it was true about the lead, too; he hadn't bothered to have it tested. It was enough now that people feared they'd have cyclops babies to keep them off the property.

The only person who had actual access to the property was Jack. Caroline had no idea what the code was to open the front gate or the front door, or where the key to the basement hatch was. If he died, they'd need to blow up the fucking place to get inside. Which was going to be a problem, since the lots surrounding the Sno-Cone Depot, which were two blocks east of Beach Boulevard, snuggled close to the foothills of Yeach, were recently zoned for medical facilities, Jack and Caroline thinking about maybe getting into the assisted living game.

As of today, Jack still had most of the block to himself. There was the shitty comic book shop, the one that had a mural of fucking Robert Green on it. He'd tried unsuccessfully to buy the damn place for close to a decade, but they wouldn't sell. Even tried to pretend he was a Japanese investment firm willing to pay double market value. That blew up in his fucking face. The newspaper started running xenophobic op-eds about foreign money influencing the town. So Jack said fuck it. No one was watching him, anyway. It became less pressing once he bought and renovated the yoga studio into the Evergreen Spot. There was also a coffee place called Heisted—clever—that also sold used records and weird clothes. If Jack were king, he'd close that shit down.

Jack pulled up to the front gate, punched in his code, parked, went into his office for a couple minutes to check the cameras, make sure no one had followed him in, make sure there were no fucking drones flying overhead, his new fear, and then headed into the Depot to take care of business.

The Depot building was almost seventy years old, a classic A-frame with a drive-thru center. Jack's grandfather built it by hand to no discernible code and for a long-ass time, it was an actual Granite Shores institution; every Biddle and every other local kid worked there over the summer, and tourists would kick off the season by posing under the huge **TREAT YOURSELF AND TREAT YOUR KIDDIES!** neon sign that was illuminated every year on Memorial Day and didn't turn off until Labor Day.

Jack fucking hated it but appreciated the grift of selling ice to snowbirds, a thought he had every time he descended into the basement, where he was now. Back in the day, Grandpa Biddle used the basement as a de facto speakeasy, running card games and beating reluctant witnesses, least that's what Jack's father told him, and which explained why it was finished so nicely. Hardwood floors, soundproof walls, a separate AC unit, even a fully operational slot machine and a craps table. And a lot of weird stains in the grout and baseboards and along the rim of the tub in the bathroom. Why Grandpa Biddle installed a tub in there in the first place was curious, but seemingly useful in the long run.

It was also where the industrial freezing system was kept, which now included a state-of-the-art SinoArctic Air Blast freezer he'd purchased a few years ago and had shipped from Jiangsu Province and then assembled piece by piece. Eighteen feet long, twelve feet high, eighteen feet deep. The size of a decent storage unit, and if he didn't own a fucking snow cone shop, that's where he'd probably need to keep it.

This baby was the Rolls-Royce of freezers.

Aluminum alloy evaporator.

Double-density air-blow return system providing high-efficiency deep freezing.

Reinforced nuclear submarine–grade polyurethane foam between the walls, ensuring that even with a prolonged electricity outage, it would remain between -40 and 0 degrees for a week.

A second, blast-fan dry-air walk-in inner freezer the size of a NYC studio apartment.

It was so cold, he had to put on RefrigiWear full-body Iron-Tuff coveralls and fitted headwear, which he did, so he wouldn't freeze to death—Jack acutely aware of not dying an ironic death—then unlocked the machine, stepped inside. He wasn't fucking around with pollen this time. Jack could fucking punch himself for that screwup. He'd figured it out while he was driving over, retracing his steps.

Instead of driving up Yeach to get high, like in the old days, at the golden hour he'd started walking down to his private beach at the bottom of his Dunes at Granite Shores property, setting down a blanket, putting in his earbuds and some Pink Floyd, sucking on forty milligrams of sativa gummies. Sometimes, if he had some work to do, he brought it with him.

Like those fucking diamond earrings a couple years ago.

They were probably worth ten or fifteen grand—they were each the size of his thumbnail—but he'd found trying to sell jewels for anywhere near their worth was a real problem. He couldn't hire some crackhead to go sell them at a pawn shop and hope to get anything like value, he couldn't go to a reputable dealer, and none of the dirtbags he did business with had any kind of taste. He'd been able to sell some while traveling overseas, but with all the bullshit with Travis, he'd curtailed his travel, and he didn't see himself stealing away for France anytime soon.

So fuck it. It would be a lucky day for the idiot who'd made the commissary payments. If he got nabbed? Just another weird part of the story. It only helped Jack.

He'd already gone to the freezer to rub the earrings between Robert's middle finger and index finger. Plucked an eyelash and a few eyebrow hairs from Robert's head, sprinkled them inside a small envelope. Then, sitting outside there, relishing the breezes coming in from the shore, he jammed it all into the larger mailer, sealed it, gloves on as per usual, then put the mailer inside a sealed evidence bag. The next day, Bobby C. drove it out to Elko, Nevada, dumped it in a mailbox.

It was a level of precaution that at the time he felt was probably overkill. He didn't realize this Mitch Diamond fucker was tracking who was making the commissary payments and would show up to confiscate the diamonds. Another dumb fucking irony. He could have paid this guy the normal way, but no, he had to get cute.

And then, couple weeks ago, when this whole Outward Bound thing came up, he was feeling down. Powerless, really, so he decided, fuck it, he'd do something to feel good again. Went and looked at what he had in storage, found the urn, remembered that in addition to ashes, it had an encrypted flash drive in it. That was weird. Did a search on Melissa Ruby. Found a woman with an employment record at the Pentagon. No photos. No social media. No nothing. What did it all mean? Jack didn't care, but clearly someone was doing something with their identity that was not on the level. That seemed moderately valuable and kind of a cool mystery for him to figure out one day after he retired and didn't have real police work to do, Jack thinking maybe there'd be a future on TV, hosting his own cold-case show . . . Yeah . . . like in a cool car . . . a '74 Dodge Charger? Maybe.

Anyway.

That would be later.

He'd need to hire a personal trainer.

So.

Wrote a letter, in care of Barer & Harris, in the name of Melissa Ruby, the client in question.

Made a request.

Three hundred grand.

Cash.

Account in Gibraltar.

He wouldn't even have the money to spend right away, it was the point of it all, that hit of dopamine, and then he'd get out to Gibraltar in a few months if need be.

Took his blanket to the shore.

Headphones.

"Comfortably Numb."

Envelope.

Next day, sent Bobby C. on a road trip to Sacramento.

*Send.*

Stupid. Lazy. Never again.

Jack opened the interior walk-in, where he had Robert Green hung like meat, his body on one hook, his head on another. After fifteen years at subzero, he still looked pretty good, all things considered. Jack had taken off bits and pieces here and there over the years, no major parts, but today was going to require a bit of surgery. Which was fine. He was prepared. He had all the tools he'd need, had spent a lot of time with Lizzie DiGiangreco, the coroner, watching her work, asking the important questions. *Why are you cutting this way? Why are you cutting that way?* Lizzie surely chalking it up to professional curiosity over the years, even inviting Jack down to watch particularly challenging cases unfold. Which he'd done. Asked if he could try a Y incision, that sort of thing, Lizzie happy to say yes. Asked all the appropriate questions. Jack always knew a rainy day was going to come, and today he had the good sense to know it could very well pour.

Jack Biddle was not going to wait around for bad shit. In Iraq, he'd been what they called a meat eater, his jobs focused almost entirely on violence, and he'd been good at it. He was Jack Biddle! He was the man who single-handedly turned Losertown around! If he had to fuck someone up to keep that, well, he was more than capable of doing that.

He would control his situation.

It took him nearly twenty minutes to yank out six of Robert Green's teeth and then another half an hour to dig out a little bit of Robert's brain—about half an inch's worth—without getting too much bone or hair involved in the sample, since that would be something a decent ME would be able to recreate in terms of velocity and impact and all that *CSI* shit. He placed it all into a vacuum-sealed medical-grade cooler for easy transport.

Then, Jack cleaned up, went back upstairs, and called Seema Nitch, who wrote up all the local gossip in *The Granite Shores Daily News*. She wasn't America's finest journalist. In fact, she wasn't even Granite Shores' finest, was prone to exclamation points, but she was good people. They'd gone to high school together, and Jack had the vague memory of her maybe giving him a hand job in the back of her VW Cabriolet after a football game.

"How you doing, Chief?"

"Real good, real good," he said, though in fact he was digging Robert Green's flesh out from under his thumbnail using an old toothpick he found in his desk. "Listen, I've got something happening and I could use your help. You got five minutes?"

"For you? I've got seven."

"You're sweet," he said and then told her about how this fella Mitch Diamond—"like the gem, yep, and I'll text you a link to his biography from the website"—from Barer & Harris had come to town and was about to announce a significant development in the Robert Green case, and while he couldn't go into too many specifics, "and in fact, if you could use the old 'sources familiar with the case' line, that would be helpful," word was there was about to be a major reward announcement to be tied to the start of the festival.

"Oh wow," Seema said. "How do we feel about this?"

"We're 100 percent in support of Mr. Green's capture, of course, but are concerned about creating a carnival atmosphere."

"Other than the actual carnival, I guess?"

Fucking journalists. It didn't matter if they gave you a handy thirty-five years ago. They'd always try to get you with a gotcha.

"We can't have those unsavory elements brought to the town. If you want law enforcement to do its job, can't have a bunch of yahoos meddling in our business."

"So I understand, though," she said, "isn't this Seattle's business? Because that's where the crimes were committed?"

Jack said. "See what I'm saying? This all seems like a publicity stunt we don't need to even entertain here. We're proud of our role in figuring out the whole heist. Hell, I took a bullet because of it, but what we can't have is a bunch of yahoos showing up and acting like fools."

"Yeah, you said that about the yahoos, I get it," Seema said. "But not seeing the local gossip interest, Jack. This sounds more like city beat stuff. You want to talk to the new kid? Plotkin? He's very much on top of things. You've met him, yeah?"

Fuck no, he didn't want to talk to Plotkin. Fucker sniffed around shit like a feral dog. He was one of those guys who went by his last name, and for some reason always wore the same hat, a wool newsboy, like it was 1938. He might actually be the finest journalist in Granite Shores, as it happened.

"Here's the kicker," Jack said, opting to press ahead. "You'll never guess who this Diamond is shacking up with on this trip into town. I'm going to email you a couple pictures. Anonymous source, of course."

# CHAPTER TWENTY-EIGHT

*Monday*

Mitch Diamond said to Penny, "That bother you?"

They sat outside, sipping overly expensive coffee at a joint called Heisted. It was up the block from Mel's Comics—the giant mural of Robert staring at them—and what used to be the Sno-Cone Depot, but which now looked like a prison camp, Mitch telling her he had a hunch. This was after Mitch called Penny and told her to pack up all their shit and get out of their Airbnb immediately, to not speak while she did so, and to make no phone calls within a hundred feet of the property, then instructed her to get an Uber to drop her off at the marina, where he'd unironically managed to rent a houseboat.

Wasn't in slip 52, so that was good.

When Mitch showed up at the marina, he'd ditched his Cadillac. Instead, he was behind the wheel of a rented brown minivan for some reason, the kind with those cool automatic doors, and enough room to ferry an entire softball team to practice.

"What's this?" Penny asked when she got in.

"We're going on a field trip," Mitch said and proceeded to tell her about what he described as the weirdest fucking meeting of his life. "And it turned out Jack Biddle was familiar with my Cadillac."

And now here they were, in disguise. Which in this case meant they both had on old-school Losertown baseball caps—the giant L wrapped around a Douglas fir *was* a nice logo—that they picked up inside Heisted, as well as some kind of hipster BluBlocker sunglasses, the frames done up in sparkly gold and silver. Mitch also had a pair of birding binoculars on a chain around his neck. He kept picking them up and staring at different sites, like any good tourist would. Drinking Heisted coffee added to the appearance—Penny thinking no one would possibly drink this shit if they had a choice—but also Heisted used these gigantic mugs that blocked half your face when you drank.

Penny gave the mural a close look. Was that a person who would let his little sister rot in prison?

"Twenty minutes with a Wagner paint sprayer," Mitch said, "it never existed. I can have it gone tonight."

"That's sweet of you." It was nice to see his face. It was a very good mural. "Probably don't need you getting arrested for vandalism."

"I'd hire it out."

Right next to Mel's was a black box venue called the Evergreen Spot, which Penny recognized as the former location of Fitness4Moms, the yoga studio Addie operated. Last time Penny saw her cousin was at 3:00 a.m. on a Hulu true crime documentary program called *Justice, Stalled,* hosted by someone named Morgan Stalled, who Penny guessed won a reality show or was a Fox personality fired for being slightly competent. Addie was in her thirties and didn't look anything like how Penny recalled.

Gone was the goth affectation. She now looked like she'd robbed a Lululemon. Morgan Stalled interviewed her in full view of rows of exercise balls, nodding inappropriately while Addie spewed conspiracy theories about the case, including her belief that a local criminal syndicate led by shadowy members of the Granite Shores police force had likely murdered Robert. She'd been hitting that same drum since the day Penny got pinched.

Wasn't until Penny read through all the documents Mitch loaded onto the iPad, however, that she found out Addie had sued the city and settled out of court for some confidential six-figure sum and then started her true crime empire. Which didn't make sense to Penny. Not the true crime part. Addie was an opportunist. Penny couldn't blame her for that. Well, she *could,* she just didn't *now. Now* was likely to become *later.*

Rather: How do you defame someone who'd been involved in a crime? Or, at least, defame her in such a way that the city thought it was cheaper to write her a check versus fight her in court, even when the city had endless pockets and Addie had nothing.

As a person who'd spent plenty of time with people who filed baseless cases, in most instances to get out of their cell for a few hours, maybe get some better coffee while meeting with their lawyers, she understood why people with no choices filed cases. But Addie wasn't that. The Seattle DA knew all about her involvement. They got all the emails. And Penny admitted to everything, including how Addie was going to fence for them, theoretically. So why did the city of Granite Shores pay? Penny had copped to everything to keep Addie out of court. That was the deal. But in retrospect, Penny wondered what they would have done? Charged a teen for thinking about doing a crime?

"I need to see Addie," Penny said.

"Not a good idea."

"You think she remembers you?"

"She called me the 'mysterious person of interest' in season two of her show, so, yeah, I think so."

"You listened to the whole show?"

"I do a lot of driving," Mitch said.

Penny could hear the Pacific roaring, the air brisk and cool today. The boardwalk and pier stretched behind them. Penny heard the familiar sounds of summer floating over the breeze: the ringing bells, buzzers, and sirens coming from the games of chance, the clack of Skee-Ball, the shrieks of joy from the kids riding the Demon. If she closed her eyes, she could be eleven. It even smelled the same, like cotton candy, meat being deep-fried, and the sticky sweetness of tanning lotion.

Problem was, her eyes were wide open.

There was a billboard advertising the New Model Home Tour, **Where Life's a Beach!** Something called the Dunes at Granite Shores was depicted on an outcrop of land that hadn't previously existed. It was right up against the beach in a part of town that in the 1980s was the county dump, until people living nearby started getting weird cancers, so they moved all the people out, put up a fence, poured a bunch of dirt on top of the garbage, and waited. Now, the whole area had been reshaped by landfill, the development a good thirty feet above the beach, a slope of rolling dunes covering the distance.

Unbelievable.

Paradise built on trash.

City workers were putting up tents for the Green Days Festival, including something called the Green Food Experience. There was a fifteen-foot-tall banner advertising appearances by celebrity Food Network chefs, including that guy who drove around eating cholesterol bombs.

"Have you been to this before?" Penny asked.

Mitch followed her gaze. "Every year."

"Every year?"

"They have a look-alike contest," Mitch said. "Wanted to make sure Robert didn't sneak in and win."

Penny didn't know if he was joking. Maybe it didn't matter.

"What do they cook?" Penny asked.

"Last year it was all food from the South American port cities on your maps. Year before that, they recreated artisan versions of Granite Shores High School's cafeteria menu from Robert's senior year. The Taco Tuesday Experience was notable."

"You're kidding."

"I wish I was," Mitch said. "That thirty-minute meal lady? She did a whole thing on healthy food you might have cooked on the boat, if you'd made it off the shore. Since they knew what you had stored onboard."

"I don't cook."

"Yeah," Mitch said, "they didn't cover that."

"This is . . . sick," Penny said. "Who is making money from all this?"

"The city," Mitch said. "There's a resort bed tax, a short-term rental tax, a transient occupancy tax, plus all the basic tourism dollars. But the festival, that's a private/public partnership."

"What does that mean?"

"City provides some key services for free," Mitch said, "like the beaches, the streets, infrastructure, that sort of thing, and in exchange gets those tax dollars. Provide the funding for the police and public safety, allow the festival to use city parking, have the city workers erect the stages. And then the private funding pays for all the talent, takes in all the ticket money, the merch, everything with a price tag; that comes back to them. With of course the sales tax going to the city, also. Each year it gets bigger. We're talking millions in revenue, split a few ways."

"And who are these private people?"

"I'll give you a hint," Mitch said. He gave Penny the binoculars from around his neck. "Take a look at the stage at the far end of the street."

About five blocks away, workers were setting up the giant cooking demo stage, which was nicer than any home she'd ever lived in. Professional-grade appliances. Blond wood counters. Overhead mirrors. Lighting. Were those . . . walk-in refrigerators? They were. There was also a full A/V bay beneath the stage, since they'd be filming all this, naturally. Spread across the back of the stage, twenty-five feet tall, was a banner for Danny Vining's Sunshine Fudge.

"You have to be kidding." She gave him back the binoculars. "How is it that my brother and I supposedly pulled off the greatest heist in the world, and the only person who *didn't* get rich from it is me?"

"Ask your friend Jack Biddle and his lovely wife. They partnered with Mr. Fudge to seed it."

Penny knew that Jack Biddle got married to Caroline Frost. Their combined generational wealth could only seed a watermelon. They all lived within three blocks of each other in the foothills. Only family that had real cash were the Vinings. Fudge paid. Plus whatever dark shit they were involved in, even back then. "Where'd they get that cash?"

"Jack sued the marina for not having proper lighting on the night he got shot," Mitch said. "So there was that. Then if I had two guesses, one would be that he then invested it wisely."

"What would be your other guess?"

"He's crooked. Has been since the first day I met him."

Well. That was true. That was family tradition among the Biddles. If you had something vaguely illegal in your possession, they'd take it from you. That didn't mean they'd arrest you. Which is fine when you're fifteen. But as an adult you tend to realize that's neither protecting nor serving.

"When did you meet him?" Penny asked, thinking out loud more than anything else.

Mitch exhaled so deeply Penny was concerned he might begin to levitate. "Day after your brother went missing." He kept his eyes focused straight ahead. "That day I told you about."

The fuck?

"With Addie?"

"Once without her, once with her." Mitch scratched at something on his neck. Which is when Penny noticed for the first time that he had a faded scar beneath his Adam's apple. Like someone had tried to slit his throat and failed at some point. "Now understand," he said, "I was a different person then—I mean that in about five ways," then told her about their meeting on the mountain and then outside the building, with Addie.

When he was done, Penny said, "I have a feeling *he* remembers."

"One day in a long life," Mitch said. "You remember everyone you met with when you were high?"

Penny said, "Pretty big day."

"Next time I saw him," Mitch said, "was when he became chief. Maybe seven, eight years later? He's never once given me even a glimmer of recognition."

She was attempting to process all of this. "And you never saw Addie again?"

"I kept track of her. It's a thing I do. But we never spoke again. I wanted to make sure she didn't get tossed up in something out here. She was a good kid. Mostly." This made Penny laugh. "Jack Biddle spent a lot of time fucking with her. Why she stayed out here, I don't know."

Penny did.

"Would you hire a person who helped a famous heist at, I don't know, Nordstrom?"

"She was a kid."

"So were you," Penny said, "when you started doing whatever ended up with you getting that scar on your neck, I bet." Mitch touched his throat absently, Penny certain he wasn't even aware he was doing it. "Here, she had a shot, at least. She's a celebrity. Whatever that's worth."

"Meeting with her," Mitch said, "is going to rip open a scab. You sure you want to do that?"

"I need to try."

"I'll wait in the car."

A thought came to Penny then. "You were tracking me, too?"

"Could be."

"How long did you wait to show up?"

"Didn't have a reason until the firm made this decision."

"If Rodney Golubev came to collect," Penny said. "What then?"

"He wouldn't have made it within a hundred miles of that bar."

"Why?"

Mitch turned and faced her. "You didn't deserve what happened to you." He touched his neck again. "This here? I was seventeen. Easter Sunday. My stepfather didn't like the marinade my mother used on the flank steak. Or me telling him to fuck himself, he should be happy she cooked for his dumb ass. Came at me with the electric carving knife, still plugged in, which is what saved me. Came out of the wall before he could find a good artery."

"That's good luck," Penny said. "You could probably get some minor plastic surgery. You'd never have to see that scar again."

"I hold on to good luck."

A truck hauling a sailboat turned onto the block, two motorcycle cops in front of it, two behind. When it rounded the corner, Penny saw the name on the back: the *Pere-a-Dice*.

"Oh shit," Penny said. "That's my boat!"

"Yeah," Mitch said. "For twenty-five bucks you can take a tour of it starting on Wednesday. They'll have it in the marina." Something caught Mitch's eye. He lifted the binoculars. "Here we go," he said. The twelve-foot-high gate of the old Sno-Cone Depot slid open. "Take a memo."

"I don't know stenography," she said. "How about I record you on my phone."

Mitch gave Penny a quick glance. Was that a . . . smile?

A tricked-out Tahoe pulled through the gate. Jack Biddle got out of the truck. What was happening?

Penny scrunched down in her seat. "Shit, he'll see us."

"He won't," Mitch said. "His situational awareness is for shit, and he's too vain to wear glasses."

"You knew he'd be here?"

"I followed him before I came and got you." He leaned forward. "And these binoculars. Hit *Record*."

Jack Biddle went to the keypad door lock on the front of the gate. Punched in numbers.

Mitch said, calmly, no rush: "And write these numbers down, too: 8, 7, 2, 8, 4, 7, 2, 4, 3, 3, 5, 3, 9, 1, 7, 2, 0, 0, 9."

Jack got back into his ride, screeched out of the driveway, going way too fast into traffic.

Penny wrote the numbers on a napkin, handed it to him. A nineteen-number code. That was a good level of encryption, unless someone saw you punch it in. Mitch read the numbers in silence. "Play me the recording," he said. Matched it to the numbers. The same. Shook his head once. Tore the napkin into little pieces, dropped them in his coffee cup. Took the phone, deleted the recording.

"You don't need that?" Penny asked.

"No," Mitch said. "I'll remember it."

"Are you also the Zodiac?"

"That lock, it's a Magus 1160. German lock. Costs a fortune. We use a version on the safe-deposit boxes at Barer & Harris now. There's a code in and a code out. Nineteen numbers. If you screw up either one, there's a second interior lock that requires a key, and then you have to reset everything. No second tries."

"Smart," Penny said.

"Yeah," Mitch said, "you should get paid for that, too. Don't know a firm that doesn't use it on its private boxes." A real smile crept across Mitch Diamond's face, Penny thinking she saw something new in this man she couldn't figure out: grudging admiration. "That code. It's his son's name and birthday, alphanumerically, like on a phone."

"You're sure?"

"Yeah," Mitch said. "It's the kind of code you use if you don't expect anyone is watching you, or if someone is, they don't know you."

"And you just happen to know his son's name and birthdate?"

"I know everything about him, Penny." Mitch dumped his coffee cup, secret code and all, into a garbage can. "Soon as he did the birthday at the end, I saw it." A Granite Shores Police cruiser came screaming down the street, lights flashing, which was some PTSD Penny did not need, but Mitch, he stared right at the driver, a woman, which was weird, Penny not sure she ever saw a woman on the force back in the day.

Mitch stood there on the corner, watching, waiting. Not averting anything.

When the cruiser disappeared, he said, "You ever seen where your brother slipped into lore?"

# CHAPTER TWENTY-NINE

*Monday*

Jack was nearly home, cruising slow along Dune Shores Parkway, the new fancy maple-shaded road leading to his gated community, feeling pretty good about his moves, liking the idea of the Russian mob killing Robert Green. That made things really current. Kept the story fresh. Not that Rodney Golubev was an actual member of the Russian mob. He happened to be of Russian descent and a criminal, had done pretty well with semilegit businesses, too, and when he and his brother operated in Granite Shores was always really good about donating to the Little League and Pop Warner fundraisers, even helped out with the Surfrider Foundation coastal trash pickup, but yeah, they were also basically scumbags, so whatever. Semilegit meant criminal.

He'd crush the Russian mob in small-town America! If Caroline was serious about this baby thing . . . *Jesus fuck if that was true* . . . that would be the perfect way to continue making money on this whole deal, without an ounce of worry. There was the memoir idea. He liked that. But if he really crushed the Russian mob, could be Jack Biddle would be in the congressional conversation. Which, under the right administration, might lead him to the top job at the FBI.

Did you need a college degree for that?

And if he could implicate Bobby C. . . . while also eliminating Bobby C. . . . well. He might get away with this without needing to kill Mitch Diamond.

In fact, now that he had what he needed in the cooler, maybe he should get rid of Robert's body? A plan started to lock into place, Jack popping a couple Oxy, thinking maybe he'd call Danny up, let him know he was cool, he was on this shit, it was handled . . . when a cruiser pulled behind him and lit him up.

*The fuck?* This was the problem with driving his own Tahoe versus the company car. Had he rolled through the last stop sign? Or maybe it was the fact that his windows were tinted so black he could pass for a cartel shooter. That was probably it, Jack thinking whoever this was behind the wheel was about to feel some healthy embarrassment, but that was okay. No one was above the law. Theoretically.

Jack pulled to the side of the road, under a canopy of maple trees they'd yanked up from Patterson Gulch and replanted over here, and waited for the cop to run his plate, realize they'd fucked the chicken but good, and move it on. He shook another Oxy and an Altoid into his mouth and chewed them up so he could really enjoy this. A few seconds later, there was a tap on his passenger side window, which was not protocol off the highway, and it was with the nightstick, which could have busted out his fucking window! He was going to talk to whoever was training the newbies, since it was only newbies they had doing traffic bullshit.

Jack took down the passenger window. Standing there was an officer he was not sure he knew. Well. He knew her. He saw her at the office. But they had sixty police officers now on the force, plus meter maids and community police volunteers and 911 operators and detectives and search-and-rescue and SWAT, Granite Shores a real town now, couldn't throw a big-ass festival and not have a team in place in case there was a terrorist attack or active shooter or some shit. Not on Jack's watch. So Jack didn't get the chance to know them all personally, like back in the day, when he was one of twenty.

This one. Her name was Betty. No. Betsy? Beth? It was something in that family. She was maybe twenty-five? Tall, broad shouldered, like an Olympic swimmer. And then he started to remember her, from when she was a kid? She'd been a lifeguard! That's right. Worked up at that beach they closed because there was some worry it was giving people cancer on account of some waste dump that was landfilled above it. She got to be locally famous for a couple days after she saved some kids who got caught in the undertow. Might have been her own brother. Jack couldn't remember. Maybe one of them died and she saved the others? Jack may have given her a medal. Yes. It was all lining up. She was probably pulling him over to thank him.

"Help you, Officer?" Jack said. He opened up his glove box, took out his registration and insurance, had it in his hand, waiting.

Betty/Betsy/Beth took off her sunglasses, leaned on the window frame. "Mr. Vining said you needed some help," she said.

"Mr. Vining?" Jack didn't understand what was happening. Had Danny called 911 on him? Did he think Jack was on drugs? He was, but he didn't know if Danny knew. Shit. What was happening?

"Danny?"

"Right. Danny."

Betty/Betsy/Beth looked up and down the street. Did she roll her eyes? Jack was not sure what he was seeing here. Was this even happening? She faced Jack again. "About the letter, Chief. I'm at your service. Ready to work."

"You?"

"Don't be so surprised," she said. "You work for him, too."

"Right," Jack said. "That's more like a business arrangement. Old friends. You understand."

"I don't, no," she said.

"How long have you been . . ." Jack stopped himself. What was the right term?

"Cleaning up your messes? About three years."

"My messes?"

"Chief," she said, "no disrespect beyond what I feel for you professionally, but there's a reason Mr. Vining hired me."

Jack stared at Betty/Betsy/Beth. She hadn't been a cop for three years, had she? "I'm sorry," he said, "when did I hire you?"

"Eighteen months ago."

Jack felt like someone had picked him up by his feet and was dangling him over Patterson Gulch. "Danny had you go through the Academy?"

"One hundred percent," she said. "He called it the 'Sunshine Fudge Law Enforcement Scholarship.'"

"Funny."

"He thought so." She looked at her watch. "My shift is over. You want, I can follow you back to the snow cone place and we can talk."

"You followed me *from* the Sno-Cone Depot?"

"Chief," she said, "I lit you up ten minutes ago. I don't know what you were doing."

What was he doing? And who was this woman? He was pretty sure her name was Beth. Her name tag said Officer Frane. No help. He gave her a long look. This was the replacement for Bobby C. in Danny's life?

"You're Danny's muscle?"

"You ever do MMA?"

"I was in the United States Army," Jack said, feeling good now, yeah, feeling it. "The original ultimate fighting."

"I was 16–1 fighting regional MMA," she said. "Could have gone national. Been on TV. Probably have a billion-dollar OnlyFans."

"What happened?"

"The allure of law enforcement." She cut her eyes to Jack's open glove box, where he had a one-hitter and his Altoids tin. Didn't say anything. Smart. Danny must have made her throw a fight. *Wonder what that was worth these days.*

"Right," Jack said. "Right." He gathered up his thoughts in a tight ball in his head, tried to focus. The Sno-Cone Depot would make good sense if there wasn't a dead fucking body hanging in the basement. If they were going to talk, it needed to be somewhere private. Or very public. "Sno-Cone Depot is no good. Best for you not to show up on the cameras there. Might make my wife nervous." What was he saying? Jesus. He had to get it together.

"Chief, we're not even on the same playing field."

"I didn't mean that in the way it came out." Shit. Everything was jumbled again. "I don't think you should show up on any cameras. Mine or anyone's."

Betty/Betsy/Beth said, "You on some cold medicine or something?"

"I've got postnasal drip."

Betty/Betsy/Beth said, "Respectfully, Chief? You look assed out."

Jack said, "That's what you call respectful?"

"I didn't say you look dope sick. But that's what I meant. So yes. Respectfully." She surveyed the block again. Took a deep breath. "Okay," she said, "I'm going to be real direct with you, Chief, because I think you've earned it. I know what you are. I find you pitiful. I don't respect you at all. How you got into this position and are in Mr. Vining's pocket makes me sick. It's where I'm headed, and that makes me want to throw up, to think I might not get the gumption and grit to fill up my tank and head east. Become a park ranger in Colorado. Maybe get a job running a police station at a small liberal arts college. These are my dreams, Chief, and in one way they're attainable: doing this shit right here, with you." She reached into the cab and slammed closed his glove box. "Lock this. Never open it in front of an LEO again. Riding dirty, for fuck's sake, Chief. And don't pull that bullshit with a touring country band again. You don't know what I had to go through to keep that under wraps."

Jack said, "Didn't I give you a medal?"

"Yeah," she said. "You were high then, too."

"Who did you save?"

"Kids. My cousins."

"But you let someone die, didn't you?"

"I didn't let them die. They died. Also my cousin, but an adult."

There it was. Now he recalled. That's probably why they gave her the medal. Help her feel better. "That must haunt you," Jack said. "Letting the person you knew longer die. That would be hard. It was me, let those kids go. Rest of their life they've probably suffered all that grief. Basically, you let a part of all of them die."

"Again. There is no *let*. Jesus." She sniffed. "You smell like a corpse." She peered into the back seat. "What's that in the cooler?"

Beth.

Her name was Beth.

He remembered because after he gave her that medal—and he was high as fuck that day, he remembered that—he sat in his Tahoe and listened to the old KISS song like ten times.

"Evidence," Jack said.

"What kind of evidence do you keep in your snow cone place? Mostly DNA?"

Jack said, "How long have you been following me?" Had she said . . . three years?

"You're sloppy," Beth said. "Mr. Vining doesn't want to worry all the time. You understand." She pointed at the ice pack Jack was sitting on. "You should get that checked out. Could be cancer. Amount of time you've spent sitting on ice packs, could be you're stage four at this point. Take the finger up the wazoo, Chief, it's worth it."

Jack said, "I think I'm good. With everything. I don't need your help."

"Yes, you do. Did you notice the surveillance van watching you today?"

"What?"

"Yeah. It was a rental. Picked you up on Beach, followed you to the Sno-Cone Depot. I was already watching you, so picking them up wasn't too hard. Didn't get a good look at the driver, but they weren't trying to hide. Rented the van using a corporate credit card. Barer & Harris. Law firm up in Seattle? You familiar?"

"Yeah," Jack said, "I'm familiar."

"Danny thinks maybe there's someone that needs to be taken care of, quick like a bunny." When Jack didn't respond right away, she said, "Name rhymes with *Bobby C.*"

"Keep your voice down," Jack said. "You don't know who's listening."

"If someone was listening," Beth said, "wouldn't that be you? So let's get to it." She patted the roof of the Tahoe. "I'll meet you in fifteen at that little spot where you like to get high and do your mail. Sound good?"

Jack managed to make it all the way home before he threw up.

# CHAPTER THIRTY

*Klamath Falls, Oregon*
*Monday*

Rodney Golubev sat in an interrogation room at the Klamath Falls police station, listening while his lawyer, Leonard Lawrence, from the esteemed firm of Barer & Harris in Seattle, informed Detective Haskell via speakerphone why Rodney would not be speaking to him. Even if he was under arrest, he wouldn't be speaking to him. Even if everyone else on the planet died via a humanity-killing asteroid, Rodney would remain silent.

"My client spends maybe one day a month in your city," Leonard said. "Half of the staff of that facility has a prison record, as Mr. Golubev is dedicated to helping those freshly released from prison gain some dignity through work again. Which, as you might imagine, means there are plenty of employees there who have lengthy records, which my client absolutely does not. Are you even certain that was a human foot you found?"

"Bigfoot is normally found further north."

"Detective," Leonard said, "these are the relevant questions we need to ask. Nevertheless, the Purple Flamingo's bathroom is available to any number of disreputable people. Mr. Golubev is a man of substance. Keeping him any longer is a violation of his civil rights. If you would like to set up a formal interview, we may put it on the schedule for early July."

"Yeah, we'll give you a call," Detective Haskell said, then clicked off the phone. "You're free to go," he said. "If you intend to flee the country, I'd advise against it."

Rodney said, "Where would I go?"

"Your motherland?"

"There is a war," Rodney said. "Maybe you have heard?"

Detective Haskell stood up. "You should have talked when you had the chance. We're going to get DNA on that foot, and then you're going to have a problem. Might be a few weeks. Might be a few months. But we're going to get it, and you'll be back here in an orange jumpsuit."

By the time Rodney pulled out of the police station onto Shasta Way—the safe in his back seat, including Dale's thumb, which was going to require a solid plan—it was already rush hour. Which in Klamath Falls meant there were four or five other cars on the road. Stopped at lights. People looking at you.

Which was fine.

Rodney was just another man in Klamath Falls driving an Outback, which made him less concerned about the fucking thumb.

Then his phone started blowing up with Google alerts. He turned down Washburn and into the parking lot of Los Potrillos, the only Mexican place in the city with anything approaching decent food, and parked. Read the notifications. He had three of them. One for his brother's name. One for his name. One for Penny Green. Tried to make sense of what he was seeing.

>@GShoresNews Look who is visiting for Green Days! Penny Green! (And sources tell us that strapping buck is Mitch Diamond from @BarerHarris)

Penny Green was in Granite Shores?

And...

She was with Mitch Diamond. Okay. Who was that? Why did he know that name?

And then he pulled up the photo.

"Motherfuck," Rodney said. There he was.

Wait. He reread the tweet. Mitch Diamond worked at Barer & Harris?

He pulled up their website. No photo. Just the bio of someone who sounded like a character from a Liam Neeson movie.

He pulled up the photo on Twitter again.

That was him all right.

Older.

Maybe a little meaner-looking now.

Nice shoes.

Nice watch.

"Motherfuck," Rodney said again.

He called his wife, Svetlana. That wasn't her real name, that was his pet name for her. She was wife #2. He called wife #1 Svetlana, too. Kept things from becoming confusing.

He told Svetlana he had to drive up the coast. That he had some business to take care of in Granite Shores. Svetlana said, "Oh it's Green Days! I saw it on the news. Bring back some Sunshine Fudge."

"Yes, I will do that, absolutely," Rodney said and hung up.

He'd be bringing something home in a box, that was for sure.

# CHAPTER THIRTY-ONE

*Monday*

The peak of Yeach Mountain reached over ten thousand feet above sea level. Just short of two miles. In the summer, the mountain was a lush canvas of green and gold, the contours of its landscape easy to see with the naked eye. Unlike the western side of the mountain, where Granite Shores stretched up the foothills, and new housing developments and resorts were already being planned on recently denuded plateaus and valleys, the eastern side was largely protected land until you reached the flatlands on the other side of Patterson Gulch and Leigh Creek. Leigh Creek was a popular—if moderately illegal—camping and fishing spot during the summer. In the fall and winter, however, it swelled into a dangerous river, Penny telling Mitch about all the kids and teens who vanished into it over her childhood. She rattled off a series of names. Alexander Birnbaum. Diana Malkin. Gwendolyn Faust. Twin sisters Minnie and Scout Cocker. A few washed up, a few never did.

"Where'd they go?" Mitch asked.

"Either the ghost of Yeach Patterson ate them," Penny said, "or bears and coyotes did. Cougars. Gray wolves. A whole host of predators out there."

It was the early evening now, and the sun was finally disappearing behind the mountain. Summer on the Oregon coast, the nights didn't get truly dark until almost nine, but on the east side of the mountain, everything descended into shadow long before that. Penny explained to Mitch that was how businesses in Granite Shores used to be able to sustain life during the long winter months when tourism came to a trickle. Those few extra hours of light, every night for an entire summer, made all the difference on the profit margins for mom-and-pop places.

That didn't seem to matter now. Mom and Pop were long gone, Mitch thinking, unless your mom was named West and your dad was named Elm.

"So you're talking about a place like the Sno-Cone Depot?" Mitch said.

"That place was strictly seasonal," Penny said. She told him how the Biddles owned that place for a hundred years. During the off-season, it was where kids met up to get high before going somewhere else to get high, the TREAT YOURSELF AND TREAT YOUR KIDDIES! sign a beacon to stoners. "Soon as spring hit," she continued, "there was a line of tourists starting on Friday, and then the locals would bring their Little League teams and cheerleading squads over Monday through Thursday. Nighttime, if you knew the secret password, Old Man Biddle would make you a frozen daiquiri."

Mitch wondered why Jack Biddle was holding on to the land the Sno-Cone Depot sat on. And why he had it secured like the White House. Jack bought and sold so much land in that town that the Sno-Cone Depot wasn't now a Tesla dealership was frankly shocking.

"You ever get the password?" Mitch asked.

"Yeah," Penny said. "You handed Jack's father five dollars, he gave you a daiquiri. Passed that on to his shithead son."

"When did it close?" Mitch asked.

"I was going to ask you that."

"Far as I know," Mitch said, "it's never been open. Not since I've been coming to town."

"Maybe Jack's near-death experience made him not want to sling frozen desserts anymore," Penny said.

"Wouldn't he be more likely to quit being a cop?"

"You don't know Jack Biddle," Penny said. "Only authority he ever got was from that badge and gun."

They'd descended to the bottom of the mountain and then turned around, so they could climb up and park at a new "scenic turnout" midway up the east side of the mountain. For the next fifteen minutes they watched the last of the traffic roll by, a summer day before the Green Days filled the mountain road with revelers. Fifteen years ago, the road alternated between two and three lanes all the way up and down the mountain, one side Patterson Gulch, the other side the granite face of the mountain. Now, after years of road construction and dynamiting, it was four solid, well-paved lanes, two in each direction, with a center divider and retaining walls on both sides. There were even lights, "selfie stations," and decent signage celebrating Yeach's indigenous history and, of course, its dark cannibal past, though that had largely been debunked in recent years when archaeologists found graves of the Patterson family, none of whom looked to have been cooked and eaten.

It was only about a quarter of a mile, as the crow flew, from the turnout to the grade sign, but Mitch and Penny weren't crows, so once the traffic petered out, they took the van up the mountain and parked on the side of the road, Mitch cracking road flares around the van. Mitch had driven up and down this mountain countless times over the years, and whenever he saw the sign **Very Steep Climb Ahead 14% Grade**, he always slowed and looked for cash flying around.

No such luck.

But he'd never gotten out of his car again, because he didn't want to get run over.

That bit where he nearly slid down the mountain was enough to keep him behind the wheel, until this moment.

Hence the flares.

A strong, cool, circling breeze blew up from the canyon below. It was a warm day in Granite Shores. Up the mountain, in the shadows, it was a good 25 degrees cooler.

"Okay," Mitch said when they got out. "Look around. What do you see?"

"Nothing."

"Look on the side of the road." Penny did. All that was there was dirt and gravel and maple leaves and evergreen needles . . . and one silver gum wrapper, which Penny pocketed.

Other than that, nothing.

Mitch fished the lucky cash out of his wallet, showed it to Penny. "The day after your brother disappeared, I found this cash. Flew into my window. Right here."

"A hundred and twenty dollars?"

"I also found a wedding photo from the 1950s and a business envelope. Those I found on the ground. Other side of where that retaining wall is now."

"How do you know it was from the 1950s?"

"It was in black and white," Mitch said. "And *1953* was stamped on the white border."

"You have those in your wallet, too?"

"I gave them to Jack Biddle, and he tore them into little pieces, dumped them on the floor of his truck."

"When?"

"That night. Right here."

"In front of you?" Like an accusation.

Mitch said, "I wasn't in a place where engaging with the police was my normal behavior. If he'd looked at my ID, I probably would have shot him."

"What about today?"

"Well," Mitch said, "situation comes up, we'll find out."

Penny said, "I have a feeling you're going to get that chance."

A Ford Explorer came roaring up the mountain, so Mitch put an arm around Penny, stepped her back against the low retaining wall. Dry leaves kicked up in the SUV's wake. Mitch caught one in the air.

"Good reflexes," Penny said.

Mitch crumpled the leaf in his hand. He showed her the dried pieces stuck to his skin. "What do you see?"

"I thought it was a metaphor."

"No," Mitch said, "object lesson. This leaf has been out here for a day or two, and it's turned to nothing." He wiped his hand on his jeans, then handed her the cash. "This money? It's fairly pristine for how old it is, because it's been folded inside my wallet for fifteen years. Which is not much different from how it looked when I found it, except it was damp from the rain. That one bill had a tear in it, but the others were perfect. And they were all relatively new at the time. Look at the dates."

She took out her phone, turned on the flashlight, shined it through the cash.

"What are you doing?"

"Looking for a secret message from my brother in disappearing ink." She handed the money back to him, Mitch thinking she must think he was a little nuts. Which was fine. He was a little nuts. "You ever look up these serial numbers? See if they were stolen?"

"That's not a real thing," Mitch said.

"What do you mean?"

"Unless the money is being compiled for a ransom. You rob a bank, you can go spend that cash at 7-Eleven on your way out of town, safely. Get blue Slurpees for the entire crew and a carton of Marlboro Reds for the wheelman."

"That's oddly specific."

Mitch shrugged. "Once you know something, you know something."

Penny took a few steps out into the road. Peered up and down the grade. Looked up at the face of Yeach. Across into Patterson Gulch. A curious look crossed her face. "Has that sign always been here?" she asked.

"That or something like it," Mitch said.

"Last time Robby and I spoke," she said, "he said he was coming up on the grade. Might have been his final words, it's hard to remember now."

She walked up to the sign. "This might have been the last thing he saw. I mean, in the dark, how would you know that the grade was about to start?" Pushed on it. Didn't move. "Solid." She stepped over the retaining wall. "Hold on to me," she said, putting her arms behind her. Mitch took one of her hands. "Both hands. Come on. Don't be shy. We're all we've got up here. Hold tight. I'm going flying." She took another couple of tiny steps and was on the edge of the world, looking down. "When we were planning this whole thing, Robby said something that stuck with me." She took another step. Lifted one leg behind her, tipped forward. Mitch could feel her grip slacken. "He said there's only one way into this life," Penny said. She looked over her shoulder at Mitch. The breeze whipped her hair. "And one way out." She let go of Mitch completely then, but it didn't matter, he had her in his grip. She hung there like that, swaying, her eyes closed.

Mitch didn't know what she was doing, not exactly, but when she grasped him again and stepped back onto both feet, he could see tears on her cheeks.

"Are you all right?" Mitch said.

"I wanted to see what it would feel like to sail over the edge."

"How was it?"

"Peaceful." She wiped her cheek, looked at her hand, like she half expected to see blood. "I don't feel him. Robert. I don't think he's still here."

"It's been a long time, Penny. They did eventually send dogs down by the creek, in case he was hiding in the woods. But they came up empty."

"After Harvard, camping to Robby was a Radisson without room service," Penny said. "And I don't mean *here* here. I mean, in this world. This . . . terrestrial plane." She looked up into the stars, Mitch thinking maybe she was trying to call the aliens in, right now, to get her, to get them both. "If he was right here, that night, seconds after we talked, he wouldn't leave me. He'd never turn around. That wasn't his nature. If he was climbing this mountain, in that weather, he was coming for us, Mitch. Not for me. Not for him. *For us.* He knew there was only one way into Granite Shores and one way out: going up and down this goddamn mountain in a torrential storm. He could have turned around. He could have spent the night in Brawton. What would it matter? No one was looking for him. He could have told me right then, but he didn't. He said he'd see me soon."

Mitch said, "So what happened?"

She sat down on the retaining wall. Mitch sat down beside her. They didn't speak for a long time.

"We got away with it," Penny said eventually. "We did the thing everyone wants to do. We got away with it. He wouldn't then punish me for our success. He spent his entire life trying to protect me. That didn't suddenly change because he had money. You didn't know my brother. You didn't know the people we grew up with. The two of us were all we had. One way in, one way out. That was our entire *lives*."

"Technically," Mitch said, "there were two ways out."

"What?"

"The water," Mitch said. "How you were literally getting out. There was a second way. He'd planned it."

Penny perked up. "Say that again."

"Your brother figured out a second way out. Where you really couldn't be caught. Not easily, anyway. Even if Barer & Harris realized what happened on Monday, you'd have three days on them. You'd be on the high seas and out of reach. The clients who got robbed of cash, they weren't going to go on the record. Same with the ones with nefarious shit. The only people who would speak publicly would be the clients who lost things that might have sentimental value, but Robert must have known the Navy wasn't going to be marshaled to go after missing photo albums. This crime that you did, it's only famous because of what's been leaked. And what's been leaked has often come from Robert." *Or me.* "The only person with anything to lose for some reason has kept the authorities engaged. He found a second way out and then spent the next fifteen years trying to make sure people kept looking for him."

Penny said, "See, it doesn't make sense." She stood up. Started to pace. Moving her hands, like she was working out an equation. "I wish I had a whiteboard," she muttered. "Have to improvise." She took her phone back out. Started typing with both of her thumbs and talking at the same time. "Do you know the principle of sufficient reason?"

"Is that a Rush cover band?"

"No," Penny said. "Parmenides came up with it." She kept typing.

"I don't know him. He also do time with Kiko?"

"Pre-Socratic Greek philosopher. I got into him one term when I was supposed to be learning quantum physics at MIT. I found myself asking why we didn't have more evidence of what came *before* the universe. The universe is what we call a brute fact. It just *is*. Yeah, there is the notion of the Big Bang. We have that, but . . . what made the superheated singularity that created the big bang?" Penny was pacing now. "There's no evidence of God. That's faith. Belief. Unprovable. Parmenides came up with the principle that everything must have a reason, cause, or ground." She stopped typing, turned her phone around:

For every x, there is a y such that y is the sufficient reason for x (formally: $\forall x \, \exists y \, Ryx$ [where "Ryx" denotes the binary relation of providing a sufficient reason])

"Get it?" she asked.

"Not remotely."

"For every fact, there must be a reason why. An explanation. Nothing is true by chance. So short of the creation of the universe, there must be . . . something. So the money you found. What's the sufficient reason it blew into your window?"

Mitch didn't know if that was possible. "Other than luck."

"Yes," Penny said. "That's the thing. Luck doesn't exist in this world I'm presenting to you. It's only facts you can source."

"You mean," Mitch said, "the fact that the day before I found $120 in cash, plus an old photo and an envelope on a frozen mountain road, a van filled with cash and personal and business mementos was, theoretically, precisely where I was?"

"Right. How does that happen?"

"Maybe Robert's got his windows open. Money and a couple pictures fly out."

"Pouring rain. Freezing cold. Gale force winds. Why is his window down?"

Mitch thought about that. "He smoke?"

"Not even salmon," Penny said.

"He gets pulled over," Mitch said. "Shows the cop his ID through the window, something flies out."

"There'd be a record. Cop would have called it in. And then, where is the van? Where is Robert, and where is the cop?"

"Maybe they get into a fight."

"Robert never hit anyone in his life. He was a pacifist. He wanted to become a lawyer to protect people. Which is silly, in retrospect." She paused. "And still, where is the van, and where is Robert, and where is the cop?"

Mitch looked over his shoulder, into Patterson Gulch. "These retaining walls weren't here then."

"When I was a kid," Penny said, "they called this Blood Highway."

"Charming," Mitch said. "Guess you don't eventually put up a retaining wall and expand the roads unless people are going off the side. Which sounds like sufficient reason."

Penny stood next to the grade sign. Pushed on it again. Then rubbed her thumb across it, leaving a long smear in the dust and dirt. Was that . . . a smirk? Was Penny Green . . . smirking? "All the DNA you've collected over the years," Penny said. "What was it?"

"What do you mean?"

"Was it fluid? Or hair or what?"

"Everything." But then Mitch thought about it. "Well, no. I mean, it used to be everything. We haven't recovered saliva in a long time."

"How long?"

"A decade? Maybe more. I'd have to look it up. It's usually hair. Or skin."

"Fingerprints?"

"Rarely."

"How rare?" Penny asked.

"A piece of mail, it's handled by a lot of hands, so we find prints, but not Robert's in a usable way. We've found consistent glove prints. Your brother has a preference for blue medical nitrile gloves."

"Why would he wear gloves?"

Mitch almost said, *So he wouldn't leave fingerprints* . . . but was able to stop himself just in time.

"Say it," Penny said. "If you keep it in your mouth, it will cause moral decay."

"So he wouldn't leave fingerprints," Mitch said, to make her happy.

"This is a man with a mural of himself flipping off the cameras that would, if he gave a shit, indict him. But Robert's not being careful. He wants you to know it's him. So why aren't you finding saliva and fingerprints on everything? Why would he wear gloves but not give a shit about leaving hair? Evidentiary facts only, Mitch, backed up by sufficient reason. Give it to me. What's the answer?"

Mitch needed to work through a few things.

Mitch needed to tell Penny about the windshield glass that was found in the last hair and skin sample they received.

Mitch needed to tell Penny that Robert was trying to blackmail a person he didn't realize was Mitch.

And a few other things.

Instead, he said, "His sister owed a bunch of Russians money, so they cut off his hands."

"Sufficient reason," Penny said, "unlikely result. And still no reason to wear gloves. Did anyone else's fingerprints or DNA show up that got pinged?"

"Well, yeah," Mitch said. "The mailroom clerks at Barer & Harris, for the ones that came to us directly. And we cleared those people. Made sure they weren't somehow in on it, too. And then the letters that were sent to Jack Biddle at the station. His material has been all over those."

"And the pollen? Where are those dunes?"

Mitch said, "His house sits on top of them."

Penny said, "Do you hear yourself?"

# CHAPTER THIRTY-TWO

*Monday*

Jack Biddle had wanted Bobby C. dead since at least the end of eighth grade.

That was when Bobby filled his locker with dogshit. Back when he was still Bobby Calhoun Jr. Back when they used to be the best of friends.

They'd gone to Granite Rock Elementary, used to catch the bus together in the morning, even, and then they'd play kickball together at recess. Bobby was a slow-baby-bouncy guy, and Jack knew how to deliver that to him in his sweet spot. They got to junior high at Foothill Middle, and for that first year, everything was cool, Jack and Bobby a little behind some of the other boys, physically, neither of them hitting their growth spurt yet, neither of them really functional around girls yet, though Jack already had it pretty bad for Caroline Frost, so they kept to each other. Read *Dune* and played D&D and collected baseball cards, walked Bobby's Great Dane, Lucy, stole candy from Sprouse Reitz, all that normal shit.

Teachers back then even liked having Jack and Bobby in class. Their homeroom teacher, Mrs. Wheaton, affectionately called them Kirk and Spock, Jack remembering how Mrs. Wheaton brought that up when he pulled her old ass over for a DUI twenty-five years later. She was coming out of the parking lot at Lolly's Diner—Jack could see Lolly's neon sign glowing in the foothills down below at this very moment, even from up here on the Granite Darklands or Granite Trashlands or Granite Highlands, whatever Caroline was calling it now—loaded on afternoon wine spritzers. When she saw Jack in her window, she said, "Either I'm drunk or you're Mr. Spock." He could have given her a warning, but Jack Biddle wasn't a warning kind of guy, not when he was working traffic, like he did for the first several years he was on the force. But he did her a solid and didn't show up to court.

Over the summer between seventh and eighth grade, Jack stayed in Granite Shores and worked at the Sno-Cone Depot with his dad and cousins, and Bobby went to some Bible camp off the Snake River outside of Walla Walla. Three months later, Bobby returned to Granite Shores close to six feet tall, had a wisp of hair on his top lip, aggressive acne, and had on a black AC/DC T-shirt, torn jeans, and low-top black Chuck Taylors. For the next year, he wore that uniform every day, sometimes adding a wool-lined denim jacket, or subbing in a Black Sabbath T-shirt. Jack was a full dungeon master now, and Bobby looked like he had a wife, two kids, a Dodge Charger, a job at the paper mill, and a warrant for possession. Bible camp also seemed to have fucked Bobby up in a more elemental way: he kept carving pentagrams into his forearm using whatever he had handy. A compass. An old pencil. His sharpened thumbnail.

They went from being best friends to nodding at each other in the halls to Bobby calling him a pussy whenever he walked by to, finally, Bobby getting his combination and dumping what had to be three bags of Lucy's shit in his locker. Lucy was a sweet old girl, but that dog took dumps like a fifty-year-old man with IBS.

To this day, Jack could see it all happening, as if he was above his body: Jack walking up to his locker, Bobby and his crew of stoners lined up against the wall behind him, watching, Jack wondering what was up, but whatever, he had to get to pre-algebra, opening his locker and a cascade of dogshit raining down on him, all over the floor, everywhere, Bobby laughing, high-fiving, Jack picking Great Dane shit out of his hair, his shirt, his pants, his shoes, all his books.

For the rest of eighth grade—before Jack had his own growth spurt that next summer, before he started fucking people up, before he ended up the kind of guy who liked to fight, who went looking for fights, who enlisted to fight in Iraq, twice—kids would walk by Jack and pretend to gag from his smell, which earned him the nickname Jack Shit. Even Caroline and her friends called him that. There were people in town, still, who probably thought of him as Jack Shit.

That was all Bobby's doing.

Soon enough, Bobby was kicked out of school and ended up at Amistad, the continuation school, until he eventually quit that and started working for the Vinings, doing odd jobs at Sunshine Fudge and dealing speed (which Jack didn't know at the time was supplied by Danny Vining's father), which is when he stopped being Bobby Calhoun Jr. and became Bobby C., because that was a more badass name.

Now, Bobby C. was four minutes late, and that was pissing Jack off. He popped a handful of Oxy-Altoids. Chewed them ruefully. Not only was Bobby C. an asshole who knew too much, this iteration of Bobby C. was also dependably hard to depend on.

Jack's cell buzzed. He was sitting on a pleasant park bench on the rim of Suicide Ridge, the skeletons of the new homes being built behind him, along with the massive landmovers that were turning this into a Vacation Paradise! Jack had a Priority Mailer on his lap, blue medical gloves on his hands, a plan in mind. He and Bobby C. met up here for years, always after dark, locals not really interested in coming to this haunted-ass place anymore, not even to kill themselves. Tourists and short-term rental owners didn't give a shit; they were happy to plunk down cash for this view. Eventually, Jack would need to find a new place for prurient shit . . . but maybe not. Maybe this was this, and this was over? Because this spot used to be dirt and rocks and coyotes, but now he was underneath a pleasant awning amid a pleasant park setting, swings, a slide, a water fountain. Suicide Ridge really pleasant now, even at this late hour.

Pleasant, pleasant, pleasant.

Provided you didn't think about all the people who'd jumped or were thrown to their death about fifty feet away. Jack didn't believe in ghosts, unless he thought about them too much, so he wasn't doing that, but yeah, it was quite *pleasant* all around. The Pacific crashed down below. The air smelled of salt water and ocean breezes and the pataki they'd planted nearby. If you looked south, and it was clear out, you could see the pier and the boardwalk and the marina. If the wind swirled you might catch a hint of Pronto Pups on the jet stream. *Pleasant.* Maybe they should rename this fucking launch point to the watery graveyard below Pleasant Ridge. He'd look into that.

His phone buzzed again.

"You all right?" Beth asked.

"Pleasant," Jack said.

"That's aces, Chief," Beth said. "He's coming up. Get straight." Jack saw lights coming up toward the ridge. The roads up to the ridge were paved now, there were lights shining up at the yellow NEW HOMES COMING SOON! flags, which lined the way toward the three models they'd already built. And then this nice park area, which was only going to be accessible to homeowners, and was to eventually include a putting green and pickleball courts, and which already had parking for the cars and golf carts of people who didn't even know they were going to eventually live here until they died of fucking boredom or tore their ACLs chasing a pickleball, whatever the hell that was.

It was all going to be very . . . pleasant.

Suicide Ridge was ancient history-ish.

All hail the Granite Darklands . . . or whatever the fuck Caroline was calling it. "You good to handle this on your own?" Beth asked.

"I've got it," Jack said. Plan was simple. He was going to give Bobby C. the mailer with some of Robert Green's teeth in it, along with a felony's worth of heroin. Tell him to drive up to the border and stick it in the mail, but instead Beth would pull him over tonight, they'd bring some dogs to search the limo, what with Bobby's C.'s record, find the heroin and the teeth, make it a whole big deal that Bobby wouldn't be able to fix. He began to talk out his neck? Danny had guys on the inside who could throw him off the top deck. Jack already felt a lessening of his concerns. One less problem in Jack's world. One less person who knew too much.

Not that Danny and Beth knew about the teeth. That was the Jack Special he'd be serving up tonight.

A few minutes later, Bobby C.'s limo parked next to Jack's Tahoe, and Bobby C. came and found Jack on the bench.

"You're a little late," Jack said.

Bobby C. said, "Getting my son to bed takes an act of Congress. You want me on time, have these meetings happen during school hours."

"It's the summer," Jack said.

"Still," Bobby C. said. "We keep him on the same schedule. So that way, school starts, he's not out of sorts. Things gotta be dependable, or everything gets tossed into flux."

*Flux.* Where the fuck did Bobby C. learn that word?

"That's a big word," Jack said.

"What?"

"*Flux.* That's a big word for you."

"It's four letters." Bobby C. gave Jack a look. "Oh you're saying because I'm a dumb fuck I shouldn't know that word. I get it. We went to the same schools, boss."

"Did you ever get your GED?"

"When you were in Iraq."

"Which time?"

"The first time. I did six months in County. Knocked it out then."

"When did you learn that word?"

"I know all the same words as you. I read the same newspaper as you read. You want to quiz me? What the fuck, Jack?" He shook his head, then spit on the ground, then snapped on some blue medical gloves of his own. "Whatever. Whatever. What do you have for me? Let's get this done."

Jack handed him the mailer. "Tomorrow, as close to Canada as you can get, stick this in the mail. Ferndale would be good."

"The carnival starts tomorrow."

"So?"

"You want me to tell Deb I took a job driving to damn near Canada on the day we're supposed to take the boy to the carnival? I won't get back until Wednesday."

"Not my problem," Jack said.

Bobby C. looked at the mailer. It had Penny Green's name on it, but no address. "Where's this going?"

"You get to Ferndale, I'll email you the address."

"She's right here in town, why you mailing her something?" He shook the envelope. It made a rattling sound. "And what would you be sending her, anyway?"

"You ask questions now?"

"Maybe I do," he said.

What was this impertinence? Jack bet that was a word Bobby C. didn't know. So he said, "Why the lip?"

"You know they're about to announce a reward to find Robert Green or that shit he stole?"

"No," Jack said, "didn't know that."

"Yeah, yeah," Bobby C. said. "I feel like maybe I have an inside track on that. So maybe watch your fucking mouth with me, okay? I can take only so much." How did Bobby C. know this?

"Where are you getting this information?"

"Ran into Seema Nitch at the new Panera. She was telling everyone. Said she thought it was going to be in the millions. You imagine that?"

"Yeah," Jack said. "Who are 'they' in this?"

"Fuck if I know," Bobby C. said. "Can I tell you something? The world is a lot bigger than this shitty place. Deb and me, we're thinking of getting out of here. Find a better medical situation for the boy. I come up on that money? You won't have me to run your errands anymore. Keep that in mind. I'm being 100 percent with you here. I've got responsibilities you can't comprehend. Lotta shit in *flux*, and I can't be pulling all-nighters to motherfucking Ferndale." He handed the mailer back to Jack. Reached into his pocket, took out a pack of smokes. Lit up. "So that's it."

"That's it?"

"A couple days from now, I could potentially be a millionaire. I have some strong working theories about where that loot might be."

"Why don't you go steal the loot, as you call it," Jack said, "then you don't have to worry about paying taxes on all those millions."

"Maybe I will."

They sat there for a moment, not speaking, Jack trying to decide if he should kill this dumb motherfucker or not, before finally saying, "So you're quitting?"

"I didn't say I was quitting," Bobby C. said. "I said that's it with your little errands. Either I get this reward or I don't, but our time doing this is done. Seeing Penny Green the other night clarified for me that the old school is about due for recess. I'm not of the mind I could successfully defend myself against that whack job. Might be you should consider the same. Secrets? Not keeping them for no one but me now."

There it was. The final disrespect. It was clear to Jack that Bobby C. had no code. He'd snitch out Jack at once. Not that he'd be able to prove anything, but that would surely be a headache.

Jack got up. Walked back toward his Tahoe.

"That's it?" Bobby said. "You got nothing smart to say, Jack?"

"You put dogshit in my locker."

"What?" Jack already opening his car door. Was maybe ten yards away.

"Eighth grade. You put dogshit in my locker."

Bobby said, "What are you on about?"

"I'm telling you something you did to me. Remember we used to be friends?"

Bobby C. stared at Jack for a long time, not saying anything. Then finally said, "That sounds like something I'd do, but I don't remember it. Why do you bring it up now?" He laughed. "I mean, didn't I also break your fucking hand?"

"No, that wasn't me. You pissed on my front door once."

"I don't remember that, either."

"What do you remember?"

Bobby C. said, "Are you all right?"

Jack Biddle was not, in fact, all right. He was trying to work up the rage he'd need to do what needed to be done, but it was like all the Oxy he'd taken in his entire life showed up at the same time in his blood. He was so calm, everything was so pleasant, he almost felt sorry for Bobby C.

"You move somewhere," Jack said, "you gonna start going by Bobby Calhoun again?"

Bobby said, "You ever think maybe this town ain't that grand for you, either? You're a drug addict, you've got a gambling problem, and everyone in the fucking town knows you're a fucking pretzel. I managed to grow up and improve, slightly. So. Yeah. Maybe I will start using my own name again. It's all in *flux*, Jack Shit."

So he *did* remember.

Jack got into his Tahoe, turned on the engine, flipped on his brights, everything flooded in his headlights now, including Bobby C., sitting there on that bench smoking a cigarette with a fucking grin on his face. Jack put the Tahoe in reverse, rolled back about twenty yards, made sure he gave himself enough room to really get moving, then gunned the V-8 engine. Judging by the angle, the bench about ten feet below the parking lot, sloping toward the ridge, Jack figured he'd need to really be moving to get Bobby's dumb ass to adhere to his hood for a few seconds. He'd then need to hit the brakes quickly to get the desired rapid deceleration to get Bobby C. to fly through the air the way he was now imagining. And so Jack wouldn't plunge to his own death. Fortunately, these were things Jack knew well. All those traffic accidents he had to investigate early in his career really came into use when running a motherfucker over.

Sudden impact + friction − deceleration rate = Bobby C. flying off Suicide Ridge.

He'd give it a shot.

Bobby C. jumped off the bench—maybe he wasn't so dumb after all, since he clearly realized what was about to happen. But he had a bad knee and a shitty back and had a BMI of about 40, so he wasn't going to outrun a Tahoe.

Or fate.

Jack plowed into Bobby C.'s back at just under sixty miles per hour, which probably killed Bobby straightaway, his whole body snapping forward likely severed his spine and broke his neck. The old double whammy, Jack thought, Bobby rag-dolling there between his headlights before Jack slammed on his brakes, and the living human formerly known as Bobby Calhoun Jr. took flight into the darkness, landing somewhere in the Pacific below.

Jack backed up. Got out, checked the damage to his car. Minimal. The bumper had a little dent. Nothing major. No blood. All things considered, this had worked out perfectly. He took the envelope with Robert Green's teeth and some heroin out of his cab, went over to Bobby C.'s limo, popped the trunk, pulled back the carpeting, dumped the teeth into the spare wheel well. That would take his people a bit to find, since Jack knew how his examine team worked, but since Bobby C. was a known felon, finding his limo out here on Suicide Ridge with no sign of him was going to be plenty suspicious. He tossed the heroin under the front seat of the limo. This was all working out. He couldn't have planned it better. Why hadn't he thought of this in the first place? So much easier!

Jack spent another thirty minutes making sure all evidence of his presence on the Suicide Plains of Granite during the demise of Bobby C. was cleaned up, then came down the hill, found Officer Beth Frane across the street in the parking lot of what was soon to be a Trader Joe's but was currently the burnt-out husk of a Dollar King, which ironically Jack had Bobby C. burn down eighteen months earlier to force those fucking assholes out of town. She sat on the hood of her cruiser with her radar gun out, pretending to speed-trap drivers. It was a nice ruse.

Jack put down his window. "Bobby C. had an accident."

"Meaning what?" Beth said.

"He's in the spirit world now. His limo is still up there."

"How did he enter the spirit world?"

"Flew. How's my front end look?"

"Dented," she said.

"In the shape of Bobby C.?"

Beth sighed. "No. Like you hit a post or something."

"He was like a post."

Beth said, "I'm going to need to unfuck this."

"He was a guy who was going to kill himself eventually. No one will be surprised by this. He washes up, I'll spearhead the investigation myself. He was a dear friend." Jack looked up the hill. "I hope he had life insurance. He's got a kid."

"They don't pay out on suicides, typically."

"No? Huh. Well. We'll set up a GoFundMe or something."

"You really think people are going to give to a GoFundMe for Bobby C.?"

Well.

He'd need to investigate that.

Jack said, "They'll find the limo in the morning. I want you on the call. Park yourself right here at 8:00 a.m. You'll be set."

"Drugs still in the car?"

"Yes."

"You don't care that his wife and kid are going to know their father and husband was a drug addict? Not bad enough that he jumped to his death?"

"Sure," Jack said.

"Sure what?"

"Sure, he was a scumbag. Some things are true. Kid would have learned that eventually. Wife must have known. She married Bobby C. for god's sake. You know, he once put dogshit in my locker? He did. That's the kind of man we're talking about."

Beth said, "My admiration for you plummets by the millisecond." She tossed her radar gun into the trunk of her cruiser. "I'm going home unless you desire to destroy more of my options for future peace."

"You drive your cruiser home, too? When I was starting out, I liked to do that. It was an honor."

"Yes sir," she said. "It's an honor. To the profession. To protect and serve. To fucking speed and run red lights and stop signs and never have to wait for anything." She got into the cruiser, Jack still standing there, feeling awfully *pleasant*. She said, "Don't do anything stupid tomorrow without telling me first, all right? Can you do that? This could have been avoided, sir, just once again being 100 percent clear with you on the profundity of your failures as a man and a police officer."

"Pleasant," Jack said.

# CHAPTER THIRTY-THREE

*Monday*

The Shore View at Granite Park hadn't changed all that much in fifteen years. It was still six-stories tall. It still hung over the Pacific. The neighborhood surrounding it still felt like the setting of a saccharine romcom, though the Meg Ryan movie from the '90s had morphed into an out-of-season Hallmark Christmas movie: SUVs in diagonal parking places, twinkling gold string lights, pretty people dining alfresco, plates of artisan meats and cheeses, men in zip sweaters who probably called themselves "girl dads" and roamed in and out of bakeries.

The senior citizen population was gone, literally and figuratively, replaced by thirtysomethings in leisurewear, judging by the people Mitch spied walking into the building's lobby. The adjacent parking lot, where he'd once parked a Caddie with a dead dog's head in the trunk, had been transformed into the private Shore View Fitness Park, replete with a climbing wall and three pickleball courts.

"You're sure about this?" Mitch asked.

"I haven't seen her since it all happened. I owe her a visit."

"Or what? She'll write another book about you?"

Penny looked up at the building. "If my grandmother still lived here," she said, "she'd jump out of the window."

"How are you going to get in?" Mitch asked.

"Used to be if you hit star, 7, 7, star, 7 the door would unlock. It's what the cops used. I'll give that a shot first."

"Why do you know that?"

"My dad knew a lot of shitty cops," Penny said. "Have to imagine Chief Biddle hasn't improved the situation."

Mitch watched Penny walk up to the door, punch in the code, and then disappear inside.

Well.

Shit.

Mitch took out his phone, entered that code into his notes, in case he needed that down the line.

He pulled up his notifications.

Looked at his missed calls.

Five from Barer & Harris.

No messages.

That wasn't good.

He hit his alerts.

There was a photo of him and Penny. It was a still from the Ring camera outside their Airbnb. Time-stamped at 8:30 this morning.

> @GShoresNews Look who is visiting for Green Days! Penny Green! (And sources tell us that strapping buck is Mitch Diamond from @BarerHarris)

Did Jack Biddle . . . snitch them out to the press?

Why would he do that? It was like he wanted every bad actor to know Penny was in town.

And then it occurred to Mitch: He wanted every bad actor to know that Penny Green was in town.

And he wanted to put Mitch's name and face on the internet.

And if he told the press Mitch and Penny were in town, it would reason he told the press why, too.

His cell phone rang.

*Barer & Harris.*
How many ways out did Mitch have now?
*Decline.*
Who was working at this hour? He clicked through to his office camera app.

There were two people in his office. The one sitting at his fucking desk, tapping away at his computer, was Bessy Mendelsohn. She was the firm's head of IT. Bessy was nice enough. She was forty-five, divorced, no kids, and in a trivia league, which Mitch joined as well. Monday nights, if he wasn't somewhere in the country doing dark shit, he was at the Good Society Brewery with Bessy, taking all the literature questions and paying for all the cheese sticks. There was also one night where they drank too much at the Good Society and ended up making poor personal decisions. It wasn't a bad time. End result was she left his computers alone.

The one pacing behind Bessy was Randall Barry, head of HR. After thirty years on the job, Randall was looking to retire, constantly going on about a mythical fishing village in Mexico where he wanted to build a cabin. Mitch was pretty sure he'd end up in Spokane. Mitch hated Randall. Under normal circumstances he'd probably avoid him at all costs. Instead, Mitch cultivated a friendship with him, took him to twenty-five Mariners games a year, forged Ken Griffey Jr.'s signature on a baseball for him one Christmas, got him loaded on twenty-dollar ballpark beers and listened to him complain.

And now they were both in his office, going through his business.

Bessy picked up Mitch's office phone. Seconds later, Mitch's cell rang again.

*Decline.*

He clicked over to the cameras in his apartment. Not that Barer & Harris knew his actual address. He rented two condos in Seattle. One that he lived in, one he did not. He'd booby-trapped the doors of both before he left, knowing he wasn't coming back. The building wasn't going to blow up. No one was getting their head cut off. Maybe they'd end up with a broken arm, a concussion, some cracked ribs. Enough to let them know he was onto them, no real harm done, but harm could have happened, which was usually enough for smart people to stop doing dumb shit.

He'd disabled the GPS on his Caddie long ago. Situation got worse, he'd need a new VIN. Easy enough. He'd swing by a dealership in Portland, take a photo of a VIN, make some new tags. Get some dealer plates while he was at it. Done that a hundred times.

His phone rang again.

He clicked back over to his office.

Randall stood on a chair, held a piece of paper up to the camera. ANSWER YOUR PHONE OR THE NEXT CALL IS THE FBI *Block.*

They'd need the CIA to get into his work computer; the FBI didn't have the skills, but everything was hackable, eventually.

He'd only been out of contact for a few days. He needed twenty-four hours more. Then he'd be free and clear. Provided the firm didn't send someone to come get him. And provided no one killed him and he didn't kill anyone. No sure thing, any of that.

# CHAPTER THIRTY-FOUR

*Monday*

"I thought you might show up here eventually," Addie said. She was standing in her doorway, a gun pointed at Penny's face. Looked like a Sig Sauer P226. A little too much gun for such a small woman, in Penny's opinion, but then Addie was always super concerned about making a first impression.

Penny said, "Why don't you put down that gun, Addie."

Addie said, "I know how to use this. I want you to know that."

"How hard could it be?" Penny said. Penny craned her neck to one side, peered into her nana's old place. Looked like Addie made some renovations. "Did you knock down a wall?"

"What?"

"Inside," Penny said. "Did you knock out the wall between the living room and the kitchen?"

Addie said, "The kitchen was tiny. So. Yeah."

Penny said, "Smart."

Addie said, "Remember you couldn't have the oven and the fridge open at the same time?"

"Right, right." They stood there like that for a few more seconds, Penny trying to make sure her nana's condo hadn't been turned into a living museum, too, Addie pointing a fucking gun at her. Finally, Penny said, "If I was here to hurt you, Addie, would I have knocked on the door?"

Addie considered this. Lowered the gun an inch, Penny not all that worried since she could see the safety was on, but whatever, she'd let her cousin have her moment. "How *did* you get in?"

"Star, 7, 7, star, 7," Penny said.

Addie said, "That still works? Unreal." She put the gun down to her side, let Penny in. "I don't know how to use this dumb thing. My ex left it here. I don't even know if it's loaded."

Addie took Penny outside onto the patio, so she could smoke a clove. It was late, the traffic on the floating bridge to Loon Island a trickle of lights across the water. "You been to the island?" Addie asked.

"No."

"I go once a month, leave flowers on my mom's grave," she said. "Your dad's, too."

"Dad wasn't really the flowers type," Penny said.

"I know," Addie said, "but it's the polite thing, isn't it?"

"Didn't know that was a concern of yours," Penny said. "You did just put a gun in my face."

Addie sighed. "My therapist makes me go." She paused. "And look, I've got some bananas fans out there. You're not the first person to show up at my door unannounced."

"Maybe don't film videos of yourself in front of the building," Penny said.

"It's on the tourist maps," Addie said. "So I'm like, whatever. The gun usually works."

"'Usually' is doing a lot of work for you there, cousin."

Addie laughed. "Wait. You've watched my videos?"

"And listened to your podcast."

"Really?"

"Well," Penny said, "the first season. A second season seemed like a reach."

"Yeah," Addie said, "but the tourism bureau gave me a car, so, what was I supposed to do? Say no? It's got a wrap for the tourism bureau on it, but whatever, it's free, and they even pay for the gas if I do public events." Addie blew smoke into the night air, then coughed in a way that sounded painful. "I need to give these up. Remember the urban legend that they made your lungs bleed? I believe that could be true. Another Big Pharma conspiracy." Addie stared at Penny for a moment. "Where have you been hiding?"

"The desert," Penny said.

"Like Saudi Arabia?"

"No," Penny said, "like Joshua Tree."

"I went there once," Addie said, brightening. "I rented a house and did ayahuasca with this crazy shaman and like, five girls all named Cheyanne. We met online."

"How was that?"

"The shaman said I'd find Robert like, in the spirit realm or whatever," Addie said.

"And?"

"I threw up for two days and ended up with a kidney stone. It was terrible. Turns out those girls weren't even really named Cheyanne. Total scam." She shook her head. "So dumb. What's it like living there?"

"Quiet."

"You going back?"

"If I can," Penny said. "It's why I'm here, actually. I wanted to talk to you about something."

"The reward and all that?"

"Where'd you hear that?"

"Costco," Addie said. "I was getting toilet paper like two hours ago. Bobby C.'s wife was there, talking her ass off." Addie flicked her clove off the balcony, down into the ocean below. "She's a piece of work. But anywho. They've got a sick kid, so I was like, whatever. I assumed it was some publicity stunt for Green Days. Couple years ago, they did the look-alike contest and rumor was Robert was going to reveal himself and give everyone diamonds or some shit. People are so random with what they believe."

"What do *you* believe?"

"About Robert? Sweetie. You don't want to know."

"Try me."

"I think he's been dead a long-ass time," Addie said. "I'd be willing to bet he had a partner here in town, and they had this like, big plan to cut you and me out of the whole thing. Something happened, they decided to kill Robert and keep all the stuff."

"Yeah," Penny said, "that was season one, wasn't it?"

"Well, yeah, but I believe that. It makes sense, yeah?"

"He didn't have any friends here."

"That he told you about," Addie said. "I found like, so much weird shit online that Robert was into. Like, message boards about Y2K and shit. He might have been into some big things, Pen, like widespread conspiracy-level shit. You don't know."

"Do you hear yourself?" Penny asked.

Addie said, "Look. It's whatever, now. What does it even matter if it's true? Who is even being hurt? If it were me doing it? I'd have broken into his apartment and stole his hairbrush and toothbrush and his nightguard and everything else I could find and be mining his DNA."

"Why stop there?" Penny said. "Why not dig up my mom and dad and see if you could *Jurassic Park* a new version of Robert altogether?"

"You mock," Addie said, "but do you have a better answer for all this?"

Thing was . . . Penny didn't. What today was showing her was that something deeply fucked-up happened. She couldn't conceive of what.

"Why'd the city pay you off?"

"Is that what this is about? You want money?"

"No," Penny said. "Not from you, anyway."

"Jack Biddle defamed me," Addie said. "Over and over and over again. So I called his bluff, got a lawyer, did that whole thing, and the city settled with me, which is all I wanted, anyway, plus to have him stop, which I guess he's done, at least on TV. They made me a good offer." She shrugged. "End of the day, it was the best thing that happened to me."

"They don't care that you spend your time spinning conspiracy theories about the local cops?"

"If they had a problem," Addie said, "they could sue me, right?" She shrugged again. It was how Penny remembered Addie: a series of continual shrugs as a life plan. "But Jack Biddle doesn't want to be examined too closely, I'd guess. And anyway. I'm good for business. I keep talking my shit, people keep coming out here, renting Airbnbs, filling up hotel rooms, getting pulled over for traffic violations, parking too close to crosswalks, buying weed, getting DUIs, every new dumb thing I say creates a financial ecosystem."

Penny said, "My bedroom is a museum exhibit."

"Yeah, I know," Addie said. "I donated pictures to help them get it right."

Penny's phone buzzed. A text from Mitch:

We need to not be here.

Penny wrote back: Almost done.

Five minutes, Mitch wrote back. And then I'm burning the building down.

"I need to go," Penny said. Penny stepped inside their nana's old apartment. It still had the plush carpeting. The walls were still painted butter yellow. Addie redecorated the kitchen and living room and filled the place with period furniture and art. It was like being stuck in an episode of *Miami Vice*, right down to the Nagel prints. And yet, Penny could still smell her nana. If she closed her eyes, she could imagine that no time at all had passed.

"You don't really believe what Bobby's wife said, that Robert's been here?" Addie asked.

"No," Penny said.

"I think he's probably dead, Penny. You may think I'm nutty, but that's what my investigation has concluded. That's going to be season three."

"And what did your investigation comprise?"

Addie smiled broadly. "I don't know," she said. "I haven't done it yet. That's the whole thing, Pen. You don't need a *real* answer. You have to have the answer you want to be true. People will believe what you want them to believe for the thirty minutes they're listening to you while they're driving or falling asleep or walking the dog or doing their dishes or whatever. And then it disappears, and you can say something totally different the next episode, and then they believe *that*. Whatever I say, I'm just filling their habit that day."

Penny thought: *There it is. There it fucking is.* Penny took one last look out the window, at the floating bridge, at the dim lights of Loon Island in the distance, listened to Addie prattle on about the lemmings and the sheep and her plan to put together a cruise to Hawaii for the real fans, and did Penny want to get in on that? Penny nodded and smiled and watched her father's ghost walk through the condo, sit down on the sofa, light up a cigarette, open up the newspaper. Nana came and sat down next to him. Clicked on the TV. And in walked Robert, impossibly young, not even twenty, bangs in his eyes, goofy smile, not a concern in the world, and then there was mom, too. She came and stood beside Penny, squeezed her arm, said, *I saw what you put on your ceiling, babe. It will get better. I promise.*

"You should sell this place," Penny said, interrupting Addie's monologue. "I bet you could get a lot of money."

"You think so?"

"I really do," Penny said. She opened the front door, looked down the long hallway, saw herself running up and down, ringing doorbells. She took Addie's hand. "Can I tell you something, Addie?"

"You want to go to Hawaii?"

"No," Penny said. "No, I never want to go anywhere with you. I went to *prison* to keep you out of this shit. And now, here you are, feasting on it." Penny took Addie in for a hug, her cousin stiff in her arms. "Robert was right. I was a fool to involve you in this. I'm so sorry." She pulled back. Stared at Addie for a long moment. "I loved you so much. What a waste."

# CHAPTER THIRTY-FIVE

*Tuesday Morning*

Soon as Penny saw the social media post, she told Mitch she'd never be able to sleep, so he gave her a book from his suitcase. It was a slim, beat-up paperback with a seagull on the cover. Five pages in, the seagull was already dispensing '70s-era pop psychology bullshit mixed with, essentially, Rudolph the Red-Nosed Reindeer's social analysis, which gave Penny what the Ambien she craved would have provided: hallucinatory sleep.

When she woke before 3:30 a.m., she was momentarily lost, as she often was in the middle of the night.

Was she in prison?

No. She could smell the water.

Was she twelve, at home, her dad and her brother down the hall, mom long gone?

No. She could feel a subtle rocking beneath her.

And then she remembered: a houseboat in Granite Shores.

With that man. Mitch. Who held her arms while she floated into the abyss.

What a strange thing. This man. She knew nothing about him other than what she'd learned in these few days—that he wasn't who he said he was, that he was probably not a good person, depending upon how one defined *good*, that he was for sure lying to her about something significant—she could feel that in her DNA—and then, for reasons she simply could not conjure, it didn't bother her. He needed her for this weird quest. And in the end she was going to have answers to the questions that plagued her.

Right?

She wasn't sure about that.

A million dollars?

She doubted that, too. It seemed ludicrous. Like some James Bond shit.

Penny got out of bed. They were staying on a forty-foot houseboat named the *C-Level*. Mitch gave Penny the bedroom, and he was sleeping on a converted sofa in the main cabin. At least that was the plan. However, when Penny stepped into the cabin to get a glass of water, Mitch wasn't to be found. She poured herself a glass from the small kitchen sink and then walked out to the main deck. Mitch sat on one of two Adirondack chairs . . . with a gun on his lap.

"Finish the book?" he asked.

"It finished me, for a little while," Penny said.

"It's one of those books where you gotta buy the concept or it's not going to work for you."

"I didn't buy the concept."

This made Mitch laugh. "First time I read it," he said, "I was in Quentin."

"With Kiko."

"With Kiko," he said. "I was in a situation where buying the concept was the least of my concerns."

"What's with the gun?"

Mitch took his phone from his pocket. Showed her that a half dozen posts from *The Granite Shores Daily News*'s various social media accounts had become a thousand other posts.

Penny felt like she might be sick. "How long have you had an alert on me?"

"Long as I've known I could," he said. "You tend to pop up in the middle of the night. During the pandemic, when everyone became a true crime detective, it was a nightly experience. Someone would tweet a theory or write a Substack about all the evidence they'd found that day."

"Did it help you find me after I got out?"

"Someone saw you hiking in Joshua Tree. So yeah."

"They say if I had good form?"

"They caught a photo of you."

"Why didn't Rodney show up in my living room?"

"I got my guy to hack into the account in five minutes, delete the post, and deactivate the account. Then I crossed my fingers Rodney wasn't looking. Got lucky. This? It's different. It's probably been seen a hundred thousand times. It was posted on every social network and on the paper's website." He showed Penny the page. "Jack didn't tell the press you were here to make you feel welcome."

"Yeah, I figured that out. Hence the need to read that talking-bird book."

"Trouble is coming. Maybe not right now. But soon."

"That's what I thought, too."

"Been a long time since I was on the right side of things." Mitch popped out the gun's magazine, examined it, shoved it back in. "Not sure I'm built that way."

"Is that where we are?"

"I think so," Mitch said.

"This trouble," Penny said. "Is it coming for me or for you?"

"No difference, now."

Penny watched Mitch for a moment, waited to see the other side of that sentence show up, but it just hung there.

"Why are you being so nice to me?"

"This when I'm supposed to say something like, 'You and me, we're not so different'?"

"I hate that," Penny said. "I always turn movies off when characters say that."

"Yeah," Mitch said, "me, too."

"You didn't answer my question."

"Let me show you something," Mitch said. He scrolled through his phone. Turned it around. "What do you see here?"

Penny was staring at a photo of herself, in handcuffs, getting perp-walked out of the Granite Shores jail to be dragged back to Seattle to be arraigned. "A bad day."

"Where was your family?"

"My dad was dead, my mom was even deader, Robert was in the wind, my grandmother and my aunt were probably sitting anticipatory shiva, Addie was likely selling her life rights. That's my best guess."

"Friends?"

Penny felt her stomach drop. "Not thick on the ground in those days."

"What about now?"

"No one I've met in the last two years even knows my name."

Mitch tucked his phone away. "That photo, it ran everywhere. It was pinned up on a bulletin board outside the HR offices at Barer & Harris, like an achievement. I walked by it every day. And every day I thought: *She won't last inside. She might survive, but she won't last.*"

"You were wrong."

"I thought, you know, *I bet she could use a friend.*"

"I had Yard-Shitting Sam," Penny said. "Then you blew up my spot."

Mitch said, "Say we had to disappear. Where would you want to go?"

"We?"

"Figure of speech."

Penny pointed out into the bay. "My boat's docked out there somewhere. I'd get on that and just keep going."

"You ever spend any time on the open ocean?"

"I grew up on the beach."

"So that's a no."

Penny said, "My dad used to play Jimmy Buffett records, until he went punk."

"When did Jimmy Buffett go punk?"

"You'd have to ask my dad. He had a real opinion about it."

"When I was a kid," Mitch said, "we used to take school field trips into the California delta. Always on some rickety science boat. All I remember is feeling sick. Maybe take that into consideration."

"You don't have your own plan?"

"I might want to visit," Mitch said.

"In this situation, do we have money?"

"We do."

Penny closed her eyes. "Okay, I'm astral-projecting into my future. I'm in the desert. But not California. Taxes are too high. So maybe Arizona. Yeah. Like near Sedona, but not in Sedona, because I can't listen to anyone talking about vortices without wanting to push them into traffic. I've got a little house, five to seven dogs, and a jukebox in the living room that plays nothing but classic country songs."

"A jukebox?"

"Yeah, like an old Wurlitzer," Penny said. "It's my dream, let me have it."

Mitch said, "I'm going to need a drink." He disappeared into the boat for a few minutes, came back with two glasses and a bottle of Macallan 18. Poured both a healthy dose. "What if," Mitch said, "I told you to go to that place right now, and I'd find you?"

"I guess I'd wonder about your motives."

"No motives," Mitch said. "You've done your time. What comes next, I don't know, I feel like it could be bad."

"Says the man with a gun on his lap."

"I'm worried that you'll find yourself in a position where you'll want one, too."

"I'm pretty sure you can't have a gun, either." Penny took a drink, felt the pleasant burn on its way down. She wasn't much of a drinker, but she could get used to good stuff, she suspected. "What did you get caught doing?"

"We're doing this now?"

"Don't you think it's time?"

Mitch took a sip, held it in his mouth for a moment, swallowed, grimaced. "Bank robbery."

"How many?"

"That I did or that I got charged for?"

Penny said, "Give me the dirty truth."

"Eleven banks," he said. "But my real specialty was safes. I took down probably thirty grocery stores, back when people still paid with cash. Never did catch me for that."

"Probably thirty?"

"Thirty-six," he said.

"I had a feeling you knew exactly."

"Different life," Mitch said. "Listen. Rodney Golubev. He finds you, he's not going to take a check. Tonight, we're probably safe. This boat is rented under a fake name. By tomorrow, the whole country will know you're here."

"I get it."

"You give me seventy-two hours, I'll have a whole new identity for you. Not just a name. A whole backstory. A week, you could run for president."

"You can't change my face," Penny said. "Or my DNA."

"I could show you how to make both irrelevant."

"The problem is I could look like anyone," Penny said, "I'd still be me." She leaned back in her chair, stared up into the sky. The fog had come in thick. "This Wurlitzer, it would play 45s, so I'd need someone who could go out shopping in old record bins for deals. You know anyone like that?"

"I do," Mitch said. He poured some more scotch in Penny's glass. "He could get you a car tonight, if you wanted. He could get you a hotel room in Flagstaff. There's a place there called the Little America. It's smack in the middle of the Ponderosa pine forest. They've got a diner inside, a bar, a sundry shop filled with wooden crap you pay double for on vacation."

"Sounds wonderful," Penny said.

"I know a guy there, he'd do me a favor. Get you a job tomorrow if you wanted. But you wouldn't need to keep it. I'd be down with the Wurlitzer before too long."

"I'd want to pick that out myself," Penny said. "I have peculiar taste."

Mitch said, "Penny. You could be there tomorrow night. You should go. I'll be right behind you with your half, one way or the other."

"You want me to believe a man who robbed thirty-six grocery stores? Who robs grocery stores?"

"I waited until they were closed."

"Still. Grocery store is a public trust."

"Didn't you rob a corn dog shop?"

"I see your point."

"I also lent you my favorite book," Mitch said. "And I've stayed up all night guarding you."

"That's your favorite book?"

"Talking animals," Mitch said. "Always appealing."

Penny finished off her scotch, got up, walked to the boat's stern, took a moment to survey the other boats: yachts, houseboats, tricked-out catamarans. Everyone was ready to take to the high seas, everyone with a way to get out.

"When will the firm's announcement go public?"

Mitch hesitated for a moment, like he was evaluating the answer, which was odd, since he was the one who was behind it. "Wednesday. That will happen Wednesday. But it doesn't matter. I'd be surprised if it wasn't out there right now. The rats are already running the streets. Maybe the firm doesn't even bother saying anything."

Penny said, "Jack never had a good reason for coming to see me that night on the boat."

"Good way to get shot," Mitch said. "He could have picked you up anytime."

"I thought it was some Losertown bullshit. Crooked cop did crooked shit and got lucky, found a multimillion-dollar heist kind of in progress."

"What would your homeboy Parmenides say?"

"That I'm in the cave." Penny went inside the cabin, came back out wrapped in a blanket, plopped herself down in the deck chair. "I'm not ever coming back here. And I'm not leaving until I get what I came for, one way or the other." She tugged the blanket under her chin. "Now tell me a bedtime story, no talking birds."

# CHAPTER THIRTY-SIX

*Tuesday*

Rodney Golubev stood in his underwear watching the Pacific roll in. He was on the patio of his home at the Dunes at Granite Shores, sipping a cup of hot tea, eating a bagel, letting nature wash him. He'd raised the Russian flag on his absolutely-not-to-code backyard flagpole. He'd get a fine from the HOA about that. Fuck them. Native pride was coming back. He'd finished cleaning his gun, which he liked to do outside, and had communed with his brother, Freddie, who he suspected was haunting him. Last few days, he'd really felt him. So he put the flag to half-staff, in his honor. He felt his presence like a shadow behind him.

Could also be that he drank too much last night, which was, fuck it, one of those things. Still.

He did not love this place. His wife did, and that was fine for her. She came with their dogs, and they would frolic on the beach. Rodney would come only sometimes. You did things for those people you love, and he did, in fact, love Svetlana #2. But Granite Shores? It was a Losertown. Maybe after today, he would like the place more, when Penny Green was not lingering in the background of his anger. He blamed her for his brother's disappearance. Simple as that. And then when he tried to make it right with her? She skipped town on him. Owing him money was one thing. Disrespecting the memory of his brother, that was a hanging offense.

Not that he'd hang her.

Seemed hard to do.

He'd shoot her. Quick, easy, dump her into the ocean, everything that is done is done, and that would be done. And then he'd handle this Mitch Diamond situation in equal measure, but with maybe some torture? He would see.

*Be calm, brother. Penny is a friend.* There was Freddie again, trying to muscle into his mind. He drank some more tea. Tried to muffle him.

"Pardon me?"

Rodney looked to his right, half expecting to see Freddie, instead finding a woman of about thirty-five standing on her balcony patio, a child beside her, Rodney not sure if it was a boy or a girl, the kid that age where it was impossible to know unless you gave over a moment of your emotional attention to the situation, read cues, engaged in rational thinking, all things Rodney was not doing today. Was she even . . . real? He had to focus. Torturing Mitch Diamond wasn't needed, strictly, but he did not like this bullshit with the foot and thumb.

"Are you real?" Rodney asked.

"Pardon me?"

He took a step toward her and immediately smelled her overwhelming perfume. Chanel number god-knows. She wore it like a tarp.

This was the problem with these houses.

They were right on top of each other.

You could even smell each other!

This woman and her spawn. He needed to pretend she did not exist or engage in pleasantries.

"I said, 'Pardon me,'" the woman said before Rodney could make his decision.

"You are pardoned." Rodney turned back to the Pacific.

"I'm sorry?"

When did people start saying *I'm sorry* to mean, "I need to bother you"? It was one of those things that irked Rodney to no end. He'd learned the English language at seven years old and he appreciated the nuance of it, but still. Words had meaning.

"I accept your apology," he said.

He watched the seagrass on the dunes wave in the wind. The grass was beautiful. Imported, was Rodney's understanding, so that the landfill they were on wouldn't slip into the ocean.

The woman clapped.

Rodney turned to her once more. She'd put one hand over her amorphous child's eyes. "I'm sorry," she said, "but I'm trying to show you something!" She pointed out toward the beach. "There's something in the water."

Rodney craned his neck, but his view was blocked.

"Do you not have someone who helped you create that child?" Rodney said.

"I'm sorry? Can you please see what this is?"

Rodney finished his tea, stepped over the low wall between the houses, stood beside the woman and child, who was a boy, Rodney saw now. He would grow up weak. Looked out over the beach. About a dozen seagulls were feasting on something big.

"Could you please check that out. I'm really worried."

She said *please*. That made up for the clapping.

Kind of.

Rodney walked down the short staircase from his neighbor's home, crossed the dunes, and stepped out onto the beach, shooed away the seagulls, found a very naked and very dead man on the shoreline. He did not have much of a face anymore. Much of his skull was on the outside of his head. Raw bone jutted from his flesh, his back was torqued backward so far his head could practically touch his heels. He must have washed up during the low tide, Rodney thinking this would not be great for his home value, but that was the problem with living on the beach. You never knew what might wash up.

"That is a dead man," Rodney said when he returned to his neighbor's patio.

"Oh my god," the woman said. "I'll call the police."

"Maybe the coroner makes better sense?" The woman stared at him, unblinking, as if she could not believe Rodney's words. "Police are useless."

"Chief Biddle lives one court over. I'm going to run over there. Will you watch Devin?"

Was there ever a boy named Devin who grew into a man people respected? "No," Rodney said.

"No? What do you mean *no*? There's a dead body!"

"*No* is a complete sentence," Rodney said. "You need a second responder. A funeral home. A hazmat team. Much fluid on the beach. Police will not be able to help this man."

"I'm sorry?"

"I again accept your apology." He looked down at the boy. He was maybe four. Rodney mussed his hair. "Cute kid. He will grow up to despise you for naming him Devin. And I would rather watch a hyena eat a puppy than babysit this weak child."

"What? What did you say? What?"

Rodney was already back over the low wall, and then he was in his house, and then, even before the cops arrived on the beach, he was mixing a vegetable-and-rum drink, doing his breathing exercises, and already on to the next things on his to-do list, none of which had to do with the dead man on the beach. Find and kill Penny Green. Find and kill Mitch Diamond. Get Svetlana fudge. See about selling this stupid house. Call child protective services on this woman for naming her son Devin.

# CHAPTER THIRTY-SEVEN

*Tuesday*

Five Granite Shores Police cruisers, two Granite Shores Police bike cops, one Granite Shores Police Tahoe, an ambulance, a fire truck, and a coroner's van lined Beach Boulevard at the entrance to the beach below the Dunes at Granite Shores.

Two cops erected a scene canopy over a corpse half covered in a white body bag sheet. The coroner and Chief Jack Biddle, dressed in a light-blue Adidas tracksuit, crouched over the exposed torso. The rest of the cops milled around the yellow tape line, drinking coffee from Heisted-branded tumblers.

The seagrass swayed.

The surf crashed.

Down the beach, on the boardwalk, the Ferris wheel spun.

"So," Mitch said, "those are the imported dunes."

"You see the body, right?"

He did. He was trying to decide if it was a metaphor for the start of the trouble coming down.

They approached the crime tape. "What's going on?" Penny asked one of the cops. She was tall, broad shouldered, hair in a ponytail. Name tag said Officer Frane.

"Floater," she said.

"Doesn't look like he's floating," Penny said.

"Colloquialism," she said.

Mitch said, "What weight did you fight?"

Officer Frane cocked her head, like she wasn't sure she heard Mitch right. Shifted her weight. Feet shoulder width apart. Hips open. Like she might, in fact, need to fight right now, Mitch wondering if Penny noticed, Penny being a person who noticed things. "You in the game?"

"Fought Goldens," Mitch said.

"That right?" Officer Frane said. Then she stared into Mitch's eyes, Mitch stared right back. "You were a real grappler, I bet. There clips on YouTube?"

"This was before you were born," Mitch said.

"What was your record?"

"Thirty-six and oh," Mitch said, hoping Penny caught that. She rolled her eyes. So that was good. "After a while it got too easy. You know how it is when the competition is practically a grocery sack."

"I'll look you up," Officer Frane said, not blinking. Mitch thinking he knew this woman. Not personally. Knew her kind. Not long for police work. If she ever was. Most fighters, they don't really want to fuck up a stranger for being strange. Officer Frane carried herself like she wanted you to swing on her. Mitch had known COs like that in Quentin.

"No need," Mitch said. "I'm right in front of you."

"What was your fight name?" she asked. "Kid Diamond or something?"

Putting her cards flat. Mitch sort of admired that. Gave her a smile. Show her that he had all his own teeth. Well, most of them. Barer & Harris's dental plan was a real benefit. "No, I went by my real name. To honor my father, you see."

"Honor, yeah, I see it."

Mitch gave her the once-over, in the most respectful way he could imagine, since he didn't want to piss her off and end up with her fist in his teeth. "Feather?"

"Bantam back then," Officer Frane said. "If I went back, I'd probably roll feather. I've bulked up." She broke eye contact with Mitch, cast her gaze down to Penny, who was a good five inches shorter than Officer Frane. A slow, appreciative nod, everyone knows everyone, how it would be with them, Mitch thinking this cop might have cliqued up before she was in uniform. "You didn't throw in prison?"

"No sanctioned bouts," Penny said.

"You in town for long?"

"Hope not."

"Saw you two in the paper this morning," she said. "You're not here to cause trouble, are you?"

"Cause it? Not us, Officer Frane," Mitch said.

"I went to school with a Frane," Penny said. "You have a brother?"

"That was my cousin Calvin. He passed."

"What happened?"

"Drowned," Officer Frane said. She pointed behind her. "Between here and the rocky point. Where the undertow gets bad. He went in after his kids. I was working as a lifeguard that day. Saw it all happen. I was a kid, too, you know. Sixteen and in charge of saving lives."

Penny said, "Why do they even let people swim there?"

"It's America, you're allowed to be your own worst enemy." Frane adjusted her belt. "Worst, best day of my life. Saved my kid cousins, went back for Calvin, he was already gone." She shuddered, like she'd just gotten out of the water. "They gave me a medal."

"He wash up?" Mitch asked.

"Never did," Frane said. "I used to do a little magical thinking and imagine he got picked up by a cruise ship out in the channel, and he decided, screw it, and started a new life somewhere else. I guess you'd understand that, Ms. Green? No disrespect."

"That's why I'm here," Penny said. "Make sure that's not him."

Officer Frane looked over her shoulder. "It's not him, I can tell you that." Officer Frane regarded Mitch again. Then took several steps toward him, stopped, the police tape between them. "Talk a little shop about your line of work?"

"Depends which line you're talking about," Mitch said.

"I saw you yesterday at the precinct, meeting with the chief and the mayor. Then I saw you again in the paper. Got interested. Poked around online a little bit. Your bio is gone from your company website. Did you know that?"

He did not.

"Probably being updated."

"Found a cached copy," Frane said. "You need to be ex–military intelligence to do your job? Or that just helps with serving subpoenas?"

"Corporate security means a lot of things. Process server is not one."

"Person who understands delicate things," Frane said. Frane pointed at Mitch's ankle. "Nine?"

"Nine."

"No half measures, I like it." She bowed slightly. Pointed at his front right pocket. "Sap?"

"Don't want to bring a sap to a gunfight. So extra magazine, instead."

"You think you're going to be in a gunfight today, Mr. Diamond, where you'd need to fire your weapons sixty times?" When Mitch didn't respond, she said, "No armor?"

"Useless. Only shows the bad guys where not to aim."

"Refreshing." She looked Mitch up and down. "Where is your primary?"

"Well," Mitch said, "it moves."

"Smart," she said. "Never know if it's someone you know who is trying to disarm you. I'll model that down the road."

"Your thinking is a little faulty."

"That so?"

"If you try to disarm me, what you're really trying to do is avoid getting killed. That's how I see it. Then I have to wonder why you'd think I needed to kill you. And that opens up a real box of shit, if you'll pardon my language."

Officer Frane smiled broadly. "Ms. Green, you have captured the right man's heart."

Penny said, "We're not like that."

"Sure you aren't." Officer Frane watched Penny for a few more seconds, then said, "What was it like being on the news and all that when you were a kid?"

"Disorienting."

"Kids now," Frane said, "be a different story."

"No," Penny said. "It's the same story. It's all about someone getting away with it. People like that."

"You did a couple nickels, didn't you?"

"Thirteen years," Penny said. "Turns out I didn't get away with anything."

"What about you, Mr. Diamond?"

"Same as you," Mitch said. "Just collecting medals for living righteously."

Chief Jack Biddle stood up under the canopy, a phone to his ear. Looked around, Mitch thinking he seemed a little frantic . . . right until he saw Officer Frane. Biddle put a finger in his mouth, whistled like he was calling a Doberman.

Penny said, "I think your boss is trying to get your attention."

"That was him with the whistle?"

"Yes," Penny said.

"Exhausting," Frane said. She turned on her heel, walked over to the canopy, checked out the body, then listened to Chief Biddle, nodded, pointed at him, pointed at the body, pointed out at the ocean. Shook her head. Looked, to Mitch at least, like she wanted to run headlong into the waves and never come back.

"What is going on?" Penny asked.

"I'm not sure," Mitch said.

"What was that whole thing about your weapons?"

"Oh," Mitch said, "that was her telling me she was going to shoot me in the face if it came right down to it."

Penny said, "I didn't get that."

"It was subtle."

"Her cousin?" Penny said. "I took him to the Sadie Hawkins Dance in eighth grade. He cried into my shoulder when we slow danced to a Boyz II Men song. Nice kid when you got to know him."

Chief Biddle went back to the body. Officer Frane headed back toward the line, seconds later was walking under the yellow tape, headed to one of the cruisers, started to get in, stopped. Regarded Penny. "If your brother was drowning and there were kids you *didn't* know, who'd you save?"

"The kids. No question."

Officer Frane thought about that, then said, "That's the right answer, isn't it?"

"You did the right thing," Penny said.

"I know that," Frane said. "Atavistically, I mean. Dark night of the soul, or someone else gets in your ear, you start to question these kinds of things. What makes a good person a good person. What makes a bad person a bad person."

"Not so easy as all that," Penny said.

"What's your opinion, Mystery Man?" Frane said.

Mitch said, "Someone tells you different, that's someone who would let you drown."

Officer Frane said, "Two things. Number one: You friends with Bobby C.?"

Penny said, "Not in this or any other life."

"Then you'll be happy to know," she said, and nodded toward the body, "he suffered first. Might not be today, might not be this week, but someone's going to figure out that wasn't a natural death." Now she pointed at Mitch. "Number two: Get this nice lady a snow cone before you leave town. Today. You're here tomorrow, think about Kevlar, and I say that with respect." And then she was gone.

# CHAPTER THIRTY-EIGHT

*Tuesday*

For the next twenty minutes, the two of them watched as Bobby C.'s body was zippered into a body bag and then hoisted onto a gurney. How they were going to push that over the sand was anyone's guess. A crowd had begun to gather at different points along the beach, including, Mitch saw, Mayor Biddle standing on her balcony, watching her husband still assisting down below. The Biddles' house was on the highest bluff and its balcony stretched long into the dunes. If they'd woken up early enough, they would have likely been the first people to see the body.

The low whine of more sirens played somewhere in the distance but didn't end up at the beach. Seemed like a lot of people were having a bad morning.

"Did anyone see you talking to Bobby C. at Shake's?" Mitch asked Penny after a while.

"Yeah," she said. "The bartender. A bunch of tourists."

"You threaten him or anything?"

"Anything," Penny said. Penny felt something tighten inside of her. Chief Biddle, she could handle. This Officer Frane seemed like another sort.

Mitch said, "You should get out of town. They could be setting you up for a big fall, Penny."

Penny said, "I got that." She exhaled deeply. "Bobby C. was a scumbag. One of the worst people on the planet."

"I'm sure he was."

"He had someone who loved him. That's weird."

"The world is a deeply weird place," Mitch said. "And you see that big house up there? The one on the highest bluff? That's where Jack Biddle lives."

"Explains the sweatsuit, at least," Penny said. They stood there another few minutes, watching, not talking. "You really think Biddle will try to take a run at me for this?"

"Your alibi is that you were on a boat with a man with no past reading a book about a talking bird."

"There must be cameras on the docks."

"You disappeared for a lot of hours," Mitch said.

"I was asleep."

"Tell it to the judge, convict," Mitch said. "Now, see that house with the Russian flag on the pole?"

"Hard to miss."

"Rodney and Svetlana Golubev's home."

"Svetlana. Really."

"Imported her from Los Angeles. Now. Watch the wind. Watch how the dunes move."

"Toward the homes," Penny said.

"The wind is always coming from the water, so the natural path is right into Jack Biddle's front lawn, but he doesn't have a lawn, he has a sand dune."

"I get it," Penny said. "I'm the smart one."

Three cops and two EMTs tried to push Bobby C.'s gurney through the sand for about a foot, then they decided, apparently, fuck it, and the five of them took Bobby off the gurney and carried him like an imitation Christmas tree. Not much care. A lot of bumping. Some jokes. The sea of people gathering at the yellow tape parted, and they put Bobby C. into the coroner's van. Five minutes later, the canopy was coming down, the van was gone, and the crowd was thinning. What a way to end a shitty life. That was not how Penny wanted to go out, that much was sure. She wasn't a woman prone to epiphanies, but this week was trying to show her something.

Mitch said, "Officer Frane. She really said to get you a snow cone? I didn't imagine that?"

"I was going to ask you the same thing."

"How old do you think she is?"

"Not more than twenty-five, twenty-six," Penny said.

"That place has been closed most of her life."

"She was driving the cruiser we saw yesterday," Penny said. She knew Mitch had seen her. Looked right at her.

"This town," Mitch said, "is not a good place."

"Used to be we'd get snow cones every day during the summer," Penny said.

"Well," Mitch said, "let's see if they'll open for us."

# CHAPTER THIRTY-NINE

*Tuesday*

If Jack Biddle knew when the lowest tide of the fucking decade was going to hit the Oregon coast, maybe he wouldn't have murdered Bobby C. in the spectacular fashion he stumbled on the night before. He was chief of police, not a meteorologist! Or whoever it was that reported on the tides.

As it was, at least he was the first on the scene, thanks to Hannah Sperry knocking on his door, telling her fucking Rodney Golubev found a dead body on the beach. Jack was able to run down and make sure his hood ornament wasn't embedded into Bobby C.'s back, not that he should have worried. Bobby was mostly broken bones and a bag of skin. His face look like an old cheeseburger after the seagulls had their way. Provided cheeseburgers had jaw bones pushed through their ears.

The coroner, Lizzie DiGiangreco, gave Bobby one look when she arrived and said, "Well, he's dead all right. You recognize any of these tattoos?"

"That's Bobby C.," Jack told her, then quickly corrected himself. "Bobby Calhoun Jr."

"Friend of yours?"

"Bullied me in middle school." He took a breath. Thought about it. Decided. No. Then. Decided. Yes. "A very close family friend of the

Vinings. Basically a brother to Danny. He'll be very upset. Wouldn't be surprised if he created a memorial fudge in his name."

Lizzie tipped Bobby over. "A real map of artistic depravity." He had two lightning bolts tattooed over his heart, his last name tatted in an Old English font on his gut, a bloody dagger buried in ink on his sternum. She got down on a knee, touched the lightning bolts. "The Vinings are friends with Nazis?"

"He did some time when he was younger."

"Those lightning bolts could have been covered up pretty easily." Lizzie shook her head. "It's a real choice to keep those. Guess he didn't go around topless very often." She waved over an EMT. "Get him covered up, and let's get him off the beach."

"What are you thinking, cause-wise?" Jack asked.

"I'm going to guess his heart stopped," Lizzie said, "then his brain died." She put on a pair of glasses, checked Bobby's broken body more closely. "He's all blunt force trauma. I doubt he was alive when he hit the water. We can autopsy him and find out for sure. See if there's water in his lungs."

"Family might not want that," Jack said.

"It would be up to you, Chief," Lizzie said. "My best guess is he probably jumped and hit all the rocks on the way down, smashed on the shore, washed out for a bit, surf roughed him up and tossed him back here, then the birds had their time." She ran a gloved hand over his ruined back. "These are compound fractures, as you can see. Profound internal injuries." She stood up, stripped off her gloves. "I'm going with jumper. Would like to say, 'No Human Involved,' but I see he has a wedding ring. If you're looking for next of kin, you'll be looking for either a woman or a man with a shaved head and a bomber jacket, probably speaking German, possibly walking a Doberman, and spouting bullshit. Need help with that, my office stands at the ready."

"We'll handle it," Jack said.

"I'm sure," Lizzie said. She looked out at the ocean, then back at the houses perched over the coast. "Did you call the body in?"

"My neighbor came to my door," Jack said. "She was very shook up."

"You seem equally traumatized."

"Oh I am very much traumatized. I'll be commanding this investigation myself."

Lizzie said, quietly, "Try harder, Jack, or I'll see you at the inquest."

Jack's phone rang, right on time. It was his deputy chief, Gil Olney. "Chief, 911 got a call about a limo parked illegally up on old Suicide Ridge, construction workers said they need it moved."

"Why am I being bothered with this?" Jack said. Though he had a good idea.

"It's registered to a Robert Calhoun. That's . . . well, you know who that is. I wanted to let you know. It's already on the scanner, so press might come sniffing around. Didn't want you to be caught unaware."

"I've got Bobby C. right here on the beach with me."

"The body?"

"Poor son of a bitch is a mess. Coroner just called it. I've got Officer Frane down here. I'll have her run up to the ridge, secure the scene." Where was she? He looked out over the beach . . . which is when he spied Penny Green and Mitch Diamond at the police line, talking to her.

Good thing?

Bad thing?

He didn't know.

What he did know?

Time was now. He put his fingers in his mouth, whistled at Frane.

"Do me a favor," Jack said to Olney. "Start running the public video footage from the last few days. I want to know where Penny Green's been. Any friendly businesses, too."

"What are we looking for?"

"Could be Bobby C. was pushed. Want to see where Ms. Green's been."

"The list of people who'd want to push Bobby C. could wallpaper the Taj Mahal."

"Just do it," Jack said and hung up, Officer Frane striding over to him.

"Never, ever whistle at me again," Frane said.

Jack said, "They've found Bobby C.'s limo. I need you to run up there, quick like a bunny, secure everything."

"I cleaned up all your shit last night," Frane said. "You left prints and DNA everywhere. I was up there with a black light and a spray bottle of bleach at three in the morning." She pointed in every direction. "Hair, fingerprints on his windows, tire tracks, looked like you'd hosted a frat party up there. Don't do crimes, Chief, you're goddamn terrible at them." She pointed at the body. "I were you? I'd get this asshole cremated ASAP." She began to walk away. Stopped. "Did you not even look at the tides?"

Jack really did not like her tone. "Did you look at the tides when you let your cousins go swimming?" When she didn't respond, he said, "Get this handled, I'll give you another medal, all right?" He clapped. "Quick-like, I've got a possible murder investigation to spearhead."

Which is how, twenty minutes later, he ended up standing on Rodney Golubev's back patio with a ziplock bag in his pocket, a good chunk of Robert Green's brain matter defrosting inside, Hannah Sperry watching him.

"You've not seen him before?" Jack asked.

"Never. We're new here," Hannah said. "He was so rude to me."

"And the body showed up when, again?"

"Minutes before I came to your house."

"And you saw Mr. Golubev when?"

Hannah said, "Well. Same time. It all happened at one time. I saw the body. I saw him."

"I see," Jack said.

"He arrived last night. Made a real commotion."

Jack tried the back door. Locked. Looked inside. Everything inside the Golubev house was white: white leather sofas, white appliances, white roses in white vases. And what wasn't white was mirrored. It was like being in a fun house or a boy-band video from the '90s, which Jack decided was maybe the idea. In any case, Rodney Golubev was gone. He surely realized that him finding a dead body was, well, not going to be great.

Or maybe he didn't care.

Probably a combination.

Jack didn't actually care, either.

He needed to figure out how to get this brain matter on Rodney's property in a believable way. Connecting him to Bobby C.'s body would be a bonus.

"Describe this commotion," Jack said.

"He paced around the patio, talking to a person who wasn't there, while drinking from a bottle of vodka. He'd stop and sing what sounded like Russian fighting songs."

"Was he on the phone?"

"No, I looked. He also was only in his underpants. Is that a sex crime?"

"Is wearing a bathing suit a sex crime?"

"Well, no, but it's about context, yes?"

Jack had to think about that. He really needed to brush up on the law.

"What did he say to the person who wasn't there?"

"He mostly cried and professed love and a desire for vengeance."

"And you'd testify to this?"

Hannah said, "Would I need to go into witness protection or something?"

"I don't think so."

"Then yes."

Jack's phone buzzed. He ignored it. It was good to be present in these situations. "Anything else you remember?"

"He was cleaning a gun. Does that count?"

Jack wondered if he could shoot Robert's corpse at this late date and somehow make that stick against Rodney, too? "That also counts." He'd need to find the gun, of course, which would mean finding Rodney with it. Well. He'd see how that went. "How long have you been here?"

"About two months," she said. "We met you and your wife at the Summer Kickoff Mixer at the clubhouse?" Jack had no memory of this. "We're seasonal."

"Must be nice," Jack said. "Wait here. I'll be back." He walked around to the side yard where a twenty-foot dog run stood vacant—gravel floor littered with desiccated dog crap, forgotten squeaky toys, a **Beware of Dog** sign, and three yellow tennis balls. The dog run was enclosed by the house on one side, a chain-link fence overlooking the ocean on the other, blocked off at one end by a block wall and gated by an eight-foot chain-link door in front of Jack.

It was a nice, perfectly secluded place for a dog to run around barking like an asshole.

Or, Jack thought, maybe to theoretically beat someone to death.

He snapped on some gloves, stepped into the run, imagined how he'd club someone to death if they were on their knees in front of him, did the spatter geometry—medium velocity, 30 to 60 degrees of arc, that was pretty standard—dumped the brain matter into his palm, and then he flung it against the wall at about a 45-degree angle. Pure muscle memory. Would be great to have some blood to teardrop around the chunkier bits, but alas, he hadn't planned that far ahead. Anyway, Granite Shores' forensics team wasn't exactly Quantico quality. This would do.

Jack came back around to the patio. Hannah was still there, gnawing on her own lip.

"That dog run. Some unusual stuff in there. What do you know about Mr. Golubev's dog?"

"His wife came with a Rottweiler once," Hannah said. "Which as you know are often used in Satanic ceremonies."

"Yeah," Jack said, "lot of those Satanic cults out this way. Really need to be careful."

Jack's phone buzzed. Again. Someone had better be dead. Another someone.

"Things like this?" she said. "They don't happen back home."

"Maybe you should stay home, then," Jack said.

He walked down into the dunes. Not far from his Fortress of Dune-y Solitude, which had inadvertently fucking doomed him. He yanked a blade of dune grass out of the sand. Ran his thumb along the sharp edge. Could you cut a throat with this? No. *But look at me,* Jack thought. *I managed to cut my own throat.* He sniffed the grass. It smelled mossy and sweet, a scent he'd come to associate with the good life he thought he deserved.

How much did he have put away?

Enough.

Cut his hair, start working out, be one of those guys who wore linen shirts? Could he do that?

Damn right he could.

He'd need a couple days to get things lined up. Maybe even do it like Robert Green had done it. Take vacation days, buy plane tickets, and then . . . go. But not, in this case, get beheaded in a Ford Econoline and spend the rest of eternity hung like meat in an old snow cone joint. He'd need to start the process now. Right now.

Jack called deputy Olney, told him he'd confirmed Rodney Golubev was seen with Bobby C.'s body, that Golubev's neighbor reported he'd been acting extremely erratically, screaming in Russian, cleaning his gun, weeping, the whole nine, Gil muttering, "Jesus, Jack," with every new detail.

"We need to get some dogs out on this," Jack continued. "I'm feeling like there might have been some kind of Satanic thing going on out here. I saw some spatter patterns on the side of the house that are deeply troubling."

"Blood?"

"Worse," Jack said.

Gil muttered, "Jesus, Jack," again.

"Put a BOLO on a Commie in a Subaru Outback," Jack said. "I'm hitting the streets right now, this feels personal to me."

"Yes, Chief," Gil said.

Jack hung up, took a deep breath. If they could get Rodney into lockup today, get the brain matter off the wall before sundown, Jack could be in Luxembourg by Sunday night.

Jack looked up, saw Rodney's Russian flag snapping in the breeze.

What was Russia like this time of year?

Did they have free medical care?

He'd look that up.

Jack Biddle's phone buzzed. Again.

Fine.

A text from his wife:

Appointment today with the adoption agency! Call me 911.

*Delete.*

A text from Officer Frane:

Ridge situation escalation. Limo is coming up registered with you as co-owner. Did you fail to mention this to me? Plotkin from newspaper is here, with camera. Also, I quit. This is your problem, shit-heel.

*Delete.*

His phone rang.

Danny Vining.

Nope. *Ignore.*

Jack didn't believe in déjà vu, but man, he was feeling something a lot like it. Sunday was off the table. He needed to solve his problems permanently, right now. If something or someone went cattywampus, well, Jack would let God sort 'em out.

# CHAPTER FORTY

*Tuesday*

During her first few weeks at MIT, Penny Green realized she wasn't the smartest person alive. She'd been led to believe otherwise. There were the newspaper articles. The *People* cover story. The TV talk shows hosted by dipshit men in expensive suits who wanted her to do complex math problems in her head, "but answer in Mandarin!"

At first, Penny enjoyed the attention.

The problem with firsts? Seconds.

Penny was convinced that by the time she was twenty, she'd probably rule the world.

When she showed up ten minutes early for her first graduate course at MIT—Cellular Neurophysiology and Computing—she found exactly one seat left in the hundred-seat lecture hall. It was in the last row of profoundly uncomfortable fixed, straight-backed theater seats, behind a post she had to crane around to see the professor. Everyone in the class a front-row person, everyone the smartest person in the world, everyone peerless until they finally met their real peers.

To be in a room filled with all the other outliers was amazing at first. She wasn't alone? There were others like her? Of course she knew that to be true on an intellectual level, but the pickings were light in Granite Shores. She never felt more out of place in her life than in the town she grew up in.

She'd adapted to the peers she had access to. And now? Here were her actual equals, and what she soon found, time and again, was . . . they were so damn boring. She thought half of what they said was a joke, only to find herself laughing in the middle of their bone-dry stories. What was the use of getting to know people who, while geniuses, had no relationship to reality?

Penny knew that most prodigies ended up doing nothing notable as adults. It's why they're so interesting. To reach your potential at fifteen and to spend the rest of your life as a trivia question? To be someone's midnight YouTube search? *Oh yes, there's that adorable child going toe to toe with David Letterman . . . and in Mandarin!*

That seemed to Penny like the worst possible life.

All of which was the beginning of Penny's long, stupid reckoning.

Today, at a closed snow cone shop in Granite Shores? This felt like the end.

Mitch pulled the van up to the gate, took down his window beside the keypad. "You ready for this?"

She was. Lucidity about both her past and her future came to Penny that very morning, when Bobby C. was dragged across the beach. All the awful shit he'd done, all the awful shit he'd been, all the awful shit he'd brought into others' lives? In the end, he was what he'd always been: trash to be taken out.

People were what they were.

Robert Green was a good brother to her.

He wasn't going to stop.

She didn't feel him in this world because he was not in this world. What happened, where he'd gone, it hardly mattered. Dead was dead. To not have hope was acutely freeing. She didn't have to be angry. She could choose to live for them both, or not.

The only person who seemed to care about the actual disposition of Robert Green was Jack Biddle.

The last person on earth Robert would even give one moment of his actual time to? Jack Biddle.

If Robert knew Jack Biddle profited from his disappearance, he'd have returned, all right. Probably with a cease and desist. He knew how to write those.

What Penny knew: Jack Biddle was a jealous, pitiless man.

If he'd had a chance to be Robert for even one minute, he'd have slipped into his skin like a new shirt, and still, he'd wear it poorly. He showed up on the *Pere-a-Dice* that night fifteen years ago not because of some stolen Pronto Pups, but to show Penny that he had her number . . . and it was not 216.

Thing was, he wasn't smart. He was a walking shortcut.

Standing on that beach, looking at those homes built on trash heaps to create a view of a dying world? Seeing Jack's very home had the best sight lines? Parmenides would tell her that the evidence of this reality was all before her. The reason it all existed.

Penny knew that if she and Mitch tested their fate in Granite Shores for much longer, they were likely to leave in a bag like Bobby C.

Penny took out a piece of paper. She'd written nineteen numbers on it. The code to get into the Fort Knox of snow cone shops. "Ready?"

"Give it to me."

Penny read them off: 3, 4, 8, 3, 3, 6, 5, 5, 2, 7, 3, 2, 4, 7, 8, 4, 7, 4, 7.

Mitch punched them into the keypad.

The gate slid open.

"You're not the only person who can crack a safe," Penny said.

"You going to tell me what that number was?" Mitch asked.

Penny said, "Alphanumeric. *Five dollar daiquiris*. It's been the password forever. I told you."

The Sno-Cone Depot, as Penny remembered it, was a charming A-frame with a drive-thru center. There was a patio with blue-and-white plastic picnic tables that dated from the 1960s, detached restrooms, a small parking area, and a giant neon sign. All of that was still behind the gates, along with a phalanx of security cameras and fifteen-foot halogen lights capable of capturing the movements of every living creature.

"Real neighborly vibe," Mitch said. They stepped out of the van. He'd left it running, however, and told Penny to leave her doors open, Penny thinking that bank-robbing background had some value in getaway situations. "It's like a training center for urban assault teams." He looked behind him. "Not real subtle."

Penny walked through the drive-thru, peered into the window on the right. There was a cash register, a stool, a whiteboard that had "86 grape" written on it, rows of empty flavor dispensers—Penny really loved that old bubble gum flavor, no one had that anymore—and then a very nice-looking snow cone machine. Brushed metal, high-visibility tempered glass, sturdy, dependable, and a time capsule from the summer of 2008, since she could even see the maintenance record on it—"Water valve replaced May 12, 2008 by JB."

The whole space was maybe six by eight feet.

"Nothing over here," Penny said. Mitch was behind her, examining the building itself.

Penny looked in the opposite window. Same snow cone machine. Same empty flavor bottles. There were old family photos on a corkboard in this box—Caroline pregnant, Jack and his dad, Owen, Jack and his own son, the family resemblance impossible not to notice, the Biddle strong in that one, so he was probably a budding sociopath—and then a closet filled with cleaning supplies.

The A-frame was two stories tall. On the right leg was the patio, on the left leg there was a rectangular outbuilding where the **TREAT YOURSELF AND TREAT YOUR KIDDIES!** neon sign hung. That's where Mitch was, his ear pressed close to the wall, like he was listening for the ticking of a bomb. Every couple seconds, he'd knock on a different part of the wall, nod, knock, nod.

Adjacent to the delivery window on the left was a door marked **EMPLOYEES ONLY!** The exclamation point was a little aftermarket Sharpie addition for emphasis. Underneath that sign: **AUTHORIZED PERSONNEL**

**ONLY**. And then one more sign, above the door: SMILE YOU'RE ON CAMERA! **ARMED RESPONSE**. Jack had ordered every sign they sold in the home security department of Walmart, as if the infrared cameras and the lights weren't enough.

Mitch said, "Very intimidating." He tried the door. Locked. Pushed against it. "This door is steel." He knocked on it, too. It made a dull *tong* sound. "It's a reinforced blast door." Got on one knee, looked closely at the setup. "S&G 2937. Best door lock on the planet. Keyed entry, plus combination lock. Solid brass. Platinum plated. Antipick pins. Nice."

Penny said, "Seems excessive."

Mitch said, "Unless you're keeping valuables inside."

"Can you get in?"

"With unlimited time, sure," he said. "But let me show you something." He walked around the building, knocking as he went, like he'd done before. He started at the door—the metallic *tong* again—kept moving, whacking on the frame, then along the side wall of the outbuilding, all reinforced with steel, until he was around the bend, under the unlit neon sign. He pounded his fist there. A gentle, hollow, wooden *thud*.

Mitch went back to the van, returned with a shotgun and a suppressor, which he screwed on. "You see this with grocery stores," he said. He pressed on the wall. "They'll reinforce everything, cake the whole facility in concrete, install state-of-the-art vaults, secure their loading docks like they're moving cartel cash." He gave the bottom of the wall a good kick. Left a dent in the shape of his shoe. "But then they make the entire front facade glass and stay open for twenty-four hours. It's an invitation for a man like me to revert to bad habits." Another kick. Another dent. "If I were still in the grocery store game, I'd be inside a different store every single night, getting rich. Or at least walking out with a fair number of expensive meats and cheeses." He took five steps back. "You're going to want to move."

Penny did as she was told.

Mitch Diamond pumped six shells in a tight circle right into the space beneath the neon sign, walked over, put his boot through the center.

"After you," Mitch said.

They stood shoulder to shoulder in what should have been a standard break room . . . albeit one surrounded by blast walls: There was a small table with two chairs, a counter with a sink and a Mr. Coffee, a stack of filters beside the coffee maker, some napkins. An Oregon OSHA poster on a corkboard. A "Caroline Biddle for Mayor" campaign poster on the back of the locked door. A refrigerator covered in Sno-Cone Depot magnets. A shelving unit stacked with Sno-Cone Depot T-shirts and red plastic cups.

It was the floor that had Penny's attention. Instead of concrete or wood or carpeting, it was covered in industrial steel tread plates. She'd seen this before in Gig Harbor, on the floors where the dog grooming happened: You could power wash it and leave nothing behind. Dog urine, for instance, or blood. Hardly made sense for a break room at the Sno-Cone Depot.

Smack in the middle of the floor was a metal hatch door leading to the basement. There was a green padlock on the door that looked imposing, plus a quasi-menacing sign that said **DANGER HIGH VOLTAGE**.

"What do you suppose is down there?" Penny asked.

Mitch squatted down, yanked on the lock. "F&C 654C. Made commercially for the military, used to lock up weapons usually. Shrouded shackle. That's nice, keeps it safe from concussion blasts. There's typically one master key, two operating keys, only top guys have them." Mitch flipped it over. "This is an older model. Probably early 2000s. Didn't Jack go to Iraq?"

"Yeah, they gave him a parade when he got back."

"Probably stole it from there," Mitch said. He dropped it back down, which made a loud clang.

"Can you crack it?"

"It's going to take all my skill and learning and precise vision and hearing." He piled up loose wood and drywall from the floor, wrapped them in two aprons, slid them under and around the lock, along with a pack of napkins. "You're going to want to stand outside, in case there's a ricochet."

Penny didn't need to be asked twice. She pushed back through the wall and stood outside, watched as Mitch put his shotgun barrel right up on the center of the hinge and fired. Inspected it. Pressed the barrel against the lock again, fired, and the hinge snapped in two and skittered across the metal floor.

"That's how you pick a lock?" Penny asked.

"People get too fancy," Mitch said. "Sometimes, you need to blow things apart." He opened the hatch door. Bright halogens flickered on, revealing a cement stairwell dying into nicely appointed hardwood floors. "I'll wait up here."

"Are you sure?" Penny said.

"You want to be trapped down there for the rest of your life?"

"Not particularly," Penny said. "Can I trust you?"

"Well," Mitch said, "we've gotten this far." He smiled faintly at her. "Listen. Whatever you find. It's yours, okay, if you want to scatter. I need a couple items and I'm good. Because Jack isn't going to let us walk. You understand that, right?"

"Could be a lot of snow cone flavors and nothing else."

"Could be."

"Could be Robert's down there playing Magic: The Gathering with D. B. Cooper."

"Could be," Mitch agreed.

"Could be we're five minutes from two million dollars."

"Less than that," Mitch said.

*Time or money?* Penny wondered and then disappeared down the stairs.

In her entire life, Penny had never seen anything like the SinoArctic. She'd stayed in apartments that were smaller. Her cell at Gig, her home for thirteen years, would fit inside five times. Hell, the house she'd grown up in, before it was turned into a museum, had to be less expensive. But the more pressing issue was: She couldn't conceive of why it was here. It was like finding the Large Hadron Collider underneath a McDonald's.

The temperature readout on the outside wall said: "-37 (main), -74 (interior)."

There was what looked like a space suit hung up next to the freezer. Penny peered through a porthole window. Pure frozen darkness.

Penny looked at the temperature gauge again. What was the coldest she'd ever been? Certainly not -37. And really not -74.

She was currently dressed in low-top Chuck Taylors, shorts, a T-shirt, and a sweatshirt she stole from the gift shop inside her old house. She figured she'd be dead in about two minutes. She saw the space suit hanging there and decided she was now firmly in her Fuck It period and went ahead and put it on, boots and all, and stepped into the SinoArctic. Flipped on the wall of light switches.

Eighteen feet of frozen darkness came into daylight, along with fifteen years of waiting and wondering. The unit was lined with shelving and each shelf was stacked with plastic container units, each with a number on them, from 1 to 324. There was a rolling five-step ladder at each end of the floor to reach the top-level storage, where Penny expected to see . . . food? Ice? Something having to do with the actual operations of the property. But instead she saw more boxes and, maybe, some kind of old seating? Was that . . . the front end of a car? Even inside the space suit, she was damn cold, so she was already feeling a little disoriented. There was also a second, interior space, the size of a walk-in closet, with its own closed door.

She started pulling out the boxes. Each was meticulously cataloged, marked, and filed. It all seemed so familiar, and then she understood why: She'd put together the original spreadsheets containing all this information. Rings of keys. Jewels. Photos. Urns. *How many people keep urns?* She remembered having that specific memory typing all this up, and now, here it all was again. Drugs. Guns. Computers. Hard drives. She kept pulling out box after box. It was a boutique of shady shit.

And it was going to be the fortune she shared with Robert.

Everything was in its place here, each and every box Robert took, recreated in a gigantic freezer beneath the Sno-Cone Depot. It was the most absurd situation she'd ever encountered, the silliest, dumbest end to a mystery that enthralled millions, and it was in a basement in Granite Shores, all this time?

She kept pulling out boxes.

There were boxes that weren't numbered, too. They were marked with "$."

She opened one.

Stacks of cash.

Brick after brick after brick. Fives. Tens. Twenties. Fifties. Twenty rows. Ten bricks per row. A hundred bills per brick. She did the math. Answered in Mandarin, for old time's sake, but in her head.

In this box alone, there was $425,000. Enough to start a new life? Enough to try.

Several other boxes were marked "Rx." Inside one, a good hundred bottles of various pills.

That explained more than Penny needed to know.

She picked up the box of cash, began to walk it outside, already buying that Wurlitzer, thinking of new names she might try on, thinking that Brooke was a pretty name. She'd never used that one before. Maybe even go with Brooke Lynn? That might be funny. She liked a good joke. Yes, this was all working out.

And then she stopped.

What was she doing?

She could leave this all here.

Mitch would claim the two million dollars, and she'd get her cut. But then . . .

One day the press would find her, again. That would happen quickly. It wasn't like it used to be. Addie would produce a whole new podcast and have it up on Spotify by next week. There'd be a hunt on for her immediately. Mitch Diamond wasn't a real person. The internet sleuths would figure that out before the cops, she wagered, and if they presented that information to him, she suspected the result would not be one the person armed with a keyboard would be expecting. Violence for violence's sake, that wasn't Mitch, but that didn't mean he wasn't capable of change. The pinpoint nature of that shotgun blast to the lock told her a few things.

She looked back at all the boxes.

People's lives.

She didn't want any of that stuff. God no. Maybe she did when she was twenty-six, at least in theory, but in practice, having the karmic weight of all that history on her? It would have been a yoke.

Whoever put this cash away, though, they weren't doing so out of convenience. It was to hide it. Who really needed to hide money? Normal person with this amount of cash, it's going into the bank, it's accruing interest, it's offshore, or it's sitting in a savings account, waiting for the flood. Even Noah was smart enough to start building his boat before the rain started to fall. The people who left their money at Barer & Harris were worse than Penny. This money would finally find some good.

Unlike whatever Jack Biddle had planned.

Though hadn't he forced people to donate to good causes? Wasn't that part of the plan she and Robert were going to execute? It was. That was always the plan. Do a little good. And Jack did that, too, but only to hide who he was.

He had all 324 boxes. How was that possible unless he'd found the van? And if he found the van, that meant he found Robert. Everything from the van was in here, and Robert wasn't sitting on a sofa watching baseball, and yet, his DNA was on every bit of blackmail. Did Jack have Robert in a cage somewhere?

Which is when Penny Green made the mistake of looking to the right, where the smaller, colder interior freezer sat.

# CHAPTER FORTY-ONE

*Tuesday*

Mitch Diamond never heard a person make that noise.

A shriek? Yes, many times.

A wail? Hundreds.

A caterwaul? Once. His stepfather. The last time he saw him.

The noise Penny Green made echoed up the stairs, into the empty room, through time, space, reason, and right through Mitch Diamond and every other name he'd ever been.

# CHAPTER FORTY-TWO

*Tuesday*

Penny yanked the boots off her feet, stripped the space suit off, tore the insulated face mask off her head, kicked them all across the room, stomped on them, spit on them, the whole time screaming in blind fury, grief, loss, woe, sacrifice, and things she wouldn't quite understand for days, weeks, months, years, might need an entire afterlife to get right, the cruelty and madness and avarice and greed of humans too much for her to ever understand now.

And then she was in Mitch Diamond's arms, and he was saying, "It's okay, it's okay, it's going to be okay, it's okay, it's okay," though how could he ever know? How could he possibly know?

"He's inside," Penny said.

"Your brother?"

"He's been there," Penny said. "Maybe the whole time."

Mitch pulled Penny back, examined her face, Penny thinking he looked like he'd been dropped on an alien planet only to find it populated with his entire family.

"Did Jack . . . kill him?"

"I don't think so. It's . . . you have to see it, yourself. I'm sorry. I can't put it to words." Mitch let go of her, moved toward the door. "No, wait, you can't walk in there. You'll freeze to death. You need these freezer clothes."

"How quickly would I die?"

"Two or three minutes until you got frostbite. You'd be dead in about ten."

He put the freezer suit on. Disappeared inside. Came back five minutes later, holding a stack of boxes—#219, #106, and the one filled with cash that Penny had left on the floor. Set them on the floor between them, removed the face mask. "You're right," he said.

"Which part?"

"Both. I don't think he killed him. I think he found him, made a really fucked-up choice, a series of them, in fact. And then kept making them." He stripped off the suit. Stood there for a few seconds, staring at Penny, then back at the freezer. "There's a lot happening in there. None of it good. Jack finds us, he's going to try to kill us. That's going to happen. Whatever happened to Bobby C., I'm going to guess it wasn't a suicide. So listen to me, okay, I want you to take all this cash, okay? Get in the van and go. I promise you, I will find you, and I will give you your share of all of this, like I told you on the boat. But get this cash before Jack gets wind, because I can't guarantee anything after that."

"He comes for me, again, I'll kill him," Penny said. "He's had my brother hanging like a side of meat for . . . for what? Jesus. It's too much."

"I know," Mitch said. "This is why I need you to go. Let me handle him. I promise you. I will find you, and I will get you yours."

Penny said, "I don't want any of this. I don't want this cash. I don't want what's in those boxes. It's someone else's life. I've given too much of mine up to take someone else's. I'm done, it's over. We need to do the right thing. We film all this. Everything. Even Robert's body, or else no one will believe it. Call the Portland police, call the Seattle police, call your law firm. However long it takes is however long it takes. You get that reward. That's what you need, I stand behind you, but I don't want anything. Not a dime."

Mitch took Penny by the hand, said, "You need to hear me. This money? Everything in the freezer? That's all there is. There's no reward. I lied. To you. To the mayor. To Biddle. To everyone."

"What? What are you talking about?" She pulled her hand from his. "What are you saying?"

"I tried to tell you last night," Mitch said. "I've been trying to tell you. I've wanted to tell you." He picked up box #219. "This box. This is mine. Everything in here is me. I was the last person he tried to blackmail, he just doesn't know it." He set it down. "And I told you, I'm not going back. The reason no one has shown up here yet, the reason it's just you and me? I only sent one letter." He picked up box #106. "To Danny Vining. The only person in Granite Shores who had a box. This one right here. I had to know what would happen. I had to know who he would go to. And he went to Jack Biddle. Things I thought I knew, you put them together. You showed me what to see. I should have known it. That Robert was here all along. But I didn't want to." He pushed Vining's box toward Penny. "This box is worth more than anything else, I'd guess. Take it and take the cash. And I'll find you."

Mitch kept talking, but Penny felt like she was back in the freezer, overwhelmed by reality.

"There's no reward?" Penny said, interrupting him.

"No."

"No press release?"

Mitch said, "No."

"Do any of the people who were robbed know anything about this?"

"No. No one does. It's not real."

"Do you even work for Barer & Harris?"

Mitch said, "I did. Up until about twenty-four hours ago. I'm guessing there's a bounty on my head right this moment. Or on Mitch Diamond's anyway. That name is cooked."

Penny couldn't compute everything Mitch was telling her. It was like sopping up a fire hose with a cotton ball. "You . . . knew? You knew Jack Biddle did something to my brother?"

"I had an idea."

"Since when?"

"Two years. Maybe longer. But I didn't have anything concrete until a few weeks ago. We found windshield glass in a DNA sample. Matched the van Robert was driving. It all started to make sense." He paused. "To give me sufficient reason."

Penny said, "No. No. You do not get that."

Mitch said, "I told you, the last person Jack tried to blackmail was me." He pointed at the box at his feet. "That's all me. Take it, too, if you want. I don't need it. If it will help you understand, take it. It's not important to me."

Penny put a hand up, to stop Mitch from talking. He did.

Penny said, "My brother is in there, hanging like meat. Are you telling me Jack-fucking-Biddle *harvested* him for his DNA all these years?"

"Yes."

"And you suspected this, let him call forth every asshole from my past, and brought me here, just to see if you were right? So you could prevent him from blackmailing *you*?"

"Yes," Mitch said, "but that's not how it ended. That's how it started. But you're not hearing me. I'm here, right now, for you. To give you what you want."

Penny hefted up the box of cash . . . then dumped it on the floor, climbed up the stairs, got into the still-running van, and did the smartest thing she'd ever done, would ever do: She got the fuck out of Losertown for good and didn't bother to lock the gate behind her.

# CHAPTER FORTY-THREE

*Tuesday*

Jack Biddle wasn't going on the run in sweatpants; his vanity wouldn't allow that, so he'd changed his clothes, packed a cooler with as many ice packs as he could fit, loaded up his Tahoe with a couple suitcases full of clothes and shoes and a couple DVDs he liked, his laptop, his PS5, some games, Jack thinking, you know, he'd need to be entertained, Jack maybe too fucking high on pills to do this all in a judicious manner, but fuck it, left a note on the kitchen table for his wife, letting her know he couldn't take his failures any longer and that he'd be ending his life, probably in Mexico, most likely in Puerto Nuevo, where they had all that good lobster, so if at least she went looking for him she'd have some decent meals. Left another note for his son, telling him to be a better man than Jack, which made Jack a little teary-eyed, thinking that Travis would have to work damn hard to do that, because Jack was a great man, would probably end up with a bronze of himself one day when history looked more fondly on him than the present was likely to, not unlike their cousin Yeach Patterson . . .

Jack snapped his department cell phone in two, which was stupid since he wasn't taking it, but he liked the image, took one last look out the window at his terrific view, then headed over to the Sno-Cone Depot. He'd get some money, some jewels, the keys to all his safe-deposit boxes around the world, a couple hundred Oxy, a few guns and ammo, grab up Robert

Green, dump him off a bridge somewhere, and he'd be free. Those brains on the wall of Rodney's place were enough to pin it all on him.

At least that was his plan until he pulled inside the Depot, saw that nothing was how he left it.

He should have replaced that wall, dammit. But he didn't want to fuck with the old sign. Which he loved. Plus, did he really need to fortify anything? No one was looking for him! He'd gotten away with it!

Until he got caught.

He opened his glove box. Shook his Altoid container. Empty. Shit. He'd refill downstairs.

Jack pulled up his security cameras on his phone, pulled up the last thirty minutes, saw the video of the van pulling in, watched Penny and Mitch wandering around, then that bastard Mitch blowing his wall to pieces. That sign and that wall and the whole damn A-frame were going to be on a historic registry if he ever, you know, tore the security fences down, moved out the corpse and the stolen items, started selling snow cones to tourists again, and ever figured out what, exactly, a historical registry was, but, that was all to be investigated at a later date.

Well. That went . . . cattywampus . . . again.

That word.

It was like a harbinger.

He clicked on the cameras in the basement, saw Penny climbing into his freezer and knew he needed to stop wasting time. If he was lucky, he had about ten minutes before the cops were here, or Danny Vining, or the media, or the whole damn city, with pitchforks.

Jack took his gun from his glove box, got out of his Tahoe, walked around the buildings, made sure Mitch and Penny weren't sitting there waiting on his ass, but their van was gone, and they had no good reason to sit and wait, regardless.

He stepped inside the wreckage. Looked around. Listened. The lock was blown off the hatch, which pissed Jack off. That was a damn good lock. He checked the basement's camera feed. It was offline.

They'd probably robbed him and didn't want the evidence.

Well, fine.

They couldn't have taken everything.

He opened the hatch an inch, listened for a moment. He could hear the freezer humming. That was good news. They must have taken what they wanted and left, which he highly doubted included his pills and guns and his keys. Everything else was . . . whatever. Jack was getting out and being unencumbered, by regrets or all that other shit, was how he'd be living from here on out.

Jack stuffed his gun into the back of his waistband, like he'd seen gangsters do, but which he'd never done because he was a holster guy, but he wasn't wearing a holster, then yanked the hatch open all the way, which was a mistake, he recognized, when Mitch Diamond shot him.

# CHAPTER FORTY-FOUR

*Tuesday*

Mitch Diamond was a done deal for Mitch Diamond.

So was Oregon. So was Washington.

He closed the rear door of Jack Biddle's Tahoe. Went around the front, made sure he could see through the rearview mirror with all those boxes.

Not that he'd be doing too much looking back.

California had promise, again. Now that he had some good identities to work with again. All the materials he'd ever need? They were packed in the back of the Tahoe. He'd need to get new plates, probably a paint job, but he had time. No one was going to find Jack Biddle for a while. He felt pretty good about that.

Mitch would pick a new name by dinner. By then, he'd be pretty close to the forests of Northern California. He'd lay low for a bit. See what the news reported. Make his next move from there. Trade the Tahoe for a Caddie. An older one. Big trunk.

He went back into the basement of the Sno-Cone Depot, took one last look around before his final chore. He wiped down everything he'd touched. He'd burn the place down but that seemed too obvious, in light of everything else.

"You need to get me to a hospital," Jack Biddle said. He was tied to a chair, not that he was going to run off. "I think you blew off my toes."

Mitch probably had, in fact, blown off a couple toes on his right foot. He'd shot him using one of Jack's own guns, a pretty nice Smith & Wesson 617 revolver he found in the freezer, loaded with .22 bullets, which wouldn't do much real damage. He didn't want to amputate the man's whole foot, not yet anyway. He wanted to hurt him, disarm him, and then figure out what to do next.

"I think you're probably right," Mitch said.

"I could bleed out."

"You could. I doubt it, but you could."

"I also gotta piss like mad," Jack Biddle said. "You have to let me piss. That's Geneva Convention."

"You're not a prisoner of war," Mitch said.

"Aren't I? I served my country, twice!"

Mitch dragged Jack's chair over to the freezer. Placed him in front of the door. Took out Jack's burner cell phone, scrolled through it absently until he found what he was looking for. "I've watched a lot of your YouTube videos," Mitch said. "You're a wonderful public speaker."

"Could I get an Oxy? There's about five thousand of them right there in that freezer. Six would take the edge off of bleeding out, I bet."

"What I like best in your videos is how confident you are about forensics and DNA and all that. I watched a talk you did in Prague once. That was really something."

"A couple Percs would work, too."

"What I thought was amazing in that video," Mitch said, "was how you discussed the need for local police to think like the criminals who were coming to their town. How they had to match their depravity—mentally—in order to catch them. Do you feel you've been able to do that, Jack?" He clicked open the camera. "Now. You're going to explain how, exactly, Robert Green's body ended up hanging in your freezer. You ready?"

"And if I don't?"

"Well, then I'm going to shoot you in the face."

"You're crazy," Jack said. "What did I even do wrong?"

"That's what this interview will be about, exactly what you did wrong. Ready?"

"If I do this," Jack said, "you'll give me something for the pain? Even Penny called 911 when I got shot."

"When you shot yourself," Mitch said.

"Everyone with that bullshit."

Mitch turned on the camera. "Go ahead," he said and for the next ten minutes, with a few digressions to complain about feeling, for sure, that he'd lost his pinkie toe, and to suggest proper ways the future might honor his valor, Jack Biddle explained everything. When he was done, Mitch clapped. "That was great, Jack. Very professional. I'm sure they will build a public square devoted to you. I'll text this to your list of contacts, and I'm sure someone will get this posted as soon as possible." Mitch then opened the freezer door and dragged Jack inside, still tied to the chair.

"What are you doing?" Jack said.

"The cold will bring down the swelling," Mitch said.

"I'll freeze to death," Jack said.

"Don't worry," Mitch said. "I'm not some kind of monster. I'm going to call 911. I'm sure the cops will get here in time to save you."

"You can't do this."

"Can and will, Jack. Can and will." He pushed the chair into the center of the floor, with a view of the open door into the smaller freezer, where Robert still hung. "Be happy you're not on one of those hooks." Mitch walked back out, but kept the door open for a moment. "I'm going to warm this up to -25. Give you a fighting chance of just losing your nose, maybe your ears. For sure a couple fingers. Won't be shooting any guns. Not that you get to carry in prison."

"I'll be dead in ten minutes."

"You'll pass out in ten minutes, for sure. It will take you a little longer to die, so here's hoping your 911 system is top of the line, Chief."

Jack Biddle's eyes went wide. "What did I ever do to you?"

Mitch said, "You hurt my friend."

And then he closed the door.

# EPILOGUE

**One Year Later**
*Torrey, Utah*

Brooke Lynn had fifty-one minutes left on her shift at the Lamplighter. She had thirty-six dollars in her pocket, her arches were on fire, and someone had put five bucks into their classic jukebox and picked the same damn song five times, which meant Bobby McGee was going to be stuck near Salinas for a long-ass time. Brooke could give a shit. She was happy. Every day, she woke up without worry. She'd seen the worst the world had to offer, and she'd survived it.

So Brooke was in the back, eating a plate of fries, when her manager, Jordyn, with a *y*, which was dumb, came back and sat across from her, ate two of her fries.

"You have a table," Jordyn said.

"I'm done for the night."

"He asked for you."

"By name?"

"No," Jordyn said. "He asked to sit in the smart female's section."

Brooke said, "Did he say 'female'?"

"Is that what I said? He said 'woman.'"

Brooke said, "Does he have an accent or anything?"

"No."

Brooke walked out onto the floor, just as the windshield wipers were doing their thing in that song, but there was no one in her section. "Oh," Jordyn said, "he was sitting at the four top in the corner. Looks like maybe he left you something?"

Brooke walked over to the table. In the center of the table, under the saltshaker, was a Post-it note affixed to a brick of bills.

The Post-it note had a name on it.

Her real name.

She flipped through the bills.

Did a quick count.

Ten thousand.

How did he find her?

How did he find her . . . again?

She peeled off two grand, put it in the tip jar at the bar, which was split by all the dishwashers and barbacks, then found Jordyn, told her those fries weren't sitting right, or maybe she was coming down with something, would it be cool if she boned out a few minutes early?

"Girl," Jordyn said, "of course. Tell me he left you his number. He did, right."

"Yep."

"Get it," Jordyn said. "Can't wait to hear all about it!"

Penny Green took off her apron, dropped her order pad into the trash can, and escaped out the back door of the Lamplighter and into the high desert night.

She only looked back once, to make sure that car in the parking lot was a big old Cadillac.

# ACKNOWLEDGMENTS

Much of this book was written while I sat in waiting rooms at the Lucy Curci Cancer Center in Rancho Mirage while my wife, Wendy, was in treatment, so before all else, I want to thank the wonderful people who took such great care of my wife and brought her back to good health. We must do more to assure everyone the level of care my wife was lucky to receive. Specifically I want to thank: Dr. Vulchi, Dr. Lingareddy, Dr. Ihde, and Courtney Le Vasseur.

Profound thanks to Grace Doyle, my editor at Thomas & Mercer, for her deft hand on all these words, but more importantly for her kindness and patience. I swear, I *usually* make my deadlines. Equal thanks to my agent, Jennie Dunham, for holding my hand throughout this process, picking me up when I was down, and for always having my best interests; and my film and TV agent Judi Farkas, for handling all that big-dream business while I was otherwise engaged, while also providing me with priceless personal advice on how to live through things beyond your control. I would be remiss if I did not thank Dan Smetanka for his grace . . . and also for his unending advice, even when it's not his job. If you want to succeed in this business, my suggestion is to surround yourself with people who care about you as a person, first and last.

This book would not exist were it not for a conversation I had one morning with my nephew Brent Dinino. He knows why. And yes, I'll buy you another bottle of good scotch when the book is released.

After that initial bit of inspiration, I needed to learn a few important things, and these folks were extremely helpful: Shannon Presby, for the law; Matt Piucci, for the science; Kathryn McGee, for understanding buildings (plus, daily, running the Low Residency MFA at UCR while I was in the clouds); my sister Karen Dinino, for more of the law; Jim Thomsen's highly informative 2009 blog post regarding the Washington Corrections Center for Women; Jennifer Hillier's equally informative 2011 post on the same. I found the very cool equation for Parmenides's principle in *Stanford's Encyclopedia of Philosophy*, and Penny's explanation is adapted from that as well. Even though I learned amazing facts from all these people and their writing, I changed things to suit my fictional pursuits. When you think you might want to send me a letter saying I got something wrong, please understand that none of this is real. It's all fiction. I made it all up, including the city where this all takes place.

Lastly, no book gets written without the support of a legion of people, personal and professional. Here is the legion that got me through this year, even though I thought it would kill me: Susan Straight, Alex Espinoza, Mark Haskell Smith, David Ulin, Ivy Pochoda, Jill Alexander Essbaum, Elizabeth Crane, Rob Roberge, Gina Frangello, Gabino Iglesias, John Schimmel, Joshua Malkin, William Rabkin, Mickey Birnbaum, Agam Patel, Ross Angelella, Maret Orliss, Rachel Kowal, Juliet Grames, Lily DeTaeye, Matthew Zapruder, Rob Bowman, Stefanie Leder, Jim Ruland, James D. F. Hannah, Nikki Dolson, Liska Jacobs, Bree Rolfe, Johnny Heller, Brenda Holcomb, and of course my siblings—Lee Goldberg, Karen Dinino, and Linda Woods—and their families.

## ABOUT THE AUTHOR

Photo © 2024 Wendy Duren

Tod Goldberg is the *New York Times* bestselling author of sixteen novels, including the Gangsterland quartet: *Gangsterland*, a finalist for the Hammett Prize; *Gangster Nation*; *The Low Desert*, a Southwest Book of the Year; and *Gangsters Don't Die*, an Amazon Best Book of 2023 and a Southwest Book of the Year. Other works include *The House of Secrets*, coauthored with Brad Meltzer; *Living Dead Girl*, a finalist for the *Los Angeles Times* Book Prize; and the Burn Notice series. His short fiction and essays have been anthologized in *Best American Mystery and Suspense* and *Best American Essays* and appear regularly in the *Los Angeles Times*, *USA Today*, and *Alta*. Tod is a professor of creative writing at the University of California, Riverside, where he founded and directs the low-residency MFA program in creative writing and writing for the performing arts. For more information, visit www.todgoldberg.com.